# DAMASK ROSE

# DAMASK ROSE

## Haywood Smith

**Five Star**
**Unity, Maine**

Copyright © 1998 by Haywood Smith

Five Star Romance.
Published in conjunction with St. Martin's Press, Inc.

Cover photograph © 1998 Diana George Chapin

January 1999
Standard Print Hardcover Edition.

Five Star Standard Print Romance Series.

The text of this edition is unabridged.

Set in 11 pt. Plantin by Al Chase.

Printed in the United States on permanent paper.

**Library of Congress Cataloging in Publication Data**

Smith, Haywood, 1949–
    Damask rose / Haywood Smith.
        p.    cm.
    ISBN 0-7862-1687-5 (hc : alk. paper)
        1. Scotland — History — 15th century — Fiction.
    I. Title.
    PS3569.M53728D36  1999
    813′.54—dc21                                    98-41986

*My life has been blessed by a rare and precious few
friends or family
who are as good-to-the-bone, yet practical, as the
heroine of this book.
Best of all is my precious sister Lisa Cross
of Houston, Texas.
This book is my tribute to you, Little Nurse,
for you have always demonstrated
the heart and hands of Christ
not only to me,
but also to everyone lucky enough to know you.*

# Acknowledgments

Special thanks go to my dear friends Doug and Suzann Bonds for permitting their precious Timothy to be the model for the character of Timothy in this book. Knowing them, and Tim, has blessed my family more than I can say. I would be remiss, though, if I did not explain that the real-life Timothy is always immaculately groomed, and he is far too well-brought-up a gentleman to do some of the things his fictional counterpart does. Thanks, Doug and Suzann, for being big-hearted enough to allow me dramatic license with that characterization. Tim really *is* an angel.

I would also like to thank Suzann Bonds, Teri Pope, and my friend Edith Puckett for providing additional inspiration for the character of Nara. You're all good as gold, and I am proud to be your friend.

Last but not least, there really are guardian angels walking around in this world (honorary ones, anyway). Dr. Marvin Royster of the Peachtree Orthopedic Group in Atlanta and his assistant, Judi, are two perfect examples. I couldn't have gotten through the past two years without their kindness, generosity, and understanding (and cortisone). God bless you both and thanks, from the bottom of my heart.

# Prologue

## Scotland (Central Highlands), 1413

Tynan MacDougald had longed for death every day of his eighth year and well into his ninth. It would have been so easy to die. But instead of giving in, he had clung ferociously to life through grief, humiliation, abuse, squalor, sickness, and starvation. He was the last of his kind, and he had a sacred vow to fulfill. That, and that alone, kept him going.

Propelled by sheer determination on this bleak January day, he forced one filthy bare foot in front of the other until he had crossed the frozen bailey of Eilean d'Ór.

*Eilean d'Ór.* The very name mocked him. This was no golden isle. It was hell on earth.

Once he gained the shelter of the stables, he stumbled past stall after stall of Laird Cullum's huge warhorses until he reached the mound of soiled hay that had been his bed these past two years.

Tynan collapsed into the hay, too cold and exhausted to care that he was covered in excrement from head to toe. With the last of his strength, he pulled the hay over his bony arms and legs for warmth.

For most of the souls who lived within its walls, Eilean d'Ór provided a haven of safety amid Scotland's endless tribal wars, but for Tynan, the massive stone fortress was a prison offering no hope of a reprieve.

His body began to quake as the pestilence that coated him invaded the rope burns beneath his armpits. The sickening

9

sensation took him back two years, to the day he'd wakened to find himself wounded, bound, alone, and hopeless — at the mercy of the very man who had stolen everything Tynan held dear. Only two years. Could that be?

It seemed like a lifetime.

Two years since he had been a strong, strapping lad — big as most full-grown men — with a close-knit family, a snug home on good land, and a keen sense of his place in the future of his people.

How quickly Laird Cullum had taken all that away.

Tynan's fevered brain echoed with the thunder of hooves that had given them scant warning of the raid. It had all happened so quickly. Yet now when the memories assailed him, it seemed as if everything played out at half-speed. Deadly, gruesome, inevitable . . . it all unrolled before him.

His father's shout of alarm. Laird Cullum and his men bursting through the door. His mother's vain efforts to shield her children. His sisters' shrieks and his brothers' futile blows against their attackers. Table overturned, benches flying, precious food scattered.

Then the sickening crunch of Laird Cullum's mace shattering flesh and bone and the dull scrape of sword in flesh. Blood everywhere, a red haze in the firelight. And then darkness.

He should have died with the rest of them. Would to God that he had. But only his innocence had died that day . . . and his hope.

A gruff, familiar voice drew him back from the brink of oblivion. "By Odin's beard, lad! What in perdition have ye gotten into?" Old Devan glared down at him in disgust.

Too weary to reply, Tynan looked up, mute, at Laird Cullum's Master of Horse.

Visibly repulsed, the old man leaned closer and gagged

10

outright. "*Hiu!* Ye smell like a cesspool!"

"Listen to the man," Tynan grumbled weakly. "Sniffs fresh horse-shite like it's violets, then has the nerve to say *I* stink." He cracked one eye to glare at the wiry little man who hovered nearby. "I smell like a cesspool because that's where I've been. The drains were clogged."

Tynan knew he had Laird Cullum to thank for being burdened with the most demeaning jobs in the castle. "But I'll wager it's the last time they use me for that. I've gotten bigger. They could barely hold me." He raised an arm to reveal his torn shirt and the raw flesh beneath. "See how the rope cut me." A dry, mirthless chuckle escaped him. "That's one nasty job I've outgrown, at least."

The stableman groaned. "Ah, lad. If I'd known it would come to this, I'd have finished ye off myself that day, instead of bringin' ye back to the livin'."

It was as close as Tynan would ever get to a declaration of concern from the only soul who had ever shown him any mercy in this place. He would have been grateful if he'd had the strength. Instead, he merely wondered yet again why Laird Cullum had let him live this long. It made no sense, despite the sadistic pleasure his father's murderer seemed to take from humiliating Tynan again and again.

Old Devan straightened, his usual brusqueness returning. "Well, I won't be standin' for this human filth in me stable. Bad for the horses, it is." He motioned for Tynan to stay where he was. "Wait here. I'll find ye some clean clothes, even if I have to steal 'em, and some warm water. Old Devan will get the boy cleaned up."

Feeling more ancient than the timeworn stones beneath him, Tynan closed his eyes and accepted, once again, the burden of living.

# Chapter I

*Near the Isle of Mist (Now Known as Skye), Eighteen Years Later*

From the first year of his manhood, Tynan's dreams were haunted by the shadow of a woman, her voice as seductive as the first scent of spring on a raw Highland breeze; again and again, she summoned him by name and whispered of his destiny:

> *I call the remnant at the root's direction,*
> *Seed of love from hate in vengeance sworn.*
> *Blood oath broken by a dark reflection*
> *Buried with the damask rose's thorn.*
> *Witch who is no witch works her protection;*
> *Death from life and life from death is born.*

Now he swore he could hear her breathe his name in the scrape of leather against the rocky shore as he dragged the small boat he had stolen through the fog.

*Tynan . . .*

She was close; he could feel her.

Was it the Isle of Mist that called him, or his own blood hunger? Once he had thought it was the ghost of his mother, long dead and unavenged, but time had convinced him otherwise.

Though he could not see the Isle of Mist for the fog, he'd been told it lay close across the narrows. The Witch, they called the place.

The witch who is no witch? he wondered.

For two long years he'd been searching, tracing and re-tracing every rumor and rabbit-trail in the Highlands in re-lentless pursuit of even the slightest clue to where Lady Cullum could have gone. He'd found precious few who'd even been alive twenty years ago, much less anyone who could remember something as unremarkable as that long-ago, furtive passage of a lone woman and child.

But he hadn't given up. Month after frustrating month, he'd cajoled, bullied, and connived answers from suspicious strangers, seeking out anyone spared by war and pestilence these past twenty years, following lead after lead only to end up staring into the empty eyes of senility or standing beside an unmarked grave.

A rational man would never have undertaken such a hope-less task, but Tynan had no use for logic. His obsession left no room for it. The moment he had struck his bargain with Laird Cullum, he had *become* the hunt — driven, insatiable. Every ounce of energy, thought, and will he funneled into his search.

At last, his stubbornness had paid off. Only days ago, he'd found the old boatman who remembered ferrying a regal, richly clad woman and her infant to the Isle of Mist two decades before.

They were there yet. They *had* to be.

All Tynan's instincts told him his destiny was waiting on the Isle of Mist. And his prey.

The fog parted briefly ahead of him, exposing a barren hummock that looked for all the world like the mossy breast of some giant, sleeping earth-goddess. Guided by that one glimpse, he pushed the boat into the cold, fast-moving waters of Caol Rhea and heaved himself inside.

Overburdened by his substantial weight, the little curragh settled alarmingly low in the swift current. The humble craft had been built for ordinary men, not the likes of Tynan, whose tall, powerful stature sent children scurrying for their mother's skirts and turned heads even among the giants of the Highlands.

Muttering an oath, he shifted cautiously to distribute the burden of his oversized frame. One false move, and he'd end up plummeting through the freezing water to an unmourned death, for no matter how many times he'd tried to learn, Tynan had never been able to swim — he sank like a stone. Judging from the whirlpools and eddies all around him, these cold, gray waters would like nothing better than to suck him to a nameless grave. Determined not to oblige them, he moved with agonizing care to lay the oars into their cradles. Tynan gauged the current and the angle of the waves, then rowed with smooth, powerful strokes toward the Witch's breast.

*Tynan . . . Deliverer,* the voice breathed above the rhythmic splash of the oars.

She had never said that before!

His name meant darkness, not deliverer.

Tynan tried to shake off the gathering sense of foreboding that swirled around him like the white oblivion of the mist.

Good thing he had brought along some cheese. Tynan believed in nothing but himself, yet like all sons of the Highlands, he took a few basic precautions. A good chunk of cheese was known to be proof against getting lost in the fog — particularly cheese that had been paraded sunwise in a basket beneath a newborn babe, as had the moldy hunk tucked into his leathern pouch. Anyway, he told himself, if the talisman didn't work, he could always eat it.

It wasn't easy to maintain his heading through the powerful crosscurrents of these narrows. Despite years of secret training with axe and broadsword, his muscles strained at the

14

oars. There were easier crossings, but he had chosen this one for brevity and stealth. If the fog should clear, he was less likely to be seen here than at An Caol.

Without slacking his pace, he turned in the eerie silence and tried to make out some sign of the shoreline, but saw only fog that seemed to thicken with every stroke of the oars. Despite the westerly currents that tempered these lands even now, in February, a sudden chill raised the flesh beneath Tynan's plaid.

Would the place itself betray his coming?

No matter. As he had sworn, he would find Laird Cullum's granddaughter and bring her safe to the old man's feet. The thought of what would follow brought a bitter smile to Tynan's lips. Laird Cullum's sins would be avenged, but the old man wouldn't be the one to pay the price. No. The sins of the father would be visited upon his seed. Only then could Tynan lay down the tormented life he had borne these twenty years and join his kin. His father and mother were waiting, along with his brothers and sisters. And the rest of his kinsmen, his sept. Only when he had kept his vow would they all have peace.

Strengthened by the prospect, he stroked harder to keep his course amid the whorling eddies of the strait. He would find the girl and bring her back, or die trying.

*Northern End of the Trotternish Peninsula, Four months later*

Beltane was two weeks past before Nara could steal a whole day to scale the Quiraing. This June morning, she and Gobhar reached the base of the mountain before the rising sun had burned away the fog that hid the mainland.

As usual, she climbed with far more agility and confidence than the little nanny goat who lagged stubbornly behind her.

"Come along, Gobhar," she urged.

Gobhar bleated reproachfully in the fog, justifiably annoyed that she'd been brought on such a trek with a full udder.

A pang of guilt brought a frown to Nara's lips. "I know you're full. I'll milk you as soon as we reach the Table. I promise. Come, sweet one." She quickened her pace up the steep, rocky track in the fog.

Nara loved these hushed, blanketed days, for they provided her only chance to roam the rugged Trotternish Peninsula without fear of being seen. Still, she kept her veil in place in case *Seanmhair* was watching. Nara was convinced her grandmother could see through the fog as clearly as she herself could see through time, and she had no wish to suffer punishment the way she had the last time *Seanmhair* had caught her bareheaded.

Nara's strong legs and youthful constitution made easy work of the thousand-foot climb up the green slopes of the Quiraing, but Gobhar dawdled and bleated every step of the way. By the time Nara had climbed above the fog and made it almost to the lip of the Table, she looked back and saw her little nanny goat plant her hooves firmly in the dirt.

Nara frowned down at Gobhar and, below her, the thick, white mantle of fog that hid the slopes. "Gobhar," she scolded, "have you forgotten you're a goat? The Good Lord *made* your breed to climb these mountains."

"Maaaa!" Gobhar reproached, obviously indifferent to her divinely ordained abilities.

"Oh, all right, you daft creature. I'll carry you." Nara retraced her steps and hoisted the animal into her arms. She ducked forward to put Gobhar across her shoulders like a shawl, then grasped all four dainty hooves to her chest with one hand. It took more than a little effort to straighten up and maintain her balance. Nara had known perfectly well Gobhar

16

disliked climbing, but lately she'd felt so lonely that she had brought her pet along, anyway — for the company as much as for the milk. "Goodness, you're heavy with all that milk in your udder," she grumbled. "So much for my clever idea of bringing lunch on the hoof. An oatcake and some cheese would have been a lot lighter."

As if to confirm the irony of the situation, Gobhar's distended udder gurgled warmly against her ear. Nara let out a guilty sigh. "Poor beastie, you're about to burst." She struggled upward, doubly cautious now that she had only one hand free for balance. "We're almost there," she panted. "I'll milk you as soon as we reach the top."

That was easier said than done with a stone's-weight of goat around her neck, but at last Nara reached the lip of the green plateau. Her heart pounding from exertion, she pushed Gobhar onto level ground ahead of her. The goat made straight for a clump of sweet grass, and Nara followed, collapsing beside her to catch her breath.

When her pulse had slowed to normal, Nara sat up and inhaled the sun-warmed aroma of green heather. No matter how many times she came here, the magic of this place never failed to awe her. All around, rugged rock outcroppings and needles of stone thrust skyward like the fingers of a hand cupping the flat, green jewel in their palm. By August, the tableland would be bright with purple heather, but now it lay fair and green before her, a private world where skylarks sang and golden eagles soared. Ever since she'd been old enough to find her way without *Seanmhair,* she'd thought of this place as the heart of her own, personal Golden Isle. For as long as she could remember, she had found security and magnificent solitude here. But lately, her hidden, impregnable refuge had begun to seem merely lonely . . . empty, even with Gobhar for company.

17

Why had she begun to feel this sense of loss, of emptiness? Nothing in her life had changed. She still had *Seanmhair* and Auntie and Gobhar.

Nara sighed, telling herself she was making too much of these moods. She was probably just hungry.

She lay down with her head beside the goat's hind leg and grasped a teat. "Lunchtime." One expert squeeze directed a stream of rich, warm milk straight into her open mouth. By the time Gobhar's udder was empty, her own stomach was full. Then the two of them curled up together for a brief, satisfying nap.

When Nara woke, a westerly wind had risen, chasing away the fog but bringing in a bank of low clouds that hid the sun. She knew from the smell of the wind and the feel of it against her cheek that the storm was hours away, yet. Nara set Gobhar to her feet and rose. "I'm going to the cliffs," she explained, convinced that her pet understood every word. "You can graze here until I return." Though the bay was but a few miles away, the path to the cliffs was treacherous, and Nara had carried Gobhar enough for one day. "I'll be back. Stay." She left the animal to graze and headed for the base of the Table.

Moving quickly once she reached the slopes, she covered the rugged track in only an hour. The closer she got to the inland straits, the harder the wind whipped at her veil and apron. Nara climbed and descended, then climbed again, until she reached the ridge that towered over a crescent bay pounded by storm waves.

She stood on the backbone of the ridge without fear, the tips of her sandals projecting over the void. Arms outstretched, she savored the powerful tug of the wind and wondered how it must feel to ride the invisible currents like a gull.

Nara closed her eyes and willed herself to become a gull —

soaring, soaring, her tiny bird-mind conscious only of flight. She could almost see the ground drop away beneath her, feel the breath of God carrying her to the clouds.

As a little girl, she had imagined beautiful palaces atop the clouds — palaces filled with kind people who never became ill or died, people who lived in peaceful kingdoms that glided safe and serene far above the dangers of her world.

Now, mounting higher and higher on the wings of her imagination, she had almost reached that cloud-kingdom when the raucous screech of a golden eagle snatched her back to herself.

Nara opened her eyes just in time to see the magnificent creature swoop past her and descend to a strange gathering of birds that swarmed just offshore. She crouched low to keep from falling and looked closer.

Never in all her life had she witnessed anything like the odd collection of gulls, terns, and cormorants that circled and dived above a drifting mass of flotsam. Usually the mere presence of an eagle would be enough to clear the skies, but these birds were so busy attacking what looked like a lump of brown fur that they ignored the intruder.

What were they pecking at so viciously?

Too far away to see, Nara wished she could fly, indeed. From the heights, the bay looked a mere stone's throw away, but it was actually more than a mile. She climbed down as fast as she could. Once she reached the gentle foothills that led to the sea, she hurried toward a basalt outcropping that overlooked the bay, her side aching with every breath.

By the time she scaled it and looked out over the choppy waves, the raft had drifted to the center of the bay. She scanned the sky for a raven — sure evidence that witchcraft was afoot — but there was none, nor any ill-omened petrels.

Nara winced at the vicious frenzy of the birds' attack.

Then she saw the lump of soggy brown fur raise up in a weak gesture of self-protection.

Was it a man? A tingle of alarm shot through her at the prospect, but her fear was tempered by a thrill of curiosity. She had never seen a man up close. From earliest memory, *Seanmhair* had warned her in the direst terms against strangers — men in particular.

She looked closer. Despite the distance, she judged its size against the birds' and decided it couldn't be a man. Too small. A dog, perhaps, or a shaggy Highland calf. Whatever it was, the birds were doing their best to peck it to pieces.

She pitied the poor creature. Nara knew that it was foolish to interfere in the cycle of life, but she could not bear to watch any living thing suffer such a brutal death.

But she didn't have to let it die. She *could* save it.

On impulse, she decided to try.

Nara slid from the rocks, then raced down the green slope toward the beach, tearing off her veil and apron as she ran. When she reached a pile of stones at the edge of the sand, she pulled off her sandals and shucked down to her shift before she hastily shoved everything into a dry crevice in the stone.

Nara paused for a moment at the edge of the churning surf. With a storm blowing in, the currents could be treacherous, even in the inland straits. But when she saw a large tern dive headlong for a vicious stab at the drifting animal, a fresh pang of sympathy strengthened her resolve. She charged into the icy water.

As always, the cold took her breath away momentarily, but she knew that swimming would stir her blood. She struck out with long, gliding strokes toward the hapless animal. Nara had scarcely traveled a dozen yards when two supple, dark shapes flanked her in the water.

She smiled. Erk and Merk, always there to protect her.

And, as always, she felt slow and clumsy compared to her seal companions. How effortlessly they streaked along below the surface while she splashed on top, all awkward arms and elbows like a grasshopper. Nara quickened her pace to keep up, yet just before she reached the tangle of driftwood, Erk swam directly into her path and surfaced with a warning bark.

"This is no time to play, Erk! Get out of my way!" She splashed a sheet of water at Erk's speckled gray head, but he slipped below the surface in time to avoid it.

Just then, a strong gust of wind — the likes of which she had never seen — spun the pile of flotsam full circle, then sent it back toward the mainland, almost as if the Isle of Mist herself were rejecting the odd raft and its contents. Nara shivered, wondering if it was an omen.

Perhaps she should turn back. The raft was farther out than she had thought. In all her gambols with the seals, she had never ventured so deep, especially with a storm coming. Already she was winded, and her legs had gone numb with cold.

While she paused to consider and catch her breath, the current nudged the raft back in her direction. The snarl of seaweed and driftwood was only a dozen yards away when Nara saw what looked like an enormous dog rear its head skyward.

Not a dog — a wolf! A big one, just like the silver image hammered into *Seanmhair*'s brooch, only this one's fur was brown!

She paddled backward a few strokes, remembering her grandmother's bloodcurdling tales of the Highland wolves that preyed upon human and kine alike, but this wolf's tortured expression halted her flight. His swollen tongue protruded from a gaunt muzzle, and his breath came in shallow, erratic spurts. Obviously, the animal was near death.

21

Nara trod water as the waves brought the animal closer. She knew she should swim away as fast as she could — no one but a fool would bring such a savage predator ashore — but just as she made up her mind to leave, the wolf opened huge, golden eyes to stare at her in mute torment.

She looked into the eyes of the wolf and saw the soul of a man. His suffering rode the invisible thread of her gaze to lodge behind her heart and bloom into a void so dark and painful she feared it might consume her.

Averting her gaze with a gasp, she recited thrice against the evil eye:

*If eye has blighted, Father, Son, and Holy Ghost have blessed.*
*If anything elfin or worldly has harmed me*
*On earth or above or in hell beneath,*
*Do Thou, God of Grace, turn it aside.*

Thank goodness it was a Thursday, so the charm could work its protection immediately!

Without warning, the Sight stirred within her. Usually she saw things clearly, but this was a vision of dark shapes that formed and diffused without meaning. She could discern only that the wolf was male, and she was destined to save him. Then she looked down the tunnel of time and saw a brilliant light, beckoning with warmth and comfort from afar at the end of darkness.

When she came back to herself, Nara was staring at the wolf. Was this the Dark Deliverer she had dreamed of? Or was it a shape-shifter, luring her to her doom with wizardry?

The wolf sighed and laid his bony skull on his paws, in just the same way her favorite puppy had when it died. She sensed that this once-powerful creature had struggled long and hard to survive adrift but no longer possessed the strength to fight for life, much less to harm her.

Unless she intervened, and quickly, he would breathe his last within sight of land.

"No!" She splashed at him. "You mustn't die, not before I save you! Wake up!"

The wolf didn't move.

After a split second of indecision, she crossed herself, swam three times sunwise around the wolf despite her fatigue, then grabbed a trailing strand of half-rotten rope and began to pull the unlikely raft toward land.

Once she reached the shore, Nara untangled several scraps of rope from the flotsam. Destiny or not, she had no intention of becoming dinner for a starving wolf. With the first length, she bound the unconscious animal's muzzle; with the second, she tied his forelegs together; a third secured his hind legs. Throughout the process, the wolf never stirred.

She spent the next hour and the last of her strength dragging the senseless creature to one of her special hiding places well above the tide. At last, Nara reached the snug little cave in the sea-cliff and struggled to pull the wolf in after her. She entered to the sound of fresh water dripping into a clear pool at the back of the cavern.

Once inside the closed space, the wolf's fur gave off a powerful, sour stench, mixed with the strong odor of decayed kelp. Gagging, Nara dragged the animal to the bed of dried heather she had left there, then collapsed, panting, beside him.

The animal lay so still, she wondered if he'd stopped breathing. Nara put her ear to his chest and heard a faint, thready heartbeat.

Water. He needed water.

She hastened to the pool, then frowned. She had no means to bring the much-needed liquid to the thirsty animal. Unless . . .

23

After only a moment's hesitation, she shucked off her shift, wrung the last of the seawater from it, then swished it in the pool. Naked and shivering, she rolled her shift into a dripping wad in her hands and carried it back to crouch self-consciously beside the wolf.

Why was she worried about being naked before a dumb beast? The wolf was merely a half-dead creature, nothing more. If he had been a wizard, surely he would have seized her before she tied him up. Still, she drew up her knees to conceal her nakedness before she untied his muzzle and pried open the animal's long, sharp fangs so she could drip water onto his parched tongue.

At first, nothing happened. Then the wolf choked and shuddered to life, his great, golden eyes flaring open. He thrashed against his bonds with surprising strength and bared his fangs to snarl a blast of acrid breath in her direction.

Nara scrambled backward, hastily covering herself with the sodden fabric of her shift. As before, she sensed manlike fear and rage in the wolf's golden gaze. And as before, she understood his anger and felt pity for his suffering.

"Shhh," she crooned from a respectful distance. "Calm down. I had to bind you, or you'd have made a meal of me, and who could blame you, poor starving beastie." One could hardly expect a wolf to be anything but a wolf, after all.

To her relief, his burst of energy was short-lived. At the sound of her soothing words, he closed his eyes and relaxed, almost as if he had understood her.

Nara extended her arms and gingerly wrung the remaining moisture from her shift into a hollow depression near the wolf's muzzle. "There. That should hold you until I can come back with some broth and cheese." After making sure that the animal's bindings were secure, she shrugged into her damp shift and crouched toward the mouth of the cave. She paused at the opening to look back.

She had saved the creature. Now, whatever in the name of blessed Saint Brigit would she *do* with the savage beast, especially if he regained his strength?

Nara wished she knew. First, she must fetch Gobhar and take her home. Then she would bring the wolf some broth and cheese. She'd worry about the rest when the time came.

Tynan had waited more than an hour for a reply to his inquiry before he heard the faint sound of approaching footsteps through the ironclad portal of the priory.

A small peephole opened level with his chest, and he saw a decidedly feminine eye take his measure. The pupil widened in alarm. Then a prim mouth replaced the eye at the opening to say, "It's against my better judgment, but our prioress has agreed to speak with you. After the bell rings, you may enter."

The peephole closed.

Shifting impatiently from foot to foot, he scanned the bleak headland that surrounded the convent on three sides. The priory was at the tip of a steep promontory, its high walls as stout as any fortress Tynan had ever seen — and in two years of searching, he had seen more than most Highlanders saw in a lifetime.

Good thing the nuns had decided to let him in. He'd have had a devil of a time scaling those walls, otherwise. After fruitless months of investigating every hovel and haven from the south end of the island to the tip of Vaternish, he knew that unless he found what he was looking for here, his instincts had betrayed him.

She'll be there, he reassured himself. His instincts had never failed him yet.

At the sound of a bell from inside the priory, he grasped the heavy metal ring on the door and pulled with all his might.

The door hardly budged, and its hinges squeaked from disuse.

Didn't anyone ever *leave* this place? he wondered. There must be another way out, though he'd seen no other opening in the walls of the ancient broch that now served as a convent.

Another mighty tug, and he was able to open the massive door just enough to slip inside a dark, narrow hallway furnished with only a mean cot and single chair. He left the door ajar, having no intention of closing himself in. Tynan hated feeling trapped, especially in a place as close as this with no windows. Squinting in the dimness, he made out a threadbare tapestry on the opposite wall and a closed door with no hardware at the end of the corridor.

A female voice caused him to jump. "Traveler, what seekest thou?" The accent was strange, unlike any he had ever heard, yet the sound of her voice seemed faintly familiar.

Tynan weighed his reply. "I wish to speak with the prioress."

"I am she. State your business, then leave us in peace. This is no place for a warrior."

"I am no warrior, Good Mother. Merely a man on a quest." Tynan's hand eased from the hilt of his father's sword. "A quest of mercy. And of honor."

Where was the woman?

Detecting a tiny flicker of light from behind one of the worn spots on the tapestry, he strolled closer but kept his eyes on the open doorway. "I come at the bidding of Laird Cullum, master of Eilean d'Ór and Chief of the Glen Achall sept of the MacKay."

A small gasp emanated from behind the hanging.

Tynan grasped the heavy fabric and pulled it aside, revealing iron bars and, behind them, the familiar features he had seen so many times before at the shrine in Laird Cullum's chapel.

26

Lady Cullum. He'd found her at last!

The prioress bent her face into her hands. "Is there no refuge in this world?"

She was older, of course, and her nun's veil covered the raven hair that glowed blue-black in her portrait at Eilean d'Ór, but Tynan was certain it was she. He'd seen that face often enough; every day, Laird Cullum lit a candle beneath her likeness and prayed for her safe return. And now Tynan had found her. His pulse thrummed with anticipation. It was only a matter of time until he located the girl.

He dismissed the notion that she might have died or moved away.

Tynan struggled to conceal the flush of triumph that tingled through him. He had to play this out carefully, or Lady Cullum might take the girl and flee, just as she had twenty years ago.

He faced the trembling woman and said softly, "Twenty years ago, Laird Cullum drove away his beloved wife with a hideous oath, an oath born of grief and rage but quickly repented." Much as he wanted to know the reasons behind the slaughter that had followed, he made no mention of it.

The nun shuddered.

"My lady has nothing to fear . . . from me or my master. I seek her at his bidding to beg her forgiveness and to ask her to return."

He had thought she'd been weeping, but when Lady Cullum raised her eyes to face him, she radiated bitterness and anger — emotions he understood all too well. "If a mere apology were sufficient to wipe out such a heinous sin," she declared, "there would be no need of the Cross, sir." She rose, her mouth set in a grim line. "The lady you seek is not here. And even if she were, she would not do as you have asked. I mean no insult, but only a fool would take the word of a stranger in such a matter."

"I agree. It is imprudent to trust the word of a stranger," Tynan replied mildly, extracting the precious letter he had guarded these past two years. He laid it on the ledge between two bars. "But these are the words of Laird Cullum himself, his shame and remorse publicly confessed and recorded before the entire fief. He swore then to grant any boon within his power to the man who safely returned his beloved wife or his granddaughter."

At the mention of her granddaughter, Lady Cullum's eyes narrowed, but her expression remained rigid. She made no move toward the letter. "And what boon would you ask, sir?" she asked with suspicion.

A wise question. It always helped to know what an adversary had at stake. Tynan answered with as much of the truth as he thought prudent. "Only what is mine by right . . . to take my place as leader of my sept."

His sept. Thanks to the "mercy" of Laird Cullum, Tynan *was* his sept — all of it. But now that the Council held Laird Cullum's written promise to restore Tynan's rights on the safe return of the granddaughter, Tynan would have the last word . . . and the last sword-stroke. Only Tynan and Laird Alexander, head of the Council, knew what would come next.

Now that he'd found Lady Cullum, Tynan could almost taste the bitter satisfaction of victory. But the grandmother was only a means to an end. He needed the girl.

He smiled. "Laird Cullum wishes to bring his granddaughter home so she may take her rightful place as his heir and choose a husband to succeed him as chieftain."

The prioress let out a derisive snort. "Choose a husband, indeed." Her voice dripped venom. "As long as it's not a MacDougald . . . assuming he didn't kill them all, as he swore

28

to. Or was that but *another* rash vow Laird Cullum didn't mean?"

"That vow, he did his best to keep," Tynan answered with deceptive softness.

He'd still been in the care of his mother when the raid had shattered his life. Not yet privy to the councils of men, he'd known nothing then of the reasons for the massacre. Like all children of the Highlands, he'd accepted the endless conflict between tribes as a simple fact of life, a bitter reality as constant and unavoidable as storm or pestilence.

Over the years, he'd managed to learn most of the sordid tale that had led to the destruction of his sept, but there were still dark questions yet to be answered.

All in good time. All in good time.

He glanced pointedly at the letter balanced between him and the prioress. "I'll leave Laird Cullum's letter in your care." He could play the game her way. "Perhaps Lady Cullum might be found, after all. If only she'd read it, I'm certain the lady would at least consider returning with me to Eilean d'Ór."

Tynan rose to bow with a dignity and grace he had copied from Alexander, Laird High Chief of the Council himself. "I have business at Duntulm, but I shall return. Until we meet again, my lady." He turned and left the priory without looking back.

Only when he was well out of sight and certain he had not been followed did he double back and set up camp in a safe place. Then he settled in to wait . . . and to watch.

# *Chapter II*

Huddled by a smoldering peat fire, Tynan shifted his plaid and tugged the clammy homespun of his tattered shirt away from his skin.

This Isle of Mist seemed colder, damper, somehow, than the Highlands, but he wasn't certain why. The same westerly winds blew across the green desolation of these moors, bringing the same drizzles and fog between spates of welcome sunshine.

Maybe it was witchcraft that chilled his bones. He'd found a fairy ring almost directly above him on the crest of the deep crevasse where he now hid.

He could always search out another hiding place, one that wasn't beneath a fairy ring, but he doubted there would be another spot so convenient or secure — at least, not within easy range of the priory. Here, a fast-flowing burn cut through the narrow, twisting crevasse just a few feet below the shallow niche where he sat, and a slab of basalt overhead sheltered him from prying eyes. Best of all, an unrelenting sea-breeze whistled through the crevasse, dispersing the smoke of his campfire so well that not even a hunting hound could sniff him out.

He poked a stick into the blood-red heart of the fire and decided to remain where he was.

Tynan feared no witch or wizard, nor any fairy cunning — not even the Banshee's shriek. He'd willingly match his hatred against any power, seen or unseen. No matter what forces came against him, he *would* find the girl and take her back.

But first, he needed to eat. He was so hollow, his belly had clapped to his backbone, but his hunger pangs had long since given way to weakness.

How long had it been?

Three days? No, four, since he'd consumed anything more substantial than roots or the rare bit of soft moss he cleaned and washed down with cold, clear streamwater. If he hadn't come upon the little goat in the fairy ring, he might well have starved.

He unsheathed his blade and set about skinning and dressing his kill. A tiny pang of guilt nagged him when he saw the haze of death in the creature's eyes — eyes that had once been dark and luminous, looking up at him with absolute trust even as he'd bent to sever the animal's throat. Most creatures fled at the quake of his footfalls, but this hapless animal had approached him freely.

Food, that's all it was, he told himself, trying not to remember the moist gurgle of blood that had spurted from flesh and sinew.

Tynan chided himself for caring. If it weren't for all he'd managed to steal, he'd never have made it this far. In this harsh land, inhabited by an even harsher people, life was a matter of survival, plain and simple. That single imperative came before all else save his duty to his sept, and he had to survive to acquit himself of that. Only then could he entertain the luxury of mercy . . . or of dying.

He finished skinning the goat, put the organs and waste aside, then fashioned a makeshift griddle of rocks and shells over the glowing heart of the fire. When the stones were hot enough to make a drop of blood dance, he laid the carcass across them to cook. Noting that the hide was supple and would make a good pouch, Tynan climbed down to the burn to wash and scrape it.

Whatever lingering reservations he might have had about the goat vanished when he returned to the mouth-watering aroma of roasting meat. One sniff, and his empty stomach growled like thunder, awakening his appetite with a vengeance. For weeks before his food had run out, he'd been skimping along on nothing but toasted oats and fish. Little wonder he was ravenous.

An hour of turning and basting later, he could wait no longer. The haunches were scarcely done, but he carved one off and bit into it anyway. The meat sizzled when it touched his tongue, scalding him.

Tynan cursed and snatched the steaming haunch from his mouth.

Chastened, he blew on the meat until it was safe to consume, then tore greedily into the hot, juicy flesh. By the nine virgins of Saint Brigit, it felt good to chew a mouthful of meat again! He stopped eating only when his distended belly could hold no more.

Full and sleepy, he stripped the remaining meat, salted and packed it into his pouch, then climbed to the moor to bury the bones and organs, reserving only the brains to soften the hide.

A waste, it was, he thought as he used his father's battle-axe to chop through the thick turf, but he could not risk attracting scavengers, especially the noisy attentions of gulls or crows.

When he was done, he climbed back down into his shallow den and curled atop a narrow bed of peat, wedging himself securely against the rock. That night, Tynan slept more soundly than he had in memory.

The next morning, the gray light of dawn had barely found its way into Nara's earth-house when she returned from the secret tunnel to the priory. "*Seanmhair,* did Gobhar come back yet?" She knew the answer before she asked. If Gobhar had come home, the little nanny goat would be tangled underfoot. Gobhar loved Nara almost as much as Nara loved her, and until last evening, the sunset always found her safe at home, eager to sleep next to her mistress. Nara frowned. "Auntie . . . I mean, Mother Esau said she hadn't seen her."

Nara had risen before first light to search for Gobhar. "Maybe she got stuck on a ledge," she offered, wishing with all her might that it were true, but knowing it was not. She bit her lip. "She might have gotten stuck on a ledge."

"Perhaps." *Seanmhair* stopped sweeping the hard-packed earthen floor and turned compassionate eyes toward her granddaughter. "Why don't you go look for her? But mind you, Nara, wear your veil. And keep a sharp eye for strangers."

Nara had heard what came next so many times, she mouthed the very words her grandmother spoke.

"No stranger must ever know we're here," *Seanmhair* continued gravely, as if she were warning Nara for the first time instead of the thousandth. "Neither one of us would be safe if we were found out." She drew close to tuck a jet-black tendril into the thick plait that hung to Nara's waist. "Promise me you'll keep your veil on."

Nara picked up the veil — a length of thick, ivory-colored wool that matched her simple gown and apron. As long as she could remember, she had dressed like the novices at the priory, and *Seanmhair* like the nuns in their drab brown habits. "I promise to keep my veil on," she said without conviction. She laid the veil low across her forehead, then se-

33

cured its ties tightly at the nape of her neck.

"There's a good girl." *Seanmhair* arranged the trailing fabric to conceal Nara's plait, leaving no evidence that she was not what she appeared to be. "Run along, then. We'll break our fast when you return." Nara's woeful expression prompted her to add, "Gobhar always turns up somewhere. You'll find her."

Nara nodded, in spite of what she knew.

At times like these, she hated having the Two Sights. How often she would have preferred the comfort of hope. Yet Nara could no more control her uncanny convictions about the present than she could her glimpses of past or future.

Perhaps she was wrong, just this once. Gobhar might still be alive.

It didn't surprise her, though, when she later found the splash of blood near the fairy ring. With shaking hand, she knelt and touched the rusty stain.

Instantly, she saw a pair of glowing, golden eyes and felt a slash of pain across her throat. Then darkness closed around her.

When she recovered, she was lying beside the patch of blood, looking up at a cloudless blue sky.

Golden eyes . . .

A desperate realization brought her to her feet.

The wolf!

Nara ran as fast as she could to the sea-cliff and scrambled recklessly down its treacherous face toward the cave. By the time she neared the entrance, she had cut her hand on a rock and badly scraped her ankle, but she felt no pain. She only knew she had to make certain the wolf was still there, safely tied.

Afraid of what she would find, she leaned back against the rocks just outside the cave opening. "Please, oh, please,

Blessed Saint Columba, let the wolf be there." As much for her own safety as for Gobhar's, she included herself in the prayer she had chanted on Beltane for the Driving of the Kine, concluding with, "The safeguard of Cormac the shapely be ours, from wolf and from bird flock."

Dear heaven, she couldn't remember the rest of the prayer, and she knew she'd left some out. Her heart pounding with dread, Nara crossed herself, then bent and entered the cave.

As she had feared, the wolf was gone. It had chewed through its bonds, leaving behind only its stink and a few shreds of rope.

Nara picked up one of the frayed cords and sank to her knees. "Gobhar!" Her cry of grief bounced back loudly from the stone walls of the little chamber. Unable to deny any longer what had happened to her pet, she burst into tears. "Oh, Gobhar," she sobbed. "Why did I save that vile beastie?" If she'd known he would kill Gobhar, she'd gladly have let the animal die at sea. *Why* had she brought him here?

But she had, and the predator had killed her pet.

A chilling question brought an abrupt halt to her tears: What else would it kill?

"*Seanmhair!*" she gasped. "I must warn her!"

Tynan had observed the priory in secret for eleven long, uneventful days before his patience was rewarded. At last, he looked up from the matted cotton-grass where he lay and saw a brown-clad nun plodding westward across the moor, her veil and habit flapping as she bent into the wind.

So there was a secret entrance! She hadn't emerged from the priory's only door. It remained closed and locked, its rusted hinges silent. That meant there was another way out, as he'd suspected.

He watched the nun approach the cliffs alongside the steep, featureless walls of the convent. Was it the prioress? She was certainly tall enough. And her shoulders were perfectly squared, just as Lady Cullum's had been. Tynan waited until her back was turned to creep into a narrow depression that paralleled her progress. Keeping low, he followed for a closer look. With luck, he'd be able to get within a few yards of her without being seen.

When she reached the crest of the cliff, she stopped, allowing him to catch a brief profile.

It was Lady Cullum, all right. But what was she doing? Why had she left the safety of the priory?

She reached up, untied her veil, and — to Tynan's amazement — pulled off the coarse brown fabric, releasing a magnificent cascade of straight black hair that fanned free behind her in the wind. Though the woman had to be at least fifty, not a single strand of gray marred the ebony perfection of her hair. It gleamed almost blue-black in the sunlight that filtered through high, streaky clouds.

In this island of fair-haired Norse descendants, such coloring instantly betrayed her Highland origins.

Tynan's brows knit. Nuns were supposed to cut off all their hair. But then again, Lady Cullum could hardly be a real nun. The woman still had a living, breathing husband! Tynan wondered irreverently if she'd made a cuckold of the Lord Himself.

He watched her begin to sway in the wind, as lithe as a young girl.

Her blue-black hair shifted and gleamed behind her, causing Tynan to marvel anew at its youthful luster. Had she used sorcery to keep it that way? Perhaps she had struck a bargain with the devil to preserve her crowning glory. Tynan knew women were particular about their hair, yet he could scarcely imagine trading one's soul for such vanity. The very idea caused his skin to pebble.

He wasn't a superstitious man, but he crossed himself and whispered a hasty prayer against witches, just to be on the safe side.

He'd scarcely murmured the "amen" before his attention was abruptly diverted by the howl of a wolf close behind him. Drawing his dagger, he pivoted and dropped to his stomach. Tynan scanned the rolling slope where the sound had come from. There was no sign of the wolf.

When he turned back to the cliffs, the prioress had disappeared.

A thrill of alarm shot from the base of his neck to his fingertips. Where was she? She couldn't be hiding; there were no trees or bushes on this barren headland, and Tynan crouched in the only depression large enough to conceal anything bigger than a rabbit.

Then it occurred to him that she might have jumped or fallen from the cliff.

The prospect brought him instantly to his feet. If Lady Cullum died, he might never find her granddaughter. Pulse thundering in his ears, he scrambled to the spot where Lady Cullum had been standing.

Tynan looked down. A hundred feet below him, churning waves charged against the dark boulders at the base of the cliff, but there was no sign of Lady Cullum.

She hadn't jumped, then. Her fair skin would have been easy to spot, even from this height. Bands of tension loosened their hold on his chest.

But if she hadn't jumped, where was she? He turned again to the empty slope.

Had he seen her fetch, then — a mere specter of the real Lady Cullum, sent to lure him to the edge of the cliff?

Perhaps he'd been wrong to dismiss the potency of magic. Tynan's scalp prickled as he carefully backed away from the precipice.

One thing was certain: No ordinary woman could have disappeared that way.

Suddenly realizing how exposed he was, Tynan crouched low and returned to his watch-place. He would see her again, and when he did, he wouldn't take his eyes off her — not even for an instant. If she turned into a hare, he would follow the hare. If she turned into a cat, he would follow the cat. He would follow her to hell, if that was what it took to find the girl.

Nara's grandmother sighed wistfully as she barred the turf-covered trapdoor to their ancient earth-house. She'd known better than to remove her veil in the open like that, but Nara wasn't the only one who loved to feel the wind tugging at her hair. Even Keriam had confessed to exposing her own cropped locks when the breeze was soft and unseasonably warm, like today.

Ah, well, Eideann thought as she climbed down the ladder, what harm had it done? They were safe — for the time being, anyway. She thanked Providence yet again for her deliverance from that golden-eyed warrior who'd shattered her security with his terrifying questions and even more terrifying revelations. If he should return, Keriam would warn them. Then Eideann would take Nara into the Quiraing to hide.

The sound of muffled sobs greeted her when she entered the subterranean chamber that had been her haven these past twenty years. "Nara?"

A loud sniff emanated from behind the arras. "Yes, *Seanmhair?*"

Eideann pushed the tapestry aside to find a red-nosed,

swollen-eyed Nara clutching her pillow the way she used to hold Gobhar. "Ah, child." She sat down and pulled her granddaughter close. "I know you miss Gobhar." She stroked Nara's shining black hair, their common legacy.

For Eideann, looking at Nara was like looking at Keriam thirty years ago. Or herself, before time and tragedy had taken their toll.

"I know how lonely it is for you here," she said softly, "but we must be grateful for this refuge God has given us."

Nara curled against her and began to sob afresh.

Eideann rocked her gently, wishing she had more than platitudes to offer. Poor child. For twenty years, Nara had been the only ray of joy in this isolated place, but ever since the girl had come to the fullness of her womanhood, she'd grown more and more distant and moody. Eideann feared what would happen if things went on this way.

Her own eyes welled. "Oh, Nara, how long must we live in the shadow of this curse?" Her throat tightening, she swiped away the single tear that escaped. "You should be long married by now, with a babe at your breast and half a dozen wee ones clinging to your skirts."

Nara stopped crying and turned her tear-stained face to her grandmother, the pain in her emerald eyes tempered by sudden inquisitiveness. "Did you have half a dozen children clinging to your skirts?"

Eideann's heart contracted. "No," she managed. In all these years, Nara had never questioned why they lived this way or what had gone before. She'd questioned everything else — continually — but never the reason for their exile.

So the reckoning had come at last. Eideann had known it would. She struggled to maintain her composure as the memories flooded back. Nara deserved the truth, no matter how painful it would be for both of them. "Of the four sons and two daughters I bore my husband, only two boys survived infancy. The younger, Curran, was killed by the MacDougalds when he was only eighteen."

Glad that her grandmother had answered with such candor, Nara nodded gravely. "That left my father, Duncan, son of Cullum." She'd been able to sing her father's lineage since she was ten — *Seanmhair* had taught her the harp for just that purpose — but that wasn't enough anymore. Summoning her courage, she made bold to ask, "And my mother? You've told me her name, but nothing more."

When *Seanmhair* did not reply, Nara summoned up all her courage to ask again what she'd been wanting to ask as long as she could remember. "Please, *Seanmhair*, may we speak of her at last? I feel like only half a person, knowing nothing of her."

*Seanmhair*'s encircling arms went rigid. For a moment, Nara feared she would never answer, but eventually she did, her voice thick with emotion. "She was a beautiful woman, as fair as you and I are dark. And she was good — everything I had prayed for my son's wife to be." *Seanmhair* let out a deep sigh of regret, speaking volumes with what remained unspoken. "Your father loved her very much. He called her his Damask Rose."

"His Damask Rose . . ." Nara rolled the name across her tongue. "Damask Rose." She liked the sound of it. *His* Damask Rose. Did that indicate affection or possessiveness on her father's part? she wondered. "But you told me her name was Grainne. Why did he call her Damask Rose?"

A faraway expression in her eyes, *Seanmhair* turned Nara's face up to hers. "Her cheeks were pink as the Damask Rose our ancestors brought back from the Great Crusade." Her thumb stroked gently across Nara's cheekbone. "As pink as your own." The weight of her sadness settled between them

40

like a cold, gray fog. "When your mother . . . came to us, she was wearing a deep pink gown of the same shade, in damask silk. It made her skin glow like an angel's. I think that was the first time your father called her his Damask Rose."

Nara risked asking further, "And my mother's father . . . who was he?"

*Seanmhair*'s face congealed. "Laird Galen of the Clan MacDougald."

A cold tingle of dread congealed around Nara's heart. "The same clan that killed my uncle?" No wonder *Seanmhair* had been loath to speak of them! Nara leaned closer to the woman who had been both father and mother to her from earliest recognition. She sensed a sickening wave of grief and remorse in her grandmother. "I'm sorry, *Seanmhair*. I was selfish to make you open old wounds. Forgive me. I shall ask no more questions about my mother's people."

"Beloved child," *Seanmhair* whispered, her arms tightening around Nara, "I knew this day would come. You have every right to know your heritage, all of it. What few names I can remember from your mother's ancestry, I will gladly share." She kissed Nara's forehead. "You must understand, though, that the pain I feel has nothing to do with you."

"What caused such sorrow, then?" Nara could no more have stopped herself from asking than she could stop her heart from beating.

"The pride of men," *Seanmhair* replied caustically, "and the same senseless hatreds that have robbed mothers of their sons, wives of their husbands, and babes of their fathers since the beginning of time." Never had she spoken with such bitterness.

Suddenly *Seanmhair* looked old far beyond her years. "Once I believed that some men were different, but life taught me otherwise. I fear now that no man is above such hatred. It's in their blood, the very taint of Adam, and when it's stirred, all else falls by the wayside, even the love they hold for their women." She gave Nara's shoulders a squeeze, then rose and crossed to the narrow table where they worked and ate. When she spoke again, frustration sharpened her tone. "Regardless of their station, the heritage of men is the same: pride and vengeance." She turned burning eyes to Nara. "That is why we must live in hiding, burrowed beneath the ground like rabbits. That is why you must never trust a stranger, nor even let one see you, Nara. A curse of pride and vengeance hangs above your head. You will be safe only if you remain hidden here, on this island."

Nara's heart constricted. "And if I should want to leave?" How could she explain the longing she felt whenever she looked across the straits to the mainland?

"Never." *Seanmhair*'s green eyes darkened with warning. "You must never leave this island, Nara. Promise me."

"Will there be no husband for me, then?" Nara asked brokenly. "Nor babe at my breast? Nor children at my skirts?" She rose, her eyes level with her grandmother's. "What life would I be saving, *Seanmhair*, without that?"

*Seanmhair* opened her arms and drew her close. "The same life we have shared these last twenty years, my treasure. Has that been so bad?"

"No," Nara confessed. To spare her grandmother further anguish, she tried to speak positively. "We have food and shelter and our own little family. That should be enough for anyone."

But it wasn't, not for her.

# Chapter III

Tynan had long since eaten the last of the salted goat meat when he decided to try for one of the speckled seals he'd seen lounging on the rocks just north of the convent. He didn't particularly like seal meat, finding it greasy and unpalatable, but he hadn't caught any game or fish in days, so hunger overrode the sensibilities of his palate.

Fortunately, the day dawned foggy enough to hide him from the seals, and from prying eyes. Glad for the mist, Tynan shouldered his bow and quiver, then followed the burn to the shore. There he climbed along the rocks until he was overlooking a little bay with a narrow beach. No seals lay on the boulders in the bay, but it was early yet.

He found a good vantage point on a rock outcropping and settled down to wait. As he nocked an arrow against the bowstring, he prayed that the seals would come and that his aim would strike true. He couldn't afford to lose any more arrows. There were only three left in his quiver, and he hadn't found a single tree fit for making shanks in this windswept, godforsaken place. What few rowans and hollies there were grew twisted and stunted, low to the ground. Prudence dictated that he save his shots until he had clear aim to the seal's eye, guaranteeing a kill. Otherwise the animal might swim away to die, taking his arrow with it.

He waited in the mist, the silence broken only by the sound of the waves lapping against the rocks. The rising sun had begun to disperse the fog before he saw a speckled gray seal poke his head above water in the middle of the bay. The animal sniffed the mist, barked, then turned to survey its surroundings with huge, dark eyes.

Tynan went still as the rocks around him. Too far out to ensure a hit, he judged. Better to wait.

The seal disappeared, then resurfaced closer, joined by another speckled gray head. Then a third head rose, facing away from Tynan, its fur black as onyx.

A black seal? Tynan blinked hard to make sure he was really seeing what he'd thought. It was black, all right. Never in his life had he come upon such an animal. Even in the diffuse light that filtered through the fog, the seal's sleek pelt glowed almost blue.

A smile spread across Tynan's lips. Such a rare pelt would fetch a premium at Duntulm. Not only would he have meat from the carcass, but money from the skin besides. He took deadly aim, holding his breath as he waited for the animal to turn.

To his frustration, the black seal slipped beneath the water along with the other two.

Bow still drawn, Tynan stepped to the edge of the rock and sighted down the arrow, scanning the gentle swells on the bay. Then the sleek, black head surfaced again, only a dozen yards ahead of him. He almost let fly before he realized it had a woman's face.

Tynan eased his bowstring with a gasp.

A selkie!

The selkie granted him only one brief tantalizing glimpse of her face before she ducked beneath the water and swam toward the steep little beach, her movements as fluid as her speckled companions'.

Tynan watched in awe as she went by below him. Every

Celt alive knew the legends of female seals who shed their skins to come ashore as women, but he had never met anyone who had actually seen one!

Her pelt! If he could find it . . . Whoever had possession of a selkie's pelt could control her at will.

He watched through the mist as the selkie rose on two legs and waded gracefully up onto the steep little beach. Her long, black hair molded a form so voluptuous that Tynan's manhood sprang to life beneath his threadbare plaid. He could clearly see the curve of her hips and buttocks beneath the covering of sleek, wet hair.

She turned to wave farewell to the two spotted seals who resurfaced just offshore. Her gesture exposed the generous curve of her breasts, the creamy flesh of her torso, and the dark vee at her loins. But before Tynan could get a good look at her face, she turned away again.

Seeing her like this, her hair gleaming to her knees, he believed the tales of mortal men lured to a watery grave by such perfection.

The selkie climbed to a level patch of beach and paused. Only when she threaded a hand behind the base of her neck to free her hair did he see that she was wearing a thin shift, made transparent by the seawater that now dripped from its hem.

Did selkies wear clothes?

Tynan forgot the question immediately when she gathered her dark tresses over her shoulder, sat on a boulder with her back to him, and began to wring the moisture from her hair, her hands squeezing and twisting with methodical grace.

By the spirits of land and sea, what he'd give to have those hands caress him like that, stroking, squeezing . . . The mere thought made Tynan's manhood throb more urgently with every beat of his heart.

Through the haze of lust, though, one of old Devan's admonitions surfaced unbidden: *Never let yer cock do the thinkin', boy. It'll kill you, every time!*

Devan was right, of course, and Tynan knew it. Though his needs were as urgent as any man's, there was no place for a woman in his life, even a selkie. True, there'd been a few women who'd wanted him, and when they'd been winsome and safely married, Tynan had obliged, making no promises. But such couplings meant no more than scratching an itch.

Until this moment, he had never let a woman into his heart or his mind. But this creature . . . Suddenly he felt as if he'd perish unless he could run his hands over those curves and bury himself inside her.

Perhaps she had bewitched him already.

Trying to think clearly, he realized he must proceed with caution. Only a fool would confront a selkie unless he'd found her pelt.

Her back still to him, the selkie rose and headed for a narrow break in the rocks.

Tynan followed, keeping his eyes on her until she entered a cleft between two huge boulders. Determined not to lose her, he leaped from rock to rock, then swiftly and silently climbed the outcropping that separated them. When he reached the top, he looked down to the other side and saw her step into a freshwater pool at the base of a waterfall.

The selkie turned her face up to the cascade and arched her back, concealing her features but exposing every inch of her charms through the thin fabric of her shift. Tynan's lungs contracted with an overwhelming paroxysm of desire.

She *must* have bewitched him, for never had he felt this way about any ordinary woman.

He watched as her hands moved over her torso, smoothing fair skin that the torrent had scrubbed to a rosy glow. Then she stepped back and disappeared into the curtain of water.

He stared at the foaming cascade for a hundred hammering heartbeats before he realized she wasn't coming out.

Tynan muttered an oath and clambered down to the pool. Heedless of the cold water, he charged through the fall, only to discover a deep fissure in the rock beyond. He turned sideways and picked his way through the crevice for several yards before it narrowed too tightly for him to squeeze through.

"Conn's balls!" he muttered in frustration.

The cave beyond was extensive; he could tell from the delayed echo and the steady stream of cool air that poured past him. But he could no more get his chest through that opening than he could thread himself through a cobbler's needle.

He had lost her.

Two more long, hungry, uneventful weeks passed before Tynan saw any sign of a nun outside the priory. This one was swathed from head to toe in creamy white, instead of brown, but he spotted her as she emerged from the sea-cliff.

The sea-cliff! Of course. The Norse had made good use of the caves that riddled these islands. She must have come from one of those. That would explain the prioress's earlier disappearance.

Despite her change of clothing, the woman's height, stance, and stride were the same as Lady Cullum's. "You'll not fool *me* that easily," Tynan murmured, determined not to lose her again.

As if she'd heard him, she glanced his way at the exact moment he shifted to a crouch. Tynan saw her freeze in place.

Whack me with the *Shachdan druiadhach*, Tynan thought. She'd spotted him! He watched her pivot and bolt for the cliffs.

"Oh, no, you don't! Not this time!" Tynan launched himself after, the ground quaking beneath his strides.

At the edge of the cliff, she glanced back at her pursuer for only an instant, but that instant was enough to cost her footing. Arms flailing, she screamed and slipped over the edge, taking Tynan's stomach with her.

"No!" He lunged for the edge. Dreading what he would find, Tynan looked down to see, to his vast relief, a tangled heap of arms, sandal-clad feet, ivory wool, and blue-black plait just below him on a narrow ledge.

"Don't move!" He found a secure spot above her and lay on his belly at the lip of the cliff. Tynan extended his hand to her. "Careful, now. Stay clear of the edge, but see if you can reach my hand! I'll pull you up!"

The heap shifted, sputtered, and sorted itself out into a woman. She flung back the veil that had covered her features. The face that looked up at him made Tynan's mouth go dry as dust.

It was the very face he'd seen so many times at Laird Cullum's shrine to his missing wife — Lady Cullum's face, only decades younger than she'd been at the convent!

Had he found the granddaughter? Or was he looking at Lady Cullum, made youthful by sorcery?

This woman looked exactly like Lady Cullum's portrait come to life. Surely no two people who were not twins could look so similar.

Tynan stared at her, perplexed, for several moments before he realized she was staring back with equal shock and recognition. But before he had time to wonder about that, she spoke, and the world turned upside down.

"You have golden eyes," she murmured tightly, her own green ones wide with fear. "And your hair is the same color of golden brown."

Tynan gave no heed to what she was saying for the voice

with which she said it. He'd recognize it anywhere! Now he realized why Lady Cullum had sounded so familiar; she spoke like *her,* only older.

But this, this was the voice that had whispered the riddle of his life throughout his dreams. He knew it as well as he knew the sound of his own heartbeat.

> *I call the remnant at the root's direction,*
> *Seed of love from hate in vengeance sworn.*
> *Blood oath broken by a dark reflection*
> *Buried with the damask rose's thorn.*
> *Witch who is no witch works her protection;*
> *Death from life and life from death is born.*

Tynan's head began to swim. Fearing the evil eye, he rolled over onto his back and tried to steady himself.

Nara saw the golden-eyed stranger go pale as porrich, then roll over, leaving only the top of his head and his muscular forearm visible — a forearm bigger than her own leg. She watched his long, elegant fingers shape the sign against the evil eye.

After all of *Seanmhair*'s warnings . . . a fine vat of waulking-soup she'd gotten herself into this time! If she stayed here, *Seanmhair* would come looking for her, and the huge intruder would have them both. But if she let him pull her up . . . Nara shuddered at the indelible impression of those golden brown eyes. Just like the wolf's.

She'd never heard of a shape-shifter who could become a wolf, but *Seanmhair* had often told her that there were stranger things in this world than anyone could imagine. He might be a shape-shifter. If so, was the wolf his true form, or the man?

Either way, he was dangerous.

Nara rolled against the cliff face and carefully pushed herself to her feet. Her shifting weight dislodged several chunks from the narrow ledge. Watching them fall, she went weak.

It wasn't safe to linger here. Perhaps if she let him pull her up, she'd be able to escape later. He mustn't find *Seanmhair*.

"Well," she shouted up at the powerful arm extended straight out above her. "Are you going to help me up, or not? This ledge is starting to crumble!" She stood on tiptoe, straining toward him. "Give me your hand!"

She wasn't prepared for the look of grim desperation on the stranger's face when he rolled over and reached down to clamp his large, callused fingers around her wrist.

"Don't move," he ordered brusquely. "Just relax and let me pull you up." He lifted her as if she weighed nothing.

As soon as her waist cleared the edge, Nara gained her footing and tried to scramble away. But the stranger was quicker and stronger.

"Oh, no, you don't!" Two corded arms closed around her and drew her backside hard against his torso. He ignored the kicks she aimed at his legs. "Who are you? Lady Cullum, made young with witchcraft? Or the granddaughter?"

"Witchcraft?" Still struggling, Nara turned on him. "How dare you insinuate such a thing!"

*Ochan*, but he was big! Until this moment, Eric the Fishmonger was the biggest man she had ever seen, but this devil was at least a head taller. Yet where Eric was heavy-boned, clumsy, and misshapen, this one looked sleek and lethal as some giant predator, all muscle and sinew.

The unnatural creature had had the brass to accuse *Seanmhair* of practicing witchcraft! Ignoring the fear that turned her bones to water, Nara confronted her captor. "What in heath and heather are you about, sir, manhandling me and making such wild accusations? There are no witches here, and I'm *not* Lady Cullum!"

The huge stranger's golden eyes narrowed. His arms tightened, drawing her buttocks harder against him. "Stop kicking me," he said mildly. "Is that any way to treat the man who saved your life?"

She glared up at the hard lines of his face. "*Hiu!* You did not save my life, sir; you almost cost it! If you hadn't frightened me, I never would have fallen." She felt something gouging into the base of her spine. "*Oof.* You're squeezing the life out of me, and your scabbard's hurting my back. Let me go!"

He bent his mouth to her ear and murmured evilly, "That's *not* my scabbard, lady."

"Well, whatever it is, it's hurting me!"

He let out an evil chuckle. "Stop fighting, and I'll give you room to breathe."

"Oh, all right," Nara huffed. She was winded from kicking and flailing, anyway. And it did no good. The man was solid as a broch.

"That's better," he said equably. The pressure around her waist eased slightly, but he still held her securely.

Nara tried to divert his attention from the direction where *Seanmhair* might open the trapdoor and emerge. "What do you want?" she demanded, an edge of panic in her voice. "Why won't you let me go?"

"For two years, I have journeyed far and wide in search of the granddaughter of Laird Cullum of the MacKay."

Nara went still. Of all the strangers in all the world, she had fallen prey to the very one her grandmother had warned against all these years! She did her best to conceal the cold tingle of dread that flooded her. "What will you do with her, this granddaughter you seek?"

A flame of bitterness glittered darkly in his golden brown gaze. "I will take her safely back to the loving arms of her grandfather. Laird Cullum is an old and broken man. He wishes to see his sole heir and descendant before he dies."

Nara didn't believe him for one second. She needed only her ordinary "sight" to read the hatred in his eyes, feel it in the heat and tension of his body. "Why would you undertake such a quest?"

He looked at her in surprise, but did not answer.

"What is this to you?" she prodded. Even as she spoke, her mind whirled with a dozen contradictory notions of escape. She forced herself to focus on her captor. "No man undertakes such a quest without a reason."

He granted her a wry smile that bespoke grudging admiration for her impertinence. "My lands and heritage, which Laird Cullum stole from me."

That explained the hatred she saw in his eyes. Nara's dread deepened. "How do you know this laird will keep his word?"

Her captor let out a brief, humorless chuckle. "I do not. But he gave me his written promise, which I took to the Council of Lords. *They* will see that he keeps his word." He scanned the headland, then started toward the priory.

"Where are you taking me?" Nara asked, terrified that he might do harm to the sisters.

"To clear up this mystery once and for all."

"What mystery?" His every stride jounced her innards against the iron arms that held her.

"How you can be old one day and young the next. And why a nun has long, black hair."

"You needn't take me there," she protested, desperate to keep him away from the others. "I confess. I *am* Lady Cullum."

52

Again, that cruel mockery of a smile twisted his lips. "Now, why don't I believe you?" He never slowed his pace. When he reached the door of the priory, he shifted Nara like a sack of turnips into the crook of one powerful arm. His free hand drew a dagger from his belt at the small of his back.

The dagger was a coarse weapon but stoutly made, not unlike its user. He pounded the ironclad door with its hilt. "Open up!" He pounded again, the sound of metal on metal ringing dully across the moor. "Open up, I say!" At a faint noise from the other side of the door, he pulled Nara upright and pinned her in front of him. He laid the blade to her throat, but did not press hard enough to cut her.

Minutes passed before the peephole in the door opened. Nara saw two familiar green eyes and heard a muffled gasp. "Do not harm her! You may open the door at the sound of the bell."

Her heart pounding like a storm-surf, Nara heard a clattering of keys and the squeal of rusted metal as the ancient lock was opened. Then the bell rang.

"Open it," the brown-haired stranger demanded.

She pulled with all her might, but only when he lent his own strength to the effort did the door open begrudgingly on complaining hinges.

He pushed her ahead of him across the dark vestibule to the arras. "Pull it back."

Only the blade to her throat kept Nara from refusing. She jerked aside the worn tapestry.

Her great-aunt Keriam was waiting, safely out of reach on the other side of the grille. Nara felt the tension in her captor ease almost imperceptibly. "Dear one," she cried to her aunt, "stay back! Don't let him take you!" Even as the stranger's callused left hand closed roughly over her mouth, Nara saw the alarm and indecision in her aunt's eyes.

"So there *are* two of you," her captor declared, not without amusement. "The resemblance is amazing." Then his tone grew deadly. "Come out, Lady Cullum, or the girl will pay."

Nara realized he had mistaken Aunt Keriam for *Seanmhair* and meant to take her, too. If he did, *Seanmhair* would come after them, endangering all three of them! Frantic, Nara bit down hard on the brackish-tasting flesh pressed against her mouth.

"Ow!" As she'd hoped, he snatched his hand away. "You wicked little vixen!"

The moment he let go, she cried, "*Seanmhair*, no matter what he threatens, he will not harm me! He has vowed to bring me safe to my grandfather! Don't let him in! If you do, we'll all be lost!" She reached toward Aunt Keriam. "He mustn't hurt *Seanmhair!*"

Tynan looked from Aunt Keriam's face to hers. "Of course. Now it all makes sense. She hid you here with her, among the nuns."

Nara turned to the man who held her. "I swear, I'll go with you of my own free will, if only you'll leave my grandmother alone." At least Aunt Keriam and her grandmother would be safe.

"No!" Aunt Keriam rushed forward and reached desperately through the bars. "You mustn't, child! It will mean your death."

Suddenly Nara went calm. She knew what she must do, just as she had known Gobhar was dead. "Greater love hath no man, than he lay down his life for his friend." She turned a long, loving look at her aunt, realizing she was not likely to see that cherished face again this side of heaven. "You taught me that, and that it applied to women as well. I will go, but you must stay. It is my wish, dear one."

Nara turned back to the stranger and crossed herself. "In the name of the Father, Son, and Holy Ghost, I swear by my immortal soul that I will freely accompany you to my grandfather, but only if you take me, and me alone."

"You are in no position to bargain, little one," the stranger scoffed. "I have you. That's all that matters. And you'll not escape me."

"We'll just see about that!" Nara landed a useless blow on his rock-hard chest. Desperate, she blurted out, "If you refuse my terms, I'll kill myself, and you won't be able to stop me! How happy will Laird Cullum be *then,* when you have nothing but a dead, decaying body to bring him?" To her infinite satisfaction, his pupils widened in alarm.

"Nay!" Keriam's shout of protest resounded against the stone walls. "By all that is good and holy, I shall not let you take her! I'll curse you, villain, and all your generations!" From the look in her eye, both Nara and the stranger could believe her.

"I have vowed to bring her back safe to Laird Cullum, lady," he offered tersely, setting Nara to her feet. Quick as a fox, he surrendered his embrace in favor of a harsh grip on her wrist. "I will accept the girl's bargain and match it with my own." He knelt to one knee and crossed himself with the hand that held the dagger. "By the Father, Son, and Holy Ghost, I vow upon my own immortal soul to bring her safe to her grandfather, protecting her with my own life, if necessary, from the harm of any other hand."

"It is done, then," Nara murmured softly. She turned to leave, but her aunt's voice stopped her.

"Wait! Grant me this one boon, sir . . ."

The stranger's eyes narrowed. "Why should I?"

"For pity's sake." Her face crumbling, the prioress reached out to him through the bars. "Mercy, sir. A simple boon . . ."

Annoyed, the giant glanced at Nara, then back to her aunt. "What do you want, then?"

"Only that you take my hand and tell me your name before you go."

Nara knew what her aunt was doing. "Please," she whispered to her captor. "What harm could it bring? I have sworn to go with you."

"Very well," he assented. Still gripping her wrist in his left hand, he pulled her over to the grille, then tucked his dagger into his belt and extended his right hand. As he spoke, Aunt Keriam grasped his long, callused fingers and closed her eyes. "My name is Tynan, son of Phelan, chief of his sept and liege warrior of the clan MacDougald."

*The clan MacDougald!* Nara's eyes widened. *He was one of her mother's kinsmen!*

Aunt Keriam remained silent for almost a minute, then opened her eyes to stare boldly into the stranger's. "Marry her," she said quietly.

"What?" Nara and the stranger exclaimed in unison.

The stranger snatched back his hand and retrieved his dagger.

Scarcely able to believe her ears, Nara bit back the *Auntie!* that would have betrayed them both. What in all of Heaven or Hades would possess her great-aunt to propose such a thing?

She grasped the bars that separated them. "Are you mad? *This* is the very man you've warned me about all these years! I have looked into his soul and seen only darkness! Yet you would have me wed him?"

Looking anything but mad, Aunt Keriam reached through the bars to caress Nara's face. Her palms felt hot as a fresh-baked bread against Nara's cold cheeks, but if she was trying to communicate something, Nara was too agitated to receive it. Instead, she heard her great-aunt say, "Aye. I would have you wed him."

Green eyes resolute, Aunt Keriam withdrew her hands. "Think, Nara. It's the only way. You cannot travel with a man alone without being dishonored. Only as your husband will he be bound by the laws of God and men to protect you . . . and your honor." Her drawn features softened. "Oh, Nara, you know I love you more than life. Trust me in this. It's the only way."

Nara stepped back, the sound of her own rapid heartbeat roaring in her ears. This couldn't be happening.

She turned to the stranger. "Don't listen to her. Obviously, she's lost her senses."

"Marry her," Aunt Keriam repeated, gripping her silver crucifix so hard her knuckles went white. "Or I'll follow and slay her myself, rather than see her driven across the country at your mercy and delivered unprotected into that devil's hands!"

Nara gasped in shock. Surely Aunt Keriam couldn't mean what she was saying. She was only trying to frighten them both into submission.

The stranger tucked his chin in consternation. "You *are* mad, lady, to think that I would believe you. I saw the fear in your face when I threatened to harm the girl. You'd never be able to kill your own granddaughter."

"Wouldn't I?" Aunt Keriam's eyes went almost black, her gaze locked on the stranger. She lifted the fist that clutched her crucifix. "There are things worse than death, sir, especially for a woman. I would willingly consign myself to hell and her to Heaven, rather than let you dishonor her."

To Nara's horror, she saw the back of Aunt Keriam's hand bulge, then erupt with an explosion of blood as the silver crucifix's shank was forced clear through from her palm.

"Believe this, then!" her aunt thundered, thrusting her

mangled fist through the bars and shaking it, splattering both Nara and her captor with blood. "Marry her!" she roared.

Nara realized her aunt's threat was not an idle one. She *would* kill Nara, rather than let the stranger take her without marrying her. The painful truth of that revelation cut straight through her heart, sundering it more surely than any weapon ever could. "How *could* you?" she whispered, but Aunt Keriam wasn't listening. She was glaring at the stranger.

Nara followed her gaze to the stranger's face. For the first time, she saw a flicker of indecision cross his chiseled features. He hesitated, obviously wrestling with his options.

Despite the numbness that had begun to curl through her like peat-smoke, she sensed an odd mixture of guilt and anger within him.

She shuddered with revulsion to see his tongue absently lick away a droplet of Aunt Keriam's blood from his lip.

The stranger nodded. "Very well. As you wish. I'll marry her."

Nara drew back, aghast, and blustered, "Well, I'll not marry you, you great, stinking brute of a lout!"

The blood of kings flowed through her veins! Cheeks throbbing, she turned to her aunt and railed, "Look at him! He's wearing rags! *Filthy* rags! And he has the hands of a common laborer!"

"And how, pray tell, would you know a common laborer from a king, you insolent bit of a girl?" Aunt Keriam snapped. "Unless you've lied to me, this is the first man who's gotten closer to you than half a league!" With visible effort, Aunt Keriam tempered her tone. "Nara, you must marry him. You said it yourself, child; if any of us were to follow you, all will be lost."

Ironic, that the same woman who had just vowed to kill her now appealed for Nara's protection. Yet despite her aunt's betrayal, Nara had no wish to see Aunt Keriam, or *Seanmhair,* endangered.

Well aware that this was the most important decision of her life, she looked at the huge, rough stranger who held her wrist so painfully. She would readily have taken her own life to keep *Seanmhair* safe, but could she face living as the wife of such a brute? Her eyes welling, she turned in mute supplication to her aunt.

The prioress sank into her chair, silent tears coursing down her own cheeks. "Do this, Nara, and there will be light at the end of darkness."

*Light at the end of darkness,* just as in the vision. Aunt Keriam had seen it, too.

Nara's throat tightened. After this moment, nothing would ever be the same. "What if that darkness is my life?" she asked in an agonized whisper. "Will my release come only in death?"

Aunt Keriam took a shuddering breath, but had the grace to grant Nara the truth. "I do not know, my little one."

Visibly shaken by their exchange, the stranger interjected gruffly, "Fetch the witnesses. If we're to marry, then let us do it and be done."

Aunt Keriam looked to Nara. "Nara?"

For a fleeting moment, Nara wondered if this was how Isaac had felt when his beloved father Abraham had raised the knife to slay him on the altar at Mount Moriah.

Then she launched herself into the darkness. "Very well. I will marry him."

# Chapter IV

Nara had scarcely begun to follow Tynan into the crevasse when a strong updraft whipped her veil over her face, forcing her to let go of the cliff with one hand to uncover her eyes. No sooner had she pulled the veil free of her face than another strong gust snatched the fabric from her grasp and sent it sailing.

Was the loss of her veil a sign? She was a married woman now, no longer entitled to wear it.

A married woman, with a husband. The brute was actually her husband.

Nara looked below her to see Tynan descending from foothold to foothold with surprising grace and speed for a man his size. Such power, governed by razor-sharp reflexes. He moved with a confidence that spoke no fear of the treacherous drop.

Was he always so reckless?

No. Not reckless, for there was no carelessness in the man. His every move was swift, calculated, and sure.

Fearless, then?

No. Ferocious . . . that was the word that fit him.

As she watched the smooth play of muscle beneath his ragged clothes, a lone ray of late afternoon sun broke through the clouds, singling Tynan out like a great, golden finger of God. It shone brightly all around him, gilding his wind-tousled mane and lighting the amber stones in the hilt of his sword so the graven wolf's eyes came alive with a chilling, golden glow.

The wolf. Nara shuddered, certain that the beast and the man were linked somehow.

And then the sunlight disappeared behind a cloud.

For the first time since her desperate vow in the priory, she considered the perils of her hasty commitment. Yoked to a complete stranger — a wild wolf of a man who dressed like a beggar yet bore the weapons and arrogance of a chieftain.

The golden warrior turned a stormy face upward to chide, "Come along." He motioned her after him. "It's tricky here, so take care. But don't dawdle."

Though she knew every rock and cranny of these cliffs, her usual confident progress was stilled now by apprehension. He'd said he was taking her to her grandfather. But to what end? Aunt Keriam had called her grandfather a devil. What evil awaited Nara when she got there? And why was Tynan in such a hurry?

He glowered up at her again. "Why have you stopped? Keep moving. This way."

Nara tried to conceal her fear. "I know my way, sir," she declared emphatically above the rush of wind and water. "The Witch has been my playground since I was a little girl. I learned very quickly to respect the perils of her cliffs and seas. I would not have lived long, otherwise." That said, she worked her way after the stranger with exaggerated care.

Tynan waited for her on a narrow ledge below, his back angled firmly against the rock. "If this island is so treacherous," he called up to her, "I'm surprised Lady Cullum didn't keep you safely tucked away in the convent all the time."

"A convent is no prison, sir," Nara replied, troubled by his ignorance. When she reached the security of the ledge, she settled to rest as far away from him as possible. "Our convent is a refuge from the world. Those who remain within do so of their own free will. My grandmother was never my jailer."

"Indeed."

She could tell from the tightness of his response he didn't believe her. What a strange creature this man was. Were all men so cynical? she wondered.

Nara had seen men before — more than a few from a safe distance as she roamed the rugged Trotternish Peninsula — but until Tynan had found her, the closest she'd ever gotten to one was when the rare traveler had sought refuge in the priory's vestibule, affording her a brief, clandestine peek through the arras when Aunt Keriam wasn't around. Even from that limited perspective, she knew this man was much larger than most. And much more dangerous.

"Come." Tynan started to rise. "I want to set out with the tide."

Nara stiffened. "I told you, the Witch won't let me go." She sought his golden brown eyes, now hard as brass. "She means to keep me here."

"Nonsense," he scoffed. "Who gave you such a notion? Lady Cullum, no doubt."

Nara shook her head in denial. She feared what he would do when she spoke the truth, yet she felt duty-bound to tell him. "I have the Two Sights."

His expression unreadable, he straightened to every inch of his formidable height, towering over her. "Old women's nonsense," he growled, "conjured up to work their sway over weak-minded folk! I told you, I set no store by such foolishness. Come." He pulled her roughly to her feet. "Or we'll miss the tide."

She felt the heat of him even through her woolen habit and smelled the sharp, masculine scent that permeated his ragged clothing. The man exuded power almost as tangibly as he radiated bitterness and anger, sending a jolt through Nara with his every touch. Pierced by the intensity of his anger, she turned wide eyes up to him. "Such a wounded soul," she murmured, gently caressing his cheek. "What horror left you thus?"

Tynan recoiled as if she'd slapped him, a brief flicker of alarm crossing his features before they settled into his usual grim expression. "My past is my own business, not yours."

Surprised by his gruff reaction, she kept her gaze locked to his even when he thrust her to arm's length. "You are my husband now. May I not know the man I've —"

"Nay," he interrupted. "You may not. Now let us go. I want to be off this island by nightfall."

Nara felt a familiar tingle in her scalp, accompanied by a distant ringing she recognized all too well.

It was happening.

"This island is a part of me, and I of her," she heard her own voice say. "She will fight us if you try to take me." Staring into the golden depths of his eyes, Nara felt as if she were being sucked backward into a dark abyss. "I belong here. The Witch will strike us both if we try to leave."

Then, as quickly as it had come, the Sight departed. Suddenly drained, she sagged against the cliff face.

Tynan stepped forward in alarm, steadying her against him with corded arms huge and hard. "Have I married a witch, then?" His question rang with accusation.

"Nay, sir. I am no witch," Nara murmured. For one brief instant, she allowed herself to be grateful for the iron-sure security of his embrace. That illusion of safety moved her to confess, "You have no way of knowing what a trial it is, to see what others cannot — what I *would* not, if I had any say in the matter." Nara straightened, pushing away from him, her palms flat against the coarse shirt and plaid that covered his chest. "But the Sight is never wrong." She looked up to find him regarding her with a curious mixture of suspicion and . . . something else, an expression she could only describe as hunger — a hunger so dark and ravenous that her heart constricted in fear. "I tell you again: If you try to take me from this island, we shall both meet with disaster."

His golden eyes narrowed. "And I remind you: I am no child, madam, to be frightened by such vapors." His huge hands tightened on her upper arms. "I have waited years for this chance to win back my birthright and put my sept at peace. I fear nothing, not even God." When Nara blanched and crossed herself, her actions elicited a cold smile from her captor. "Do you really think anything you could say would deter me? Well, think again, lady. If Fate counted for anything, I would have been dead a hundred times over." Bitterness radiated from his every pore. "I stand before you as proof that a man makes his own luck."

Nara drew back, convinced that God would strike him dead on the spot for such arrogance. "True, you are here, sir," she corrected gently, "but only by Divine Providence, as God has allowed."

Tynan let out a derisive snort. "*Hiu!* Why do I bother to speak the truth to you? It's wasted effort." He motioned her after him. "We've delayed long enough. Come."

When they reached the shallow indentation in the face of the rock where Tynan had camped, Nara marveled at the meagerness of his belongings: two stout oaken oars, a few smoked fish, and several sealskins that caused her a moment's panic. Then she saw that the pelts were not familiar. He hadn't killed Erk or Merk. Not yet, anyway.

But what would happen when they put to sea? If Erk and Merk should happen to sense her presence and follow, this savage would probably try to kill them.

Not if she could help it. Nara sank miserably against the stone and resolved to do everything she could to protect her precious seal companions.

She watched in tense silence as Tynan pulled a leathern pouch from a wide fissure in the stone. The worn pouch's bulges suggested a few crude cooking implements and sparse provisions. Then he reached back into the niche and drew out a gleaming, lethal-looking axe, its curved blade sharp as a razor. Nara had never seen such an implement, but she judged from its short handle and huge, crescent blade that it was meant to fell men, not trees. The thought sent a chill straight through her.

Tynan wrapped the axe in one of the seal pelts, securing it with strips of hide. Last, he pulled from his hiding place a stout longbow and quiver with only three arrows. When he turned, Nara was granted a closer look at the hilt of his magnificent sword. Polished to a silvery glow, it was finely wrought, the carving of a wolf's head so real she could almost imagine it snarling. Below the wolf's graven fangs, three large, tear-shaped rubies glistened like drops of blood.

Nara noted the practiced precision with which Tynan slipped bow and quiver over his shoulder. He tossed his leathern pouch at her feet. "You carry these. I'll manage the rest." He then scooped up the oars and axe as if they weighed nothing.

Nara felt her mouth go dry as she rose, the pouch gripped tightly in her hands. He was really going to do it, try to take her from the safety of her island despite her warnings. Suddenly her feet felt as if they had sent down roots into the stone. "Where are we going?" she asked shakily.

"I told you; I've hidden a boat nearby." Tynan cocked his head, his chiseled features betraying his impatience. "Come along, then. I'm not going to eat you, woman."

She willed her feet to move, but they would not. How could she expect them to? If the Witch had her way, Nara was heading for disaster. "Your boat . . . how big is it?"

"Big enough. And it's not mine. I stole it."

Indignation momentarily supplanted her misgivings. "You *stole* it?" By Dugall the Brown, she had married a thief! His blighted soul was now united with hers, staining them both. "You stole it."

"Aye, lady, I stole it," he declared, calm as you please. "You might as well know it: You've married a man who takes what he needs, whenever the circumstances require, and I make no apologies about that."

Nara couldn't begin to imagine what had spawned such hardness in him. But surely he realized . . . "Why, some poor family is probably starving now for lack of their livelihood, thanks to you," she blurted. "Didn't you stop to think —"

"Silence," he roared, cutting short her reproach.

As if the island herself had taken offense, the ground began to tremble beneath them. An ominous rumble overhead drew Nara's eyes to the cliff above Tynan just in time to see the rock face vibrate, then slowly squeeze out a huge slab of basalt, accompanied by a hail of rocks, soil, and gravel — all headed straight for Tynan.

But instead of seeing the danger above him, Tynan seemed more concerned with Nara's safety, his eyes betraying fear for the first time — not for himself, but for her.

There wasn't time to warn him. Instead, she hurled herself in his direction, shoving him onto his back on the narrow strip of ledge just beyond the path of the boulder. Her body hard against his, their faces only inches apart, she closed her eyes to the tide of stone and soil that rained down on both of them. But the massive boulder rumbled past harmlessly behind their feet.

When the tumult subsided, she found herself crushed against the unforgiving resistance of her husband's muscular torso by a heavy mound of rock-studded soil. Only their heads protruded. Still, the weight of soil was so great Nara could scarcely breathe, and her nostrils were thick with the musty smell of earth sharpened by a hint of bruised bracken and a pungent stab of gorse.

She tried to inhale, but took in only a faint gasp before her chest met unyielding resistance.

Would she die this way?

Tynan turned his face clear of hers, spat the dirt from his mouth, then let loose a fit of coughing that released a fresh cascade of dirt and gravel into her hair. She arched her neck, trying desperately to get more air, but succeeded only in bringing down more debris atop their heads.

"Don't move," Tynan choked out.

Feeling dizzy and strangely detached, she subsided against him and lay very still.

The Witch's warning had been no idle threat. Nara was convinced that Tynan's rash declaration been enough to provoke this disaster.

The sound of his voice, hoarse with effort, drew her back from the brink of unconsciousness. "Nara! Speak! Are you injured?"

"Can't . . . breathe," she managed.

"Calm yourself. You'll be fine," he urged, his own words shallow. "The soil is loose. I can dig us free, but it will take a little time. When I breathe out, you breathe in."

She did as he asked. It worked to some small degree, but there was precious little space for either of them. As if from a great distance, she heard the muffled sound of his hands clawing frantically beneath the soil. Loose gravel and dirt tumbled noisily over the precipice as he worked. She didn't know how long it took, but she was seeing stars by the time she felt him scooping aside the debris that pressed against her ribs.

The moment there was room, she inhaled, filling the hard-won space. But her silent prayer of thanks was rudely interrupted by a stab of pain as Tynan's excavations shifted a sharp rock hard against her back. "Ouch! Take care, sir! Things are poking me all over. My back, my belly."

Despite the concern etched on his dirt-streaked face, a rueful smile curved Tynan's lips. "One breath, and you use it to chide me." The bulge against her abdomen seemed to grow even harder. "Are you always so ungrateful when someone saves your life? This is the second time today I've —"

"What?" Nara reared back as far as their confinement allowed. "Why, you great goggling beastie! It was I who saved your life just now, although why I did escapes me!" She sputtered a stray clod of dirt away from her mouth and into his face. "You'd have been squashed thinner than a bishop's conscience if I hadn't pushed you out of that boulder's way." A spasm in her neck sent her face helplessly against his. "You should be thankful I didn't let that stone take you to perdition," she muttered into the golden stubble on his cheek.

He rumbled with mirthless amusement beneath her. "Perhaps I should." In a matter of minutes, he was scooping off the last of the dirt and rocks from her back. "Careful, now," he cautioned. "We don't know what the landslide did to this ledge. Try to roll free of me toward the cliff, but move slowly, lest we start more trouble."

Nara did as he instructed, pulling her legs from the remaining debris with agonizing care before easing clear of Tynan against the cliff face. Tynan followed, his movements equally deliberate. Only when they were both safely standing did Nara venture a look at the path of the boulder.

It had carved a wide channel deep into the face of the cliff, from top to bottom. Seeing the force of its destruction, she began to tremble uncontrollably.

Tynan caught her to him. "Hold, woman. I didn't save you only to have you swoon and topple off this ledge."

Too rattled to let go, she murmured, "Just give me a moment to collect myself." As soon as she trusted her legs to bear her, she pulled free of him. "Thank you. I'm fine now." She made a futile swipe at the grime that coated her once-snowy habit, then turned a worried frown to her captor. "We've foiled the Witch this once, but mark me, if you persist in trying to take me from this place, she will try again."

Tynan's eyes narrowed. "Let her try." His golden features hardened in challenge. "I am not afraid. And I *will* take you safely back to your grandsire. Not god nor witch shall keep me from it. Not even the devil himself."

Was there no limit to the man's arrogance? Nara sent up a hasty, silent prayer asking God's forgiveness for Tynan's evil declaration. Then she took a deep breath and ventured, "Lead on, then, sir. Even though it mean my death, I shall go with you." With that, she followed this Lord of Darkness toward certain disaster.

# Chapter V

At Tynan's gruff instruction, Nara settled reluctantly into the stolen boat he had hidden near the mouth of the estuary. Only when the dark intruder was busy lashing their meager belongings to the crosspiece did she dare to scan the inlet for signs of Erk and Merk. Blessedly, no speckled heads broke the water's choppy surface.

Odd, though, that they weren't there. Usually the two creatures were waiting just offshore whenever and wherever she came to the sea. Yet under the circumstances, she was supremely grateful they'd stayed away. Perhaps they had sensed, in the mystic way of animals, the threat of Tynan's presence.

Then it occurred to Nara that there might be an even more powerful reason for the seals' absence. In the gathering darkness, she looked up at the low, heavy-hanging clouds that churned overhead and realized just what that reason was. "There's a storm brewing," she cautioned Tynan. "I can feel it, smell it on the wind. We'd better wait till morning."

Tynan acted as if he hadn't heard. Instead he leaped into the shallow water, circled to the bow, then pulled the boat free of the rocky shore as easily as if the heavy hull were made of straw instead of stout Scottish oak. He reserved his reply until he had heaved himself back aboard. "The storm will keep anyone from following us."

"But it's almost dark," Nara protested, realizing even as

she spoke that logic would probably mean nothing to a man as driven as Tynan. Still, she felt compelled to try. "We cannot see the stars. How will you be able to navigate?"

"The wind is from the west. It will drive us to the mainland." Tynan set the oars and began to row for open water. With each stroke, the smooth ripple of corded muscle in his arms and shoulders seemed to mimic the rhythmic power of the swells beneath them.

Even in the waning light, she could see the dark determination in his face. Mindless and inexorable as a predator driven by the scent of fresh blood. Shivering, Nara settled low astern, a cold tingle of fear curling inside her as she gripped the crosspiece. "This is madness," she called above the creak of the oars. "I beg you, turn back while we still can."

"There will be no turning back — not now, not ever," Tynan growled, his pace increasing as they reached the turbulent waters of the strait. "Now quiet yourself and leave me to my labor."

Nara's lips clamped shut, less from obedience than from sudden queasiness. For ten summers past she had swum these waters with the ease and familiarity of a wild sea-creature, but riding the storm-tossed surface was another matter entirely. Now that they'd reached the open strait, their ill-gotten boat bobbed up and down two feet for every foot of progress, causing her stomach to crest and plummet with every wave. Nara dared not open her mouth for fear of being ill. Instead, she huddled against the hull in miserable silence, her knuckles white on the crosspiece as the storm broke full force.

Tynan rowed with all his might against the storm, straining for some sign of shore ahead. He tried not to think of the cold, dark depths beneath them; instead, he focused on fighting the fitful gusts and currents that threatened to pull them off course.

A pox on the girl and her talk of the island as if it were a living, breathing sorceress! Her wild tales had him imagining the Witch's laughter on every shriek of the storm.

Laugh all you want! You shall not have us, he thought. He had not come this far only to fail. Witch or no Witch, he would survive, and the girl along with him.

They'd be all right as long as he kept heading toward the mainland. But after wrestling the oars until his arms quaked with fatigue, he realized he no longer had any idea which way they were going. The Witch was winning.

Despite the strength of his strokes, Tynan's efforts had little effect. Cold, driving rain obliterated all signs of shore, and the wind gusted from so many directions that the sturdy craft was blown about like a leaf. He gave up rowing and shipped the oars, then settled low in the stern, using the tiller in an effort to keep them headed into the waves.

Tynan peered into the darkness just ahead of him, scarcely able to make out the rain-pelted heap of dirty wool that was Nara, clinging for dear life to the crosspiece. Drenched and no doubt terrified, she'd ridden the storm without a word of complaint or recrimination.

An uncharacteristic pang of remorse struck home.

Now he understood why Nara had been so nervous about getting into the boat. He knew she wasn't afraid of the water; she swam like a seal. But swim though she might, Tynan mused, she was no more a sailor than he was.

Yet even the seals knew better than to risk a storm like this one.

Nara had been right to warn him. They should have waited till morning, but he'd been too stubborn to listen, too driven by the compulsion to escape her eerie island.

Now they'd both be lucky not to drown.

Tynan's one comfort lay in the fact that the outer isles

stood between them and open sea. Even if the storm should shift the prevailing westerly winds to the east, at least they wouldn't be blown off the edge of the world. His best guess was that they were now being blown almost due north, but he couldn't be sure of anything. Regardless of what direction they were headed, they were bound to make landfall somewhere, and soon. The question was, where? And how?

Cursing the folly of his own stubbornness, Tynan struggled with the tiller. In the future, he vowed to give more credence to this Sight that guided Nara.

If he got the chance.

He was beginning to think this might be his final, fatal mistake. Another scan of the dark, heaving waves eroded his confidence even further.

Then an ominous sound drew his attention directly ahead: the unmistakable thunder of breakers on rock.

Tynan's gut sang with the same discordant howl of energy he experienced racing into battle, only this time he had no weapons against his enemy. The tiller was no match for the raw force of nature that was driving them toward destruction.

The Witch had all the power, and she seemed determined to send them to a watery grave.

A huge sheet of foam arched overhead, then came crashing down, almost sinking them. He felt the rudder catch, then shatter. Tynan lurched forward to shelter Nara with his body. "We're going aground!" he shouted into her ear, pulling her hard against him. "No matter what happens, hold on to me. I'll get you safe to shore."

He felt her nod beneath his chin.

A huge swell caught the boat and bore it aloft, sending the craft hard between two jagged peaks of rock. No sooner had they cleared that obstacle than they were tossed against an unrelenting wall of stone. Tynan heard the sound of splintering wood at the same instant the impact drove the air from his lungs.

The next thing he knew, he was lying — chilled, wet, and battered — in absolute darkness, his back hard against cold stone and his head resting on something soggy but resilient. He swallowed and tasted salt, his throat and nose scalded by seawater.

He could still hear the storm, yet it sounded far away, and he felt no rain.

Where was he? It was dark as the inside of a blind man's eyelids . . .

Air currents moved fitfully around him, but they lacked the force of wind. Close by, he heard dripping and the trickle of water on rock. And breathing, not his own.

He moved his leg, only to find it baptized in cold water. "What the . . ."

"Thanks be to God," Nara's exhausted whisper murmured from the darkness nearby. "You're not drowned after all."

He tried to sit up, but gentle hands urged him back.

"Please lie still, sir," she cautioned. "This ledge is narrow, and the water is hard by us. I haven't the strength to pull you to safety a second time. I fear we'll both perish if I try to save you again."

Save him again?

*She* had pulled *him* from the storm-sea?

True, he had no memory of anything beyond being thrown into the water . . . As suspicious as he was grateful, Tynan subsided gingerly to the pillow of her thigh.

She must have saved him.

The realization confused his already muddled thoughts even further.

He knew how much she feared him, that she'd only married him to protect her grandmother. It made no sense to save him, and yet she had. But why? The question lodged in the deepest, darkest recesses of his mind, dogging him.

"Where are we?" he croaked.

"In a sea-cave. I have no idea where."

"My weapons —" His father's axe and sword! Tynan sat up abruptly, loosing a merciless throb in his skull.

"Pray be still, sir." Nara pulled him back into her lap. "You've a knot the size of a turnip on your head."

"My father's weapons . . . I cannot lose them," he protested. "They're all I have left —"

"Calm yourself," she soothed. "Your sword and axe aren't going anywhere. They're at the bottom of the lagoon, along with the rest of our supplies and what's left of your ill-gotten boat." He felt her settle back to rest, her voice growing softer. "Everything will still be there in the morning. Sleep now. We've had enough danger for this night."

Tynan didn't believe for a second that he could sleep, but, exhausted from fighting the storm and weakened from his near-drowning, he soon lapsed back into a dreamless slumber.

When the first glimmers of daylight crept through the crevices of the sea-cave, he rolled onto his back and opened his eyes to an impressive vault of natural stone overhead. Here and there, a small fissure opened to the sky, but he saw no evidence of an exit to the outside world.

He stilled, listening to the sound of Nara's breathing. It rose and fell in easy rhythm, despite the cold stone beneath her and the weight of his head on her thigh.

Slowly, lest he wake her, he eased himself into a sitting position to assess their situation. Let her sleep. She would face the cold and hunger soon enough.

A dull throb echoing through his brain, Tynan rubbed the

knot on his head and looked about. Somehow, Nara had managed to drag him onto the only level surface in the sea-cave. Everywhere else, the sheer stone walls descended precipitously into the dark water.

He shivered, wondering what forces had guided her to this place.

As if she had read his thoughts, Nara spoke. "When we hit the rocks, I saw you go under." He turned to find her sitting up, her fingers unconsciously trying to put her wet, filthy habit in order. Even in the unnatural twilight of this hidden place, her green eyes shone clear. "I grabbed hold of you and tried my best to keep your head above water, but you were so heavy, you pulled us both down. When I finally managed to get you back to the surface, we came up in here."

Tynan scanned the stone cavern, whose musty smell and dripping ceiling reminded him far too much of Eilean d'Ór's dungeons. "You may have merely exchanged a quick drowning for a lingering entombment. I see no way out."

She cocked her head at him in obvious surprise. "We shall leave the same way we came. Obviously, there's an underwater passage," she said in a tone fit for a child or a simpleton. "When the day brightens, we'll be able to see our way out."

Hard as it was for him to admit it, she was right. Within hours, the sun shone through a shallow opening three feet below the water's surface. No sooner had Nara pointed it out to Tynan than she dove gracefully into the cold water.

Stymied, he waited what seemed like an eternity until she came back.

At last her sleek head broke the surface. "What are you waiting for? It's glorious outside. The sun is shining, and the wind is fair. Why do you tarry in the darkness?"

Tynan glared at her, scarcely able to speak what he knew he must. "I like this place no better than you do," he growled,

76

"but I cannot follow." His fist curled against the rock ledge in frustration. "I do not swim."

There. He'd said it.

Nara's green eyes widened. "And you put to sea in a storm?" She peered at him through the gloom. "You must have been desperate, indeed, to take such a risk."

Tynan eased himself into the chest-deep, icy water. "I told you; I fear nothing." He extended a hand to Nara. "You pulled me into this place; now pull me out."

"You trust me to deliver you safely?" she asked, her grave expression revealing that she was fully aware of his misgivings.

"I said, take me out, woman!" he snapped, "before I freeze to death. This water's so cold, my balls are in my throat!" His huge hand closed around her slender wrist. "Do it. Now."

Nara arched a dark eyebrow. "Very well. Hold your breath."

Tynan took a deep breath, squeezed his eyes shut, pinched his nose between thumb and forefinger of his free hand, and forced himself to relax so she could draw him under. As the cold waters closed in around him, he fought back a mindless surge of panic.

Concentrate, he told himself. Keep your eyes closed and remain limber, so she can pull you through. If she'd wanted to drown you, she'd have done it last night.

He felt the smooth flow of her feet kicking beside him. Then the darkness behind his lids grew lighter, reddening until he broke clear of the water and into the sunshine. Drawing in a grateful breath, he found his feet and stood in the lagoon.

Now that the storm was over, the water was only chest deep. Tynan turned, rapidly assessing their predicament. While Nara hoisted herself nimbly onto the sun-warmed rocks, he saw that most of the hull lay wedged onto a narrow strip of sand. Pieces of seaweed and debris floated all about him in the shallow lagoon, and he could see several dark outlines on the bottom.

He'd worry about the boat later. First things first.

Tynan squeezed his eyes shut, held his breath, and groped the bottom until he had found his sword and axe. Once they were safely recovered, he rose from the water triumphant, a bundled weapon in each hand. "Ah-hah!"

A soft chuckle drew his attention to Nara's perch. Wide-eyed and innocent as some wild sea-creature, she asked, "What use are such weapons here?" Her hand waved the scope of their tiny little island. "I would gladly trade your sword and battle-axe for a sharp saw, some nails, and a hammer. We are shipwrecked."

"I can repair the boat," he assured her, more than a little defensive, "but it will take some time." Tynan heaved his precious weapons onto the little beach, then retrieved the almost-empty flagon, his pouch of supplies, and most of the hull fragments. Only his bow and quiver had been lost.

Numbed by cold from the waist down, he clambered up onto the sand to rest and warm himself in the welcome sunlight.

The island was tiny — smaller than the bailey of Eilean d'Ór.

He looked up at Nara and frowned. What manner of woman was she, sitting there, calm as you please? She must be as cold and hungry as he, yet she made no complaint. "After you've warmed yourself in the sun," he directed, "we'll eat what's left of the meal in my pouch." He opened the flap and drew out a dripping bag of parched oats, now bloated with seawater. "They'll be a might salty, but filling."

"We'll need fresh water, then," Nara informed him. "I

78

heard a steady trickle in the cave. I'll go back and search out the source. If we're lucky, perhaps it's a spring." She stood and turned her back. To Tynan's amazement, she began to pull off her sodden clothes, laying them neatly across the rocks to dry. As easily and unselfconsciously as if she were alone in the privacy of her bedchamber, she stripped down to her almost-transparent shift.

Tynan's mouth went dry with desire when she revealed the tantalizing curves and shadows that had haunted his dreams since he'd first seen her that morning in the mist. Now, just as before, her damp shift concealed nothing. Rather, it made the untouched treasures underneath even more alluring.

He scarcely breathed, for fear she would realize he was watching and cover herself. But instead of covering herself, Nara merely picked up the limp wine-flagon and offered it to him. "It's almost empty, but you should drink what's left. It will fortify your blood."

She looked so fragile and exposed, standing almost naked before him, that Tynan was moved to uncharacteristic concern. "Nay," he blustered. "You drink it. If anyone's blood needs fortifying, it's yours."

"No. No." Even as her cheeks ruddied with embarrassment, her laughter danced like sun rays on the wave tops. "It's terribly childish, but I can't abide spirits of any kind. Even beer." She shook her head. "Silly, isn't it?" She sobered, yet the sparkle did not leave her green eyes as she pressed the flagon into his hand. "Please drink it. If you refuse, I shall have to pour it out to make way for our water, and that would be a waste."

Underneath his soggy plaid, Tynan's manhood swelled to painful proportions. Trying his best — with only limited success — to avoid staring at the tempting details that showed through her shift, he raised the flagon and drained it in a single, searing gulp. He tasted nothing, too preoccupied with the nubile form before him. She stood so close he could feel the heat of her skin through his damp clothes.

He knew he should say something, thank her. Why was he suddenly tongue-tied?

This wasn't the first time he'd been with a nearly naked woman, and it wasn't likely to be the last. But there was something so disarming about Nara's lack of awareness that Tynan couldn't think straight, much less speak.

Silent, he returned the empty flagon.

"Thank you." She took it from him. As agile as a seal, she spun and launched herself smoothly into the water, disappearing back into the cave.

Tynan watched the soles of her feet disappear with misgiving. True, they needed water, but what if some accident befell her in the cave? He had to bring her safe to her grandfather. If anything happened to her before then, all would be lost.

Tynan told himself that was the only reason for his worry. Still, he did not rest easy until her smiling face broke the surface of the lagoon. She lifted the bulging flagon. "Thanks be to God, it was a spring, as sweet and clear as the one back home." Nara waded ashore, her shift all but invisible now. Heedless of Tynan's burning attention, she climbed to a good vantage point and scanned the horizon. "I can see land all around us. I would swim for help, but the sea is far too cold, even this time of year, for such a distance. I'd never make it." A brief shadow darkened her features. "I fear the Witch has made us her prisoners. For the time being, anyway."

Nara descended and drew close, facing him. "I'm very cold. May I warm myself on you?" Before he could reply, she slipped her arms around his waist and snuggled close.

"Mmm. I knew you would be warm, waiting for me in the sun." Her hands smoothed the wide planes of his back. "And your back is almost hot. I wish I could wrap myself around you and soak up all that warmth at once." She nestled even closer, blissfully ignorant of the effect she was having on him.

Everywhere she touched, Tynan's blood ignited, singing through his veins until it concentrated painfully at the core of his arousal.

Nara tipped her face to his. "There's that scabbard again, poking me in the belly."

Tynan gripped her upper arms, not certain whether to ravage her or push her away like a willful, but ignorant, child. "I told you. That's not my scabbard."

Nara's expression went blank. Then her brows drew together in concentration. "Is it your man-thing, then?"

"Conn's balls, woman," Tynan thundered, thoroughly done out. "Have you no shame? Not even a tavern wench would speak so boldly! It isn't proper."

Nara seemed to take the question literally. She considered, then shook her head. "No. I don't believe I do have any shame. Is that bad, then? I shouldn't think so." She looked up at him in challenge. "And as for what's proper, how in heath and heather am I supposed to know what's proper when it comes to such matters, especially between a man and a woman? I've been in a convent all my life!"

Her eyes glittering with undisguised curiosity, she drew back for a better look at the formidable bulge at his loins. "I do know that it's expected for a husband to plant his seed in his wife. I can only surmise that his man-thing is made for that purpose. It seems logical that his wife would have to see it, then, wouldn't she?" She met his shocked expression with equanimity. "I am your wife, you know. Why should you be ashamed to show me your man-thing?"

81

His deepening scowl caused her cheerful smile to fade. "Is there something the matter with it, then?"

"Nay! There's nothing the matter with it!" The idiot girl was playing with fire, only she was too ignorant to realize it! Tynan shoved her farther away, outraged, yet at the same time fascinated, by her ignorance.

No. It wasn't ignorance. It was innocence, of a kind he could not remember knowing.

What in all the shades of Hades was he supposed to do now? What he saw set his body afire. And now this brazen talk . . . it left him clamoring to taste her, to slake his growing hunger inside her, but he dared not let himself for fear of what would happen.

He could not need her, or even want her. He was the executioner, and she the sacrifice. She was a means to an end, nothing more.

Misreading his silence, she granted him a saucy smile. "You've seen just about all there is to see of me, and I don't mind. Why would you hide your man-thing from me?"

"Because! It's not . . . it's . . . ." Tynan struggled in vain to find words where there should be none. "I'm not hiding it from you!" he exploded at last. "A man just doesn't pull out his . . ." he actually felt a rush of blood to his cheeks, "his 'man-thing' on demand, just to satisfy the curiosity of a mere chit like you. Wife or no wife, it simply isn't done."

Undaunted, Nara studied the telltale bulge even more intensely. "Is it like a dog's, then?" She looked up at him, all earnestness. "I've seen male dogs often enough when they mate out on the headlands. Their male-thing comes out all pink and shiny —"

"Silence! I will hear no more of this!" Tynan rushed past her, desperate to put out the fire her unbridled talk had ignited. He charged recklessly into the ice-cold lagoon until the freezing water lapped at his ribcage, accomplishing in a matter of seconds what no amount of self-control could have.

"And why have you done that, then?" Nara asked, perplexed.

Gasping from the cold, he did not trust himself to speak for what seemed like an aeon. "Prepare the food, woman!" he ordered at last. "And no more talk of my man-thing! Do you understand me?"

"Aye, I understand." Nara shook her head, clearly not understanding at all. "You're a strange man, Tynan. A strange man, indeed."

"Strange?" Somehow the word nettled, coming from her. "And how would you know whether I'm strange or not?" he shot back. "You, who've been in a convent all your life!"

She considered his question as if he were actually expecting a response. "True, I am ignorant of men, for the most part," she confessed without rancor. "What little I know of them comes from the Holy Writ. And from what my grandmother has told me." She studied him acutely. "But judging from what I've seen of you, I think *Seanmhair* is wise in the ways of men, indeed."

"You know nothing of me," he growled, "and neither did she."

Nara peered at him with an odd look on her face. "I wish I did know you." Her green eyes softened, never wavering. "Perhaps then I would understand how to heal the darkness I sense within you."

Tynan could almost see the cold anger from his heart reaching out, riding her gaze until it snuffed the glow from those wide, innocent green eyes. When it did, she gasped, her pupils contracting. "How can you live with such anger?"

His own gaze bored into hers. "I would never have survived without it."

Two days later, while Tynan struggled to repair their boat, Nara huddled behind a rock in an effort to hide from the cold currents of air that sliced across the water. The weather had turned chill, and the past two nights and days had been the longest, coldest, and most desolate of her life. To ward away the cold, they'd endured the darkness huddled together for warmth in a crude stone structure that let in as much wind and rain as it kept out. Judging from the tension with which he held her, Nara surmised that Tynan was as uncomfortable about their forced intimacy as she was. He had not offered so much as a single consoling gesture.

Not that she expected it. Nara had rescued many a wounded animal in the wild, but never had she encountered such an angry, isolated creature as Tynan. He wore his bitterness like armor, letting nothing in, not even the warmth he so obviously needed.

Were all men that way? she wondered. Mayhaps she was spinning fairie-webs to think that he might need a friend, especially a mere girl who had been forced upon him.

Her empty stomach set up such a growl that Tynan actually heard it grumble above the whistle of the wind.

He turned, his brows drawn together in concern. "Check the driftwood. Has it dried enough to burn?"

She reached to where they'd piled the scant supply of flotsam. "Dry enough." Warmed by the mere prospect of a fire, she crawled back out into the open. "If your flint will work."

"It will spark." He tossed her the flint. "If *you* keep it dry." Tynan picked up his pouch and rummaged through it until he found a neatly wound bundle of fishing line with a hook at the end. "Lay in a fire, then. I'm going to catch us some fish."

Nara assessed the length of his line from the size of the

84

bundle, then scanned the cloudy sky and whitecapped straits. "You'll catch no fish from shore today. The shallows are too rough. And too cold. All the fish have gone deep."

Tynan paused, his powerful frame making the cramped proportions of their exile all too evident. "And how would you know? The Sight?" He said it more like an accusation than a question, as if she must be some sort of witch to divine such a thing.

Nara hugged her knees against the cold. "The Sight has nothing to do with such matters."

"I see. Then you're an expert on fishing."

Stung by the sarcasm in his voice, Nara glanced down into her lap. "Nay. Merely an observer of nature."

Tynan let out a chortle of derision.

For some reason, she felt the need to defend herself from his scorn. She looked up at the muscular giant who towered over her. "I learned from the seals. When the water's as cold and choppy as it is today, the seals take much longer to bring my fish. I reasoned that they must dive deep to catch them."

"Bring your fish?" His golden brows lifted in surprise. "What are you saying?"

How could she explain without fueling his suspicions? The truth sounded damning indeed, but she could no more lie than she could breathe underwater. Perhaps he would believe the truth. "My two pet seals, Erk and Merk. I found them on the beach when they were just babies, nestled against their dead mother. They were so adorable and so helpless. I fed them with goat's milk and mashed cod livers until they were old enough to hunt for themselves."

Thinking about Erk and Merk made the corners of her mouth tremble. She missed her pets. And *Seanmhair* and Aunt Keriam and her home. A ragged sigh escaped her.

"After Erk and Merk were grown," she explained, "they

were always waiting for me whenever and wherever I came to the shore."

"And they brought you fish," he repeated, openly skeptical.

"First they greeted me," she clarified, "then they brought me fish."

Tynan regarded her with an unreadable expression. Then he turned abruptly. "Lay in a fire. I'll be back with fish."

No, you won't, she thought as she watched him go.

# Chapter VI

Tynan had been fishing with no luck for hours when he smelled the first whiff of smoke.

Smoke!

He clambered up a nearby boulder for a better look at the far side of the island. Sure enough, a telltale thread of gray rose from the jagged fingers of rock that concealed their campsite.

Fool girl. What was she doing? He'd told her to lay in a fire, not light it! As it was, they had scarce enough wood to cook a fish . . . assuming he could catch one. Why was she wasting precious fuel?

Then it occurred to him that she might have good reason. Had she seen a ship? Tynan's pulse quickened at the possibility. A signal fire . . .

He hastily wound in his line and tucked it behind his belt, then scaled a tall needle of stone for a better look at the surrounding waters.

No ship. Only the cold, choppy strait that stood between them and the tantalizing silhouettes of land in the distance.

A brief puff of smoke reminded him of Nara's folly.

Tynan dropped to the rocky beach. By all the demons in dark places, he fumed. She'd probably have most of the wood burned up before he could get back to stop her, and their bellies empty but for the prospect of raw fish.

Raw fish. Even Tynan's cast-iron innards rebelled at the

thought. Though he had survived for two decades on the leavings of others, he did not relish the idea of biting into a raw fish.

He hastened back to the campsite, but even with his long legs and steady foot, the trip from spray-slickened rock to rock was treacherous and time-consuming.

As he neared the shallow lagoon, a gust of wind brought him a fresh whiff of smoldering wood. And something else.

Tynan could have sworn it was the aroma of broiling fish.

Hunger must be making his imagination play tricks with his senses. But why now? He'd gone hungry far longer than this without imagining the smell of food. Was this more of the Witch's sorcery? Or the girl's?

Scaling the last large boulder that overshadowed their camp, he looked down, but could see only smoke pouring forth from the many crevices in their crude stone shelter. With one powerful leap, he descended to the narrow strip of sand, the ground quaking beneath the solid impact of his weight.

Nara stuck her head out of the shelter. "Oh, good. You're back. Supper's almost ready."

"Supper? And what would that be?" he asked acidly.

Nara smiled with the innocence of a child proffering a handful of posies. "Fish. Two nice, fat cod." She disappeared inside, then reemerged, her hands full of fish guts. Oblivious to Tynan's suspicious scowl, she stepped to the water's edge, lifted the smelly offering skyward, and executed a medley of squawks and bird cries that sounded for all the world like a pack of raucous gulls and terns.

In only moments, a dozen seabirds appeared from nowhere, circling hungrily. Tynan watched in silence as they fed from her open hand, some of them lighting on her arms like tamed falcons.

A cold thread of warning spread through his chest. Surely no ordinary woman could conjure such an unnatural event.

Nara turned to him with a delighted grin on her face, but one look at his expression, and her smile faded. "What's wrong? Don't you like the birds?" When he didn't answer, she looked to the three terns roosting contentedly on her outstretched arms. "Poor birds. They must work so hard to stay alive." She turned troubled green eyes back to his. "I didn't think you'd mind my giving them the fish-waste . . ."

The hurt and confusion in her gaze prompted an unwelcome pang of remorse in Tynan. "I care not what you do with the fish-waste," he growled. But he did care about the pain in those lucid green eyes, and that disturbed him.

He could not allow himself to care. One day soon, he would have to look into those emerald eyes and slay her. He would do so because he had to, Tynan told himself, deliberately hardening himself to her.

"Where did you get the fish?" he accused.

Nara drew back as if his words had the force of impact. "Erk and Merk. Somehow they found me."

"That's difficult to believe. We must be a dozen leagues from the Isle of Mist." Tynan's eyes narrowed. "Unless you summoned them with a spell . . ."

Her wounded expression bloomed into one of amusement. "A spell? That's silly." She cocked her head, sobering. "I thought you believed in nothing but yourself. Surely you don't think I'm a witch." She studied him intently. "You do," she breathed softly. "You really think I'm a sorceress. I can see it in your eyes."

Averting his gaze, Tynan made the sign against the evil eye behind his back. He fully expected her to deny being a witch — considering the dire penalties for sorcery. But instead she laughed long and hard, sending the birds scattering.

When she recovered herself, Nara stooped to scrub her hands clean with sand and saltwater. "Such nonsense. Why, you're just as superstitious as the rest of them."

To Tynan's consternation, her accusation stung almost as much as her laughter. He rounded on her, determined to take the upper hand. "The rest of them? And who would that be?"

"*Seanmhair*. The other sisters." She straightened, gracefully shaking the water from her sand-reddened hands. "It's merely ignorance," she continued matter-of-factly. "What they cannot explain, they call witchcraft. *Seanmhair* and the others always seem so caught up in the business of surviving that they haven't taken the time to observe the secrets of nature."

"And you? Howbeit you've taken the time?"

"As I told you," she said evenly, "*Seanmhair* was never my jailer. She allowed me the freedom to explore, and I saw and remembered much. But there is far more, still, to learn."

A nostalgic light in her eyes, she stared toward the blue-gray lands on the horizon. "Have you ever run with the wind before a summer storm? Followed it to a high place and stretched out on the ground, listening to Thor's hammer spark the anvil of heaven and letting the rain drench you until lightning strikes so close that every hair on your body stands on end?" She closed her eyes, her face transformed by the wonder of that memory.

"Or lain in the heather on a warm August day and listened, really listened, to the hum of life around you? Stared into the sky until you felt at one with every rock and flower, a part of the earth beneath you and every living, breathing thing? Lain so still that even the wild creatures felt safe to graze beside you?"

Hearing her describe it, Tynan could not stop himself from remembering that he, too, had once been free to roam.

Nara's vivid description evoked the long-forgotten perfume of summer in the Highland moors; the whisper of the wind through fields of blooming heather; the pride and excitement of hunting with his father; the reckless joy of running free with his brothers. But he had long ago put to rest those memories of his early childhood, and the pain that came with them.

Now Nara had awakened something of the boy he once was, and with that boy, a piercing stab of grief and loss. "These past twenty years, I've had no idle hours," he said harshly, "nor sleeping in the sun."

"No?" Nara regarded him with melting compassion. She reached out and took his huge, callused hand into her own small, soft ones. "When the fullness of summer comes, we must lie in the sun together."

Tynan pulled his hand away. *When the fullness of summer comes . . .*

They might well lie together then, but in eternal darkness, not in sun.

A cold wind blustered in abruptly from the east, gaining force with each new gust.

"Brrr." Nara shivered and drew her habit higher around her neck. "Come. I can smell the fish is ready." She started for the shelter, but paused halfway there and listened as if she'd heard a summons from afar. "This will be the last night we sleep here," she murmured vacantly. Then, as quickly as it had come, her distant expression vanished. She granted Tynan a slow, sad smile. "Who knows what tomorrow will bring? At least we'll eat our fill of fish and sleep warm tonight."

*. . . sleep warm.* For the past three nights, they had shared the heat of their bodies to ward off the chill. Watching her graceful movements now, Tynan realized he wasn't as hungry

for food or fire as he was for the feel of her soft, supple body cradled against his in the night.

The thought sent a disconcerting flush of desire to his loins, prompting him to reassure himself that the reaction was merely a mindless reflex. He was a man, after all, with a man's needs. Any woman would have affected him thusly. It signified nothing about Nara.

Still, there was no reason for him not to enjoy the warmth and softness she afforded.

"Let's eat, then," he said as he crawled in after her.

Whatever new trials awaited them on the morrow, he'd been granted one more night with Nara in his arms.

"Tynan, come quickly!" Nara's voice roused him from an unnaturally deep slumber. He squinted in the predawn dimness, barely able to make out her silhouette before him. She was kneeling, half in and half out of the shelter.

"What's happened?" he grumbled, sitting up so quickly his head dislodged a stone from their makeshift shelter. "Ouch!" Stiff as an old woman, he pushed the offending rock back into place, then rubbed his skull. Every bone in his body felt as if it had worked its way through to the stone beneath him.

"Get up!" She tugged at his hand. "It's a miracle."

Yawning, Tynan rubbed his eyes, then scraped his palms across his stubbled cheeks. "Mmmm. Well, Heaven forefend I should sleep through a miracle." One of Nara's miracles . . . probably a tern hatching in a crevice nearby.

"I would have swum for it already," she declared fervently, pulling with surprising strength for a lass her size, "but the water's so cold, I dare not swim without someone watching . . . to see I get back safely."

The urgency in her voice convinced him she had seen

92

more than a nestling. Frowning, Tynan allowed himself to be dragged into the raw morning. Outside the shelter, the air was cold, but still.

Tynan focused belatedly on what she'd been saying. Swim? What in blazes was she thinking of? She knew he couldn't swim.

He yawned hugely, stretching out the kinks he'd gotten from sleeping curled in the little shelter. When he opened his eyes, he saw Nara clamber over the rocks that shielded them from the open strait. Reaching the top, she looked across the water and crossed herself. "Thanks be to God. It's still there." Without further explanation, she began pulling off her clothes even as she disappeared on the other side.

"Wait!" Fool girl. This time of day, even the shallows were cold enough to stop the stoutest heart from beating. Tynan scrambled after her. When he spotted her at the water's edge, he was so preoccupied with her safety that he didn't look past her. "Hold, woman!" He slid down beside her and grasped her now-bare arm. True to form, she had stripped down to her shift, despite the fact that the air was so cold their breath shot forth in clouds as white as dragon's smoke. "Are you *trying* to catch lung fever? It's too cold to take off your clothes, much less swim!"

She pulled impatiently at the fingers that encircled her arm. "Let me go! It's close enough now, but if I wait, it might drift away!"

"It?" he demanded. "What in the devil are you talking about, it?"

Nara pointed past him to the glassy waters of the strait. "That. The boat."

He whirled around just in time to see two spotted seals slip beneath the surface on either side of a small leathern boat a dozen yards offshore.

A boat! But where had it come from?

The seals — surely they hadn't . . .

"Well, I'll be an Englishman," he breathed. His mind conjured up a number of explanations, none of which he was willing to address. He turned to Nara. "Don't tell me that was Erk and Merk I just saw."

She shifted uncomfortably beneath his trenchant stare. "Very well. If you do not wish me to tell you it was Erk and Merk, I shall not tell you it was Erk and Merk." She looked pointedly to the huge hand that still held her upper arm. "Please let me go. The boat's so light, even a puff of wind could blow it out of reach."

Tynan hesitated. Even if the cold water didn't drown her, the swim might chill her so badly she would take the ague. But if she didn't fetch the boat while it lay close to shore, they might very well lose their chance to escape and end up starving or freezing before he could repair their damaged craft.

He looked down to find her head bowed and her hands folded in prayer. "Why are you doing that?" he demanded.

Without opening her eyes or raising her head, she answered quietly, "I know you're worried about my swimming in the cold, so I'm asking God what to do."

Tynan snorted. "*Hiu!* And you think He'll answer?" He shook his head. "You're touched, woman."

Nara opened worried eyes and crossed herself, but when she looked past him, her expression cleared.

Tynan turned, following her line of sight.

Though there was no wind or evidence of current, the boat was moving decisively toward them. As the hull scraped aground on the rocky shore, he thought he heard two soft splashes behind the stern.

The seals?

He shoved the nagging question aside and concentrated

on the very real presence of the boat. Tynan waded into the icy water and drew it safely ashore, noting the storm debris floating in the bilge. Once the hull was on dry land, he inspected it carefully for signs of leakage before emptying out the water.

Delivered. But by what power?

Not that he cared. All that mattered was that they had a way off this godforsaken island, and he meant to leave as soon as humanly possible. "Nara," he ordered, "gather our belongings. I'll get my weapons and the oars."

"Your weapons?" Nara took Tynan's measure, then turned a concerned frown to the small, lightweight craft. "I know your weapons mean a great deal to you, sir, but are you willing to risk sinking just to bring them along?" Her green eyes darkened with fear and compassion. "You are so big, and our boat is so small. Even without the added weight of your weapons, one good wave could sink us."

She had a point, but Tynan could no more abandon his father's weapons than he could leave behind the very bones that allowed him to stand. "Wherever I go, my weapons go."

Nara's eyes flared even wider, and the usually soft line of her mouth went rigid with fear.

"Why do you look at me that way?" he countered, "as if I were dooming us to a watery grave? We'll be all right." Goaded by the apprehension in her face, he added, "We'll be fine, Nara. My weapons won't sink us. I'll lash them to the boat-rails. The ballast will make the craft more stable. Now run along and fetch our things." His scowl shifted to a leer. "You'd best put your clothes on first, though."

Nara looked down and gasped. Every inch of her exposed skin flushed pinker than the sunrise now brightening the east. "Aye. I'll be quick, then, and so should you." Snatching up her garments, she scanned the mirror-smooth strait. "A calm like this never lasts long. We'd do well to paddle as far as we can before the wind kicks up." With that, she shrugged into her clothes and made her way back to camp.

Once there, she stooped into the shelter and drew Tynan's pouch from its resting place. Good thing the flagon was full of fresh water. At least she wouldn't have to dive to the sea-cave before setting out.

Placing the flagon securely into the pouch, she caught an oddly jarring glimpse of color in the bottom of the pouch. She turned toward the rising sun and opened the drawstring as wide as it would go for a better look. There, folded neatly at the bottom of the pouch, was a smooth, shiny pelt of short fur.

Nara's heart skipped a beat. No. It couldn't be. Cold dread bloomed through her like a chilling fog. With shaking hand, she drew out the pelt and unfolded it.

*Gobhar!*

She knew those markings as well as the contours of her own body.

"Gobhar!" She didn't realize she'd cried the word aloud until she saw Tynan drop what he was doing and hasten to the shelter.

"Yes, it's a goat." His golden brows drew together. "You're white as frost! What's wrong?"

Nara thrust the skin toward him, scarcely able to endure looking at the proof of her beloved pet's death. She asked tremulously, "Where did you get this?"

Tynan shrugged, his expression guarded. "I was starving. The goat was there." His angular features hardened. "I told you, Nara: I take what I need."

"Gobhar." Hot, bitter tears blurred her vision. "You killed her." Nara clutched the skin to her aching heart. How could anyone slay a creature as gentle and trusting as

96

Gobhar? She looked up at Tynan. "She was my pet. My beloved companion. And you killed her. It was you."

Not the wolf.

"Aye," he said without remorse. "And I would do it again to keep from starving."

Maybe he *was* the wolf . . .

Against her will, Nara felt her gaze drawn to his. Even through her tears, she could see the mindless hunger in the glint of predatory defiance reflected back at her.

The hunt. Was that all that moved him?

No, something deep inside told her. Tynan MacDougald did not live for the hunt. He lived for the kill.

And he would kill her if the need presented itself, just as coldly as he had slain Gobhar.

Numbed by that realization, she allowed Tynan to pull the goatskin from her hands and shove it back into the pouch.

"Come," he chided. "There's no time to waste. God willing, we will make the mainland by nightfall."

Nara tried to collect her shattered feelings, but she could not stop her tears of grief — for sweet Gobhar; for *Seanmhair* and Auntie Keriam; for the solitary freedom she would never know again; but most of all, for the terrible darkness that blighted the soul of the man who was her husband.

"I will go with you, sir," she said softly, "for I have given my word to do so." She forced herself to straighten and face him eye-to-eye. "But if we *do* reach the mainland, I think that God will have had little part in it." That said, she made for the boat with heavy tread, less frightened of drowning than she was of what Tynan MacDougald meant to do with her once he'd delivered her to her grandfather.

# Chapter VII

Distraught though she was about Gobhar, Nara soon had weightier matters to worry about. Their boat was dangerously overloaded. One false move and Tynan would be tossed into an unforgiving sea.

In an effort to balance his weight in the little craft, he lay stretched out along the shallow craft behind her, his shoulders braced against the stern. His legs were wedged hot against her on either side, making it difficult to concentrate on paddling, but Nara resisted the irrational urge to brush her arm along the muscular calves that bracketed her.

Not that his physical presence was easy to ignore, especially in such close quarters. With every awkward stroke of the makeshift paddle he was using, the boat threatened to capsize. If he were to fall in now that they were so far from land, he would surely drown. But much as she hated what he'd done to Gobhar, she could not wish him dead. After all, he'd said he was starving, and after the past few days with only fish and a few salty groats, Nara was beginning to understand for the first time what it meant to be truly hungry.

How fortunate she had been, never to have known starvation. Tynan couldn't say the same.

Remembering the Scriptural imperative for forgiveness, Nara sighed and made a deliberate sacrifice of will. *Oh, all right, Lord. I forgive Tynan. But only because You command it.*

She stole a glance at her husband's grim expression and felt a genuine pang of sympathy. *He was starving. I suppose it's wrong to value the life of my pet above that of a man.* A lump the size of a mill-wheel seemed to form in her chest. *But Gobhar was as good and gentle as any friend could ever be, dear Lord, and I loved her. You were a shepherd, and I know you loved your sheep. So you can see why it's not easy to forgive Tynan for killing her, but I do. All I ask is that you take Gobhar's sweet spirit into your fold in heaven. And that you forgive Tynan. He did not know what he was doing.*

She exhaled heavily, willing away the anger and grief she'd felt toward Tynan. For now, determining to forgive him was the best she could do. Release from anguish would take longer, but it would come in time.

*The soul of a true believer must always hold dominion over the emotions,* Aunt Keriam had taught her, *or all is lost.* Nara believed it.

Her soul purged, she felt free to ask, *And please bring us safe to shore, dear Lord. I could not bear to think of Tynan drowning unshriven, even if he did kill Gobhar.*

Nara did her best to focus on paddling without tipping the boat.

Stroke after precarious stroke stretched the minutes into an endless, grim monotony. To her surprise, Nara felt her fear fade into a strained sense of boredom. One could only remain perched on the razor's edge for so long, she imagined, before even that became routine.

Knowing that Tynan's plaid was stretched wide above his knees just behind her, she was seized with the perverse idea of sneaking a look at his man-thing to break the monotony.

This was no time for such idle notions, though. So she leaned as far forward as she could in the prow of the little boat and kept her eyes focused to their eastward destination.

*Don't think about his legs, or the heat of him. Or his man-thing.*

Nara forced herself to consider his soul, instead. Just as his powerful body radiated heat, his physical presence radiated a dark momentum — something hot and hard and indefinable: an inner compulsion as seductive as it was terrifying in its intensity. Yet underneath his cloak of shadows lay the key to Tynan's anger, and she was determined to find it.

Stroke after stroke, she heard him carefully lift his paddle from one side to the other, despite the awkwardness of his position. It couldn't have been easy. It must have been awkward, paddling from the stern instead of rowing.

As the day wore on, Nara grew more and more weary, her side aching from the constant contact with the framework of the little boat, but she doggedly kept up the pace, knowing that Tynan must be even more uncomfortable than she.

One false move from either of them and they'd sink — a sure death sentence for Tynan. Luckily, the strait was as still as a pond, the air now warm and oddly breathless, but Nara felt a growing sense of foreboding.

What if the Witch was merely toying with them, waiting to capsize them with a sudden wind or an unexpected wave?

Keep your eyes on the mainland, she told herself. We're almost there.

No longer was Wester Ross a distant strip of gray on the horizon. Now the coastline loomed larger and larger, its emerald slopes softened to jade and celadon by the hazy stillness.

So many years, she had gazed with longing toward this very shore.

But what dark purpose awaited her when they got there?

She stole a glance at Tynan, careful to keep her eyes well above the taut spread of his plaid. Despite the discomfort and

100

exhaustion that lined his features, his eyes were lit by a hard glint of triumph.

Success was in sight.

Had they beaten the Witch after all?

Nara wasn't so sure. She was certain of only one thing: Once they reached the mainland, there would be a reckoning.

Hundreds of labored strokes later, they glided, at last, within yards of a narrow beach.

Nara peered over the side. The gray waters beneath them gave no hint of depth, and the beach was steep.

"Hold," Tynan ordered. "Let me get out first, then I'll carry you ashore." When he moved, the little boat tipped precariously.

"No, wait," Nara cautioned. "We don't know how deep the water is. Let me get out first, but not until we feel the hull scrape bottom." Seeing his impatient scowl, she hastened to explain, "You're so much heavier than I. If you'll only be still, your weight will steady the boat so it won't turn —"

"Nonsense." Tynan's voice betrayed his fatigue. "It can't be deep at all; I can spit and hit the shore." He grasped the boat-rails to steady himself and tried to rise. "If I stay one moment longer in this position, my neck is likely never to be straight again. I cannot —"

He didn't finish. His next words were drowned out when the craft flipped over, tossing them both into the murky water.

Nara surfaced immediately. "Tynan!" Several yards away, he flailed and sputtered, his face rising for only a brief gasp of air above the cold water.

The Witch wasn't through with them yet.

Immediately Nara struck out with long, solid strokes until she reached him. She dived for him, grabbed a fistful of his hair, and marshaled every ounce of her remaining strength to pull his face out of the water.

His expression shifted rapidly from fury to relief to confusion, then back to fury. Tynan coughed, gasped in a ragged breath of air, then began to sink — and thrash — again.

"Stop fighting me, or we'll both drown!" Nara used the last of her failing strength to pull his head back above water. "Relax! Turn onto your back and let your body go limp, so I can drag you to shore."

To her vast relief, his thrashing subsided abruptly. But before he turned onto his back, he began to rise. Nara still had a death-grip on his hair when he bent over her, dripping and swiping the stinging saltwater from his eyes, and sputtered, "*Phtt!* You needn't snatch me bald, woman! I'm not likely to drown. The water only comes to my ribs."

Nara lowered her feet and, sure enough, met with gritty resistance with her shoulders still above the surface.

All that panic for nothing.

"Thank God," she said with absolute sincerity. "I doubt I could have pulled you another inch, much less all the way to the shore. We both would have perished."

Visibly perplexed, Tynan shepherded her toward shore. "You would have died yourself, trying to save me." He shook his head. "It makes no sense."

"I could not let you drown," she stated simply. "You are my lord husband."

He shook his head again, then reached for the overturned boat. With one mighty heave, he set it aright. Half-filled with water, it settled low on the surface, the pouch and weapons still securely lashed to the frame.

Seeing the patent relief on his face, Nara couldn't help wondering which meant more to him — her or his blessed weapons. Then she chided herself for the cynical thought.

Tynan gave the stern a mighty shove, and the craft drifted

past Nara toward shore.

She turned and followed, only to hear him wade up noisily and scoop her into his arms. Though his muscles quivered with fatigue, he held her close. "I do not understand you, Nara."

Why was it so hard to believe she would want to save him? "Nor I, you," she answered frankly.

It felt good, being in his arms. The unnatural heat of his torso radiated even through their wet clothes, warming her. Nara threw her hand over his shoulder and relaxed against the rapid thrumming of her husband's labored heartbeat. "We are bound together by honor and by troth. But don't worry, Tynan. We have a lifetime to figure each other out." She felt him tense and wondered why.

"Give it time," she added wearily. "We shall learn each other in time."

Once ashore, Tynan climbed beyond the irregular strip of debris that marked the tide and collapsed onto the sand, drawing Nara close beside him, her head to his chest. In only minutes, they both fell into exhausted slumber. It was late afternoon before hunger, aching muscles, and the coldness of their sodden clothing roused them.

Nara winced as she stretched the stiffness from her arms. The raw patch across her ribs stung as if she'd laid it to the mouth of a hornet's nest. "I'll be happy if I never strike another stroke with a paddle as long as I live."

Tynan sat up beside her, his salt-stiffened hair full of sand and sticking out at odd angles. "And aye for me, too." He rose awkwardly, obviously as stiff and sore as she. "Up you go." He pulled her to her feet. "We've slept away most of the afternoon. Only a few hours remain to find water and food."

Nara looked around her. "So this is Wester Ross." She didn't know what she had expected, but she had expected something different. Yet this particular spot looked and felt for all the world like a dozen places on the Isle of Mist. "It's not so different from home."

"Not here," Tynan countered, turning to the northeast. "But when we reach the Highlands . . ." A fierce gleam of pride lit his distant expression. "My mother used to say that the Highlands are God's footstool. There are places there where even a boy can reach up and grab a fistful of heaven."

For a split second, Nara caught a glimpse of the lad Tynan had once been — a child filled with wonder who believed he could touch the hem of God. Then she saw a crushing sorrow sweep across him, erasing the wonder and twisting his features as it must have twisted his soul.

His voice turned harsh. "Make haste. We need to find fresh water."

Tynan was grateful that it took him less than an hour to locate a freshwater stream that cascaded into an estuary. His throat was so raw from the seawater he'd taken in, he could scarcely swallow, and after all that paddling, even the negligible weight of his pouch, sword, and axe were proving too much for him. He dropped his belongings within easy reach, stooped to scoop up a mouthful of water from the stream, found it sweet, and beckoned Nara to drink first. Only after she rose refreshed did he satisfy his own thirst.

When he sat up, quenched, he saw Nara step into the stream wearing only her shift. Her soggy clothing hung limp from her arm. Then she bent to rinse the garments in the cascade, exposing the shredded, bloody patch of shift against her ribs.

Tynan's eyes widened in alarm. By King James and all the saints! She'd rubbed the flesh from her bones paddling and never said a word.

He experienced an unfamiliar stab of guilt, then wondered why he should feel guilty. They had both done what was needed. It wasn't his fault that they'd been cast away —

But it *was* his fault, a still, small inner voice reminded. He was the one who had ignored her warnings and insisted they put to sea . . .

He looked up to find Nara staring at him, a quizzical expression on her face. She smiled, waved, then plunged beneath the coursing torrent.

In spite of himself, Tynan's heart contracted at the brilliance of that smile. She rose from the cascade like a water sprite, her black hair slicked tight to every curve of her body and her thin shift all but transparent, just as when he had mistaken her for a selkie.

And just as it had then, the sleek, molded veil of black hair proved far more seductive than bare flesh.

Not that he wouldn't enjoy exploring her bare flesh. Suddenly Tynan realized just how much he *would* enjoy touching her, tasting her, slaking the hunger that rose within him at the sight of her.

A surge of lust pulsed through him, stirring his manhood to life.

She knew he was looking at her. Why this sudden teasing, this coyness? Nara was anything but coy. Frank to a fault, yes, but never coy.

Then she turned and met his piercing stare with one of her own, a look that crackled with challenge.

Conn's balls! Did she *want* him to take her?

Tynan's heartbeat deepened, growing lower and stronger by the second until he could scarcely think. She was a woman, all right, and he hadn't had a woman in months.

He imagined peeling the wet shift from her skin, laying her naked before him, then thrusting himself past her clean, stream-cooled skin to the heat within. Plunging harder and harder until he found release . . .

The mere thought was almost enough to spill his seed. Yet all his instincts warned Tynan that if he did take her, Nara would work a hold on him, a hold that could ruin everything.

Determined not to let that happen, he waded into the frigid stream and submerged himself to his chin. The icy shock should have been enough to quell any man's ardor, but it merely tempered Tynan's.

He rose, gasping and frustrated, then held his breath and thrust his head beneath the water, as much to clear his brain as to rinse the stink of salt from his hair. When he straightened, throwing his head back to cast the wet hair from his eyes, it was to find Nara standing close beside him, her attention fixed on the plaid that clung to his loins.

The contours clearly betrayed him.

Oblivious to the fact that her shift concealed nothing, she smiled up at him with open curiosity. "Does your man-thing change size, then? I don't remember its being so large before." She smelled of clean water and heather and something indefinably feminine that set his senses on edge.

Faith, had she cast a spell on him, truly? For as much as he wanted to turn and walk away, he could not. He could do nothing but grasp her upper arms and pull her close, burying his face into the hollow of her neck.

To his amazement, she gasped, then wrapped her legs around his hips, pulling herself closer.

Tynan didn't remember carrying her out of the stream or setting her to her feet before a smooth slab of rock. All he knew was that his wet clothes were strangling him. Pulse thundering in his ears, he snatched his body free of the sodden plaid. With a single motion, he peeled away his shirt, and then he was standing naked before her, his flushed skin radiating the heat of his desire.

Nara's green eyes sparkled with an odd light, but she never looked away. She inspected him with undisguised inquisitiveness and more than a hint of approval.

It was that boldness that undid him.

He had to see her, all of her. Tynan's eyes roamed the length of her transparent shift, stopping only briefly at the dark triangle at the apex of her legs. He watched his hands, moving as if at their own direction, pull the shift away from her skin and draw it up over her head.

He expected resistance, yet she did not fight him. Instead, she made it easier, lifting her arms as if she, too, were eager to be free of the restraining fabric.

Then she actually pushed herself against him, her damp skin cool against his hot torso. "Mmm," she murmured. "You feel good. So warm. Makes me want to get closer, but I know not how —"

Tynan silenced her with a kiss, a kiss so hungry it shook him to his heels.

He felt her hands slide up his chest, then thread into the hair at the base of his neck and draw him closer even as her bare legs circled his hips, bringing the seat of her desire into contact with his erection.

By Odin, her flesh wept for him already. She wanted him, truly she must.

Such brazen seduction, from a virgin? questioned a distant inner warning, but Tynan was beyond listening. He was beyond anything but satisfying the lust that now consumed him.

As if she could read his thoughts, Nara tightened her fingers in his hair. She wiggled hard against him, letting out a whimper of surprised pleasure at the sensations the movement released.

Tynan could endure no more. He lifted her buttocks, then drove himself hard inside her, sensing only the slightest resistance upon entry. She let out a startled gasp, then held him tighter, giving herself over to the frantic rhythm of mating. Faster and faster, deeper and deeper, and with every thrust, Nara's legs drew him closer, as if she knew already how to take the most of him.

Tynan opened his eyes to find hers glazed with desire, focused intently at the point of joining. Then she looked up at him with such undisguised heat that he thought he would explode where he stood.

She ground a savage kiss into his lips, then arched her back, presenting her breasts to him. Tynan buried his face in their smooth, resilient softness, reveling in the gentle scrape of his beard against her flesh. He took her nipple into his mouth and tasted.

"Ah!" Nara cried out, her hands bracketing his head. "Do the other, or I shall die."

Tynan was only too happy to oblige.

Frenzied now, she clung to him, her short nails digging into his back. Tynan could withhold his release no longer when she let out a final cry of exultation and went still in his arms.

He spilled his seed inside her, then staggered back against the rock ledge to sit with her still wrapped around him, both of them panting.

Why wasn't she angry? He had taken her virginity roughly, like an animal in rut. But instead of being angry, she had met him with a hunger as fierce as his own. How could this be?

Nara pulled free of him and rolled onto her back on the smooth, sun-warmed rock, her flesh rosy with the afterglow of their union and her breasts marked by their contact with the stubble on his chin. Beneath her, the shining curtain of her dark hair gleamed across the rock.

By the three virgins, but she looked wanton . . . and glorious.

Never in all his manhood had Tynan experienced such a potent joining.

"Mmm." Completely unselfconscious in her nakedness, she closed her eyes and stretched like a cat. Nara looked up at him with a self-satisfied smile. "If I had known *that* was what it was going to be like, I'd have demanded you do your husbandly duty the first night we were married." A wicked chuckle escaped her. "No wonder *Seanmhair* said it was sinful. That was far too much fun to be holy."

Her gaze dropped to his now-flagging manhood, and she sat up abruptly. "Oh, goodness. It's going limp." Genuine concern clouded her expression. "Did I do something wrong? Hurt you, somehow?"

"Nay. It only gets stiff when I'm . . . aroused." Why was he explaining? And why in perdition was she asking about such things? Had the wench no proper sense of propriety? Tynan shook his head in consternation. A hundred years would not be enough to understand *this* woman.

And you have no time at all to try, came a dark whisper from within.

No time at all.

That single thread of reality was enough to bring him back to his senses. He shot a baleful glance at Nara, then snatched up his clothes, weapons, and pouch. "Wait here. I'll try to find some food."

He saw her wither beneath his anger. "Whatever is the matter, Tynan?" Her injured tone firmed. "And don't try to tell me you regret our mating. You enjoyed it as much as I did. I could tell." She rose to follow him.

"Silence," he ordered. The truth in what she spoke stung him even further. He *had* enjoyed their mating, entirely too much. "Guard your tongue, woman. No trueborn lady would ever speak of such things."

She faltered beneath the venom in his voice. "Have I done something wrong, then?" She clutched his naked arm. "You must tell me. This is the first time I've ever mated, so I had no way of knowing —"

"I said, be quiet!" Tynan pulled free of her, hardening himself against the hurt in her eyes. He could not allow himself to care or all would be lost — his honor, his duty, his sacred vow.

He shook the sand from his cold, wet shirt, put it on, then hastily donned his plaid. "Stay here. I will bring back food and fuel. We set out for the Highlands at dawn."

"Aye, then," she said softly, her voice thick with tears. "I will do as you bid."

Tynan left her without looking back.

Nara watched him go, feeling as if a part of her had been brutally amputated.

He had reveled in their mating just as much as she; she was certain of it. Why, now, had he turned against her?

A squeezing pain tightened around her heart. If only she knew what had gone wrong . . .

Wiping the tears from her cheeks, she gathered her clothes and spread them out to dry. Sitting down beside them in the afternoon sunlight, she resolved to find out what had gone amiss, no matter what it took.

Time was on her side. They had a long journey ahead of them, and a lifetime together beyond that. There would be time to win the truth from Tynan. Plenty of time.

One week of endless walking later, Tynan looked back

down the ridge and saw that Nara had dropped even farther behind.

As if she sensed the weight of his gaze, she tipped her face toward his, her mouth set in a weary line of hunger and fatigue. She slowed, her posture wavering, then sank to the damp ground.

He stifled an oath of frustration. He'd driven her too hard, and he knew it. She was only a girl, and a pampered one at that. How could he expect her to keep up a pace that strained even his hardened endurance?

Majestic as they were, the Highlands made quick sacrifice of the weak or unwary. If he didn't find food soon . . .

"Wait there," he called, "I'll come to you." He doubled back, scanning the bleak slopes for some sign of shelter. The sun would soon be gone, leaving them at the mercy of the chill, dank wind that swept across these barren hills even now, in summer.

Nara lay back into a patch of bracken, clearly exhausted.

As he approached her, something in the valley below caught his eye.

Movement.

A deer?

Tynan peered into the shadowed hollow far below and was gratified to see a small lake and the faint outline of a round, thatched cottage nestled fifty paces beyond it.

Shelter. And water.

But there was no sign of light from the distant hovel, nor any smoke rising from the opening at the center of its cone-shaped roof.

Probably abandoned, which meant no food inside, but there might be fish in the lake.

"Come." Tynan leaned down and drew Nara upright.

111

"There's a cottage in that valley below. We'll rest there, out of the wind."

"Rest," she murmured gratefully, her body conforming to his in absolute trust. "May I lean against you for just a moment longer? I can't seem to make my feet work." Her head curled against his chest, the faint sweet scent of her ebon hair rising to his nostrils.

Summoning a strength he did not know he had, Tynan lifted her into his arms. "I'll carry you, then." Hunger and exertion had taken their toll on Nara since they'd begun the trek to Eilean d'Ór. Holding her now, he could tell that she weighed far less than when he'd placed her into the boat ten days ago on the Isle of Mist.

Step by weary step, he descended into the darkened vale. He'd scarcely covered a dozen yards before he felt Nara relax, her breathing deep and even.

She always did that — lapsed easily into profound, untroubled slumber. Tynan envied her the ability. His rest was never so secure. With so much hanging on his getting her safely to her grandfather, he had to sleep with one eye open and both ears cocked for the slightest sign of danger.

He forced now-leaden feet to take one more cautious downward step on the unfamiliar, rock-strewn ground, then another, then another.

By the time he reached the hovel, it was so dark he could barely see where he was going, and his human burden weighed heavier than a caber.

Without warning, a squawking apparition fluttered past, waking Nara and sending a jolt of alarm through Tynan. In one swift motion, he set her abruptly to her feet and drew his sword.

Nara clung to his side in alarm. "What was that?" she whispered hoarsely.

112

"A chicken, I think," he muttered, every muscle tensed. Perhaps the cottage wasn't deserted after all. "Wait here while I make sure it's safe."

Her arms tightened around his waist. "I'm coming with you."

"All right," he whispered, "but at least get behind me. I can't defend either of us with you latched on under my sword-arm like that."

"Sorry." She transferred her grip to the pelts that covered the axe bound to his back.

Tynan took great care to step softly on the hard-packed earth surrounding the cottage. When he reached an open window on the shadowed side, he leaned close and listened.

No sound. Only the faint breeze blowing past him.

He strained to make out the dim interior. The fire pit in the center of the single room lay cold, its ashes dank and neglected. A ragged curtain hung halfway across one-third of the hovel, obscuring part of a rough wooden bed covered with rushes and a jumbled blanket. Aside from a crude table and one bench, the rest of the room was bare.

The knot in Tynan's stomach eased somewhat. He turned to Nara. "It's not much, but at least we'll have a roof over our heads."

Once they were inside, he eased the pouch and axe from his back with a sigh of relief, but kept his sword at the ready. "Poke around in here. If we're lucky, the last occupants might have left behind some provisions." He stepped toward the low doorway. "I'll see if I can find fuel for a fire." A humorless smile tugged at his lips. "That chicken will make a good meal, if I can catch it. Otherwise, I'll have to try for some fish."

Nara nodded, too tired to speak. Stiff as an old woman, she rose as Tynan disappeared into the silvered night. She watched him go with an unexplainable sense of disquiet.

There was something wrong about this place.

Her eyes went to the ragged curtain and the bed beyond. Whose house was this? And who had last slept in that bed?

A shiver raised the hair on the back of her neck, prompting her to rub the chill from her upper arms. If only she had some light.

She knew there was a flint in Tynan's pouch, but she could not bear the prospect of coming in contact with Gobhar's pelt, even in the dark.

Once her eyes had adjusted to the dim obscurity of the cottage, she crept to the fire pit and felt around the edges of the crude stone hearth until she found a flint. A groping search of the wall behind her yielded a bundle of soiled rushes, enough to make a torch of sorts.

With her back to the ragged curtain, she pulled out a flexible strand of reed and bound the rushes together, then laid them on the hearth and struck the flint to the stone.

It took several tries, but soon she managed to coax a spark into the reeds. Relieved, she puffed gently on the smoldering embers until the torch flickered into an open flame.

Again, the back of her neck began to tingle. In a single motion, Nara rose and turned, lifting her torch to light the sleeping area behind her.

What she saw beside the curtain tore a terrified scream from the depths of her soul.

# Chapter VIII

There, only a few feet from her, stood a tall, twisted parody of a man dressed in rags, his emaciated arms drawn unnaturally to a bony, protruding chest. He'd been standing absolutely still when she'd first seen him, but the moment she reacted, he shrieked, his head jerking back and the dark eyes in his sunken face unfocused.

Too frightened to move, Nara gripped the torch and stared at the cranelike apparition. Every inch of six feet tall, he was so thin she could clearly see the outline of the bones in his filthy arms and legs.

Was he young or old? Nara couldn't tell. One moment he looked like an old man; the next, scarcely older than twenty.

"I'm hungry," he said in a strange, chirping voice, his eyes never meeting hers. "Eat now? Can we eat now?" He shifted awkwardly on his feet, executing an odd hop before he swayed back to an uncertain equilibrium.

Heavy, wide-spaced footsteps thundered closer and closer outside. Tynan must have heard her scream. At least, she hoped it was Tynan . . .

His shout preceded him. "Nara!" Sword drawn, he burst through the doorway and leaped between her and the source of her terrified expression.

The stick-man let out a high-pitched shriek of his own, then stumbled backward to hide behind the bed, his panicked cries punctuated with something that sounded like "Mooma."

Tynan pushed Nara safely behind him. One powerful arc of his sword swept back the tattered curtain that shielded the terrified stick-man.

Nara and Tynan gasped as one, not from what they saw on the far side of the bed, but from what was lying in it.

There beneath the tumbled blanket lay an emaciated old woman, her sallow skin drawn tight in death.

The frightened stick-man scuttled nearer the headboard and hid his face in the hollow of the dead woman's neck. "Hep me, Mooma! Wake up! Please wake up! There's a bad man! He'll huht me." Miserable and defenseless, he wept like a small child.

Suddenly Nara understood, and her heart twisted within her. Her eyes welling in sympathy, she laid a staying hand on Tynan's sword-arm. "Put away your weapon, Tynan. This poor man poses no threat to us. Can't you see? He has no idea whether he's afoot or on horseback. He's simple as a little child." She raised the torch to illuminate the pitiful scene. "This must be his mother."

"Mooma, Mooma, Mooma," the terrified man confirmed, nuzzling even closer to his dead mother.

When Tynan failed to stand down, Nara frowned up at his fierce expression. "Please stop scowling like that. The poor man's lost his mother, and he can't care for himself."

She turned to the frightened stick-man, her tone softening. "Heaven only knows how long she was too ill to care for him. From the look of her, she hasn't been dead for more than a day. But that must have seemed like ages to him, hiding here, alone and hungry in the dark. We must have frightened him half to death."

"Frightened *him?*" Tynan growled. "More the other way 'round, I should think." He did, however, lower his sword. "The way you screamed, I thought the Banshee'd gotten you.

Startled me so, I let go of the damned chicken before I had a chance to wring its neck. Now we'll all go hungry."

"Bother the chicken," she said smoothly, her eyes still on the shivering stick-man. "Here." She thrust the torch toward Tynan. "Hold this. Perhaps I can comfort him."

Moving slowly lest she terrify the poor creature further, she rounded the footboard and approached the filthy, ragged stranger. As she came closer in the narrow arc of space between the bed and the wall, the stick-man whimpered louder and clung to his dead mother.

Nara eased herself to sit beside him. "There, there. I'm not going to hurt you." She reached out to pat his shoulder with a gentle hand, just the way she did when coaxing a wild creature at home on the moors. The stick-man flinched only briefly, then rolled his head to the side for a brief look at her.

"Shhh. Don't cry," she soothed. "Everything will be all right. You're safe now." She offered him a reassuring smile, her fingers stroking his grimy hair away from those distant, disturbing eyes. "My name is Nara. What's yours?"

"Tim," the stick-man croaked. He lurched upright, his head rolling jerkily from side to side. Nara wondered how he could see anything; his eyes never seemed to focus, but clearly he wasn't blind. "Tim, Tim, Timothy. Toady-boy," he chanted in an awkward singsong.

"Tim," she repeated. "That's a nice name. I like it." Nara paused. She didn't want to upset him, but there were things she needed to know. "Is this your mother, Tim?"

"Mooma. Sweet Mooma. Tim's sweet girl. Hahnd." He grasped his mother's work-worn, lifeless hand and drew it to his nose, then sniffed it, frowning. "Cold. Mooma's hahnds are cold." His eyes welling with tears, he laid down the dead woman's hand and haphazardly tugged the blanket over it. "Sing to me, Mooma. Mooma sing to Tim."

117

Abruptly, his eyes wandered in Nara's direction. " 'M hungry. Eat now? Can we eat now?" Hunger and fatigue were evident in the dull, unfocused irises. "Thirsty. No more water, but Tim can't go to the pond without Mooma."

Nara's heart broke for the poor afflicted soul. Ignoring the filth that covered him, she circled his bony shoulders and drew him close, rocking him gently. "There, there. We'll get Tim some water. And some food." Her own cheeks wet with tears, she looked past Tim's tangled hair to find Tynan staring at her in open disapproval.

"Please, Tynan," she asked, "bring in some water. And see if there's any wood or peat for a fire. The poor man's cold as stone."

"I'll bring the water," Tynan growled, "and find some fuel. And, God willing, I'll catch that blessed chicken. But when morning comes, we're on our way." He glared at Tim. "Without him."

Disbelief brought a halt to her tears. "We can't leave him here. He'll die."

"People die every day," Tynan said without emotion. "If we hadn't come along, he'd have died soon enough, anyway." The lines beside his mouth hardened. "He has no one, Nara. Life can be a torment when a person has lost everything and everyone he cares about, and death can be a kindness."

Was he talking about Timothy, she wondered, or himself?

"If you truly cared for this wretched soul," Tynan said with conviction, "you'd let me put an end to his suffering with my blade. That would be mercy. 'Rescuing' him will only prolong his suffering. And his grief."

Struck to the core by Tynan's harshness, Nara crossed herself. "Life and death are God's to give, not ours." Surely he couldn't be serious. But she saw no shred of sympathy in his cold amber eyes.

Suddenly frightened by the man who was her husband, she let go of Timothy and turned to shield him. "Tynan, we must extend our hospitality to this stranger. Christian charity commands it, as does the Holy Writ." She quoted from memory, "Let brotherly love abide, and deny your hospitality to no one, for thus have some entertained angels unawares."

Tynan's only response was to snort derisively, but her words had a miraculous effect on Timothy. He stepped out from behind her with uncharacteristic ease, his palsied movements stilled. A beatific smile on his face, he looked directly at Nara and said clearly, "I know all about angels."

Nara didn't know what to make of it. But before she could respond, his eyes glazed over and his head rolled back, limp hands drawn once again to his bird-chested rib cage.

The odd, chirping speech returned. "Mooma said the angels were coming. Angels coming to take her to heaven. Are you the angels?"

"Perhaps we are, in a strange sort of way," she answered quietly. She believed in Divine Providence. The same force that had allowed Tynan to find her was now at work here.

Nara's eyes sought Tynan's. "Our coming is surely no accident. God has ordered our steps to this place. And Christ Himself said, 'As ye have done it unto the least of these, ye have done it to me.' We cannot abandon this man."

"It is I, not God, who have ordered our steps, lady," Tynan retorted, "and I shall continue to do so."

Nara turned her attention back to Timothy. Seeing a flicker of hope in his vague expression, she smiled. "Don't worry, Tim. Nara's here. Nara will take care of Tim."

"Nara's here," Tim mimicked, visibly relaxing. "Nara will take care of Tim."

"You do him no service by making promises you cannot keep," Tynan interjected. He hesitated, then laid the torch into the fire pit. "I saw what looked like a stack of peat nearby. I'll bring some in and start a fire, then we'll see about supper."

Nara nodded, grateful that he hadn't frightened Timothy further. "Very good. After we've eaten, I'll wash the body and prepare it for burial. We can lay her to rest in the morning."

Tynan halted halfway to the door. "We've neither time nor energy for a proper burial. But there's no sense letting a corpse take up a perfectly good bed." He strode past the curtain and lifted the dead woman as if she weighed nothing.

"Mooma!" Timothy shrieked and lunged for his mother. "Don't huht her!"

"Tynan" — Nara drew the distraught Tim into the shelter of her arms — "have you no heart?"

She turned to Tim, trying vainly to follow the agitated wandering of his eyes. "Tim. Look at me, Tim. It's all right." When his gaze angled in her direction, she crooned, "Remember, Mooma said the angels would come to take her to heaven. It's all right for Tynan to take her."

"Angels?" Tim asked, his panic subsiding.

"Aye, Tim. Angels."

Tynan scowled. "Angels, indeed. No one has ever mistaken *me* for an angel."

Nara shot him an ironic glance. If he was an angel, it would have to be a *fallen* one. "Lucifer, perhaps," she retorted. "Aye. Lucifer was God's brightest and most beautiful angel, but his stubborn self-will sundered heaven."

But just when she'd decided her husband had no heart, he surprised her by reacting with a brief flicker of shame.

"I'll take the body to the far side of the hill," he said gruffly, his hardness wavering. "It's the best I can do for the woman if I'm to have any strength left to catch our supper."

Harsh as it was, he had a point. Nara knew she must be

even wearier than she. After all, he had carried her the last half-mile to this place. She nodded. "I understand. But if you can possibly manage it, please cover her with stones, at least," she implored as he left, "to keep the animals from getting her."

"We'll see," he responded.

Nara gathered Tim close and rocked him the way *Seanmhair* had rocked her whenever her world had fallen apart. "Don't worry, Tim. Nara's here. Nara will take care of Tim."

"Nara," he chirped, mimicking her inflection. "Nara will take care of Tim."

It must have been well past midnight before the fire was built and the chicken caught, plucked, cleaned, and roasted. By the time the meat was done, Nara could scarcely keep her eyes open. The meat was scarce and stringy, but at least it was hot. She chewed each morsel slowly, making it last as long as she could.

Timothy, on the other hand, smacked and stuffed down his joint of chicken with such frantic alacrity that Nara felt compelled to take it from him and separate the flesh from the bones, for fear he'd eat everything at once and choke.

Tynan took his food to the far side of the fire and sat, silently aloof, watching Nara with an odd mixture of wariness and curiosity.

When the last precious morsel had been consumed, Nara gathered the bones and placed them with some water into a small iron kettle she'd found beneath the bed. There would be broth for breakfast, at least. She added the head and organs, then set the kettle in the smoldering peat, glad that there remained only one more chore before they could all rest.

One more chore, and not a small one. Tynan wouldn't like it, but she couldn't very well do it herself.

Glad that the blanket, at least, seemed clean, she drew it from the bed and addressed a skeptical Tynan. "We must get Tim cleaned up. Now that the fire is going so well, he can come back inside to warm himself once he's bathed."

She felt a flush of embarrassment rise to her cheeks. "Please take him outside and see that he . . . does whatever he needs to do. Then go to the pond and give him a good scrubbing. And his clothes." She handed Tynan the blanket. "You can wrap him in this until his things have dried by the fire."

Regarding her through narrowed eyes, Tynan made no move to rise. "I told you, we're not taking him with us. So it makes no difference to me how bad he smells."

Nara knew better than to confront Tynan about tomorrow. She'd think of some way to convince him to take Tim with them, but for now, the matter of a bath was paramount. "Tynan," she reproached gently. "How can you imagine sleeping with a stink like that for even one night? I have to breathe out of my mouth to keep from gagging every time I get near the poor —"

"Sleep with him!" Tynan interrupted. "What in blazes do you mean, sleep with him? I have no intention —"

Now it was Nara's turn to interrupt. "This is his house. His bed. We certainly can't put him on the floor while we sleep in comfort." Ignoring her husband's indignation, she shot an appraising look at the bed in question. "It may be crude, but it's sturdy enough to hold the three of us. And big enough." She offered him an innocent smile. "Don't worry. You won't have to sleep next to Tim. I'll take the middle and make certain he doesn't disturb you."

"Disturb me?" Tynan railed, his face ruddying even deeper. He pointed to Tim, who now cowered away from the outrage in his voice. "That . . . *thing* may have the mind of a child, but he has the body of a grown man. How do you think he'll respond to being cuddled against a woman's softness? Like a man, that's how." Obviously, Tynan had no intention of sharing Nara with any man, least of all this one. He glared at the stick-man, who whimpered in fear. "He can sleep on the floor."

"Tynan, Tynan." Nara drew Tim close for a reassuring hug. "He's as innocent as a babe. If he grabs anything he shouldn't, I'll just move his hand away." She drew Tim toward the door. "Come, Tim. Tynan is going to take Tim to the pond for a bath."

"Bath?" Tim pulled away from her in alarm. "No bath. Tim can't go to the pond without Mooma," he said earnestly.

Nara suppressed a smile. Perhaps he wasn't quite as simple as she'd first thought. He'd certainly been quick to come up with an excuse to avoid bathing. "It's all right, Tim." She coaxed him back. "Mooma is in heaven now, so God has sent Tynan and Nara to look after Tim." She cupped his wandering chin. "Tim can go to the pond with Tynan."

"I'll not do it," Tynan huffed. "I am no chambermaid, lady, and no saint, either, to be scrubbing some simpleton's arse. I shan't."

"I don't blame you for not wanting to." Nara directed a trenchant glance at the rags that covered Tim's bony loins. "Most of the stink seems to be coming from his privates." She sighed, rolling up her sleeves. "I suppose it is too much to ask of you. I'll do it myself, then."

Her tone became philosophical. "I wonder how he'll respond to having me scrub his man-thing?" She aimed a wry smile at Tynan. "At least it will give me something to compare yours to. Of course, I didn't get a very good look at yours when it went down. But I should imagine a good scrubbing will be more than enough to put Tim's at attention, so —"

"Conn's balls, woman!" Tynan thundered, snatching a startled Timothy's hand and dragging him out the door. "You are without a doubt the most brazen, shameless descendant of Eve I have ever heard. You speak as though you were brought up in a brothel instead of a convent!" Tynan's colorful harangue continued all the way to the pond and well into his begrudging completion of the task he'd vowed not to do.

Nara stood in the doorway and watched the distant silhouettes outlined against the faint shimmer of the pond until her own eyes fluttered from exhaustion. From what little she could make out, Tynan's ministrations were anything but gentle, yet they were thorough.

Her smile of satisfaction bloomed into an enormous yawn. She returned to the hearth, stirred the embers, shifted the kettle to a slow simmer at the edge of the fire, then at last lay down on the blessed comfort of Timothy's bed.

As her aching bones relaxed, she managed only a brief prayer before sleep claimed her. *Dear Lord, thank You for keeping us safe and giving us the strength to make it this far. And thank You for the food, and for the shelter, and most of all, for Timothy. I know You sent us to watch over him. Please show me a way to convince Tynan to bring him with us. I ask it in Jesus' name and for His sake. Amen.*

It would take a miracle. Good thing God was in the business of miracles.


A distant howling interrupted Nara's dreams. Louder and louder it grew, until she woke to the resonance of the chilling sound in the night.

It took her a moment to remember where she was. She lay on her side with Tim curled contentedly in the shelter of her arms, the thin blanket their only covering. But her back was cold.

Where had Tynan gone? He had been there before; she vaguely remembered the heat of him behind her, warming her from head to toe.

Yet he wasn't in the cottage any longer; she would sense his presence if he were. Perhaps he had gone outside to tend to his bodily functions.

But as the long, tense minutes passed, she realized that if that had been his mission, he would have been back by now.

Then she heard the unearthly keening again, only this time it was real, and her insides tightened in fear. The howl of a wolf, and close.

Her mind flashed on the vivid impression she'd experienced when first looking into the castaway wolf's eyes at the Isle of Mist. Then she remembered the same golden glint she had seen in Tynan's gaze, and a chill of foreboding threaded through her.

Was the wolf following them? It didn't seem possible. Yet the distinctive call sounded identical to the one she'd heard back on the Isle of Mist.

The howl sounded again, a hungry cry — tormented, unearthly, and far too close for comfort.

Nara's eyes opened wide in the darkness, her gaze locked to the outline of the unprotected window. Had the wolf followed their scent to the cottage? What if he decided to attack?

Tynan's war axe lay near the door, but the massive weapon was still securely bound in sealskin. Even if she had time to unwrap it, there was no guarantee she could wield the thing. And if she got up, Timothy was sure to waken, jabbering, and cause a commotion that might well draw the wolf's unwelcome attentions.

No. Better to lie still and pray that God would send angels to protect them.

Again the wolf howled, farther away this time. Or was the distance merely wishful thinking?

Timothy twitched in his sleep at the sound, but did not waken.

Nara's neck and shoulders tingled, the hairs standing on end. There was something very odd about this wolf business.

The silence that followed was broken only by the erratic gurgle of Timothy's snoring. She tightened her arms protectively around her sleeping charge and waited for Tynan to return, but the dark, endless moments crawled by with no sign of him.

Why had she never seen nor heard the wolf when Tynan was present?

She had wondered once before if her husband might be a wizard or a shape-shifter. Now the prospect seemed unsettlingly plausible.

She could think of no purpose for him to be roaming about outside at this hour of the night, otherwise.

Yet if the wolf was real, and Tynan was alone outside . . .

Unable to remain still any longer, Nara eased herself free of Timothy with agonizing slowness, then felt her way to the window. She peered outside to the darkened hills that rose in stark relief against the silvered night sky. Then she heard the howl again. Her gaze pivoted in that direction, and she saw a distinct canine silhouette on the horizon. She blinked, and the shape was gone. Another blink, and the unmistakable outline of a man loomed where the wolf had been. As he crested the ridge, Nara swore she could see the hilt of Tynan's sword over his shoulder — the sword that she knew bore the image of a wolf.

She remembered the real wolf — a wolf with the eyes of a man.

And the man with the eyes of the wolf.

Nara crossed herself and hurried back to bed. Fortunately, Timothy only snuggled closer when she resumed her place behind him. Seconds dragged into minutes before she heard Tynan open the crude wooden door, latch it behind him, then pad softly across the dirt floor and around the footboard to the far side of the bed.

Her eyes squeezed shut, she heard the whisper of metal sliding against leather as he freed his sword. With a dull thud, he laid it at the ready beside the bed, then crawled in behind her.

In spite of everything, she could not help welcoming the unnatural heat of his presence behind her.

Whether or not he had been a wolf only moments earlier, she did not know. But he was a man now. And his man's hand slid, warm and possessive, over her bottom before it curled over her ribs to draw her against him. Nara lay very still, wondering if the man and the wolf were one creature, until exhausted slumber claimed her, at last.

Tynan was dead asleep when clumsy fingers tried to open his right eye.

Lightning-quick, he captured the bony wrist attached to the hand that had molested him.

"Ow!" Timothy let out, recoiling. "That huhts!"

Sleep-tousled, Nara sat up abruptly, her features a study in confusion. "What?" She took in the scene and frowned. "Tynan, you're hurting him. Let go."

"He's lucky I didn't break his neck," Tynan growled. He turned to the frightened scarecrow of a man. "Never touch a stranger when he's sleeping. You're liable to end up dead."

"He has no idea what you're talking about, Tynan," Nara scolded. She pried Tynan's fingers from Timothy's wrist. "It's all right, Timothy. Tynan won't hurt you."

She nudged her still-skeptical charge out of bed ahead of her. "Come. There's warm broth to break our fast. Then we shall set out for Eilean d'Ór."

Tynan rose slowly at the far side of the bed, feeling even worse for the few hours of sleep he'd managed to steal. A foolish waste of energy, what he'd spent the better part of the night doing. For the life of him, he couldn't reason why he'd even bothered.

Nara. That was why. Nara, and the trusting calm in those still, green eyes of hers. The same trust with which she now regarded him.

Tynan sighed and rubbed the ache of fatigue in his own eyes, knowing they were red with sleeplessness. "I told you, Nara," he said firmly, "we're not taking him with us."

Nara shifted the kettle to the glowing embers she had uncovered. "And I told you, we cannot leave him behind."

"The matter is not open to discussion. You have sworn to follow me, and willingly. As soon as we've eaten, we leave. Without Timothy."

"I'm afraid I couldn't do that." Nara's voice remained calm as she raised the kettle lid, releasing the tempting aroma of broth into the cool morning air.

"Hungry," Tim asserted. "Can we eat now? Tim's hungry. I like soup."

Tynan sobered. "Nara, we *cannot* take him, for his sake as well as our own." He frowned, wondering how much he could risk telling her. "You have no idea how dangerous it is out there. Half a dozen warring baronies lie between us and our destination. Timothy would slow us down so much, I could not guarantee even our own safety."

At the sound of his name, Tim piped up with, "Gotta pee. Tim's gotta pee."

Nara's answering laughter was as melodic as the birdsong that had erupted from the wakening valley beyond the cottage walls. She grinned up at Tynan. "I suppose you'd better take him outside, before he has an accident."

"By the beard of Collum the Gray," Tynan muttered, "he can't even do *that* by himself."

"Go with Tynan, Tim." Nara urged him toward the door. "Hurry up, Tynan, or the consequences will be yours to deal with." She arched a dark eyebrow. "Unless you want to give him another bath afterward."

"How is it," Tynan grumbled, "you always manage to make it my fault, somehow, if things go awry?"

Not relishing the prospect of having to scrub Timothy's clothes and arse again, though, he took the stick-man's fragile upper arm in hand and led him outside. "I'll take him to the privy, then, but no farther. He is *not* going with us when we leave," Tynan shot back at his wife, "and that's final."

# Chapter IX

Nine nights and ten long days later, Tynan reached a familiar rock outcropping at the crest of a ridge. He knew this place; a small spring hid nestled in the stone.

Almost there.

Laird Cullum's holdings lay just beyond the next peak, and the Abbey and its surrounding burgh where he could safely provision for the last leg of their journey to Eilean d'Ór.

He should have been glad, knowing his life's goal was within reach, but because of his feelings for Nara, he felt a nagging tug of dread deep within his chest.

Tynan couldn't help wondering if Nara's Two Sights had warned her of what he'd sworn to do. If it had, she'd given no indication.

He looked back down the hill to find her holding Tim's hand and patiently matching her pace to the labored cadence of his slew-footed gait.

There was the matter of Timothy to deal with. What would happen to the helpless creature after . . .

He couldn't let himself think about that.

Tynan still wasn't certain just how Nara had managed to talk him into bringing Tim along in the first place. One moment, he'd been explaining for the fiftieth time why Timothy must be left behind, and the next, Nara was thanking him for changing his mind. He'd done no such thing, but his protests had fallen on deaf ears. She simply refused to acknowledge his denials. Tim in hand, she had set out with a smile on her face. In the end, Tynan's protests had served only to wear him out.

The woman was baffling. She never raised her voice or acted unpleasant. Yet despite her winsome manner, once she made up her mind Nara proved as intractable as the rugged peaks that now surrounded them.

At least they had avoided hostile encounters along the way, which was most fortunate, since Timothy slowed their progress to a snail's pace. Nara claimed the lack of trouble was God's reward for rescuing Timothy.

Tynan had to admit that ever since they'd found the hapless man, the weather had remained fair and he had managed to capture an unnatural abundance of hare, fish, and wild fowl for their cookpot — enough to satisfy even Timothy's prodigious appetite.

Nonsense, he grumbled to himself. The animals would have been there, regardless. Coincidence, that's all it was. He'd have to be as simple as Tim to believe there had been more food simply because Tim was with them.

Only a few more days' walk and Tynan would bring Nara to Laird Cullum at last. Twenty years of waiting and suffering would end.

Yet with every landmark that brought them closer, he grew more troubled about the dark destiny that awaited them there. Things had been so simple for so long, but suddenly, with the advent of Nara into his life, nothing seemed as simple as it once had.

He tried to strengthen his resolve by visualizing the execution to come, but every time, the image of Nara's lucid, trusting gaze fixed on his stopped him cold.

By all the powers of darkness and of light, how could he look into those eyes and end her life?

But he had no choice. As the sole remnant of his sept, it fell to him, and him alone, to avenge his people. In this matter, honor and vengeance were one. The blood oath he had sworn could not be taken back.

Watching Nara and Timothy now, Tynan found himself wishing devoutly that he had no heart, for the very sight of her loosed a bittersweet ache deep inside him.

Timothy crested the ridge and loped across the level ground that separated him from Tynan. "Look, Tynan, look," he chirped, his hand extended. "A surprise."

Tim's 'surprise' had become a regular evening ritual.

Grinning, he plopped down beside Tynan and spread his fingers to reveal yet another handful of shiny pebbles, bracken fronds, bird feathers, wilted flowers, and leaves. "See?" he said proudly. "Treasures."

Nara plodded slowly to where the two men sat, the rigid set of her benign expression the only indication of her hunger and fatigue. As usual, her smile softened when she looked at Timothy.

Sitting beside him, she stroked a straggling tangle back from his face. "Such a sweeting. Every day's 'treasures' are a wonder, even if we gathered the same kinds of flowers and feathers the day before."

Her gaze shifted to Tynan. "Perhaps there's something to be said for not having much of a memory." She arched the stiffness from her back, then reached down to massage her calves as she spoke. "Imagine what it would be like to own no regrets from the past or fears for the future — to live only in the moment as Tim does. I envy him that." She granted Tynan an ironic smile. "He's the lucky one, really, whereas you and I . . ."

Her green eyes clouded. "We wake each morning to the burden of what *might* happen and what *must* happen, and

132

every night our failures follow us to bed."

It was the first time Tynan had heard her speak so wistfully. Usually she was brisk and resolutely cheerful. Did she sense what he'd been thinking? "You're tired, aren't you?" he heard himself ask.

"No more than you must be," Nara responded. "And poor Timothy. Walking is so difficult for him. He must be exhausted." She forced herself to her feet. "There's cold rabbit left from yesterday for supper, but that's the end of our provisions. Shall we have a fire, anyway?"

Tynan shook his head. "Nay. There's a town nearby. Smoke might attract unwelcome attention."

Nara made no complaint, but when he saw her chafe her upper arms against the evening chill, he felt loath to add, "The rocks will shelter us from the wind, Nara, and I'll keep you warm."

The truth was, she kept *him* warm, entirely too warm, not with the heat of her body, but with the feel of her soft body against his, the faint scent of her hair, and the gentle rhythm of her breathing as she lay in his arms every night. It rankled, just how much he had come to enjoy holding her, despite Tim's noisy, restless presence just beyond her.

Merely thinking about it was enough to evoke the vivid memory of her lying naked and sated in the sunlight on the shining black curtain of her hair, a droplet of his seed still clinging to the dark curls between her legs. The image sent a bolt of pure lust straight through him, and he shifted uncomfortably at the fullness in his loins.

He could thank Timothy for one thing, at least: his childlike presence had made it far easier for Tynan to ignore the recurring urge to repeat his initial lapse with Nara. But Timothy's presence did little to diminish the memory of their coupling that haunted Tynan, asleep and awake.

He couldn't help wondering if that single, glowing event — the one spark of brilliance in the darkness that was his existence — would haunt him forever. If in fact there was a hell, the memory of that fleeting moment of joy would make a fitting punishment in the emptiness of eternal darkness.

The thought of hell should have given Tynan pause, but it didn't. He had lived in hell for the past twenty years. His eternal destination would be familiar, at least.

Tynan shoved the disturbing thoughts into a closed place deep inside him. "Let us eat quickly, then, and go to sleep."

Hearing the magic word, Timothy piped up with, "Eat now? Can we eat now? 'M hungry. Tim's hungry."

Nara chuckled. "You're always hungry, though where you put it, I'll never know."

"He must have a gobble-ghost," Tynan grumbled without conviction. "The rascal eats more than both of us put together." Yet despite Tim's prodigious appetite, the man remained as emaciated as he'd been the first day they'd found him.

Again, Tynan wondered what would happen to Tim . . . after.

Stung by an uncharacteristic pang of guilt, he felt an overwhelming urge to put as much distance as possible between himself and his traveling companions. But all that he was and all who had gone before him kept Tynan from running away.

By allowing him to live, Laird Cullum had damned Tynan in this world, as well as the next.

He could not run away. "I'll gather some dry brush for us to sleep on. Keep a sharp eye out for strangers." With that, he left them . . . and the feelings they stirred within him.

When Tynan returned with an armful of pungent gorse fronds, he found Nara busy with the preparation of their meal, while Tim was turning awkward circles near the rocks, executing an odd, hopping movement with each step.

"What's he doing?" Tynan asked.

Nara paused. Even in the waning light, Tynan could see the glow of curiosity and affection that lit her face when she regarded Tim's odd behavior. After a moment, she declared, "Dancing to the music of his life, I should imagine." She went back to her work as if Tim's behavior were the most natural thing in the world.

Dancing to the music of his life. What nonsense.

What music could there possibly be in Tim's life? Or in Tynan's?

In a rare display of perception, Tim stopped spinning and turned his roaming gaze toward Tynan. "Hulloo, Tynan," he fairly crowed. His tone shifted. "Tynan doesn't mean it, Tim," he said in a surprisingly accurate imitation of Nara's inflection. "Tynan is Timothy's boon friend. Brings food for Timothy, and keeps us safe. Tynan is Timothy's friend."

Tynan didn't know why it rankled to hear proof of Nara's intervention on his behalf, but it did. His annoyance must have been evident, because when he looked at her, Nara's mouth flattened with embarrassment, her cheeks flushing.

Was she always so transparent? Such openness would only spell trouble for all of them once they reached Laird Cullum's stronghold.

"Hush, Tim," Nara said without rancor.

But Timothy, as usual, would not be distracted. "Tynan doesn't mean it," he repeated, "Tynan is Timothy's friend. Tynan will protect us."

Nara hurried over and laid her hand across Tim's mouth in an effort to silence him, but succeeded only in diverting his attention to her. In a characteristic gesture, he grabbed her hand and pulled it to his nostrils. "Hahnd." As usual, she suffered him to sniff her fingers. "Hahnd." Tim snuffled, then groped across her for the other hand and drew it to his nose. "Mmmm. Smells good, like Mooma." Sudden tears ran down his gaunt cheeks.

Nara's own eyes welled. "Don't cry, precious boy." She drew him close. "Mooma is with the angels now. Tynan and Nara will take care of Tim."

They made an odd picture; Timothy was so much taller he could barely bend low enough to put his head on her shoulder.

The moment Tim's quaking tears ceased, his mood shifted abruptly. He giggled like a little child and flung his arms around Nara. "I like this guhl. Nara is Timothy's boon guhl. Sweet Nara," he chanted. "Tim, Tim, Toady-boy's sweeting girl."

Nara laughed and hugged him back. "Ah, 'tis you who are a sweeting, Tim." She turned a hopeful smile to Tynan. "What a joy Timothy is — as innocent as a newborn fawn. He could no more deceive anyone than he could fly. And he's happy with so little." She gazed at her palsied charge with undisguised admiration. "The smallest kindness earns his whole heart and trust. What is wit, compared to such sincerity?" When Tynan made no reply, she said quietly, "God knew what he was doing when He made you as you are, sweet Tim."

Troubled by the irony of that statement, and troubled even more by Nara's endless kindness and patience, Tynan turned his back on her. Where did it *come* from, this self-sacrificing goodwill? He wondered afresh if she could truly be as selfless — and as guileless — as she seemed.

A guileless woman? Now, there was irony. Everything in Tynan's experience told him it was a contradiction in terms.

Yet every day with Nara proved otherwise.

She and Timothy were much alike, in an odd sort of way.

Both spoke freely whatever came to mind. Both were open and generous in their affection. Both unwilling, or unable, to see the dark realities of life.

Both as different from Tynan as noon from midnight.

Determined to put an end to the disturbing thoughts, Tynan called out, "Let's eat."

Three days and he would stand before Laird Cullum and acquit himself of the vow he had made. Then, and only then, could he let go and allow the darkness to swallow him up, and Nara along with him.

He felt an odd comfort, though, in knowing that the darkness could not hold her. Nothing he did could consign her to eternal torment, for she was light, itself.

As for Timothy . . . Tynan would cross that bridge when he got to it.

Early the next day, crouched behind Tynan with Timothy dozing beside her, Nara looked across the narrow valley to the magnificent abbey on the next hillside and marveled. Never in all her life had she seen such an imposing structure. And the burgh! So many buildings huddled against the monastery's walls, the twisted, narrow streets between them teeming with people.

Nara had never seen so many people in one place. Even half a mile away, she could hear them across the narrow valley: shouts and laughter, clattering footsteps on cobblestones, a distant pounding, and the rhythmic clank of metal on metal.

And she could smell them, too — a foul undercurrent of garbage, dung, and humanity tempered the tang of woodsmoke and jumbled aromas of food from a hundred kitchen fires.

"This burgh lies within Laird Cullum's holdings," Tynan

declared. "But two years is a long time. I can't be certain which way the wind blows until I get there." He rose. "I'll find a place for you and Tim to hide while I nose about for news of what's happened since I left."

"If there's a risk, why go to the burgh at all?" Nara asked, genuinely curious. "Wouldn't it make sense just to go directly to my grandfather?"

"Nay," Tynan answered. His frown left no doubt that he resented having to explain himself to her. "Ochan, but you have no idea what life is all about." He shifted the heavy axe to a more comfortable position on his back. "Have you any idea what's been going on in the world while you were holed up in that convent?"

"No." But she wanted to know. "I do not wish to remain ignorant, though. Tell me, Tynan."

"Our king is a Judas," he spat out. "In James, the crown of Scotland sits above an English heart, and the 'royal scepter' is planted nightly in an Englishwoman's womb." He shouldered the half-empty pouch.

Equally fascinated and repelled by Tynan's coarseness, Nara listened intently. Could such a thing be true?

"First, King James murdered the Regent Alban and his sons," Tynan continued bitterly. "Then, four years ago, the traitorous bastard had full forty of the Highland chieftains imprisoned, some of them killed."

He said it so matter-of-factly, as if it were a common occurrence. Nara could scarcely grasp such treachery. What sort of country *was* this?

"Those who escaped — your grandfather among them — rallied a year later behind Laird Alexander of the Isles." Tynan's expression became haughty. "Laird Cullum armed every able-bodied man in the fief . . . even the lowly likes of me." His golden eyes darkened with hatred. "I followed, and

I fought, but not for him."

He paused, visibly struggling to contain the darkness that roiled within him. "As overlaird, Alexander of the Isles owns my honor and my sword, and those well-earned. I fought for him then, and I'd do it again." A cruel smile stretched his lips. "We burned Inverness to the ground." Then his smile faded. "But I would never lift so much as a hand for the likes of Laird Cullum MacKay, much less my sword. Never."

Nara shivered at the bitterness resonant in that declaration. Almost afraid to hear his answer, she nevertheless had to ask, "What did my grandfather *do* to merit such contempt?"

"You will find out soon enough," Tynan replied. He nodded toward Timothy. "Wake him. I want to finish my business in the burgh before nightfall."

Three hours later, in the valley just below the burgh, Tynan settled Nara and Timothy safely out of sight in a small grove at the edge of the forest. "Wait here. I'll be back before dark. With food."

"Food?" Tim chirped. "Tim's hungry. Can we eat now?"

"Hush, Tim," Nara cautioned. Before she thought, she turned to Tynan and asked, "But how will you get food? We haven't any money. No one will give us food without —"

Tynan silenced her with a caustic look.

"Oh, yes." How could she have forgotten? "You take what you need." Her chin lifted in challenge. "No matter who might be harmed as a consequence."

Tynan grew still. "Soon enough, Nara, I shall steal no more. Content yourself with that."

"I'll believe *that* when I see it," she retorted.

"You shall not see it," he said cryptically, "but you may believe it. You have my word on that." A certain grim dignity claimed his features. "I may be a thief, but I am not a liar. My word and my sword are the only honor I have left." He started to leave, but she caught hold of his forearm.

"Tynan, wait. I did not mean to give offense." Something was wrong here. Very wrong. She looked deep into his eyes, trying to reach past the boundaries of the flesh, but felt only an odd void where once she had been able to share the emotions of anyone she touched.

Nothing.

Nara tried again, but to no avail. Her only reaction was the warmth of her palm against the unnatural heat of his skin.

As quickly as she had accosted him, she snatched her hand away.

"What?" Tynan tensed. "Have you received a warning from the Sight?"

"No," she answered honestly. Had she lost the ability to touch the souls of others? The notion frightened her. "It wasn't the Sight." Nara looked up at him. "The Sight has not visited me since . . ." When was the last time? Not since . . . "Not since we joined."

Could that have something to do with it?

Nara's mind raced. Auntie Keriam had the Sight, but *Seanmhair* did not. Why one, yet not the other? Mirror-twins, the two were identical.

Except for one thing: Auntie Keriam had married Christ at eleven; she'd never known a man. Had Nara given up more than her virginity on that windswept shore?

The truth dawned on her with crystalline clarity. No longer would she be burdened — or protected — by glimpses of the future.

"Wait here," Tynan instructed, "but don't let anyone see you. And try to keep him quiet. I'll be back before dark."

Nara watched with misgiving as he strode away. As much as she had hated the Sight's intrusions, she had often benefited from its protection. Now, left alone with Timothy to care for, she felt exposed and vulnerable in a way she never had before.

"Come, Timothy," she said with pretended enthusiasm. "Let's sit down in the shade behind that nice big bush. You can put your head in my lap and take a nap. I know you're tired."

" 'M tired," Tim confirmed. "Tim, Tim, Toady-boy needs a nap."

In no time, he was sound asleep, his head in her lap and his arms around her waist.

Nara was tired, too, but with Tynan gone, every rustle of breeze and snap of a twig sent a chill of alarm through her. Only after several hours did she begin to relax. She didn't remember falling asleep herself, but woke to the sound of voices nearby.

Male voices, and coarse ones.

Nara stiffened.

It was still broad daylight. Tynan might not be back for hours.

She sat up with agonizing care, lest she disturb Tim. Blessedly, he remained inert, drooling peacefully into her lap.

Through the bushes, Nara could just make out the figures of three . . . no, four men. Their coarse conversation left no doubt about what was on their minds. To raw oaths and hoots of encouragement, the largest of the four regaled his companions with graphic tales of how one young boy — *young boy* — had entertained him with sexual acts that would have been scandalous enough between man and woman, much less between two males!

Nara could scarcely believe what she was hearing. Sodomites! The Bible spoke of them, but she'd never considered the possibility that there might actually be such creatures alive in the world today.

141

The blood ran cold in her veins.

*Dear Lord! Please don't let them find us!*

If they should find Timothy — sweet, innocent Timothy, who knew nothing of sin and such depravity . . . The prospect was too horrible to imagine.

She began to pray in earnest as the men moved even closer.

# Chapter X

"Tim," Nara said directly into his ear, her voice tight with fear. "Wake up, Tim. This is important. You must listen."

Tim's eyes fluttered open.

"Shhh," she whispered. "Don't make a sound." She couldn't be certain, but she thought his usual jerky head movements stilled somewhat. Encouraged, she murmured, "We must be very, very quiet. Those are bad men. If they catch you, they will hurt you. We must not let them find us."

For once, Tim said nothing. Nara was relieved, but unsure whether her warning had sunk in.

She wrapped her arms around his bony shoulders and held him tight. *Blessed Virgin and Saint Columba, please intercede on our behalf and keep us safe from these Philistines. Holy Mary, Mother of God —*

Her prayer was cut short by the approach of heavy footsteps.

"Don't start without me, lads," the coarse voice said. "Got to let the sap out of the old *arbor vitae* afore we commence the fun and games."

To Nara's horror, he stopped at the clump of brush where they were hiding, fumbled with his breeches, and pulled out his member. The next thing she knew, a heavy stream of urine splashed through the bushes and struck the ground not two feet from her.

Repulsed, she squeezed her eyes shut and hung on to Timothy for dear life, only vaguely aware that the quaking that rocked her came not from Tim's infirmity, but from her own fear. Her heart pounded so loudly, she could have sworn the man could hear it.

Escape was not an option. Nara's legs were swift, but Timothy . . . they'd catch him for sure. No. She would simply have to lie low and pray they wouldn't be discovered.

Blessedly, the stream of urine stopped.

Then she heard the bushes rustle and the coarse voice rumble in her direction, "What the . . ."

Nara looked up to see the branches part, revealing a gap-toothed leer surrounded by a scraggly beard and topped by a bulbous nose that seemed to draw two glistening, beady eyes even closer together.

"Hoy, lads!" the ruffian called to the others. "Look what we have here! A puss in the bushes, and a simpleton." He stepped toward her, directing a blast of fetid breath in her direction. "Here, puss, puss. We won't hurt ye none. Just havin' a little sport is all."

His beady eyes fixed with interest on Tim. "Big feet on that one, lads," he called to the others, who by now had begun to come forward. "Makes me wonder if ennythin' else about him is big." He cocked his head at Nara. "Why don't ye bring him out to play, missie?"

The predatory hunger in his face made the bile rise in Nara's throat. She had to do something . . .

Spurred by a supernatural burst of energy, Nara shot to her feet, bringing Timothy with her, then thrust him behind her toward the forest. "Run, Tim! Run away and hide!"

Perhaps it was the roughness of her treatment or the desperation in her voice, but for once, Timothy did as she ordered without question. Slew-footed as ever, he loped away far faster than Nara would have thought possible. Before the

144

others reached their companion, Timothy had disappeared into the undergrowth.

But they still might catch up with him.

She had to stop them. Nara turned and hurled herself at the approaching ruffian with the fury of an avenging angel. "Leave him alone! Don't you dare harm us, you cretinous lout!" She swung her fists with all her might, pommeling, kicking, and roaring her indignation. Her foot struck the man's shin with satisfying impact. "I'll curse you to the twelfth generation if you so much as lay a hand on either one of us! And I have the power to do it! I have the Evil Eye!"

"Ow! Ye little witch!" Taken off guard, the ruffian lost his balance and toppled backward. But in only a matter of seconds, she was surrounded. Strong hands closed on her arms and pulled her off the bewildered intruder.

Huffing and puffing, he rose to his feet.

Nara noted with relish the thin trickle of blood coming from his enormous pocked nose.

"Well, now," he said with ominous calm. "And what do ye think we should do with this little booby bitch, me lads?"

"Whatever ye say, Mog," came the general reply.

The two young men holding Nara seemed almost as frightened of their leader as she was, but neither made a move to help her.

Nara planted her feet firmly and resolved that no matter what they did to her, she would go down defending her honor. Anything to keep them from violating Tim.

The man called Mog approached within inches of her face. He smelled, and what few teeth he had left were partially rotted out. Nara glared at him defiantly.

He smiled back, a chilling mockery of a smile, then slapped her with such force she feared her neck would snap. "Bitch." He turned to the watching group. "I never could stand women." Then he delivered a particularly brutal blow directly to her stomach.

Unprepared, Nara doubled over and vomited onto the loamy earth.

"Hold." The command was not shouted, but it carried with the force of thunder across the little clearing.

All heads but Nara's turned to see the golden warrior who stood with his great, gleaming sword poised to strike.

Tynan! The minute she heard his voice, Nara went limp with relief even as she shuddered in shame for the state in which he'd found her.

Immediately the hands that had held her let go. She heard the men step back. Pushing herself up onto all fours, Nara looked up to see Tynan move between her and her attackers, bloodlust patent in his grim expression.

Dear God! He meant to kill them. He *wanted* to kill them, hungered for it, the way a starving man lusted for food!

In that moment, Nara caught a devastating glimpse of what lay at the heart of the man who was her husband: revenge. He ached for it, lived for it, breathed for it.

But Nara could not allow it. Not on her account.

"Tynan, no," she managed to croak out. "They did me no lasting harm. Please, do not kill them. I could not bear the stain of their blood on my soul." She forced herself to her feet.

Tynan was visibly quaking with the effort to restrain himself. "I vowed that no other hand should harm you, Nara. They have harmed you. They deserve whatever I do to them."

"No!" she said, terrified by the dark energy that radiated from his hate-filled gaze. "I struck the first blow, and only the big one struck back. Let them go, Tynan, I beg you."

His sword still at the ready, Tynan looked at her, incredulous. "Let them go? After what I saw that . . . that *swine* do to you? He struck you full force while you were held helpless."

"Aye," she reasoned desperately, "but the insult is mine to bear, and I beg mercy for my attacker. Mercy, Tynan." Nara didn't realize she was crying until she felt the droplets strike the bib of her apron. Sore, nauseated, and exhausted, she crumpled at his feet. "Please, Tynan. Let them go."

Tynan remained silent for long seconds, then snarled through clenched teeth, "My lady wife has begged mercy for you, you cowardly bastards. It is for her, and her alone, that I grant it." He glared at each of their faces. "But I know your faces. If any of you should so much as glance at her or anyone with her again, I will hunt you down, cut off your balls, and stuff them down your throats until you choke to death."

One of the younger men let loose a trill of hysterical laughter.

"By all that's holy, Dan, shut up," an ashen Mog ordered. Wringing his hands as he backed away, he bowed to Tynan. "Beggin' pardon, sir, most humbly, and the lady's. No offense meant." With that, he turned and ran in the opposite direction from the one Tim had taken, his fellows following close behind.

"Cowards!" Tynan roared after them. But he did not pursue them.

"Thank you, Tynan." Nara leaned against his muscular leg. He was shaking still. She looked up. "That took great courage. I am in your debt."

"Courage?" he fairly shouted. "It was weak!" Tynan stomped over to a low rock and sat clenching his sword.

"Not weak," Nara protested gently. "It took great strength and self-control to keep from killing them."

"Why do I listen to you?" He turned his anger toward her. "Those men were scum. The world would have been far better without them." His face reddened with renewed rage. "They hurt you, Nara, and God knows what else they would have done had I not arrived when I did. Yet you begged mercy for them. I do not understand it."

"And I do not understand what makes men such as those the way they are." Nara sat beside him, suddenly too weary and shaken to stand. "But they did not deserve to die, not for what they did to me — a simple blow, from which I am already recovered. Death would be too harsh a judgment."

"Not nearly harsh enough," Tynan ground out. He glared at her as if he were about to say more, then thought better of it and let out a deep sigh, sheathing his sword at last. "Where is Timothy?"

"Timothy!" Nara leapt to her feet. "Dear heaven! Why am I sitting here? I sent him into the forest to hide." She pointed to the spot where she had last seen him. "Quickly, Tynan. He has no food, no blanket, and he's frightened half to death. We must find him."

Tynan stopped her from running after Tim. "Wait. I left a poke full of fresh provisions just beyond the clearing. I'll fetch it, then we'll search for him together."

They did search. And search. And search, calling Tim's name in the forest, but he seemed to have disappeared without a trace.

Dusk was hard upon them when Tynan finally said, "We can do no more good today, Nara. And I don't want to risk spending the night in these woods. Too dangerous."

"But Timothy —"

"Timothy will manage for this night, at least." He put his arm around her waist with surprising gentleness. "Come. You are so weary, you can't even pick your feet up. Admit it."

"I'll be fine. I just need to rest for a moment. Then we can look again."

Tynan shook his head. "Tomorrow. Tonight, we shall seek sanctuary in the abbey." When Nara inhaled to protest, Tynan cut her off with, "I have sworn a sacred vow to bring you, alive and well, to your grandfather. After today, I dare not risk your safety in these woods. Look what happened in broad daylight. One can only imagine who lurks about this place at night." He straightened resolutely. "We'll go to the abbey."

Seeing the spark of rebellion in her eye, he finished with, "I am your lord husband, lady, and you are bound by the laws of God and man to obey me. The abbey it is."

Had he said it with less concern, she might have argued, but Nara merely nodded, saying a silent prayer for Timothy's safety. "Very well. The abbey." She plodded in the direction of the burgh. "But we return at first light to hunt for Timothy."

"We'll see," Tynan said. "We'll see."

So weary she could scarcely stand, Nara waited while Tynan rapped the hilt of his sword hard against the brass-studded door of the abbey. Long minutes passed before a small peephole opened in the upper half of the door.

"Who goes there?" a rough voice challenged. "Speak, in the name of the Father and the Son and the Holy Ghost."

Tynan kept his sword in hand beyond the peephole's range. "My wife and I. We travel under Laird Cullum's protection, on an express mission from the laird himself."

After an assessing pause, the voice declared, "You look no knight to me, sir. More a beggar, I would say."

"Are you calling me a liar?"

Nara tensed at the deadly calm in Tynan's challenge and wondered how often he had been insulted thus merely because of his humble raiments.

"Nay, sir," the voice hastily capitulated. " 'Twas but an honest observation. These are perilous times. I dare not risk the security of our community."

Annoyed, Nara piped up with, "And what sort of Christian charity is this, sir, that puts your own comfort over the need of strangers? Shame!"

The voice grew petulant. "I would be remiss to risk the safety of our community. This is, after all, a house of God, yet you come to our doorstep armed. The sanctity of God's house must not be violated."

"I bear arms only to protect my lady wife," Tynan said calmly. "As you said, these are perilous times." He did not, however, put away his sword. "Refuse us if you will, but Laird Cullum will hear of it. Should any harm come to us as a result, the laird will lay it at your doorstep."

"Laird Cullum, eh?" The voice hesitated. "Wait here."

Long minutes passed before they heard the metallic rattle of a key turning in the door's massive lock, followed by the labored scrape of bolts being drawn. Then the huge door swung toward them, revealing a lone monk in coarse brown robes, his face obscured beneath a deep hood.

Nara looked past him to the cold gray stone interior of the dark hallway and shivered. There was something oppressive about this place that unsettled her. She sensed evil, as clearly as she could smell the overcooked cabbage that permeated the monastery's dank interior.

"Come," the faceless monk instructed. They were scarcely inside before he closed the door behind them and secured it. "Follow me." The monk strode forward, stopping briefly beside Nara without looking at her.

"The woman will remain there." He spat out the word "woman" like an epithet. "I will bring food for the woman. The . . ." he paused, his hooded face pointedly scanning Tynan's humble attire, "*gentleman* may dine with the community."

Nara saw Tynan's eyes narrow. "Nay," he countered. "I shall remain with my wife."

The monk straightened. "Our order forbids cohabitation of male and female within these walls. This is a house of prayer, sir," he fairly growled. "Would you repay our hospitality by defiling it with fleshly commerce? Leave the woman here. She will be safe."

"I mean to see to that, sir." Tynan ran a finger down the blade of his sword, as if to verify its sharpness. "Bring enough food for both of us."

The spectral monk disappeared without further comment. Fully an hour later, he — or one of his brethren — returned with a tray bearing two thick slices of black bread, a small lump of goat cheese, a bowl of greasy gray cabbage, and two wooden cups half-filled with sour wine. After depositing the tray on the floor, he retreated into the abbey, locking them in.

Nara shuddered at the sound of the key turning in the massive door. Though she had spent the better part of her life underground, there had been no locks to keep her in. "Tynan," she asked shakily, "what if they don't let us out when we want them to?"

Tynan picked up the tray and carried it to a narrow cot she had missed in the gloom. "The lock hasn't been made that can keep me in." After setting the food down, he patted the bed beside him. "Come. We'll eat, then sleep." Unconcerned by their circumstances, he picked up a piece of bread and tore hungrily at it.

Suddenly ravenous, Nara sat beside him. If he wasn't worried, why should she be? And she was hungry. After weeks of nothing but game, fish, and berries, she mashed her portion of cheese onto her slice of bread and ate with relish. She didn't even mind the strong taste and heavy consistency of

151

the coarse bread, but the raw, red wine was another matter. She barely managed to choke it down.

Typically, Tynan ate in silence, his posture guarded as if he feared someone might try to take his food. Seeing him like that reminded Nara of the rare stray dogs she had glimpsed on the headlands — desperate, emaciated creatures that gulped down whatever they could find, always glancing about for fear some stronger, swifter predator would come along and steal their sustenance.

Did Tynan really think Nara would take his food? She was the only one there.

No, she told herself. He probably didn't even realize what he was doing. She recognized a long-standing habit when she saw one. Tynan must have had to fight for every morsel for a long, long time. She looked at him again, and her heart ached for the sad, lonely boy he must have been.

Would he ever heal? she wondered. Ever trust?

Nara looked back on the abundance and security of the life she had left behind and shuddered at the prospect of what lay ahead. Tynan had taken her from her world into his. From freedom, safety, and love, to desperate obligations, danger, and a husband so wounded by his secret past that he seemed incapable of the slightest tender emotion.

Now that Timothy was no longer there to provide a distraction, Nara realized just how lonely she felt in Tynan's presence. She sat so near to him, yet might as well have been beyond the edge of the world for the vast, unspoken gulf that separated them.

She glanced up at him. "Why do you keep yourself so aloof from me, Tynan? You hold me every night, but never caress me, never seem to want what I would gladly give as your wife."

She felt him stiffen beside her. "It is not fitting for a wife to

152

speak of such things, Nara."

"Nonsense," she declared, deliberately keeping her tone light. "I should think such a subject would be fitting only for a wife, indeed. My body is yours, and freely given. Do you not want me? Am I so inept a lover that I have offended you?"

"Saints, Nara," he blustered, rising to pace the dim hallway. The narrow corridor seemed even smaller when he stood, his broad shoulders reaching almost from one side to the other. "I told you, I do not wish to speak of such things."

But Nara would not be put off. "We are man and wife for a lifetime, Tynan. I should think you would be as eager as I to become friends, at least." She peered through the gloom to his pained expression. "If not friends, then at least allies, who by God's covenant are entitled to share the comforts of our bed and the pleasures of our bodies. Is that too much to ask?"

"For other men and other wives, it is not so much to ask." The lines in his face seemed to deepen, and when he spoke, his voice was thick with suppressed emotion. "But for me . . ." She saw a terrible resignation steal the life from his eyes. "What you ask, I cannot give."

"A lifetime can be a very long time to live with a stranger," Nara said, more frightened by that resignation than by any threat he had ever hurled at her.

Feeling more alone than she ever had in her life, Nara set the tray aside and lay facing the wall to conceal the tears that somehow managed to escape despite her best efforts to hold them back.

Her woman's instincts told her that Tynan remained aloof to protect himself. But from what? And why? Nara had never given him cause to mistrust her.

Tynan lay down behind her, his arm circling her protectively, but there was no solace nor desire in his touch. He was there to keep her safe, nothing more.

A searing wave of homesickness surged through her. She missed *Seanmhair*'s loving hugs and comforting advice. And Auntie Keriam — she'd never thought she would, but she even missed Auntie Keriam's gruff affection and stern admonitions, for they came from a loving heart.

Curled now against Tynan's unrelenting hardness in this dank, constricted space, Nara faced her own naïveté. She had thought herself lonely when she'd roamed her beloved island in solitude, but now she knew what real loneliness was. It was experiencing one glorious, explosive physical union with her husband, only to have him turn away from her in anger, without explanation. It was lying in Tynan's strong arms night after night, warmed by the heat of his body, yet never having him reach for the comfort of her embrace. It was sharing all the hours of all their days without catching more than a brief glimpse of the man beneath the mask he showed the world.

It was trying to reach him, again and again, yet knowing that a vast, insurmountable chasm of secrecy and pain kept them as far apart as heaven and hell.

Was this the way the rest of her life would be spent?

Shame on you! she chided herself, wiping away her tears. Feeling sorry for yourself, when poor Timothy is out there in the woods, cold, alone, and hungry.

Sniffing at the last of her tears, she offered a silent, heartfelt prayer for Timothy's safety.

"Rest easy, little Nara," Tynan said drowsily. "No other hand shall harm you, not as long as I am here."

She remembered what he had said: *I may be a thief, but I am not a liar. My word and my sword are the only honor I have left.*

Nara had that to be thankful for, at least. When she drifted off to sleep, it was with a heavy heart, but not a fearful one.

★ ★ ★ ★ ★

Sometime during the small hours of the night, Nara dreamed that the sodomites were chasing Timothy. Over and over, he cried her name as he tried to evade his attackers.

"Nara! Hep me! The bad men will huht me! Hep! Nara!"

"No!" Nara cried, running, running, running, but getting no closer. "Don't hurt him!"

"Nara! Hep me!" Tim's plaintive cry resonated through her.

She woke sitting up, with Tynan grasping her upper arms. He gave her a gentle shake. "Nara, wake up. It's just a dream. A nightmare."

"A nightmare?" she repeated, her heart still galloping as she ran a shaking hand through her disheveled hair. "But it seemed so real."

Then she heard it again. "Nara! Hep me!" It was faint, but there was no mistaking Timothy's voice, even when a distant chorus of cries and shrieks rose to cover it.

A chill of alarm shot straight through her. "Listen. That was no dream. That was Timothy." She peered through the darkness at Tynan. "He's here."

Nara leapt to her feet. "Shoes. Where are my shoes?"

"And where, pray tell, are you planning on going, my lady wife?" Tynan asked with more than a hint of amusement.

"To find him." Nara groped around until she found her shoes, then hastily stuffed her feet inside them.

"In case you hadn't remembered, we're locked in," Tynan reminded her.

"So?" Nara stood in front of him, her fists braced on her hips. "You said you could pick any lock. Then do it."

"And set you loose in the dead of night to wander through an abbey full of frustrated celibates? I don't think so." He stood, towering over her.

155

But Nara would not be intimidated. "We must find him, Tynan."

"Nara! Hep! Nara!" came the distant, chilling wail, setting off another chorus of disturbed cries.

"Dear God." Nara wrapped her arms tight around her ribs. "Why would they bring him here? And what are those shrieks? Are they torturing him?" She couldn't bear the thought.

"Who knows?" Tynan asked cynically. "Stranger things have happened in the abbeys. Perhaps it's all that penance. And the celibacy. Men are not made for celibacy; it warps them. And monks are, after all, merely men, subject to the same urges as any."

She could not see his face, but she knew it was grim. "They wouldn't . . . *use* him, would they?" Nara asked. Dear heaven, surely Timothy had not escaped the sodomites only to fall victim to the same perversion here, of all places. "Would they?"

"You think too much," Tynan clipped out. He rummaged in his pouch for something, then felt his way to the door that led into the abbey. "Wait here," he said quietly. Nara heard the click of metal against metal, wiggling, testing. "I'll go into the abbey and search for Tim. If I find him, I'll bring him back. If not, we'll have to wait until morning and go to the abbot."

"But what if someone comes?" Nara peered around her into the darkness. "I don't like being left alone in this hallway."

"I'll leave the inner door ajar so you can hear," Tynan said. "If anyone tries anything, don't hesitate to use the axe." He added wryly, "But before you start swinging, make certain it's not me."

With a click, the door opened, breaking the gloom only

156

slightly. Tynan's silhouette more than filled the opening. "But no matter what happens, do not follow me into the abbey. Is that clear?"

"Aye," she acknowledged. " 'Tis clear enough." She did not, however, promise not to follow.

With that, he disappeared into the abbey, his bare footsteps almost inaudible on the hard stone floors.

Nara waited for what seemed like hours before she heard Timothy again. This time his cry was so wrenching she could not ignore it. Somehow she knew, just knew, she must go to him. At least her eyes had adjusted to the darkness. She could almost make out her surroundings.

She crossed herself, praying a silent, "May God forgive me," and slipped into the sleeping monastery.

# Chapter XI

Tynan had covered what seemed like miles of halls before he ran into trouble, and trouble it was.

Just as he rounded the corner in a torchlit hallway, he caught sight of an odd little hooded monk at the far end of the corridor. More importantly, the monk caught sight of him. And ran.

*Damn!* The fleeing friar was probably on the way to raise the alarm.

Something about the monk's gait nagged at Tynan, but he was too preoccupied with trying to remember where that particular corridor went to dwell on such a triviality. The monk had such a long lead that Tynan would never be able to catch up, but if that corridor met the main hallway where Tynan thought it did, he just might be able to cut him off.

Tynan drew his sword. Trying to keep his steps as quiet as possible, he broke into a run and managed to reach the intersection just before the escaping monk.

In one swift movement, he caught the monk from behind and covered the lower half of his hooded face to silence him, jerking the little fellow right off his feet. A stifled screech of protest emanated from behind Tynan's hand, but he paid more attention to the soft, round buttocks that shifted against him with every kick of the "monk's" flailing legs.

"Well, I'll be damned," he murmured into his captive's hooded ear. "A woman." He let loose a dry chuckle. "I wondered why you didn't raise the alarm the moment you saw me."

The woman went still.

"Since neither of us has any business being here," Tynan purred, "I think I'll propose a truce." He laid his sword to the woman's neck. "If I let you go, will you swear to remain silent?"

His captive nodded.

Before he released her, he added, "Break that vow, and the sound you make will be your last."

Another curt nod.

Tynan released her and pulled back the hood at the same time.

He and his captive regarded each other in mutual shock.

"Tynan."

"Lady Margaret."

They each spoke in the same breath.

Tynan would sooner have confronted the Banshee herself than Laird Cullum's sister. "And what brings Lady Margaret here at this time of night?" he heard himself ask.

"I might pose the same question to you," she retorted, only momentarily flustered.

Tynan arched an eyebrow. "I asked you first, my lady."

"So it's Tynan." Lady Margaret changed the subject, her lined face tightening with feral interest. "My, my, my. The little fellow with the big secret."

"Not so little now," he said coolly.

"Ah, Tynan," she fairly purred. "How well you have grown. The last time I saw you, you were just a scrawny lad who reeked of horse shite."

"That was no accident, milady." After what he had seen her do, Tynan had deliberately rubbed himself in steaming dung whenever she had come sniffing around. "If that was what kept my cock out of your mouth, milady, then I'm glad of it."

Notoriously dissolute and old enough to be his mother, Lady Margaret had helped herself to almost every base-born male virgin at Eilean d'Ór. Except Tynan.

Her aristocratic features unruffled, she slapped him soundly, but Tynan held himself in check. "Bold words, from the likes of you," she said almost idly. "How dare you speak thus to your betters?"

Tynan managed an insolent grin despite the rage that shuddered through him. "I acknowledge no betters here, madam. Merely an aging degenerate who uses her position to steal the dignity . . . and the lives," he said with emphasis, "of those she should protect."

Lady Margaret did not rise to the bait. Instead, she regarded him with renewed ardor.

"You know," she remarked casually, "the only reason my brother allowed you to live was for the pleasure of planning how he would kill you with his bare hands." She reached up and circled his neck with her hands, applying just a little more pressure than was comfortable. "Every time Cullum was in his cups, he raved about some new torture he'd devised to prolong your death. It was quite a game to him." She ran her thumbs up his throat, but Tynan didn't flinch.

"I *told* him to quit talking about it and *do* it," she purred, "but then some interfering tell-a-tale informed Laird Alexander that you still lived, and our dear Laird Alexander placed you under his personal protection." She let out an evil chuckle. "Ah, how that rankled my dear, beloved brother. All those years he'd kept you under the heel of his boot, poised to crush you like an adder, and suddenly it was too late. He couldn't touch you."

She sniffed. "Frankly, I had no idea Alexander was capable of such delicious irony."

So that was why Laird Cullum hadn't killed him! Tynan had always wondered why his tormentor had allowed him to grow to manhood. Determined not to give Lady Margaret the satisfaction of knowing he'd been ignorant of the truth, he glared at her without comment.

She withdrew her hands from his neck with visible regret. "Seeing you now, I'm glad Cullum didn't take my advice and do away with you." An evil light sparked in her pale gray eyes. "I find I'm growing bored with the abbot."

"The abbot," Tynan repeated. She had sunk lower than even he would have imagined.

Lady Margaret giggled, a wholly inappropriate mannerism in a woman of her advanced years — she had to be fifty, if she was a day. "It was fun, at first. I don't know which I enjoyed more — the fact that I could force him again and again to the meanest depravity, or his guilt afterward." She granted Tynan a demure smile. "I especially liked tying a rosary around his cock and leading him about a bit before I sucked him dry."

In a prim gesture completely at odds with what she was, she smoothed the monk's vestments she was wearing, then lifted the crucifix that hung from her belt. "Ah, the things he did to me with this."

She was entirely too confident, too relaxed. Tynan didn't like it.

"But as I said," she murmured idly, "I have begun to get bored with the whole thing. The abbot's completely tamed. No sport in that. But you . . ." A hard glimmer of desire lit her face. "Now, *there's* a challenge I'd gladly undertake."

Smooth as a snake, she slid her hand under his plaid and gripped his manhood. To his disgust, his member pulsed to life at her demanding touch, despite his hatred of her. "Very nice," Lady Margaret said. "More than a mouthful, I should imagine."

"Take your filthy hand off me," Tynan growled, snatching her arm away. He had been too long without a woman if the likes of Lady Margaret could cause such a reaction. "You MacKays have abused me for the last time."

He shoved her roughly from him. "I warn you, Lady Margaret, leave me alone. I have something your brother wants — very badly. It will not go well with you should you interfere."

Her eyes narrowed. "My brother has everything. What could you possibly —"

"Not quite everything," Tynan said quietly.

Nara chose just that moment to steal around the corner. When she saw the strange woman dressed as a monk beside Tynan, she halted abruptly with a gasp.

Lady Margaret took one look at her and drained of color. "Eideann . . ."

*Damn!* Tynan had *told* Nara not to follow him! Now Lady Margaret had seen her.

As quickly as she had appeared, Nara retreated.

Then Tynan realized what Lady Margaret had said. Like him, she had mistaken Nara for her grandmother. He decided to try something. "What?"

"You saw her," Lady Margaret hissed. "It was Eideann, just as she was the day I drove her away. But that cannot be . . ."

*. . . the day I drove her away,* she had said.

Tynan hastily reviewed all that he had learned about Lady Cullum's sudden flight.

So Lady Margaret had been behind it! Lady Margaret, whose two sons stood next in line to inherit all that was Nara's, by right.

It rankled that the depraved witch would end up getting

162

her way, thanks to him, but Tynan didn't have time to dwell on that. Instead, he repeated the same words she had said to him that awful night eighteen years ago when he'd caught her getting rid of her young victim's body. "What did you see?" he asked. "There was no one."

"You had to have seen her," Lady Margaret replied, not picking up on his reference to the past. She pointed to the spot where Nara had been. "She was standing right there."

Tynan only hoped Nara had the sense to return to their bed. "I saw nothing. Perhaps it was a fetch."

"A fetch?" Lady Margaret backed away, visibly shaken. "Aye. That's all it was. A specter from the past, nothing more. Perhaps the abbot used the black arts I taught him to summon it up as a torment. It's nothing real. Eideann is long dead. She *must* be, and that misbegotten brat with her."

Nara . . . *that misbegotten brat.*

Tynan watched Lady Margaret retreat. He looked into her eyes and said, "And neither one of us has been here."

She paused, momentarily confused, then took his meaning and remembered: She had said just that to *him* eighteen years ago, when he was only ten. "Aye. You have not been here, nor have I."

"And it shall remain that way. Unless, of course, you change your mind." Tynan's voice grew hard as stone. "In which case, I shall be obliged to notify the bishop. And Laird Cullum. It won't be so easy for you this time."

For only the second time since he had known her, Lady Margaret actually betrayed her fear. It was no secret that Laird Cullum held little affection and even less respect for his errant sister, and Tynan now knew two damning secrets about her.

"No one shall hear of this from my lips, rest assured." She drew up her hood, then turned her shadowed face in his di-

163

rection for one long, parting look. "Pity. I could have given you much pleasure, Tynan, and exquisite suffering."

"Not in this life," he spat out. He watched with relief as she headed silently down a corridor that led to the kitchens.

Now to find Nara, before someone else did.

Nara had scarcely had time to wonder who the old woman beside Tynan was before she saw the anger in her husband's eyes. But there had been more than anger in Tynan's expression. His eyes had widened in shock, as if her arrival had put them both in jeopardy.

And the old woman . . . why was she dressed like a monk? And why had she looked at Nara as if she were a demon?

Nara hadn't waited to find out. All too aware that she was in the wrong place at the wrong time, she'd melted into the shadows and fled back toward the abbey's entrance. But before she had even gone halfway, she heard from an adjacent hallway a familiar, chilling sound that brought her to a halt on the cold stone floor.

Faint. Tortured. "Nara! Hep me! Mooma, Mooma, Mooma!"

After glancing left, then right, to be certain no one was about, she followed the sound down the darkened hallway. Fifty feet farther on, the passage took a sharp turn, then descended a flight of narrow stairs.

At the bottom of the stairway she came upon a low-ceilinged square room furnished with a single sturdy table. The gloomy atmosphere was so thick with the smell of human waste she could scarcely breathe. Gagging, she drew her apron up over her nose. A massive door faced the stair, and in the stone wall to its right, several high, barred openings admitted a frail light along with the rattle of chains and a faint rustle of movement that stirred fresh currents of stench.

A dungeon, in a monastery?

Nara gingerly tried the door, but wasn't surprised to find it locked. She groped her way around the room looking for a key, but found none.

Then she heard him. "Nara. Mooma. Hep me."

Timothy!

Nara resolved to get a look into the chamber beyond. A rush of desperate energy enabled her to shove the heavy table below the barred openings. Moving it into place made an awful racket, but she could only hope that if anyone heard her, they would mistake the sound as coming from the dungeon.

She scrambled atop the table and stood on tiptoe, but the barred opening was still well above eye level. So she grabbed the bars and hauled her chin over the ledge.

What she saw in the dim chamber beyond was so terrible, she let go and slithered to the table, too stunned and dizzy to stand.

It wasn't a prison. It was a lunatic asylum.

On the other side of that wall, scores of helpless demented souls were crowded into a dank, windowless room lit by a single candle in a high niche. Children, boys, men. Some were clad in rags, some naked but for their own filth. Some shackled by the arms or ankles, some — like Timothy — in heavy iron collars chained to the wall.

The horrific, vivid image burned in her consciousness as indelibly as a brand. They had put Timothy — harmless, gentle Timothy — in a lunatic asylum! Nara clutched her chest, feeling as if a great, jagged stone were pressing against her heart.

Timothy chained, like a beast. Nara couldn't bear it. She did not want to look again, but she had to, for Timothy's sake.

After a few steadying breaths, she rose and pulled herself back up again. This time it wasn't as easy. Her arms felt weak and quivered from the effort, but she managed to raise her chin above the ledge. "Timothy," she whispered, setting off a fresh commotion among the inmates.

Tim didn't seem to have heard her. Nara's vision blurred when she saw the raw flesh beneath his collar and the blood on his fingertips. "Timothy!" she choked over the din.

This time he reacted. Eyes wandering in the general direction of her voice, he cocked his head, reached for her, and wailed, "Nara! Hep me!" He tugged vainly at his collar, lunging forward as far as the chain would allow. "Hep me!"

"We'll get you out, Timothy," she said through her tears. "We'll get you out."

No longer caring who she disturbed, Nara leapt down from the table and raced for Tynan. Tynan could get Tim out. The lock hadn't been made that Tynan couldn't get the best of. With luck, they would be far away from the abbey before anyone knew Tim was gone.

She had to find Tynan.

And find him she did. Racing around yet another darkened corner, she ran headlong into his unrelenting hardness.

"Oof!" Nara looked up, relieved, and whispered, "Oh, thank goodness it's you."

Breathless from running, she grabbed Tynan's hand and pulled. "Quickly. There's no time to waste. I've found Timothy." She waved her hand in the direction from which she'd come. "He's imprisoned at the end of the third hallway to the left, down a flight of stairs. There's a big door, and it's locked, but I know you can get it open. Hurry. We must get him out."

"So *you* found him, did you?" Tynan didn't budge.

"Tynan!" she whispered in reproach. "We must hurry.

Our poor Tim is chained in a lunatic asylum, the cruelest place I have ever seen." Nara's voice thickened with tears. "He's frightened and bleeding and, dear God, the filth. We must get him out."

"I thought I told you to stay put."

Nara squirmed under his fierce expression. "I know you did. But then I heard Tim calling. He sounded so wounded, so . . ." Tynan seemed distinctly unmoved. Though she knew it was not realistic to expect Tynan to show emotion, still she had hoped . . . "Tynan, don't you even care? Timothy loves you, looks to you for protection." She tried to collect herself. "Come. We must get whatever implements you need to unlock the asylum and free him of his chains."

"Did it ever occur to you, Nara, that we might simply wait until morning, then ask the abbot to hand Timothy over to us?"

Nara shook her head. "No, it didn't occur to me." She placed her fists on her hips. "You wouldn't even suggest waiting if you had any idea how horrible it is for Tim. He's chained by the neck. Would you want to spend one second more than you had to in chains?"

"You needn't lecture *me* about chains, madam." He took her firmly by the arm and led her back toward the abbey's entrance. "I spent many months in chains, thanks to your grandfather, and I was but a child."

No wonder Tynan hated her grandfather.

Barely able to keep up with Tynan's long strides, Nara asked, "But why, Tynan? Why in the name of heaven would my grandfather do such a thing?"

"Because I didn't die when he struck me down at my own supper table," he said bitterly.

"And you a child? Dear God," she breathed. "What sort of monster is he?"

"The same sort of monster as his sister, Lady Margaret, who thank goodness mistook you for the fetch of your grandmother when you came upon us in the hallway." Tynan's grip grew tighter on her arm. "The same sort of monster as the compassionate friar who chained Timothy in that hellhole you described."

Eyes burning, he glared at her. "The real world, the world we live in, is populated with just such monsters, Nara. Not with kindness and innocence, but with cruelty and injustice."

Nara shrank from him, but he continued to drag her along beside him.

"I'm sorry you believe that, Tynan," she responded. "You must have good reason to feel as you do, but there is more to life than evil." Her words fell on deaf ears, but she had no intention of giving up.

She tried another tack. "If, as you say, the evil resides with men, then we must hide away from men." Frightened now by the grim resolution she saw in him, Nara pressed further. "We could go back to the Isle of Mist. Take Timothy with us. We could be happy there, and free, as I was. *Seanmhair* would take us in." She was babbling, and she knew it, but she couldn't help herself, for she sensed that he was right about the evil — at least in this place, which should have been a sanctuary of God.

"In two days, we reach Eilean d'Ór," he said. "There is no need to talk of after."

Tynan turned the corner and pointed to the open door of their chamber. "I expect you to stay put this time," he said reasonably. "Swear it."

"Only if you promise to free Timothy. Now. Tonight."

"You shall stay here, and that's an end to it." Tynan escorted her into the narrow hallway where their meager belongings still lay. "I have enough to worry about without your

168

popping up in the worst possible place at the worst possible moment." From behind his belt, he retrieved the thin metal strip he'd used to pick the lock. He pointed it at Nara. "You *shall* stay here."

Nara lifted her chin, her mouth tight with determination. "Will you fetch Timothy?"

"Yes!" he snapped. Then, visibly annoyed that she'd managed to make him lose control, he whispered, "Where else did you think I was going?" Tynan stepped back inside the abbey and closed the door behind him. Nara heard him wiggle the metal strip in the lock until the mechanism clicked.

He'd locked her in!

Well, at least he'd promised to fetch Timothy.

Nara went straight to her knees and began praying for Divine Providence to protect Tynan as he rescued Timothy.

Less than half an hour later, she was still in prayer when she heard the metal strip slide into the lock, wiggle about, then click the mechanism open.

Tynan! And Timothy!

Nara leapt to her feet.

But it was only Tynan who slipped inside the door and hastily locked it behind him.

"Tynan," she asked, her heart pounding in dread, "where is Timothy?"

He took her upper arms and looked at her with what Nara could have sworn was compassion. "He wasn't there. I found the asylum. The table was still beneath the vents where you left it, and the door was old, easy to open. But Timothy wasn't there."

"He has to be," she countered. "I saw him. He was chained to the wall opposite the vents."

"I looked where you told me, but found only an empty collar. There was fresh blood on it, and the straw was still warm beneath it, but Tim was gone. I even checked the inmates twice, one at a time, to make certain he wasn't hiding behind someone. He's gone, Nara."

"Tynan, he was there."

"Of that I have no doubt. But he's not there now. Are you certain no one saw you?"

"Only those within the asylum. I saw no guard, no friars there."

"I don't understand it." Tynan ran his fingers through his thick, wavy hair. "Someone must have moved him, taken him somewhere else, but I'll be damned if I know why. Or where."

Nara looked stricken. "Don't say that, Tynan."

"What? That they took him?"

"No," she said, stricken. "That you'll be damned. I know it's just an oath, but I cannot bear to hear it. Oh, Tynan." Nara leaned against his chest and circled him with her arms. "What could they have done with Tim?" She needed something solid to hold on to, and Tynan was very, very real.

To her surprise, he drew her closer, as if he craved the feel of her body as much as she craved the warmth of his.

"We'll find Tim again, Nara. But for now, rest." He swept her easily into his arms and carried her to the bed, then settled close behind her, like two spoons, nested.

Nara turned to face him, her hand gentle on his cheek. "Thank you, Tynan." She paused, then confessed, "I apologize for turning up at the wrong time. I only wanted to help Timothy."

Tynan sighed, peering at her in the darkness. "I know you only wanted to help. You always want to help." Then, to her amazement, he pulled her close and kissed her, deep and hard. The bulge pressing into her abdomen left no doubt that he wanted her — wanted her badly.

Encouraged by that confirmation, she reached beneath his

170

plaid and stroked his manhood. He gasped, but did not pull away. "Love me, Tynan," she made bold to say. "I want you inside me. Let us make something good, at least, of this terrible night."

Tynan's always-warm body temperature went from hot to steaming at her touch. "What? Fleshly commerce?" he mocked huskily. "Here, in the house of God?"

"Somehow, I do not think that God will mind," Nara whispered, her hand closing on his erection. He was hers, and he wanted her, even if he did not care for her. Nara decided that was enough . . . for this night, at least.

Tynan answered with his lips, and his hands. Fiercely, he covered her mouth with his, his tongue hungrily exploring even as his hands roamed the shape of her body, stroking her breasts, her ribs, her buttocks. Then abruptly he stood and stripped away his plaid, then his shirt.

Even in the gloom, Nara could see that he was magnificent, as magnificent as he had been that day on the beach. Suddenly constricted by her own clothing, she rose to her knees and untied her belt, then stripped away her apron, dress, and shift as one. There, kneeling before him, she unbound her hair, then placed her hands on his hips and leaned forward to kiss the pulsing shaft of his erection.

Tynan gasped aloud, his head thrown back, and threaded his fingers into the straight, silky hair at the base of her skull, drawing her closer.

Sheltered by the darkness, Nara followed impulse and gently rubbed her lips across the flesh at the tip of his erection. Soft. So soft.

Tynan gasped again, and his erection leapt beneath her lips.

She breathed in the sharp, wild smell of him and rubbed her forehead in the nest of curls low on his belly.

This was how a man should be, she decided. Untamed. Unpredictable. And ravenous with desire.

Tynan drew her swiftly up against him and kissed her again, ferocious in his hunger, and Nara liked it that way. She wanted him to want her.

She wanted him inside her. But not yet. Not quite yet.

Suspended between heaven and earth by the corded muscles of his arms and the strength of his thighs, his knees slightly bent, she wrapped her legs around his hips to maintain close contact.

Nara threaded her own fingers into his tawny mane and drew his head closer, deepening their kiss. By tightening her legs around him, she increased the pressure of that contact, setting off an explosion of ecstasy, yet she still was empty, weeping to be filled.

As if he'd read her mind, Tynan lifted her buttocks in one powerful motion and thrust himself inside her, then lifted her again and again, his own thrusts matching her downward motion with fierce intensity.

Almost delirious with ardor, Nara leaned into the hollow of his neck and tasted his flesh, then arched her back, her breasts begging for his touch. Tynan kissed them, suckled them, made love to them with his mouth, even as he buried himself to the hilt inside her with a sweet, savage rhythm that went on and on.

She never wanted it to end. But when Tynan's strokes became faster and faster, he brought her to a shuddering release that radiated like molten fire from the center of her desire to the very tips of her toes.

Collapsing against him, Nara felt as if her bones had melted into nothing. Hot. So hot.

Two more mighty thrusts, and Tynan let out a guttural cry of consummation, then went still, his legs locking in place.

172

Still joined in flesh, he cradled Nara to him and staggered back onto the bed. Their panting breaths and the sweat of their bodies mingled in a golden, wordless afterglow.

This time, Nara said nothing. She simply held on to her husband and drifted into sated, exhausted slumber.

Tynan held Nara in the darkness, trying to prolong for even a little while the sense of wholeness she had brought him.

From the first day she had met him, she had given so much, yet asked so little, and never anything for herself.

But she had also made him feel. At the very moment of glorious union, he had known the bitter knowledge of the separation to come. Even at the zenith of sexual fulfillment, he had writhed under the rasping agony of the betrayal he must commit.

And Timothy. Tynan had tried not to care, but what he had witnessed tonight . . .

Seeing the place where they had taken Tim, picking up that iron collar and coming away with Timothy's blood on his hands . . . Tynan had cursed in the name of the God he did not believe in.

That asylum . . . in a single, searing flash, the horror of it had ripped open emotional scars Tynan had taken years to form, causing him to relive the degradation and aching loneliness of his own imprisonment as if it had happened only yesterday.

And Lady Margaret. He smoldered with hatred at the very thought of her. When she'd struck him as if he were a disobedient slave, it had taken every ounce of his self-control to keep from throttling the bitch.

And the way she had spoken so blithely of Laird Cullum's talk of killing him. Rage, dark and boundless, bloomed inside him until he shook with it.

But instead of lashing out as he once would have, Tynan looked at the woman sleeping in his arms and stilled.

Completely vulnerable, naked and innocent as the day she was born, Nara curled against him in absolute trust, never suspecting the dark purpose that pulsed through him with every beat of his heart — a heart that ached now as it hadn't since he was eight years old.

Silently he cursed her for making him feel again.

Then he saw the irony of such a curse. She was cursed, already. Nara deserved everything that was good and wholesome and pure, and instead she had given herself — wholly and completely, without reservation or judgment — to him.

He was curse enough. He, her husband and executioner. And God help him, he cared for her.

Cared for her? Nay, it was more, far more than that. Why not admit the truth?

He loved her.

That made their hell complete.

A month ago, Tynan wouldn't have known the meaning of the word "love." Yet Nara . . . in a few short weeks, she had taught him what love meant. She *defined* it, by all that she was.

Rocking her gently, he stifled a tortured groan.

He gladly would have died for her, easily would have killed for her. But could he sacrifice his honor, all that he had sworn? Could he turn his back on his family, deny them eternal rest?

Soul-sick and wishing that he were anyone but who he was, Tynan sat awake in the darkness and held her close until the first hint of dawn broke the gloom.

# *Chapter XII*

Nara opened her eyes at first light. She lay curled in Tynan's arms, the faint chill of dawn on her exposed skin a sharp contrast to the warmth where her bare flesh met his. He was naked, too, just as he had been when she'd fallen into sated, dreamless slumber. Lulled by the steady rhythm of his heart and the deep, even cadence of his breathing, she closed her eyes and tried to go back to sleep, but she soon opened her eyes again. She was wide awake, too alive to every sound, every sensation of this quiet moment.

Had he held her all night?

Somehow, she knew he had. She lifted up a silent prayer of heartfelt thanks, then ventured aloud, "Wouldn't it be lovely if 'Brother-No-Fleshly-Commerce' walked in and found us this way?"

A pleasant, rolling rumble sounded beneath her ear. Nara looked up in amazement. Tynan had actually laughed! And he was smiling . . . not a soulless smile, but a genuine grin, tempered though it was by weariness and — what? She saw a certain sadness in his eyes that caused her heart to catch, but she was so grateful for the miracle of his smile that she blurted out, "By heaven, but you are beautiful when you smile. It's as if someone lit a candle inside you."

As quickly as the gift had been given, his smile was withdrawn. Tynan sobered, setting her away from him on the bed as he rose. Magnificent and wholly unselfconscious in his nakedness, he retrieved his clothes and began to dress. "When they bring our food, I'll request an audience with the abbot. Perhaps he knows where Timothy has been taken."

Timothy. How could she have forgotten, even for a moment?

Suddenly cold, Nara located her shift and dress, then pulled them on. "But what if the abbot won't tell us where Timothy is?" She knelt and groped for her stockings beneath the bed.

"Then we must leave without him." Tynan granted her a look of genuine compassion. "I know you don't want to leave Timothy behind, but now that Lady Margaret has seen us, we dare not tarry here. If she should realize who you really are" — his golden eyes darkened — "she will stop at nothing to keep us from reaching your grandfather."

Lady Margaret. Tynan had called her a monster. Nara could scarcely believe it of such a poised, attractive older woman, yet she knew Tynan never made idle accusations. If he said Lady Margaret was a monster, he must have had good reason.

Nara sat on the side of the bed, her gaze meeting his. "She would have us killed?"

"Without a qualm." He calmly gathered his weapons.

"But she's my aunt." What sort of family had Nara sprung from? "We share the same blood. Surely my grandfather would not allow her to harm us. She wouldn't dare —"

"Your grandfather would never know," Tynan interrupted. "We would simply disappear, long before we ever reached him. It has happened before. That is why we must leave."

"She's killed before?" A cold breath of alarm caused Nara to shiver. "And she got away with it?"

"Aye, she got away with it." He turned the old, hard, hateful look on her. "Lady Margaret is a powerful woman — sister to the laird — and clever. Too clever to leave any proof of her crimes."

"If there is no proof," she challenged, pulling on her heavy woolen stockings, "then how can you make such an accusation?"

Tynan radiated offense. "I've seen her kill, with my own eyes."

She could almost taste the bitterness in his voice.

"I was only ten," he continued. "Late one night, Lady Margaret cornered one of the other stableboys, another orphan scarcely older than I."

Tynan's movements stilled, his eyes focused beyond the present. "She had an affinity for virgins, the younger the better. But this boy was too young, even for her. When she tried to molest him, he thought she meant to bite off his cock, so he fought her and cried for help. With one deft motion, she broke his neck to silence him." Tynan snapped his fingers, and the hair rose on the back of Nara's own neck. "Just that quickly, and he was dead, his mouth and eyes still wide open."

For a brief instant, Tynan's face betrayed the horror and frustration of that long-buried incident. "I was too frightened to do anything but hide in the shadows and watch. When she carried his naked body to the cesspool, I crept after her and saw her throw him in, as if he were nothing more than excrement."

Nara's stomach roiled. Lady Margaret was guilty of worse than murder. Such evil, in her own bloodline! "You saw her do this . . ."

"Aye," Tynan said coldly, "and she saw me. I didn't think she had, but after she disposed of the body, she looked straight at the spot where I was hiding and laughed."

He reached for his axe. "All that time, she'd known I was watching. Helpless." His eyes closed briefly, then opened again, the life leaving them along with the pain. "She said, 'What did you see? You saw nothing.' "

Tynan sucked in an unsteady breath. "It should never have happened. I should have done something," he murmured dully, "tried to stop her somehow."

"Dear heaven." Nara's heart ached for the helpless, friendless boy who had witnessed such horrors, but she knew better than to voice her sympathy. Tynan, the man, wanted pity from no one, least of all her. "You were only a child," she offered. "What could you have possibly done to stop her?"

"Nothing, probably. But I should have tried." Tynan leveled a piercing gaze at Nara. "She robbed me of my soul that night, as surely as if she were Satan himself."

Now Nara understood at least part of what had shaped him into the hard, guarded creature he had become. Yet some miracle had kept him from growing as twisted and cruel as his tormentors. That alone gave her hope. "I'm surprised she didn't kill you, too, to keep her secret safe."

He shook his head. "She had no need to trouble herself, and we both knew it."

"But you had seen her," Nara asserted. "You were the proof."

"Aye." Tynan busied himself rewrapping his axe and checking the contents of his pouch. "But she was the laird's sister, and I . . ." His eyes met hers. "I was alone, Nara, the basest menial in the castle, with no one to protect me." He went back to his packing. "Had I brought such an accusation, they would have tortured me, at the very least. Even if I'd managed to endure the torture, it would have been my word against hers in the end.

"Both of us knew how *that* would end up. Her maid would

have sworn Lady Margaret never left her room that night, and I'd have been sent to the gallows for a crime she committed."

"So she got away with murder," Nara breathed.

"That's the least of it. There are worse things than dying, Nara. Far worse." Tynan picked up the pouch. "As time passed, I came to envy that boy she killed. He was still innocent when he crossed over to the Yonder World. He was free." Tynan lifted his sword and looked at it as if seeing it for the first time, prompting Nara to wonder how many men he had "freed" with that weapon.

With a cynical arch of his brow, Tynan slid the blade into place along his back. "Thanks to last night's meeting, Lady Margaret knows I've returned, no longer a defenseless child. And she's seen you. That's why we must leave this place as soon as possible. We'll take an indirect route to Eilean d'Ór."

Nara forced her thoughts away from the wickedness of her aunt. "But Timothy. What about Timothy?" After learning about Lady Margaret, she had real reservations about bringing Timothy into a place as evil as Eilean d'Ór. Yet nothing could be worse than the asylum.

"If he's still here, the abbot will return him to us. If he's not . . ." Tynan paused. "Once I've brought you to your grandfather . . ." His already hard expression solidified into an impenetrable mask. "We'll sort things out about Timothy after."

"After what?" Nara asked with a prickle of foreboding. It wasn't the Sight, but she sensed something huge and dark and frightening behind that mask.

Tynan looked away. "After I take you to your grandfather."

"I see." Whatever it was, she would discover the truth soon enough. Deeply unsettled, Nara found her comb and began to work the tangles from her hair. She had almost finished plaiting the jet-black tresses into a thick braid when a hooded friar — she had no way of knowing if it was Brother-No-Fleshly-Commerce — brought in a meal identical to the one they'd been served the night before, except for the beer that properly replaced last night's wine.

"I would speak with the abbot," Tynan challenged the hooded monk. "Straightaway."

His arrogance surprised Nara, and she wondered if it might have something to do with the fact that Tynan had caught Lady Margaret here in the small hours of the night. Her mind churned. What could the abbot and Lady Margaret possibly have —

The truth dawned on her with sickening clarity. The *abbot*, and Lady Margaret! No wonder she had sensed evil in this place.

Nara wasn't the only one surprised by Tynan's high-handed attitude. The nameless, faceless monk who had delivered their food straightened abruptly, his forearms clasped inside the deep bell sleeves of his vestment. "Father Abbot," he snapped, "is occupied with his holy office, sir, and does not disturb his routine at the whim of strangers."

"Ah, but the abbot and I share a close acquaintance," Tynan said smoothly. "Lady Margaret confides everything to me. Tell him that. And be quick about it."

The monk hesitated, bowed, then left them.

Minutes later, an immensely fat man who had to be the abbot himself — visibly flustered — swept into their room and closed the door behind him. "All right, then. What is it?"

When he turned to face them and saw Nara, his mouth dropped open as if he had seen a ghost.

Nara realized he must have known *Seanmhair*, but she was still put off by the way people reacted to the resemblance.

Tynan did not acknowledge the Abbot's reaction. "Ah,

Brother Abbot." Not *Father* Abbot. Neither Nara nor the abbot missed the subtle slur. "I thought you'd come."

Tynan bowed with more than a hint of irony. "I am Tynan MacDougald." The cleric's attention snapped to Tynan at the mention of his surname. "Allow me to present my lady wife, Nara."

The abbot looked ominously from Nara to Tynan, then back to Nara. Quite obviously, the introduction had significance far beyond Nara's understanding.

She was tempted to ask just what was going on, but the abbot didn't give her the chance. Turning his attention to Tynan, he settled his considerable bulk onto the cot, his hands gripping widespread knees. "I am at your service, sir. What would you have of me?"

As usual, Tynan minced no words. "There was a man here last night, chained in that travesty of an asylum. I wish to know what has been done with him."

The abbot scowled, visibly annoyed. "Our asylum provides refuge for more than seventy souls, many of whom are chained for their own safety and the safety of their fellows."

Tynan colored slightly, but his tone remained even. "This man posed no threat to anyone." Nostrils flaring, he inhaled deeply. "His name is Timothy. We want him back."

"He's my brother," Nara piped up, surprising even herself with the audacity of that lie. Not a complete falsehood . . . he *was* her brother in Christ.

Tynan shot her an incredulous look before continuing. "As I said, his name is Timothy. He was with us until yesterday, when he got lost in the forest."

The abbot pursed his lips and rolled his eyes toward the ceiling in thought. Then his expression cleared. "Ah, yes. I remember the fellow. Tall, very thin. Wild, that one." He tucked his chin, causing the folds of fat beneath to swell. "He

181

was brought in yester eve. Found wandering at the edge of the burgh. Frightened the children half to death. The burgesses had him brought to us."

Tynan's next question was more a command. "And where is he now?" He conducted himself like a chieftain, a man who would brook no opposition despite the humble raiment he wore.

"Still in the asylum, of course," the abbot said impatiently. "Unless he knows how to pick a padlock with straw."

"He's not there." Tynan leaned closer, invading the abbot's very breath. "Someone moved him. In the small hours of the night."

"That's preposterous!" Intimidated by Tynan's powerful presence, the abbot blustered to his feet and sidestepped until a safe distance separated them. Only then did he risk pointing a fat finger in Tynan's direction. "And what, pray tell, would lead you to make such a statement?"

Tynan remained cool. "Long past midnight, I heard Timothy calling, so I unlocked that door and searched the abbey for him."

"You violated the hospitality of this order?" the abbot railed. "And now you have the gall to make such idle accusations. Fie on't, sir!"

"It seems the hospitality of this order extends to some rather unorthodox activities," Tynan said smoothly. "Odd whom one meets in the hallways in the dark of night."

Nara thought the abbot was going to expire on the spot. His face went from red to gray, and he clutched his chest as if his heart had seized.

Served him right, the reprobate! He deserved to die unshriven, but she didn't want him to do so without telling them where Timothy had been taken.

"Where is he?" she demanded. "Tell us what you've done

182

with him, you wicked old man."

Tynan actually smiled at her, a proud smile. Two smiles in one day. "Return Timothy to us," he said to the gasping abbot, "and we will be on our way." He paused, then added, "If, that is, you can provide us with some provisions for our journey. And a little traveling money. Does the hospitality of your order extend to that?"

Nara gasped. "Tynan, that's extortion."

"The Church invented it," Tynan retorted, unruffled. "Give, or go to hell." Turning back to the abbot, he smiled his familiar cold, heartless smile. "I like my version better, though: Give, or I shall tell."

"You soulless son of a . . ." The Abbot's hue shifted back to dusky red, his face betraying an inner Armageddon as duty battled self-preservation. He paced, hands wringing, for several anxious, desperate moments before self-preservation won out. "Aye, then, you Godless heathen," he spat toward Tynan, the fat finger waggling. "Food, and fifty marks, but not a cent more."

Tynan nodded. "Most generous, good brother. I hadn't hoped for more than ten marks. Fifty shall do nicely."

Seeing the abbot's consternation, Nara barely managed to suppress a smile. She had to give her husband credit; Tynan had deftly gained the upper hand with a man far more powerful and far less honorable than he.

The abbot stomped toward the door. "Wait here. I will bring the man. And the food." He scarcely seemed able to spit out what came next. "And the money."

Tynan couldn't resist a parting stab. "Do not keep us waiting long."

When the door closed behind the abbot, Nara collapsed onto the bed, laughing. "Tynan, you should be ashamed of yourself."

"*Me?*" He stood beside the bed, arms akimbo. "What about you? 'He's my brother.' " A sly approval smoothed his features. "Well done, Nara. I had no idea such deception lurked behind your innocence."

"So I lied." A flush of shame rose to Nara's cheeks. "It was wrong, I know. But I thought it would make it easier to get Timothy back."

"I wasn't scolding you," he said wryly. "I was congratulating you."

"Tynan," she said without conviction, "I fear you are a bad influence on me. Absolutely incorrigible."

"I am that, lady," he said with just a little too much conviction for comfort. "I am that, indeed."

Only a few minutes later, the abbot returned, his color ashen. He swept into the room bearing a heavy bundle. "Here." He thrust the bundle at Tynan. "Food, drink, and fifty marks."

Tynan accepted the ransom for his silence. "And where is Timothy?"

The abbot retrieved a fine linen kerchief from behind his scapular and mopped the sheen of perspiration from his brow. "He wasn't there. Brother Artis had the prayer vigil last night. When he made his usual rounds an hour before matins, the man was gone. I've questioned all the others on penalty of their immortal souls, but no one knows what happened."

Seeing Tynan's cold, unbelieving stare, the abbot stepped closer, his hands folded as if in prayer. "As God is my witness, sir, I do not know what happened to the man. He simply disappeared."

"And you expect me to believe that?" Tynan gripped the abbot's flaccid upper arms and snatched him straight into the air.

Nara watched in awe. The abbot must have weighed

twenty stones, yet Tynan held him suspended with his sandaled feet flailing a few inches above the floor.

Eye-to-eye, Tynan growled, "If you're lying to me —"

"Nay, sir, I speak the truth." A stream of urine trickled from the abbot's right foot. "As God is my witness, I speak the truth."

Tynan looked at the growing puddle with contempt. "You wouldn't know the truth if it climbed your skirts and kissed your cock, you self-righteous sack of —"

Nara had heard enough. "Stop! Let him go, Tynan." Seeing the abbot for the miserable reprobate he was, she actually felt sorry for the man. How far he had fallen. "He will answer to God for his crimes. It is enough."

"No, it's not enough!" Tynan ground out, his face coloring. He dropped his captive back to his feet, then clamped a huge, powerful hand into the folds of the abbot's neck. "Look at him. He's grown fat, while feeding those poor bastards in the asylum only slops." Tynan shook with anger, his fingers closing. "He issues penance to the brothers for merely *thinking* about the sins of the flesh, and all the while, he's learning the Black Arts from Lady Margaret . . . when he's not too busy fucking her."

"Tynan, stop it! You're killing him!" Nara stepped between the two men. She grasped the corded muscles of Tynan's forearm with both hands and tried to pull him away, but lacked the strength to move him.

"He's not worth it, Tynan. They'll hang you if you kill him! Let go!" She hung all her weight on his arm, but to no effect.

Tynan was crazed. She'd seen that look before, when he'd come upon the men in the forest. Bloodlust, a killing rage. But this time, he had his hand around the offender's throat. Dear heaven, she had to stop him. But how?

185

She could think of only one way. "Forgive me," she pleaded, "but you leave me no choice." That said, she brought her knee up into his groin with all the desperate force she could muster.

Tynan let out a strangled cry and doubled over, releasing the abbot.

Nara knew there was little time to waste. She shoved the abbot, gasping like a codfish, toward the door to the cloister. "Quickly. Before he recovers." They had almost reached the portal when she realized she needed something from him. "The key to the outer door! We must have it to leave."

"But . . ." The abbot might have given them money, but his keys were another matter. He shot a terrified glance at Tynan, who was now writhing on the bed, cursing Nara and all her ancestors in a strangled voice.

"Give me the key," Nara demanded. She crossed herself, then whispered, "I swear by my immortal soul, once we're outside, I'll lock the door behind us and throw the key back over the wall."

Both of them turned back to see that Tynan, still cursing, had rolled into a sitting position and was trying to stand.

That was enough to convince the abbot. He fumbled briefly behind his scapular, produced two keys, handed one to Nara, then — with impressive speed for a man of his girth — put the inner door between them and locked it.

Nara turned. Time to pay the piper.

Hastily gathering their ill-gotten supplies along with Tynan's pouch, she did her best to quiet the fear that tingled tightly through her chest. Tynan wouldn't hurt her. He had sworn to bring her safely to her grandfather.

She hurried to the main entrance and with shaking hand put the key into the lock and tripped the mechanism. Only when the door was open did she turn to face Tynan. At least now she could run for her life if she had to.

He wanted to strike her. She could see it, yet she could hardly blame him for feeling that way after what she'd done. But he made no move in her direction. Instead, his hands cradling his injured manhood through his plaid, Tynan just stood there bent over like an old man, glaring at her as if he were about to say something. But he merely clamped his lips into a grim line and hobbled over to his weapons, releasing his groin only long enough to collect his axe and position it for travel.

Then, with obvious effort, he straightened to his full height and limped past her.

Nara heaved a sigh of relief. Stopping only to lock the door behind them and hurl the key over the wall, she followed Tynan into the cool, foggy morning.

God willing, she would never see that place again. She only hoped the same could not be said of Timothy.

Two strained, arduous days later, Nara followed Tynan up yet another stony crag. Since they'd left the abbey, he'd kept several paces ahead of her. He spoke to her only when necessary, and then only in monosyllables. So she was surprised to see him stop, looking into the valley beyond with an odd mixture of anticipation and dread.

Tired though she was, Nara quickened her pace until she was standing beside him.

In the sheltered valley below, an enormous lake spread from one end to the other, its calm waters as clear and bright as the eye of God. At the lake's center, a steep island was crowned by a rectangular castle of yellow stone whose turrets and battlements glowed almost gold in the afternoon sun.

Eilean d'Ór. It had to be. Fear and anticipation tightened Nara's innards.

Ironic. She had left the home she called her Golden Island only to end her journey at this castle of the same name.

She scanned the shoreline. Neat cottages, each with its own little boat hard by, and ripening fields surrounded the lake. Yet there was something wrong with the idyllic scene.

Nara stilled, her senses on edge. Then she realized that no smoke rose from the conical roofs of the cottages. No chickens fluttered in the stone-walled yards. No cattle grazed the deep green pastures. No farmers worked the fields.

She scanned the lake. No fishermen plied its waters.

The only signs of life were several thin trails of smoke that rose from the castle.

"Eilean d'Ór," Tynan said, his voice oddly tight. He did not look at her.

Despite its beauty, Nara was beginning to get a bad feeling about the golden castle. "Where is everyone?"

He turned a look of shrewd assessment on her. "You noticed." Tynan scanned the valley. "I don't know where everyone is. Normally these hills are bristling with sentries. Something is afoot."

He scrutinized the castle, then turned and headed back the way they had come. "Come. There's a safe hiding place not far from here. We can rest there. Once it's dark, I'll take a boat over to the castle and find out what's happened."

Nara hastened after him. "Not without me, you won't."

Tynan's lips curled inward, baring his white, even teeth. "Must you always question my judgment?" His strides lengthening, he let out an exasperated breath. Nara had to trot to keep up. "I told you, Nara, the barons in these parts are constantly at war with each other and the king. The one good thing I can say for your grandfather is that he's refused to bend his knee to King James. Laird Cullum has sworn his sword and his men to Donald Balloch of Islay, so he's fair game for the king's armies."

He cocked his head in the direction of the castle. "For all we know, The Earl of Caithness might have taken Eilean d'Ór. Or the Earl of Mar."

Trotting backward so she could see his face, Nara challenged, "You certainly seem to know a lot about politics, for the 'basest menial in the castle,' as you described yourself." She fell in beside him.

Tynan's eyes narrowed. "I told you, Nara. I fought for Laird Alexander. A man must know what he's fighting for."

"I don't believe that for one second," she countered. Keeping up with Tynan was taking its toll; she scarcely had the breath to speak. "*Seanmhair* says that the men of Scotland love to make war, regardless of the reason. They love war even more than they love their own kin. She says it's in their blood."

Tynan actually laughed. Again. "Perhaps she's right," he said. "But *this* man needs to know why he's fighting. And who he's fighting for." Tynan would not be distracted, even by talk of war. "Now, as I was saying — *you,* my lady wife, shall wait where I bid you wait. You shall not go to Eilean d'Ór until I have seen which way the wind blows there."

He grew serious. "I cannot risk letting you fall into the hands of the king's men. With you as hostage, they could force Laird Cullum to support James instead of Alexander."

"Tynan, that makes little sense." Nara stopped walking to catch her breath. "You said yourself that my grandfather is a monster. He doesn't even know me. Why would he sacrifice his honor for someone he does not even know, much less care about?"

Tynan halted ahead of her and turned to regard her with unsettling intensity. "He cares, Nara. He cares a great deal. That is why you must remain in hiding until I make certain the castle is safe."

"So you would traipse away and leave me, alone and un-protected? *Again,*" Nara grumbled. "A brilliant strategy, es-pecially considering what happened to Tim and me the *last* time you left us."

The look on his face told her she had struck deep, square at the heart of his warrior's pride.

"I'm sorry, Tynan. That wasn't fair of me," she said, gen-uinely contrite. "It's not your fault that Timothy ran away. You couldn't have known those men would come."

"Spare your pity, Nara," he said without emotion. "Spend it on someone who cares, like your grandfather." He pivoted and started up a nearby hill crowned with ruins.

Stung by his coldness, she followed him in silence.

When they reached the ruins, Nara realized she was star-ing at what was left of a church. Only one small, roofless chamber remained standing. Tumbled, blackened stones and a few fragments of charred beam testified to the fire that had destroyed the building.

Tynan picked his way through the rubble to a canted slab of stone. With a mighty heave and a groan, he shifted the slab aside, revealing a dusty, cobweb-laden stairway that led down into darkness. "Come. No one will bother us here." He descended, motioning her to follow.

Nara did so with trepidation. Blinking in the gloom, she followed Tynan into the underworld.

No sooner had her eyes adjusted to the dim light than she realized she was surrounded by death. Row upon row of stone platforms bore the bones and decayed burial trappings of fully two dozen corpses. "Tynan," she said in a strangled voice, "this is the crypt. We cannot hide here."

He crossed to the farthest corner, pulled the bound axe from his back, and used it to swipe two skeletons from the platform, stirring an explosion of dust in the muted darkness.

Tynan coughed and covered his mouth and nose with his plaid. "There. That should do nicely for both of us tonight."

He turned hard eyes on Nara. "If anyone comes nosing about while we sleep, all we need to do is sit up. That should scare them off." He reached into a dark niche and retrieved an ancient, misshapen candle. "Ah. Just where I left it."

Nara quailed. "Have you no respect for those who have passed on to the Yonder World?" She huddled next to him, her flesh pebbling. "Anywhere but here, Tynan. I cannot sleep among corpses. You may not fear those who have been transformed, but I do. What if their ghosts —"

Tynan didn't let her finish. "Listen to me, Nara. There is no other safe place to hide. Believe me, I know." He gestured to the skeletons draped in cobwebs. "These wretched souls — or what's left of them — are the only ones you *can* trust. They've departed this life for another. They can't hurt you."

He drew Nara into his arms, pulling her head against his heart. "Only the living can hurt you, Nara. Not the dead."

Grateful for the strength that surrounded her, she trembled nonetheless. "But what about tonight? Surely the spirits we have disturbed will come back to haunt us."

Tynan shook his head. "Many years ago, this was my sanctuary when I was finally trusted to leave the castle on errands for the stablemaster." He sighed. "Ironically fitting, that I should find refuge among the dead." He tipped Nara's chin up until her eyes met his. "Never once, in all the days — and the nights — I hid here, did I see or hear the first evidence of a ghost." He granted her a hard smile. "You will be safe here, Nara."

Unconvinced, she pushed away from him. "Tynan, I believe you could keep me safe in hell itself, but I'd rather not spend the night there." Nara wanted to run . . . anywhere but here.

Groping in his pouch, Tynan used his foot to clear away the bones he had knocked to the ground. Casual as you please, he pulled out the flint and laid it and the candle alongside the cobweb-covered occupant on the next bier. "We could both use some sleep." He unwrapped his axe, shook out the seal pelt, and laid it, fur side up, onto the empty slab. "I'll sleep until dark, then I'll head for the castle." He stretched out next to the pelt, settled his pouch beneath his head for a pillow, and closed his eyes.

"You want me to wait here all night. Alone." Nara looked about her. A crypt. He actually expected her to lie beside him where dead bodies had been only moments before. And spend the night here, alone!

He was right about one thing, though: No mortal in his right mind would go poking about a crypt, so she would be safe from human intervention. But she wasn't as convinced as Tynan that the dead posed no threat.

Chilled and frightened, she crossed herself, then crawled atop the slab and into the welcome heat of Tynan's embrace. That comfort, at least, was real, as was the silky pelt beneath her. "I shall wait for you, then, but only until morning. If you haven't returned by midmorning, I shall come looking for you."

"If I haven't returned by midmorning," he said ominously without opening his eyes, "you need not bother looking for me. I will be beyond any help that you can give." And on that cheerful note, he rolled onto his back and promptly went to sleep, leaving Nara to lie awake, robbed of slumber by every whisper of wind and rustle of leaves.

# Chapter XIII

Tynan waited as long as possible before untangling himself from Nara's warmth. She'd been restless at first — owing, no doubt, to her superstitious fears — and hadn't fallen asleep for a long time. But once she had settled down, she'd slept unmoving until he eased free of her to light the candle and prepare for his midnight foray to Eilean d'Ór.

Only when he covered her with their one blanket did she stir, a troubled frown drawing her dark brows together. Even then, she was so lovely Tynan's breath caught in his throat. He stood watching her, transfixed.

He'd long since given up hope that anyone like Nara actually existed. He wouldn't believe it now, but for having witnessed her unfailing kindness, day in and day out. How could anyone be so open, so honest, so selfless, so innocent?

Nara was all those things, which left her dangerously vulnerable to the brutal realities of the world to which he had brought her.

He told himself that he would be doing her a boon by ending her life. If she were to remain at Eilean d'Ór, her innocence would soon wither. The best part of her would die there by degrees, her hope smothered by oppression, her faith in humanity bleeding from a thousand daily cuts.

Tynan knew. He had managed to survive for eighteen years in that place, but his soul had not, and neither would Nara's. The evil was too strong.

Her brow smoothing, Nara exhaled softly and rolled over onto her back, one hand resting gently atop the blanket that covered her breast and the other across her stomach. For just a moment she lay so still and silent, Tynan was seized with the notion that she looked as if she belonged there, on the bier.

This was how she would be in death — motionless, her beauty luminous, even without life. Until the worms began their work . . .

Don't think about that, he commanded himself. Yet he shuddered in revulsion at the idea of what decay would do to her, and suddenly he needed to reassure himself that she was, in fact, alive.

He bent over her, close enough to feel the gentle warmth of her breath against his face and see the subtle rise and fall of her belly. The mere scent of her was enough to tighten his loins.

Not dead yet, thank God. Not yet.

She was still alive, still his, even if for only a little while. And she cared for him, just as he was. Cared for him far more deeply than he could ever care for any living soul.

So little time, and her innocence would be lost forever. And he would be the instrument of destruction.

He looked at her with longing. God help him, he wanted her, wanted to take her away and live in the glow of her goodness until they were both old. He wanted to plant his seed in her womb and watch her belly swell with life. He wanted to see their sons and daughters grow brave and tall, blessed by his strength and Nara's joy. He wanted everything that life could offer them.

The hint of a beatific smile curved her lips.

So beautiful she was, inside and out.

Looking at her, Tynan felt the stone around his heart

194

begin to shatter. And as the hard shell crumbled, his soul was rent by the pain and joy Nara had awakened within him.

By all that was holy, he hadn't hurt so deeply or yearned for what could never be since he was eight years old, twenty long years ago.

Or felt as alive.

But he was dying inside all over again, and only Nara could fill the howling emptiness that threatened to swallow him.

Unable to stop himself, he lowered his lips to hers. It was a gentle kiss, almost chaste, born of the futile hope that somehow he might partake of her innocence and so dispel, even for a moment, the bitterness that had poisoned him for so long.

Sweet. So sweet, the taste of her, the feel of her lips.

If only he could undo what had been done — change the past and make things different. If they were anyone else, anywhere else . . .

But Tynan was the last of his sept. On his shoulders alone rested the honor of all his ancestors. And it was honor, in the end, that must be served, above longing, above mercy, above life itself.

Tynan pulled away the blanket and kissed Nara again, this time more urgently. His hands slid up under her clothes to stroke her thighs and roam familiar curves of her body, marking her by touch as his and his alone. Then his fingers descended to probe for the seat of her desire. She was still half asleep when he found it, and she writhed beneath him, letting out a tantalizing moan of pleasure.

Nara's tongue sought his and her arms drew him closer. Oblivious to everything but the pulsing need his touch had awakened, she responded as naturally as a wild creature driven by instinct alone, showing him with her hands and mouth that she wanted him just as much as he wanted her.

Hot. He was so hot. His throbbing pulse pumped blood into his loins until his manhood swelled to exquisite torment.

And then Nara was pulling loose the laces of his shirt. She wrenched her mouth free of his. "Take me, Tynan," she whispered, her eyes open and dilated almost black in the guttering light of the candle. "Drive away the death around us. Make me know we're both alive."

Frantic now, he snatched his shirt over his head with one hand and unbuckled his belt with the other. Arms tangling, they each removed the last of the other's clothing. And then she was lying before him, the dark silken curls between her legs exposed, her nipples peaked, her flawless skin flushed with desire.

Tynan buried his face in the velvet flesh of her abdomen, and she threaded her fingers into his hair, drawing him even closer. He could not get enough of her. So many smooth, seductive places he needed to feel, to touch, to taste. If he could have, he would have stretched out atop her and willed his being into hers, so that the two of them occupied only one space.

And all the while, Nara's hands and lips urgently sought and tasted every part of him.

When Tynan could hold back no longer, he straddled her and drove himself inside her again and again until she cried out, unrestrained, her nails digging into his shoulders.

His heart breaking for all that would be lost after tomorrow, he arched his back and spent himself inside her. Then he collapsed, turning his face away so she could not see the agony he felt.

God, how he wished it were all over.

Tynan inhaled deeply, struggling to regain his self-control.

It wasn't easy, but he managed to will himself back to the distant, untouchable place that had been his refuge all these years. Then he rose and dressed in silence. He did not dare to look at Nara. If he did, he might not have the strength to leave.

After he had dressed, he picked up his sword and slid it into place along his back. Tynan reminded himself of the grim vow he had made, then remembered the stableboy who had died by Lady Margaret's hand that night so long ago.

Perhaps it was best, after all, that he must execute Nara.

She was too good for any of them, including Tynan. Too good for this world.

He left her without looking back.

It took almost an hour to find a boat, and another half-hour to reach the secret entrance at the base of the ancient broch that anchored the eastern corner of the castle. Luckily for him, a few rats were the only occupants Tynan encountered in the dank, debris-strewn corridor that led to a hidden door just above the dungeon.

The hinges squeaked when he opened the ancient door, but no sentry was waiting in the torchlit hallway beyond. He managed to reach the stable without waking any of the women, children, and old people who had taken refuge in the bailey.

The castle was obviously prepared for a siege.

Tynan opened the stable door and slipped inside without incident. There he found the stalls occupied not by warhorses, but by an odd assortment of kine. He was inside the stablemaster's room with his hand over Devan's mouth before the old man even knew he was there.

"Shhh," he whispered when the old man struggled. "Hold, Devan. It's me, Tynan. I'd hate to have to run you through, after the kindness you showed me as a boy."

Devan stopped struggling, so Tynan released him and sat facing his mentor on the edge of the cot.

"By Odin's beard," Devan said. He ran gnarled, shaking hands over Tynan's shoulders. "I feared ye were long dead, lad."

"Still alive, old man." Careful of the swollen knuckles, he took Devan's hand into his. "Still alive." Tynan bent closer. "Where is Laird Cullum? I see that all the stallions are gone."

"All save one." Devan lowered his voice even further. "Last week, we got word that King James had taken our over-laird Alexander prisoner again. This time, he's held at Tantallon, and there's no getting to him there." Even Tynan knew that the isolated fortress on the north coast was impregnable. "So Donald Balloch has rallied every loyal islander, man and boy, to fight. Laird Cullum armed his men and sailed last Tuesday to meet Balloch."

"Damn!" Laird Cullum was gone. But part of him rejoiced that the execution had been delayed.

And if he could catch up with Donald Balloch and his men, he could fight to free Laird Alexander. That would help even the score for Laird Alexander's intervention on his behalf.

But he had to get Nara to her grandfather before Laird Cullum risked himself in battle. The old reprobate would do Tynan no good dead.

"Where were they bound, Devan?" Tynan demanded. "I must know. I have to reach Laird Cullum before the fight."

Devan hesitated. "Do ye mean to kill him, lad? Because if ye do, I'll not be tellin' ye. Laid Cullum has his faults, but he's still my chieftain."

"I swear on my mother's grave," Tynan hissed, "I'll do the blackhearted bastard no harm. But I must reach him while he's still alive."

"That's what ye said that time you were thirteen, and huntin' the muckin-boy who stole yer blanket." Devan's advancing years obviously hadn't impaired his memory. "As I recall, there was scarcely anythin' left to bind together after you finished with the lad. Not that I blame ye, of course. But ye did swear —"

"You *would* remember that," Tynan interjected. Devan would never believe him. Unless . . . hell, he might as well tell the truth. Part of it, anyway. "I've found Laird Cullum's granddaughter."

Devan gasped. "The wee Lady Nara? But how? Where?" He paused. "What about the mistress?"

"I don't have time to explain all that now, old man." Tynan grasped Devan's frail shoulders. "Laird Cullum has sworn to restore my lands to me — and my right to lead my own sept — if I return his granddaughter to him, whole and safe. So you see, I *must* find him before the battle. If he's killed before we get to him, all is lost."

"Ah, my boy." Devan's voice thickened with emotion. "Ye make me glad I saved ye, after all."

Devan dropped his face, no longer able to look Tynan in the eye. "There are things I never told ye, lad . . ." He glanced up in supplication. "I wasn't bein' cruel, only tryin' to protect ye from yerself." The old man wrung his gnarled hands. "If ye'd known the truth, I was certain ye'd run away, givin' Laird Cullum just the excuse he was lookin' for to kill ye." He stilled. "When ye hear the whole story, I pray ye'll forgive an old man who only meant well."

Tynan frowned. "I've no time for riddles, Devan. Where has Laird Cullum gone?"

Those same gnarled hands clasped Tynan's upper arms. "They've sailed for Loch Linnhe. The barons mean to rally at

Carna, then march on Inverlochy. But I doubt anythin' will commence for a month or more. You know how the barons argue over every little thing. It'll take 'em weeks just to agree on a battle plan."

"I hope you're right," Tynan muttered. "For heaven only knows how long it will take us to reach Carna afoot."

"Afoot, aye," the old man reasoned, "but perhaps there's a faster way to get there."

Tynan stilled. "And what might that be?"

"Laird Cullum took all the stallions but one — a homely beast who showed an instant dislike to the master. Threw him three times before the laird banished him across the lake to pull Torran MacGinty's plow." It was too dark to see, but Tynan could almost hear Devan's grin in his next words. "Now, I could hardly imagine how the laird would object if a fit fightin' man like yerself was to borrow that horse so's he could join the fray."

Tynan's black mood evaporated.

Devan went on, "After all, the laird armed every male in the district, man and boy, who could hold a sword or bolt a crossbow. And ye've fought for Laird Alexander before."

"Aye. That I have." There was a chance, after all.

The stablemaster lifted his misshapen hands. "I tried to go meself, but these claws is useless. So I had to stay behind, in case of siege."

"My good luck that you did," Tynan said, and meant it. "But I'll not borrow the horse, if it's all the same to you. I'd rather buy it."

"Buy it?" Tynan might as well have said he could fly. "Pray, with what?"

"Name your price. And make it fair."

Devan remained skeptical. "Ten marks, and not a penny less. The beast is ugly, and he's spent a year behind the plow,

200

but he's young and strong — I trained him fer a warhorse meself. He'll serve ye well . . . unless he takes a dislike to you the way he did to Laird Cullum."

"Done." Tynan retrieved the leathern pouch tucked behind his belt and counted out ten marks.

"The devil's pitchfork! How'd such riches come to the likes of ye, boy?" Devan asked in amazement. "Ye haven't fallen to thieven', have ye?"

"Nay, Devan," Tynan answered. "Merely to blackmail."

"Well, all right, then," Devan declared with obvious relief. "I mean, it's hardly a crime to make a man pay for keepin' quiet about his sins when he's done somethin' wrong, now, is it?"

"My sentiments exactly," Tynan said, rising.

"Oh, by the by," Devan added, "the horse's name is Horrible."

"Horrible?" Why wasn't Tynan surprised? The first thing he had actually purchased, and the beast's name was Horrible.

He took the old man's hand into his own one last time. "You've come to my rescue yet again, Devan, and I'm grateful." Tynan's throat tightened. "We're not likely to meet again, so I'll tell you now, after all these years: I'm glad you saved me. I thank you, and my ancestors thank you, as well."

"I pray ye'll always feel that way. God bless ye, lad," the stablemaster whispered. Those were the last words Tynan heard as he crept back out into the stables on his way to Torran MacGinty's farm.

Nara did not rise until well past dawn, and then only because her stomach complained so loudly she couldn't sleep. She had been hurt when Tynan had turned away and left her without a word, but she had known better than to voice her disappointment.

It was foolish to want more than he could give. So she had watched him dress in silence, trying to be grateful for the brief joy their union had afforded.

After he had gone, she'd dressed and huddled back under the blanket, trying not to think about where she was. She'd slept only fitfully.

Accustomed to the unrelenting warmth of Tynan's embrace, she'd wakened often to find herself cold and alone. Every time she woke, Nara covered herself completely with the blanket, recited every charm she knew against ghosts, and tried not to think about the ghoulish remains lying all around her. She'd forced herself back to sleep in hopes that the next waking would find Tynan returned, his arms around her again.

It hadn't happened.

Now she was alone in this gruesome crypt and stiff as a day-old corpse. She still hadn't grown accustomed to sleeping on bare stone, much less a burial slab. Nara sat up and rubbed the countless places where it felt as if she'd been beaten with a stout rod.

Silly of her to think Tynan would be back so soon, she told herself. It was still early yet.

She opened their ill-gotten provisions and helped herself to a reasonably fresh bun. While she chewed the rich, gray maslin bread, she worked the cork from the only wine she could find in the bundle, then washed her breakfast down with a startlingly fiery swig of the bottle's contents.

Nara gasped, her eyes watering. Not wine. Definitely not wine.

Whiskey! It had to be.

By Glory, but it tasted nasty! And it burned.

Nara could almost hear *Seanmhair*'s admonition: "Well-born ladies *never* partake of strong drink, and gentlemen should use it only sparingly. The love of whiskey will steal even a good man's soul more surely than any pact with the devil."

The love of whiskey . . .

How could anyone in his right mind *like* such a dreadful brew, let alone love it?

Scrutinizing the bottle, Nara saw the faint reflection of the awful face she was making and couldn't help smiling.

But when the burning in her throat and stomach settled to a warm glow, she had to admit that whiskey might just have a salutary effect after all, if one could get past the odious taste.

Nara shivered from the frigid air that seeped through her thin blanket. The dark stone crypt held on to the night's cold, making it impossible to get warm. Cold though she was, she knew better than to think of building a fire. But she couldn't remain huddled beneath her thin blanket, not without taking a chill.

Holding her nose, she took another swig of whiskey. This mouthful didn't taste nearly as vile as the first. And the warm glow began to radiate from her belly, stirring her blood.

How long would it be before Tynan returned? she wondered.

What if he didn't return at all?

She took another swig. She was beginning to get used to the taste. In a matter of minutes, the warmth spread to her toes and fingertips. Very relaxing. She yawned, stretched, then laid back down atop the seal pelt, careful not to look at the grisly remains around her.

The soreness in her backside had eased a little, but it occurred to her that a few more sips might ease things even more.

Nara wasn't sure when her sense of well-being gave way to worry, but by the time she had consumed almost half the bottle's contents, the possibility that something might have happened to Tynan loomed huge and terrifying, as did the frightening presence of the spirit world all around her.

What would she do if Tynan didn't come back? She'd be alone and unprotected in this hostile land.

Where would she go?

She'd never make it back to the Isle of Mist alone, even if Tynan hadn't taken the money with him. And she dared not go to Eilean d'Ór — not if something happened to Tynan there.

Nara took another swig, then curled onto her side and closed her eyes.

Tynan would return before midday. He *must*.

She had no idea what time it was when she woke to find him towering above her, sniffing the contents of the half-empty bottle. He shoved the cork back into place. "Nara," he demanded, "what in perdition have you done?"

He hadn't shouted, but the sound of his voice thundered between her ears like an echo in an empty cavern, setting off waves of pain. Blessed Saint Brigit, but she felt horrible! Her tongue had grown fur while she slept, and there was a vile taste in her mouth. Nara's head pounded so brutally, she feared she would lose her breakfast. She tried to sit up, setting the world atilt.

"Tynan," she gasped, subsiding onto the seal pelt. "What's happening to me? Is it the plague?"

"Hardly," he said without the slightest trace of sympathy.

How could he be so uncaring, when she was obviously ill? Not merely ill. Nara tried to look up at him, but he was a silhouette. Every brilliant shard of sunlight that filtered into the crypt stabbed at her eyeballs like a dagger. "Dear heaven," she managed, "I think I'm dying. Truly, I have never felt so ill."

"Let me guess." Tynan sat beside her on the slab. "This is the first time you ever drank any whiskey, isn't it?"

"Aye." She closed her eyes in an effort to stop the bier from lurching beneath her. "But that couldn't be it. I only took a few sips to keep warm and ease the soreness in my bones. Certainly not enough to —"

A fresh surge of nausea silenced her. Faith, but she *must* be dying. An alarming idea shaped itself in her fuddled mind. Nara's eyes flew open. "The abbot. Perhaps he put poison —"

Tynan stopped her before she could finish. "He wouldn't dare." He exhaled deeply. "Anyway, if there had been poison in that whiskey, you wouldn't be talking to me now. You'd be as dead as the rest of these poor bastards. As it is, you're merely drunk."

"Drunk?" Nara did her best to focus, wishing devoutly that Tynan's image would stop multiplying at random. "If this is how drunk feels, sir, I cannot fathom why anyone would ever touch a drop of whiskey." She scowled at him. "Obviously, you speak from experience." Why was it so difficult to express herself?

"Oh, aye, I've been drunk a time or two, but never from anything so fine as whiskey." Tynan looked at the bottle, then took a swallow. "Mmm. Smooth, but potent. Better than what my father used to make." A smug smile shaped his mouth. "The abbot must have been frightened, indeed, to offer his private stock."

He glanced at Nara. "Perhaps I spoke too soon when I said you were drunk." Tynan studied her more closely. "Can you feel your lips?"

She bit down gingerly on her lower lip, then nodded.

"Hmmm." Judging from Tynan's expression, Nara suspected he was enjoying her predicament. He actually had the gall to grin. "I do believe you've moved beyond drunk to 'sin's repentance,' as my father used to call it."

He chuckled, his face easing. "By Odin, it's been a long time since I thought about that. My father wasn't in his cups too often, but whenever he was, none of us dared get near him until he'd plunged his head into the trough and taken a long walk."

Miserable though she was, Nara realized this was the first time Tynan had ever spoken of his family. "You were fond of him. I can hear it in your voice."

"Aye." Tynan removed his sword and propped it within easy reach. "But that was another life, not this one." He lay down beside her. "Go back to sleep, Nara. You'll feel better when you wake."

Though she was hardly fit to meet anyone, much less her infamous grandfather, Nara felt compelled to ask, "You're not taking me to my grandfather right away?"

"He isn't there," Tynan stated simply.

His casual tone and demeanor took Nara by surprise. If she hadn't known better, she would have sworn he was relieved.

"We missed him by a week," Tynan continued. "Laird Alexander is held prisoner by the king, and Donald Balloch has rallied the barons to free him. They'll meet at Carna, then challenge Mar at Inverlochy. I only hope we can reach him before the battle."

Nara rolled onto her back and stared up at the ancient stone ceiling. War. So that was why he didn't mind. *Seanmhair* had been right about men. "You want to fight."

"For Laird Alexander?" Tynan paused. "Aye, and I have good reason." He exhaled. "Nothing like a battle to clear a man's mind." He shifted the pouch beneath his head. "But I need to find your grandfather before the conflict. He can do me little good dead."

That, too, was unexpected. "I should think you'd want him dead," she ventured, "after he put you in chains and treated you like a slave."

"We must reach him while he's still alive," Tynan answered grimly. "We *must.*"

Nara closed her eyes, too ill to address the unexplained intensity in Tynan's statement. She shifted the conversation to a safer topic. "How far is it to Inverlochy?"

"As far as we have come from the Isle of Mist. Clear down to where Loch Eil meets Loch Linnhe."

Half the length of Scotland! Nara groaned. "Another week of walking."

Though her eyes were closed, she could have sworn Tynan was smiling when he said, "There will be no more walking for us. But I trow, you'll wish you were afoot a hundred times before this next night is done."

Nara's eyes flew open. "And what, sir, do you mean by that?" She heard an eerie shuffle near the opening to the crypt, then a gruff snort.

Tynan turned his back to her. "I've bought us a stallion. We ride."

"A stallion?" Nara forgot all about her headache and the fact that she and Tynan now shared a bier where only the day before some nameless couple's bones had rested. "Stallions are proof against witches, I know, but I can't ride a stallion, Tynan." They might be safe from the Witch's magic on such a beast, but Nara had often heard that stallions were powerful, unpredictable animals. Far too dangerous for novices. "I've never ridden a horse in my life," she confessed.

"You'll have to learn in a hurry, then, won't you?" Tynan

yawned loudly, stretched, then punched at the pouch beneath his head. "Now go to sleep, Nara. If I weren't so weary, I'd set out this moment. As it is, we could both use a few hours' sleep."

Above them, the horse snorted again.

She'd never get to sleep with that animal thumping about overhead. "Aren't you afraid someone will steal him?" she whispered.

Tynan sat up and glared at her. "I hid him well in what's left of the sacristy. Now go to sleep." He lay back down facing her and drew her into the heat of his embrace. "There will be precious little rest along the way, so try to enjoy it while you can."

Enjoy it? They were in a crypt! And Nara was hardly looking forward to mounting a huge, dangerous beast and riding behind Tynan half the length of Scotland.

Why couldn't things ever get simpler? she wondered.

That night after sunset, Nara got her first look at the destrier who was to bear them to Inverlochy. She hadn't seen many horses in her life, but this particular animal had to be one of the ugliest ever created. His muzzle was covered by the feed bag, but the rest of his coloring was a muddied assortment of gray, brown, and brindle. And his stance was hardly heroic. "He seems a bit swaybacked," she murmured. Still, she tried to reserve judgment. "Do you know his name?"

Tynan nodded. "Horrible."

"That's his name?" Nara turned wide eyes to her husband. "Did you know it before you bought him?" A disturbing suspicion occurred to her. "You did buy him, didn't you?"

Tynan smiled a wicked, winsome smile. "Aye, I bought him. And I knew his name when I made the bargain."

He approached the animal and stroked its mottled neck.

"Good evening to you, Horrible." Tynan untied the now-empty feedbag and stowed it away. "I know good horse-flesh, Nara. Horrible will suit us nicely. He's strong, reasonably young, and steady. If he were handsome, too, we'd not have been able to afford him." He tied the pouch to the bundle of provisions, then slung them over Horrible's neck. "We'd better hurry. I want to find our way to the road before those clouds roll in." Tynan took the reins, then with one graceful motion heaved himself atop the huge beast.

Nara marveled afresh that a man of his size could be so sure and swift in his movements.

Tynan extended his hand to her. "Put your left foot atop mine and give me your left hand. When I pull you up, settle yourself astride behind me. Then hold on tight."

Nara did as he instructed her, but it took several tries before she managed to position herself behind Tynan. At last she wrapped her arms around Tynan's waist and held on for dear life.

"Not quite so tight," he cautioned in a slightly strangled voice. When she eased her grip, he reverted to his normal tone. "That's better. We're off, then."

Tynan had been right when he'd predicted that she would long for the comfort of walking. Three hours after they set out, they had found the road south, but Nara hurt all over. Her arms were numb, her legs ached with every step of the horse's gait, and her back felt as if it would snap any moment.

"Don't worry," Tynan assured her as if he had read her mind. "You'll get used to it after a day or two."

"A day or two?" Silent tears escaped Nara's eyes. "I'm not certain I'll last that long."

"You'll last, Nara. You'll last."

Nara didn't know how he could be so sure.

# *Chapter XIV*

Evening was upon them three days later when Tynan directed Horrible toward the forest looming ahead. Nara grew apprehensive when she saw the other campfires flickering along its edges in the distance, but Tynan remained relaxed. His body gave off none of the subtle signals that told her there was danger. Still, she was worried.

Keeping a safe distance from the other camps, Tynan guided Horrible to a small meadow at the edge of the forest. When they reached a patch of sweet grass alongside a clear-flowing stream, he reined Horrible to a halt. "We'll make camp here for the night."

Tynan dropped their supplies onto the grass, then offered Nara his arm to help her down first. She gladly took it and slid to her feet, rejoicing that one more day of torture was at an end. "Thanks be to God."

Grateful as she was to set foot on solid ground, she could scarcely stand. After three relentless days on horseback, her rear end felt as if she'd been paddled soundly with a breadboard. She gingerly massaged her aching buttocks as she turned to Tynan. "You said I'd be used to this by now."

"I thought you would." He dismounted with his own subtle grunt of relief. His golden eyes weary, he uncinched the girth and removed Horrible's worn saddle.

It seemed so peaceful here. All around them, summer insects sang their twilight songs, but Nara knew better than to relax completely. She had seen the other campfires. Campfires meant strangers, and strangers meant peril.

She tried to overcome her disquiet with conversation. "I wonder how long it *will* take to grow accustomed to riding." She granted Tynan a rueful smile. "If I could only get used to it, traveling by horseback would be pleasant. I like sitting up high; one can see so much more."

Such scenery she had taken in from her perch! They had headed South toward Sgurr Mor until they reached Loch Glascarnoch, then followed the Black Water through twisting valleys strewn with heather. Beyond Loch Garve, Nara had caught a glimpse of Castle Leod, but Tynan had given it wide berth.

After that, he'd avoided the more populous routes alongside the rivers, opting instead to travel overland by way of Glen Convinth to the shores of Loch Ness. There, he'd told such convincing bedtime stories of fabled monsters lurking in the deeps that she'd badgered him until he moved their camp fully a mile away from the shoreline.

They had passed the southern end of that vast, narrow lake just this morning, and none too soon, by Nara's reckoning. Her life was complicated enough without *more* monsters; judging from Tynan's stories, Lady Margaret and Laird Cullum were monsters enough for anyone.

"How much farther is it to Inverlochy?" she asked as she had every night.

"Another day's ride," Tynan said mechanically. He'd given up chiding her for her impatience. "Maybe two." He unwrapped his axe and gingerly bent to lay it alongside the saddle.

Was it her imagination, or was he moving slower than usual?

Nara made a show of checking their supplies, all the while

studying Tynan from the corner of her eye. He definitely had difficulty squatting or rising. And instead of his usual straight stance, his legs looked as if he'd been strapped to a barrel. Whenever he thought she wasn't looking, he kneaded his lower back.

Nara couldn't resist saying, "Why, you're just as sore as I am, aren't you?"

Tynan frowned, patently annoyed that she had detected any weakness on his part. "Don't be ridiculous." He snatched up double handfuls of long grass and used them to rub down Horrible's flanks and legs. "Riding is second nature to me. I exercised horses every day at Eilean d'Ór."

Nara knew she should let the matter rest, but she couldn't resist goading him just a bit. "Aye. But that was . . . what? Two years ago? I'll marry, you haven't ridden since." It was wicked of her, but just knowing that his legs and backside were sore as hers made Nara's own discomfort more bearable.

Tynan shot her a baleful look and pointed a shock of grass toward their sole cooking vessel. "Stop your prattling, woman, and fetch us some water."

"Very well." She picked up the pot and took a few steps toward the stream. But when Tynan turned his back, she pivoted and tiptoed toward him.

He was sore, too, and she knew how to prove it. Quiet as a fog, she crept close enough to slip her hand between his legs and give the corded muscle of one inner thigh a playful pinch.

Tynan's response was not the simple "Ouch!" she'd expected.

Instead, he reacted on instinct. Quick as lightning, he grasped her wrist and jerked her forward. Before she could cry out, he had thrown himself atop her, pinning her down and knocking the wind from her. She felt something sharp

212

wedged solidly against the soft flesh below her ribs.

"Tynan!" she managed to gasp out. "It's me, Nara." Her neck bulged from the crushing force of his weight atop her, and she was beginning to see sparkles at the edge of her vision. She spent what little breath she had left on a strangled, "Get off . . ."

Tynan's whole body shook with desperate energy. His breath heaved hot and ragged in her ear, and she could feel his rapid heartbeat pounding against her back. Nara was all too aware of his inner struggle as he forced himself back from the unthinking, overwhelming urge to kill or be killed.

At long last he let out a heavy breath and rolled off her. "*Never* creep up behind me like that again," he managed hoarsely. "I might have killed you."

Her own heart thumping wildly, Nara scrambled a safe distance away. How easily she had awakened the lethal beast within him! "I was jesting, Tynan. I only meant to tease you."

He sat up and leaned forward, his arms stretched out atop his knees, hands limp. Tynan turned hollow eyes to Nara. "This is hardly the time or the place for such a 'jest,' Nara. When I think what almost happened . . ."

One look at the turmoil in his eyes was enough to shame her. He was obviously distraught at having come so close to killing her.

"I'm sorry," she offered, genuinely contrite. "It was very foolish of me." Nara was sure Tynan cared for her in his own way — though she doubted he would admit it, even to himself. But she had no illusions about why the near miss had upset him so. Her death would have cost him the chance to reclaim the lands her grandfather had stolen from him. That was behind the haunted look he now fixed on her.

She sighed, suddenly feeling very much alone.

Then Tynan dropped his head, closing his eyes. The

simple gesture communicated such despair that she forgot her own troubles.

He was alone, too. Far more alone than she would ever be.

For though the miles might separate them now, *Seanmhair*'s love, and Aunt Keriam's, were as much a part of Nara as the blood within her veins. Nothing could take that from her.

But Tynan . . .

Though she craved warmth and fellowship, Tynan's isolation was of his own choosing.

Nara didn't have to know the details of his past to see that he had survived her grandfather's cruelties by putting his soul to sleep.

If only she could revive it. But how?

*Seanmhair* had told her often enough, *Give what you wish to receive, and in God's good time, it will be given back to you.*

How could she expect tenderness from Tynan, or even friendship? He'd lived too long without either.

But Nara could offer him both. And in time, perhaps he could give them back to her.

She closed the distance between them and settled next to him on the grass. "I meant no harm, Tynan. Truly." Nara bent her forehead against his knee. "After you told me what my grandfather had done to you, I vowed never to cause your dignity further injury. Now I've done just that. Can you forgive me?"

She felt his palm smooth across the crown of her head. "It is not you who should ask pardon, Nara, but I. If I had thrust my dagger any harder —"

"But you didn't." She ached to put her arms around him and comfort him but did not dare. Instead, she stroked the golden curls that covered his muscular calf. His skin gave off the scent of horseflesh and man and a sharp, lingering note of

214

the battle-surge her misguided prank had caused.

The quiet communion of that moment was broken by the sound of a twig snapping at the edge of the forest.

"Get down!" Tynan whispered abruptly, shoving her into the grass as he rose to a crouch. Nara stayed low, but looked up to see that he had pivoted toward the darkening forest, his sword at the ready. "Who goes there?" he called. "Speak now, or you'll not live to speak again."

Thirty yards away the undergrowth rustled, causing the skin on Nara's arms and neck to pebble in alarm.

A gruff, male voice responded irreverently, "Feadain Chisolm. Who wants to know?"

Tynan's defensive crouch eased abruptly. Nara had never seen him let down his guard so readily. She heard him ask in an oddly incredulous tone, "Any kin to Feadain Chisolm, grandson of Balcor MacGregor?"

"That's me. What of it?"

"It cannot be," Tynan countered, straightening to his full height. "Feadain Chisolm is dead."

"Not the last time I looked," the hidden stranger retorted. The bushes rustled again. "By God, is that you, Mac-Dougald?"

To Nara's amazement, Tynan lowered the tip of his sword to the grass and grasped its inverted hilt. The gesture placed him at the mercy of the unseen intruder. Obviously, he knew the man and trusted him not to attack, but Tynan's face remained drawn. "Show yourself, man."

A gray-haired old warrior — almost as large as Tynan himself — emerged from the edge of the forest. "Boil me head fer a turnip if it isn't you, MacDougald," the stranger exclaimed. "We thought ye were slain in the massacre!" He strode forward a few steps, then stopped in his tracks. "Ye *were* slain, and all yer kith." Chisolm took a halting pace backward. "Are ye a fetch, then?"

"Nay. No fetch," Tynan breathed. "Feadain, it *is* you."

Nara could see the muscles working in his throat, but Tynan's face gave away nothing.

"It's Tynan, Feadain. Tynan, your kinsman." He said it like a dying man reaching toward heaven.

"But Tynan crossed over with the others!" The old man approached with caution, but he did lower his sword. When he got close enough for a good look, he bellowed, "Lay me low for a Sassenach if it isn't you, fer sure! Aye, an' 'tis, the very image of yer father, only bigger, if that's possible!" He bounded up to Tynan, caught him in a bear hug that lifted the younger man clear off his feet, and pounded his back as he spun him around. "It's a miracle! A hair-raisin', drink-me-dead miracle! Where have ye been keepin' yerself these past twenty years, lad? If only we'd known . . ."

Nara would never have believed that Tynan would allow himself to be whirled about like a rag doll, but to her amazement, he did just that, his face bearing the stunned expression of an ox that had taken a blow between the eyes.

Breathless from the effort of lifting a man Tynan's size, Feadain Chisolm stopped turning, dropped Tynan to his feet, then thrust his long-lost friend to arm's length. "Faith, but yer a welcome sight for these old eyes. Wait until me old Mary gets a peek at you. She'll faint dead away."

He let out a malicious chuckle. "She always did have a bit of a crush on yer father, ye know. I was fair jealous, I'll confess, but yer father never so much as looked at another woman besides yer mother."

"Feadain. It's really you." Tynan cupped his hands on either side of the old man's head and gazed at him as if he feared the grizzled warrior would evaporate into the evening mist any minute.

Nara cleared her throat, hoping for an introduction. But Tynan remained oblivious to everything around him. Everything but Feadain.

Taking advantage of the lull in conversation, she approached the two men and curtsied. "Pray, sir, forgive my husband's bad manners. Allow me to present myself. I am Tynan's wife, Nara."

Feadain put his arm around Tynan's shoulder and looked her up and down, a grin of approval splitting his beard. "By Saint Columba, boy, but she's a beauty." He gave Tynan's back an affectionate clout, then acknowledged Nara with a nod. "Who are yer people, then, good lady?"

Tynan's head shook in warning even as Nara said, "My mother was of the Dougald line, but my father was of the Kays."

She might just as well have announced that she had the Black Death.

Feadain's boisterous good humor disappeared, replaced by a cold, hard glare of outrage. He turned a piercing stare on Tynan.

The next few seconds of silence seemed endless, but at last Feadain spoke. "Come, lad. We must converse." He shot Nara a look of scalding hatred. "In private." Without so much as a word to her, he drew Tynan back toward the forest.

Bewildered, Nara watched the two men walk away and stop just short of the trees. She could hear Feadain's voice rising in anger, but he was too far for her to make out the actual words. He gestured heatedly, pointing in her direction as he spoke.

For the longest time, Tynan said nothing. He merely stood there, poised and silent, with his sword once more at the ready. Then he murmured something and granted Chisolm a nod of insulting brevity.

The two parted without amenities.

Tynan did not look at her when he returned to their camp. "I asked you to fetch water, Nara. Do it." He slid his sword into place along his back, then resumed rubbing the day's toll from Horrible's coat. "No fire tonight. Bread and cheese will be enough."

Wondering what he was hiding behind his grim expression, Nara almost wished she still had the Sight. But she did not need the Sight to know that something was very wrong — something to do with Tynan and Feadain Chisolm.

"Aye, my lord husband," she responded to Tynan's abrupt order. "I shall fetch the water." If only she could fetch the truth from him as easily.

They ate their meal in strained silence. Tynan stared off absently at the forest or the ground. Not once did he meet Nara's eyes. She sensed something huge and terrible going on inside him but knew better than to try to pry it out of him.

Half an hour later, as she wrapped up what little was left of the hard, stale bread and cheese, Nara heard the distant jingle of harnesses and the creak of an approaching wagon. "Tynan," she said, trying not to betray the surge of fear she felt, "someone's coming."

Tynan listened intently. "Grab the provisions. Quickly," he instructed. Luckily, the moon had not yet risen. He gathered his weapons, then seized Horrible's reins and led the horse toward the forest. "Follow me, Nara."

As quickly as she could, Nara stuffed the food into the bundle bearing the remainder of their dwindling supplies, then hastened after him into the same clump of underbrush that had concealed Feadain. Once hidden, they waited and watched as a torchlit caravan of colorfully dressed strangers rolled into their campsite.

"Romanies," Tynan murmured ominously.

218

Nara counted more than a dozen torches illuminating a ragtag company of men, women, and children who herded a collection of goats, sheep, and even a few pigs alongside six elaborately painted wagons.

As the wagons drew into a rough circle, raucous laughter carried across the meadow. Soon a fire was lit at the center of their camp, giving Nara a better look at the tattered but colorfully dressed strangers.

Despite their ragged clothing, she saw constant flashes of gold and silver reflected in the firelight. Brightly polished earrings adorned the men who set up camp. Their women moved among them with calculated ease, coins on their foreheads, bracelets and anklets tinkling.

Then Nara heard the clear, soulful sound of a female voice singing sadly in an unknown tongue. A lute joined the melancholy tune, then a fiddle, then several stringed instruments she did not recognize. One by one, the Romany nomads settled by the campfire to listen.

Though she could not understand their language, the melody pulled at Nara's heart. When the last note faded into silence, there were tears in her eyes. But the next piece was loud and lively, made even more so by the addition of tambourines and pounding drums. Soon the whole company was dancing wildly, laughing, and singing.

These dark-skinned wanderers seemed so carefree. But *Seanmhair* had spoken of the Romany nomads and how they moved from town to town, never welcome anywhere because of their evil magic and thieving ways.

*Seanmhair* had said the Romanies were the remnant of Israel, condemned to eternal wandering for their rejection of the Messiah, but Aunt Keriam dismissed such a notion, claiming that the wanderers came from the heathen peoples of India, a land far beyond even Jerusalem.

Nara had thought it tragic to live as permanent aliens with no home, no roots, but these people seemed anything but sad. They might be outcasts, yet they laughed and sang with gusto. Even at a distance, their merriment lifted her spirits.

"Come," Tynan said curtly. "We must leave."

"Can't we stay a little longer?" she asked, reluctant to leave the distant celebration. "I love to listen to their music."

"We left tracks, Nara. One of them is bound to find them soon. We must go, while they're distracted."

As usual, he was right. "Very well." She stood, but something indefinable drew her gaze back to the camp, where an unmistakable silhouette near the edge of the firelight caught her eye. "Tynan!" she whispered. "Look." She grasped Tynan's arm and turned him back toward the camp.

"What?" He jerked free of her as if her very touch contaminated him.

"See?" She pointed to the wagon farthest from the campfire. "Over there."

There was no mistaking that distinctive silhouette or the odd, jerking hop of the tall, thin figure's "dance."

"It's Tim!" Nara breathed. Despite the length of rope that tethered him by the neck to the wagon, he was moved by the music, too.

"Poor Tim," she murmured, her throat tight with sympathy. "They have him bound, just like in the asylum."

Tynan's eyes narrowed. "One of the monks must have sold him to the Romanies." He said it almost as if he were talking to himself, not her.

"Why would they buy him?" Nara frowned up at him. "What good would Tim do anyone? He cannot work."

"No," Tynan said grimly, "but he could earn a coin or two as a curiosity."

Nara felt physically ill at the thought of Timothy's being

put on display as a freak. "Oh, Tynan. We must rescue him."

"Rescue him?" Tynan fastened a hard look on her. "Are you mad? There are thirty Romanies in that camp, every one of them — including the children — ready and willing to slip a poisoned dagger into anyone stupid enough to go there uninvited." He shook his head. "Only a fool would try something like that, and I'm no fool."

"I see." Nara paused to consider. Then she nodded. "Never mind, then. I'll do it myself." She took a step toward the undergrowth that bordered the forest.

Tynan caught her arm. "You are *not* going into that camp."

"Oh, yes, I am." Nara looked up at him with absolute assurance. "Don't you see, Tynan? This is no random coincidence. We allowed Timothy to fall into evil circumstances after God granted him into our care." She placed her hand over his, prompting him to snatch his away.

Why wouldn't he let her touch him?

"You cannot imagine the burden of guilt I have borne since that night in the abbey," she confessed. Stung by Tynan's rejection, Nara's eyes welled with tears, but she knew he would see her tears as a sign of weakness, so she held them back. "This may be our only chance to redeem him. Please, Tynan. If you do not save him, I must."

Growing darkness made it difficult to read the subtle play of emotion across Tynan's features, but after a lengthy pause, he spat out, "Damn it, woman, you are without a doubt the most disobedient, manipulative wench I have ever had the misfortune to meet, much less marry." To her dismay, he seemed to mean every word. "Purgatory. That's what this is. My sins have caught up with me at last, and you, madam, are the penance."

It didn't sound like a surrender, but Nara knew it was as

close to one as she would ever get from Tynan. "I thought you didn't believe in such things as purgatory," she said gravely.

"I didn't," he retorted, "until you came into my life and convinced me there was a price to be paid for one's sins."

Nara recoiled at the venom in his voice, but she did not allow it to intimidate her. "You'll go get Tim, then?"

"Why not?" he said with sarcasm. "The more, the merrier. Why settle for purgatory when I can have hell itself?"

"Tynan," Nara chided mildly. "Tim has nothing to do with hell, and you know it. He's an angel, with a soul as pure as a babe's."

Tynan waggled his sword in her direction, whispering hotly, "I'll do this, but know one thing: If anything goes wrong, it's on your head."

It was as good as a curse.

Nara crossed herself. "Nothing will happen to you, Tynan," she said with absolute conviction.

"You seem awfully sure of that."

"I am," she responded. "God never punishes us for doing His will."

"The martyrs might have something to say about that," Tynan snapped, remembering his own brothers and sisters, and his mother. They had done nothing wrong, yet God had not protected them.

His own soul withered at Nara's naive expression of faith. She would learn, soon enough, how God protected the innocent. "God didn't protect Timothy from the asylum, did He? Or from the Romanies. What makes you think He'll protect me now?"

"He's been protecting both of us for a long, long time, Tynan," she said with the calm assurance of a seer. "He will not abandon either one of us."

"If the past twenty years are any example of His protection, madam, then you can have it. I'd rather take my chances."

Nara's eyes lost focus. "God has not taken His hand from you, Tynan. You are the Dark Deliverer, the remnant who shall bring life from death."

Tynan's skin pebbled as if a cold wind had blown down his back. The riddle. How could he have forgotten? His brain echoed with the memory of Nara's voice chanting:

> *I call the remnant at the root's direction.*
> *Seed of love from hate in vengeance sworn.*
> *Blood oath broken by a dark reflection*
> *Buried with the damask rose's thorn.*
> *Witch who is no witch works her protection;*
> *Death from life and life from death is born.*

The Isle of Mist had to be the "witch who is no witch."

Now Nara had revealed that he himself was the remnant. If that was true, then the root must be Laird Cullum.

Of course. Laird Cullum's pledge had prompted Tynan to find Nara. These past two years, he *had* been acting at "the root's direction."

Little by little, the riddle was playing itself out. But Tynan still had no idea what the dark reflection and the damask rose's thorn represented, or what the last line signified.

Even in the silvered darkness, he could see that Nara's eyes remained as blank as her expression. "Whose death shall bring life, Nara? Is it yours?" he asked.

If she said yes, perhaps he could put an end to the dread and guilt that ate at the deepest, most vulnerable part of him whenever he thought of his dreadful vow to kill her in front of her grandfather.

"What?" she asked vacantly. Her eyes clearing, Nara sank

to the ground. She shook her head to dispel the trance that had overtaken her. "Goodness. I've gone all lightheaded. Should have eaten more at supper." She looked up at Tynan. "You needn't look so worried. I'm fine. Really."

Tynan turned to Horrible. Maybe it was his death, not hers, to which the riddle alluded. If so, he hoped the Romanies *would* kill him. But to what new hell would he awaken then?

He handed Nara the reins and the axe. "Keep a sharp eye out. If anything happens to me, find Donald Balloch. Your grandfather will be with him." He pointed to the southwest. "Inverlochy is that way, but take care to avoid strangers."

"Nothing's going to happen to you, Tynan," she repeated, her face radiating an assurance he wished he could share.

"Blast it, Nara," he whispered tightly, "swear that you will obey me in this, at least."

"If it comes to that, of course I shall obey you," she said, "but it won't come to that."

In spite of himself, Tynan felt a grudging admiration. For him, the world was painted in shades of gray, but Nara saw everything in black and white. She seemed so certain of everything. Arguing with her was like trying to move a sailboat using only the force of his own breath. In the end, he was completely worn out, and the boat remained right where it had always been.

How did she *do* that?

He scowled at her and whispered, "Remember, wait here unless I'm hurt or captured."

"You won't be hurt, Tynan," she reiterated, "or captured."

Like all women, she had to have the last word. Tynan gave up.

Better to risk the Romanies' poisoned blades than stay here and put up with this nonsense. Tynan crept along behind the underbrush until he was even with the wagon to which Timothy was tied.

He waited to approach the wagon until the Romanies struck up a particularly lively tune. Fortunately, the women had piled a number of boxes and supplies between the wagon and the campfire, leaving the undercarriage in shadow. But Tynan still felt dangerously exposed as he crawled beneath the axles to the corner where Timothy stood.

Just when Tynan was about to make his move, the howl of a wolf rang out over the music. In seconds, the camp fell silent.

No singing. No dancing. No rustle of leaves in the wind. No insects. No flutter of night birds. Only the hiss and pop of the campfire.

Tynan lay flattened beneath the wagon, his back dampened by a clammy film of alarm.

Again, the haunting call of the wolf sounded, more distant this time.

Damn that wolf! Had it followed them all the way from the Isle of Mist?

Nonsense, he told himself. It couldn't possibly be the same wolf.

He lay there, ready to defend himself, the sound of his breathing loud in his own ears. Then a single drum took up the rhythm the Romanies had abandoned. A tambourine joined in. Then a fiddle. Then another drum. Slowly but surely, the Romanies reclaimed their celebration.

Oblivious to everything but the music, Timothy chirped tunelessly and hopped his own awkward dance as he watched the festivities. He never even noticed when Tynan cut the rope free of the wagon.

At least the Romanies had allowed Timothy a decent length of tether. Tynan crawled backward the way he had come, carefully handing the cut end of the rope past each wheel until he reached the corner farthest from the campfire. Then he crept out from underneath the wagon and crouched beside the rear wheel.

So far, so good. The Romanies were still caught up in their dancing and singing.

With agonizing slowness, he began to draw Timothy back toward him.

As he had hoped, Timothy was too interested in the dancing to realize what was happening. He tugged occasionally at the increased tension on the loop around his neck, but only when he could no longer see the dancers did he turn to see Tynan.

"Tynan!" he shrieked over the music and clamor, loud enough to cause Tynan to wince. He gestured for silence, but knew better than to hope Tim would oblige.

A wide, lopsided grin on his face, Tim loped over and enveloped his rescuer in an awkward embrace.

Tynan clamped a hand over Tim's mouth and suppressed a gag. He'd forgotten just how bad Timothy smelled when he'd been neglected.

"Quiet, Tim," he whispered directly into Tim's ear. "I'm taking you to Nara, but we must be quiet, or the bad men will catch us and tie you up again." He waited until Tim fell silent to pull him toward the forest.

Tim tried to keep up but succeeded only in getting tangled in his own feet and falling down.

Tynan grabbed the reeking man under the arms and dragged him backward for a few yards before deciding they'd never get through the bushes that way without attracting attention. Loath to throw Tim over his shoulder because of the stench, he instead scooped him into his arms and carried him like the child Tim really was.

Tim's scrawny legs and arms dangled every which way, but Tynan was able to cover the remaining distance to the forest quickly, for despite his height, Tim hardly weighed more than Nara. Soon they were beyond the underbrush and well on their way back to Nara's hiding place.

It never occurred to Tynan what a ludicrous sight he and Timothy made until Nara saw them coming and exploded into muffled laughter.

To his horror, Tynan felt his face flush with embarrassment. He clamped his mouth into a grim line and brushed past her.

Still struggling to stifle her laughter, Nara waved her hand and winced at the stench that followed in Tim's wake.

With one powerful heave, Tynan placed Tim astride their mount. Then he turned and grasped Nara's waist from behind. "You'll have to ride with him to keep him from falling off," he whispered. That would stop her laughing, for sure. "Hold on to him." Nara gagged when he set her behind Tim, but she did as Tynan instructed.

Tynan took up the reins and led Horrible in the direction of Feadain's camp.

Feadain would not turn them away, despite Nara's unwelcome presence. Tynan knew he could rely on the old warrior's loyalty to his father.

Alert to any sound that might betray an attack, Tynan led them deeper and deeper into the forest. For once, Timothy remained silent. Feadain had said his camp was at the heart of the wood.

Just thinking about Feadain renewed the hollow feeling in Tynan's stomach. All these years, he'd thought that Laird Cullum had killed every last member of his father's sept, including Feadain. It had been quite a shock to find the old warrior alive.

Tynan had hardly been able to swallow a bite of dinner for thinking about it.

He remembered Feadain well. Tynan couldn't have been more than six when Feadain had come to Tynan's father seeking permission to marry Cousin Mary. Since she was an orphan, it fell to Tynan's father as chieftain to settle a marriage for his cousin.

Tynan could still remember the daring tales of battle the huge warrior had spun to impress his father. After a dozen tales and as many whiskeys, Tynan's father had not only granted Feadain's suit, but had also invited the warrior to pledge his sword to Mary's sept.

Tynan had never been sure if it was the whiskey or his father's own battle stories that had prompted Feadain to accept, but accept he did, and afterward, the Chisolms were frequent guests at the chieftain's hearth. Duncan, their first-born, had idolized Tynan, following him around like a puppy.

Duncan was alive.

Tynan could scarcely take it in.

And Cousin Mary was alive, and all her children. Feadain had revealed that they'd been away visiting kinsmen in Easter Ross when the massacre was unleashed.

And there were others, Feadain had said. Some had managed to escape into the night. Others had evaded the attackers by hiding in secret places beneath their burning homes. There weren't many — only eight or nine families — but they had found each other after the slaughter and fled to the hills, then intercepted Feadain on his return. He had led them southeast to sanctuary in these woods.

According to Feadain, though, none of the survivors had forgotten Laird Cullum's treachery. Even now every man and woman burned with hatred, craving revenge and passing their hatred on to their children.

All these years, Tynan had believed Laird Cullum's lies. Why?

His steps faltered on the forest path, but he quickly regained his balance.

Why hadn't he questioned it when they'd told him everyone else was dead?

If only he'd known . . . he never would have given up trying to escape, no matter how long Laird Cullum kept him in chains. He'd have gotten away, somehow, and found his way back to his people.

Devan's words came back to him: *There are things I haven't told ye . . .*

Had the old man known? Tynan's heart contracted at the thought.

All these years, he'd felt so alone. And his kinsmen had been there, alive, thinking *he* was dead.

The irony of it pierced him to the core, resurrecting the pain and grief and hatred as fresh as it had been twenty years ago. Laird Cullum had to have known there were survivors, yet he had continued to torment Tynan with the lie that he was alone.

And that had been the cruelest torment of all. Denied by Laird Alexander of the right to murder Tynan, Laird Cullum had been forced to settle for maintaining the slow torture of loneliness, along with all the endless humiliations he'd heaped on Tynan.

No punishment could be too harsh for such calculated abominations.

Walking now through the darkened forest, Tynan clad his heart in steel. He knew how to make Laird Cullum suffer for his crimes. The question was, how to take revenge and survive.

Until tonight, he had counted his own death a fair exchange for what he planned to do. But now he reconsidered. The sept was there, his for the asking. Feadain had told him so.

Except for Nara.

Feadain had made it clear the survivors would never tolerate Laird Cullum's own granddaughter in their midst. But she would be gone soon enough.

A spark of remorse flared deep within him at the thought of killing her, but Tynan snuffed it out.

Instead, he resolved to find some way to have his revenge and walk away.

For the first time in his adult life, Tynan said a silent prayer for help and meant it, but his prayer wasn't lifted toward heaven. It was offered to the darkness that surrounded him, for he belonged to the darkness now, more than he ever had.

# Chapter XV

Barely able to make out the narrow path before them, Tynan kept his ears and eyes wide open. Horrible's every step crunched like thunder on the dried leaves carpeting the forest floor. Each snap of a twig seemed loud as the crack of a whip.

He glanced up through the canopy of ancient oaks overhead and saw a few bright stars in the silvered night sky. Not so much as a cloud, blast it. This was one time he'd have given his left thumb for rain.

The distant song of a night bird echoed through the wood, prompting Tynan to halt and stop Horrible alongside him. The birdcall might have been genuine, but then again, it might have been a signal.

He glanced up at Nara, motioning her to silence, and saw that Tim had fallen asleep against her. Though she had to be exhausted herself, Nara patiently held her lanky charge around his middle, his head tipped back on her shoulder and his gangly arms and legs limp.

An irrational stab of jealousy pierced Tynan.

Now, why in blue blazes should he feel jealous? Tim, for all his size, loved Nara purely, the way a child loves his mother. There was nothing to be jealous of . . . unless it was the easy way Tim cuddled next to her. Or Nara's fierce protectiveness.

Ridiculous, even thinking about it.

Tynan turned his attention to the subtle sounds of the

forest. The normal chorus of insects hummed in every direction, reassuring him that for the moment, at least, they were safe. Then, just above him, the flutter of an unseen owl stood the hairs on the back of his neck aright.

A true Highlander, he distrusted any forest, for though he wasn't superstitious, only a fool would ignore the evil spirits that were known to lurk in such overgrown, sunless places as this.

Give him the vast bleakness of the Highlands any day, where a man could see his enemy coming. Here, any one of the myriad darkened tree trunks might be hiding a predator, human or otherwise.

A hundred tense, wary paces passed before he caught sight of a golden glimmer through the undergrowth ahead.

The steady glow of a bonfire beckoned him to the heart of the woodland.

Feadain's camp. It had to be.

He signaled once more for Nara to keep quiet, then proceeded with renewed caution. When they reached a wild privet just beyond the amber circle of firelight, he halted and peered through the branches. Feadain's directions had led him straight to this large clearing ringed by almost a dozen crude shelters and bordered on the south by a narrow stream.

The encampment hardly seemed temporary. Though the hovels were made of peat, sod, branches, and thatch, they looked quite sturdy. Tynan counted fifteen adults going about the business of living by the light of the campfire, and almost twice as many children. It wasn't easy to tally the children, for they darted in and out of the shadows, chasing each other and laughing while their parents spun, carved, cooked, and mended.

Tynan had seen many encampments and more than a few villages in the past two years, but most of those settlements —

temporary or permanent — had closed up tight and retired by sunset. This camp was different. Its occupants hardly seemed ready for bed.

Had they become creatures of the night, he wondered, like so many of the other elusive, hunted animals of the forest?

"Wait here," he whispered to Nara. "I want to make certain it's safe before I let them know you're with me."

Sword drawn, he worked his way with agonizing care to the other side of the camp. Just as he was about to come forward, the howl of a wolf — right behind him — prompted Tynan to crouch low and pivot, searching the darkness. That howl had been far too close for comfort, and it hadn't lasted long enough to cover the sound of Horrible's brief, terrified whinny.

Nara! She and Tim were defenseless. Tynan had to act quickly.

He watched as several of the women cried out and ran to gather in their children, while two others fell to their knees in frightened prayer.

Tynan dared not delay coming forward, even though the camp's occupants were sure to see the wolf's howl as an evil omen.

He signaled his presence with the distinctive whistle Feadain had taught him. The men, whose attention had already been drawn in his direction by the wolf, took a decidedly defensive stance, the common implements of everyday life now held ready to use as weapons. Tynan decided to put away his own sword before stepping forward.

Every muscle tense, he moved with deliberate slowness into the firelight, his empty hands raised to show he held no weapon. "Stand easy," he said to the frightened strangers. "I mean you no harm."

A woman ran for one of the largest huts as the men regarded Tynan with suspicion.

Reasonably certain that the occupants of the camp possessed neither the means nor the mind to do them harm, Tynan backed toward Nara's hiding place, every eye following him. "Nara! Are you all right?"

"Aye. We're fine." Her answer sent a fresh wave of alarm through the woodsmen.

"My wife is with me," Tynan hastened to explain, "and a foundling. They're unarmed."

He motioned for Nara to come forward. "It's all right. You can come out now." He heard her cluck to Horrible, then the horse ambled into the firelight. Even riding through the bushes didn't waken Tim. He remained sprawled back against Nara, his mouth wide open in sleep.

The sight of Tim alone would have been enough to cause a sensation, but the fact that the intruders had a horse was doubtless even more surprising. A buzz of startled speculation passed through the camp's inhabitants.

Tynan addressed the men before him. "We, too, are remnants of the Wolf of Cothran."

His use of the sept's unofficial name for his father had an unexpected effect on Nara. She gasped aloud and looked at Tynan as if he had invoked the powers of darkness.

Perhaps he had, Tynan thought grimly, considering the elusive presence of the wolf that seemed to have followed them all the way from the Isle of Mist.

"Do not speak to him," one of the woodsmen advised his cohorts. "He's brought a wolf to our midst. It's an evil omen, for sure."

Tynan arched an eyebrow and offered dryly, "Perhaps that is the spirit of my long-dead father welcoming me to this gathering of his kinsmen."

His jest did little to lighten the situation. Clearly disturbed by the dark omen, the men maintained their defensive postures and murmured among themselves. Tynan saw no sign of Feadain, and none of the troubled faces looked familiar.

A tingling thread of alarm coursed through his veins. Had he stumbled into the wrong camp, then?

His palm itched for the feel of his sword. Approaching a strange camp empty-handed might well prove to be a fatal misjudgment.

"Hie, *hiu!*" an older woman's voice exclaimed from the doorway of the largest hut. "And what's all this I'm hearing?" Arms akimbo, she strode forward and pushed her way through the assembly, challenging the intruders with, "Who claims to be kinsman to the Wolf of Cothran?"

At first she didn't seem familiar, but as she came closer to the forefront, Tynan was relieved to recognize Mary Chisolm. His palm stopped itching.

She looked so old! Time and tragedy had ravaged Mary's once-pretty face, and her once-firm roundness had shifted and sagged with age, but nothing had changed her distinctive underbite or dimmed the fire in those big brown eyes.

Confronted for the first time in twenty years by the woman who had been his second mother, Tynan felt a childlike surge of joy so pure it almost hurt. He wanted to pick Mary up and swing her in his arms until they were both dizzy, but the man he was would not allow it. Instead, he merely stood and drank in the sight of her.

But seeing her brought back the past, so his joy turned bittersweet, sunlight edged in black.

"Mary," he ventured at last, "don't you know me? It's Tynan."

"Tynan?" Mary's eyes widened. Clearly, Feadain had told her nothing of their earlier encounter, for after a searching look at her long-lost cousin, Mary fainted dead away. If one of the women hadn't caught her, she'd have fallen right into the fire.

In the resulting flurry of activity and chatter that followed, Tynan did not hear Nara dismount and help Tim down off the horse behind him. But the brush of her hem against the back of his legs told him she was sticking close, hiding from the others in the obscurity of his shadow.

Tim, too. Tynan felt the flutter of Tim's fingers on his arm from time to time, as if Tim were reassuring himself of Tynan's protective presence with every touch.

Tynan addressed the remnants of his sept. "I am Tynan, sole surviving heir of Phelan MacDougald, the Wolf of Cothran." He drew Nara from behind him. "This is my lady wife, Nara" — she executed a nervous curtsy — "and her . . . *brother* Timothy."

When Timothy lagged back, Nara coaxed him into the open.

The sight of his tall, quaking frame, unfocused eyes, and nodding head sent a fresh ripple of shocked whispers through the watching strangers.

"They act as if he's some sort of monster," Nara muttered, her cheeks coloring in outrage.

Tynan was surprised to realize that he, too, was stung by the morbid curiosity directed at Timothy.

"Timothy is perfectly harmless," Nara declared loudly. "Truly, he's as sweet as an angel." When her reassurances had no effect, she spared Tim further embarrassment by allowing him to scuttle back into the shelter of Tynan's shadow.

Tynan spoke with authority above the chatter of the crowd. "We seek refuge with our kinsman, Feadain Chisolm."

At the mention of his name, Feadain stuck his head out of

the same hovel from which Mary had emerged, followed by a stout, bowlegged fellow whose stance seemed vaguely familiar. "Tynan," Feadain acknowledged coldly. "So it's you."

The second man stayed close behind Feadain as the old warrior strode to the forefront of his kinsmen. "Why have you come, then?" Feadain asked, his expression as grim as his greeting. "I thought we agreed it would be best for you and your *lady*" — he shot a pointed glance at Nara — "to keep to yourselves."

Almost as if he sensed a diversion was needed to break the tension, Tim chose just that moment to come forward and execute his odd hop-step of a dance.

Feadain's eyebrows shot skyward. "Who the hell is *that?*"

"He's with us." Tynan was in no mood to explain Timothy. "A tribe of Romanies took over our camp." If there was anything Tynan hated more than being where he wasn't wanted, it was asking for help, but there was no way around it. He said through locked teeth, "I come seeking your protection as kinsmen."

Mary, her sensibilities recovered at last, approached her husband. "Feadain, it's our dear Tynan!" She rushed forward and embraced Tynan, her dark eyes bright with unshed tears. "Ah, Tynan, Tynan. How it heals me soul to see ye again."

She thrust him to arm's length. "Look at ye, lad! I can scarce believe it. It's as if time's turned backward twenty years, and I'm seein' me dear cousin, your father, all young again." She let go of him to cross herself with one hand while the other brought the corner of her apron up to dab her tears. "Praise be to God, the good Lord has delivered you from that underhanded coward who slew —"

Feadain strode forward and whispered into her ear, cutting her off in midsentence. Tynan didn't have to guess what he had told her, for Mary's eyes widened in alarm and shifted immediately to Nara. She sized up Cullum MacKay's granddaughter with open misgiving, then retreated to pass the dreadful news to the two women nearest her.

One by one, the women spread the truth of Nara's birth to each other, then to their husbands. And one by one, the men's looks of guarded curiosity turned to hatred. Their gossiping done, the women hurried to their makeshift homes.

Left with only the men, Nara felt even more exposed and out of place. "I'll take our things over by the stream," she volunteered. When Tynan did not ask her to stay, she gathered their belongings and led Timothy toward a rock outcropping on the bank.

" 'M hungry," Timothy whined, head bobbing. "Eat now, Nara."

"I'm surprised you haven't asked before." She chose a relatively secluded spot, sat down, and dug the last stale bun and bit of salted meat from their bundle of provisions.

When Tim plopped down beside her, she handed him the food. "Eat them slowly, Tim, or you'll choke."

She needn't have worried. It took all of Tim's limited abilities to worry loose so much as a bite from the tough bread and the overdried meat.

After he'd eaten, Nara took him to the stream for a drink, supervised his relieving himself behind a bush, then, since it was too cool to bathe him, she was forced to settle for scraping the worst of the filth from his breeches and body with green leaves. Tim stank clear to Norway.

"Poor Tim," she murmured as she worked. "They didn't take proper care of you, did they?" How could anyone let him get this way? It was inhuman. Nara doubled her efforts to clean him. It helped a little, but not much.

Still, she was glad for something to do and grateful for Timothy's presence in more ways than one. Until they had lost him, she hadn't realized how much she had come to rely upon his affection. Now she fed on it. It offered a shield against Tynan's sudden coldness and the hostile glares and whispers of his kinsmen. So did the humble tasks of caring for Tim's needs. It was a constant job, but even the most distasteful chore made her feel needed.

Tynan needed no one — or so he wanted her to believe.

Nara gathered a pallet of dried leaves, removed the twigs, then laid a shaking Timothy down on them. Even here, at the far edge of the campsite, the firelight was bright enough to show that he was paler than usual, clearly exhausted from the day's ordeals. "No bath for you tonight," she reassured him. "It's too cold. But the first sunny day, it's into the water with you." She covered him with their one blanket, then laid more leaves atop it for warmth.

"Hug Nara," Tim murmured sleepily. "Lap. Head in Nara's lap."

"All right, then, sweeting." Nara settled with her back against a cold boulder and allowed Tim to use her lap for a pillow. The smell wasn't so bad, really; she'd almost gotten used to it. She smoothed the tangled hair away from his face and began to sing the lullaby *Seanmhair* had sung to her:

> *Close your eyes, little one,*
> *Take the moon for your boat.*
> *Ride the skies, little one,*
> *On the stars you shall float.*
> *God is nigh, little one,*
> *Hear his voice in each note.*
> *Do not cry, little one,*
> *Wear His love for your coat.*

Over and over she sang it, until her own eyes grew heavy. When she couldn't keep her lids open any longer, a deep yawn interrupted her singing, but she resumed singing after. Just as she was falling asleep, she could have sworn she heard another voice, faint and distant, singing with her. The last thing she remembered, she inhaled and smelled the strong scent of roses. And when she dreamed, she dreamed of a fair-haired woman who took her into her arms and wept for joy. But it was only a dream.

"I thought you were all dead." Tynan peered into Feadain's eyes. "If I'd known even one of you was still alive, no power on earth could have forced me to marry Cullum MacKay's granddaughter. But I didn't know, and it was the only way her grandmother would let me take her."

Feadain snorted. "*Let* ye take her?" He looked Tynan up and down. "Ye appear to be sound enough to fight any man I can think of, lad, and yer tellin' me a woman wouldn't *let* ye take her?"

Tynan's blood grew hot, but he kept his temper in check. "Lady Cullum said she'd kill the girl with her own hand rather than let me take her without marriage, and she meant it. So I married the girl." One by one, he met the eyes of his kinsmen in challenge. "It's done, and can't be undone. Why should you care, as long as you get your lands back?"

"By takin' a MacKay into our midst?" a middle-aged survivor exclaimed. "Why, that's puttin' an adder to our very breast! Fie on't!"

One of the younger men stepped forward, his fist raised. "We can *fight* to *win* our lands back!"

"Oh, aye," Tynan answered dryly. "The twelve of us, against MacKay's hundreds. That'll show 'em." A closer look at the rash fellow revealed a strong resemblance to Feadain. "Is that you, Duncan?"

"Aye." Tynan's recognition clearly surprised the man who had idolized him as a child, but Duncan Chisolm stood his ground. "And I mean what I said."

Tynan curbed the scorn in his voice. "Hear me, men. No one knows more about Laird Cullum's strengths and weaknesses than I do. I lived as a slave beneath him for the past twenty years."

He searched the circle of hostile faces around him. "Fight him, and the only land we'll win is a piece two feet wide, six feet long, and six feet deep for every man here." He hardened. "My way, we all win." He paused to let that sink in. "Feadain told me you would have me lead you as my father did. Well, I'll be your chieftain, but you must trust me enough to go along with my advice, even in this. Agreed?"

The men shifted uneasily, each looking to his companions for some indication of a consensus.

"Let's have it out now. Speak up," Tynan demanded. Better to know now than later. "Either you're with me, every man of you, or I walk away and do this alone."

Feadain looked to Duncan in question. Duncan frowned, then nodded. Slowly, nod by nod, the others followed until it was unanimous, except for Feadain. The old warrior took his time, probably just to torment Tynan, but at last he, too, nodded. "Done, then, my laird," he said to Tynan.

*My laird* . . . From lowly slave to chieftain. Just as he'd dreamed.

Tynan could scarcely believe it, but something about this moment felt right, as apt as a sword sliding home in its sheath.

Was this how it had been with his father? he wondered. Tynan would have given anything to have had Phelan

241

MacDougald witness this moment.

Perhaps he was watching through the mists of the Yonder World.

One by one, each man stepped forward, bent to one knee, and swore loyalty to the son of their slain chieftain. And one by one, Tynan grasped each man by his forearm and drew him to his feet, eye-to-eye.

They were his. Only death would separate them now.

"Are ye ready fer the truth, then, lad?" Feadain asked him after all had sworn.

"The truth about what?"

"About her." Feadain cocked his head in Nara's direction.

Tynan felt the blood rush to his face. The other men were listening. "For good or ill, she is my wife, sir, and I would not take it kindly should anyone" — he put a subtle emphasis on that last word — "speak badly of her."

Feadain shook his head. "Nothing but the truth, my laird."

"Aye, then," Tynan agreed, wholly uncomfortable with the subject.

"Come," Feadain motioned toward the fire. "Let us sit. The story is not a short one. Nor a simple one." As was now fitting, he and all the others waited until Tynan sat to join him.

"Bring us drink," Feadain bellowed in the general direction of his hut. Then he looked sheepishly to Tynan. "Pray forgive me, Laird. I'm so used to givin' the orders that I fergot —"

Tynan shook his head in dismissal. "No offense taken." He soothed Feadain's misgivings with a good-natured, "Good that you thought of it. I am thirsty, as a matter of fact."

Half a dozen women hurried from the hovels, each bearing

242

crude wooden mugs and clay pitchers of beer. They served the men without comment, but Tynan didn't miss the worried looks on their faces and the brief, curious glances they shot him.

It might take some time for them to accept him as chieftain, but he was confident they would. Nara, though . . . he doubted they would ever accept her.

Feadain waited until the last of the women had gone before he spoke. "Twenty-one years ago, less a month or two," he began, "Laird Cullum's only son crossed into MacDougald pastures on a cattle raid." He took a swig of beer. "That was to be expected. MacKays have been raidin' MacDougald pastures and MacDougalds, MacKay's fer generations. Neither side gave it much thought, as long as no one got too greedy and there wasn't any killin'."

The few older men nodded in agreement, while their sons listened intently.

"But the sole heir to that sept of MacKay did somethin' unforgivable this time: He stumbled upon the only child of our overlaird, Morgan MacDougald. A daughter." Feadain's eyes focused into the night.

"Grainne was her name. Aye, and she was a lovely thing. Hair like sunlight. Skin as white as pearls; cheeks as pink as dawn. Blue eyes brighter than a summer sky. And sweet . . ." He shook his head, a nostalgic smile on his face. "Laird Morgan doted on her, as did her mother. All of us did."

His expression clouded. "Unfortunately, she was bad to run off, escapin' her ladies to wander the hillsides alone. That's how young MacKay chanced to find her there unguarded, asleep under a rowan tree at the edge of the pasture."

The men exchanged murmured confirmations of the dangers of women wandering unprotected.

"We all had warned her," Feadain said. "Her father had even beaten her for goin' out without an escort — the only time I've ever known him to strike her — but she *would* do it, no matter how we tried to stop her." He sighed. "Lady Grainne was too clever for her own good. It was a game to her. But that game brought down disaster upon us all."

Tynan waited impatiently for the rest, but Feadain had always loved to tell stories, and he was playing this one to the hilt.

After a dramatic pause, he resumed. "And so it was, she'd crept out of the castle and fallen asleep under a rowan tree, where young MacKay found her and took her." He leaned forward. "The bother of it bein' that she didn't seem to mind when he took her. From the moment she woke in MacKay's arms, she was smitten, and he with her." He nodded dramatically.

"Of course, his men were outraged, but he would hear none of it. No sooner had they gained MacKay lands than damned if the young fool didn't search out the first priest he could find and marry the girl! And her the only heir of his father's sworn enemy!

"Knowing how angry his father would be, the rascal hid away with his bride for three months, which was long enough to make sure he'd planted his child within her. Only then did he dare bring her home to his family."

A child. Tynan's skin pebbled. Nara?

More murmurs from the listeners.

"Laird Cullum was beside himself with rage," Feadain continued. "He threatened to kill the girl with his bare hands, but young MacKay stood between her and his father and vowed he'd slay Laird Cullum himself if the old man tried anything. So Laird Cullum waited."

"What about Laird Morgan?" Tynan asked. "As I recall,

he had a fierce temper. Did he not go after her?"

Feadain's lips folded inward in a scowl. "At first no one knew what had happened to Lady Grainne. But after a few weeks, we got wind that young MacKay and all his men had gone missin' on a raid in our lands, so we fit shoe to foot and figured out what had happened."

He sat a bit taller. "Ach, what a commotion! Laird and Lady Morgan carried on so, I began to wonder if they hadn't rather the lass were dead than carried off by a MacKay." Feadain picked up a stick and traced idly in the dirt.

Duncan couldn't contain himself. "What happened next, Da?"

"Ye know well enough, lad," Feadain chided. "Ye've heard the tale a dozen times."

"We haven't," several of the younger men said almost in unison.

Duncan shrugged. "I know I've heard it, but I forget. You tell so many stories . . ."

"Well, remember this one, lad," Feadain said with all gravity. He pointed the stick toward each of the younger men. "This is the true saga of our people, and it's up to you lads to remember it, word for word, so you can pass it on to yer children, and they to theirs."

They nodded, confirming the spread of hatred between MacKay and MacDougald for generations to come.

Feadain resumed. "Our men were ready to take up arms and bring Lady Grainne back. Then we found out she was with child, and the whole castle went into mournin' as if she'd died." He stared again into the night. "Laird Morgan had her portrait taken down, and no one was allowed so much as to mention her name again."

"The massacre . . ." Tynan could not keep from asking, "how did that come about?"

245

"Patience, my laird," Feadain responded. "Yer gettin' ahead of me." He settled forward, intent on his story. "Back at Eilean d'Ór, Laird Cullum waited to make his move until his unwelcome daughter-in-law was delivered of a healthy daughter. No sooner had Lady Cullum and her attendants taken the child from the room to bathe it than one of Laird Cullum's creatures, a servin' woman, smothered Lady Grainne in her bed.

"Poor Lady Grainne was still warm when young MacKay came in and found her dead. He almost went mad. The wench claimed her mistress had died in childbirth, but young MacKay had seen his wife whole and healthy only minutes earlier, so he knew what had happened. He slew the woman in a rage, swearing Laird Cullum would be next."

By then, every one of Feadain's listeners was leaning forward, hanging on his every word.

"But Laird Cullum was no fool," he confided. "He'd left the castle the moment he heard the child was not a boy." Feadain braced his palms on his knees. "I've often wondered if Laird Cullum would have ordered Lady Grainne murdered had she given birth to a boy. But that's neither here nor there. Still, think how different things might have been . . ."

Seeing the impatient frowns of his audience, he stopped his musing and got back to cases. "Lady Cullum heard her son shoutin' and the maid screamin', so she ran in just in time to see young MacKay slay the servin' woman. When Lady Cullum found out Lady Grainne was murdered and Laird Cullum behind it, she tore at her hair and clothes, then took the baby and the wet nurse to her room and locked herself in.

"Young MacKay searched the castle for his father, but when he could not find him, he, too, locked himself into his rooms."

"No offense intended, Feadain," Tynan interjected, "but

how came you to know what happened in such detail inside the castle of your enemy?"

"A distant kinsman of mine has been Laird Cullum's Master of Horse these past thirty years."

"Old Devan?" Tynan felt his stomach wrench.

*There are things I haven't told ye . . .*

"Aye, my laird." Feadain looked up in surprise. "How —"

"I knew him. He was kind to me, in his own way." Another betrayal, from a man he'd thought of as his friend. "He knew. All that time, he knew I had kinsmen, yet he let me go on believing I was all alone in the world." The last remaining fragments of Tynan's deepest, hidden illusions turned to dust.

"He certainly never told me about you," Feadain offered. "If he had, I'd have come for ye."

Tynan heard the words but took no comfort from them. "He was afraid. For you, and for me." Tynan wanted to forgive Devan, but there was precious little forgiveness left in him. No more than there was comfort left in the world. Not for him.

"Get back to the story," one of the lads said.

"Where was I?" Feadain asked, visibly troubled by the hard, vacant look in Tynan's eyes.

Duncan was quick to answer, "Lady Cullum is locked in her room with the baby."

"And young MacKay has taken to his chamber in grief," offered another.

"And that devil Laird Cullum has fled justice like the craven cur he is," one of the older men growled.

"Aye, then," Feadain continued. "No sooner did we get word of what had happened than our own Laird Morgan sends a challenge to Eilean d'Ór. Hand-to-hand combat, man to man. It's directed to Laird Cullum, but since he's not there, young MacKay himself answers the challenge."

Feadain stroked his grizzled beard. "With only three unarmed witnesses from each side in attendance, they met at the broch in Meager's acre. I meself was one of the witnesses," he said solemnly.

"And I, Magnus MacDougald, another," said the bowlegged man who was obviously Feadain's second-in-command.

The same man who had served in that capacity for Tynan's father. Now Tynan knew why he looked so familiar.

"It was a cold day," Feadain intoned. "Cloudy, with a wind that went right through ye. Fittin', I suppose. Young MacKay looked terrible, like he hadn't had a decent meal in a month. Though it was just past dawn, he reeked of whiskey. His hair blew wild, and his black beard was untrimmed. And his eyes . . ." Feadain shivered. "Those eyes . . . I swear, they looked like he was dead already."

He drew in a long breath, then exhaled. "Laird Morgan had his heart set on killin' Laird Cullum, not the boy. The truth is, I don't think he'd even considered killin' the boy, for his daughter had written that she loved him and he treated her well. So Laird Morgan offered to postpone the challenge until Laird Cullum returned, but young MacKay wouldn't let him."

"What did he do?" one of the younger men asked breathlessly.

"He marched right up to within a sword's length of Laird Morgan and flicked the tip of his blade across the old man's face." Feadain shook his head ominously. "Once blood was drawn, there was no turning back.

"Laird Morgan touched his hand to this cheek and it came away red. 'I'll give ye yer fight, then,' he growled to the lad.

"We witnesses followed them into the broch and took up our places around the courtyard. The pavin' was uneven, but the yard was sound enough."

"And?" Tynan was growing weary of the embellishments. He wanted the story to end so he could lie down and rest. Sleep offered the only escape now.

"And," Feadain obliged, "they started fightin', but young MacKay, he seemed to be toyin' with Laird Morgan. Haggard though he was, the lad had the advantage. He was far younger and swifter. Yet the only time he seemed to get serious was when Laird Morgan tried to back off. Then the lad went after the old man with a vengeance, but not to kill, only to goad him. The truth is, I think he wanted Laird Morgan to kill him."

"Aye," Magnus MacDougald chimed in. "Never saw such a challenge, before or since. Neither one seemed to want to kill the other. They danced around for full half an hour before young MacKay goaded His Lairdship into striking."

" 'Tis true," Feadain confirmed. "And after Laird Morgan had run him through, young MacKay thanked him."

"Thanked him?" a chorus of disbelieving voices asked.

"Aye. Thanked him."

"And the massacre?" Tynan prodded.

"I'm gettin' to that," Feadain retorted. "When Laird Cullum returned and learned his only son had been slain by the MacDougald, he went berserk, poundin' on Lady Cullum's door and demandin' the babe, so he could kill her, too. But Eilean d'Ór is built solid as a mountain, so he couldn't get in. Furious, he swore to drain the baby of MacDougald blood when he returned, then he armed his men and set out to slay every MacDougald that drew breath."

"He damn near succeeded," Magnus declared.

"Tell 'em, Magnus," Feadain said solemnly.

"It was almost dark when they rode in on us," Magnus's gravelly voice intoned. "There was no warning. They found us at our tables or in our beds and killed without mercy. Children. Babes."

Tynan raised his hand to stop them. "I was there. I know." He stood to his feet, bringing the others to theirs. "I've heard enough, Feadain."

"But *they* haven't heard enough," Feadain said quietly. He addressed the others. "Laird Cullum's wife fled to protect her granddaughter. That granddaughter is the Lady Nara, and now Laird Tynan has brought her back as his wife."

Feadain glared at his men. "As he is our chieftain, we must leave it to him to settle the matter. For no man has suffered more injury at the hands of Laird Cullum than he."

Bitterness rose in Tynan's throat, almost choking him. "Rest assured, men, I shall settle the matter in my own good time. I have sworn it on my father's soul."

It would be the most difficult thing he had ever done, but he would take Nara before her grandfather and slay her. "But for now, I bid you good night."

"We shall keep watch over you, my laird," Magnus volunteered. He cocked his head to the rocks where Nara and Timothy now slept. "All of you."

"Then I shall rest easy," Tynan responded.

His head throbbing with dark images from the past, he crossed to where Nara was lying. For the first night since he had found her, Tynan elected not to sleep alongside his wife. The camp sentries allowed him the security to sleep close by, but he would not sleep entangled in her arms.

Now that he knew the depth of Laird Cullum's treachery, Tynan could not bear the feel of her gentle, trusting touch. The same touch that had stirred him to lust or admiration would now sear like a brand.

Tynan chose a patch of moss to lie on and closed his eyes.

He had kinsmen. Kinsmen who were as eager as he to take

vengeance on Laird Cullum. Kinsmen who had sworn allegiance to him, just as they had once sworn to his father. Yet they wanted no part of Nara. And they had told Tynan the truth — all of it.

It was as if history were repeating itself, in an odd sort of way. Once again, the sole heirs to both septs had wed. And once again, their marriage would bring destruction. But Tynan didn't want to think about that now.

First he would take his men to join Donald Balloch against the earls of Mar and Caithness. Now, more than ever, he had to be certain the Lairds of the Isles would back him against Laird Cullum, and he could think of no better way to win their gratitude than by helping Donald Balloch free Laird Alexander from King James — even if it meant fighting on the same side as Laird Cullum MacKay.

Then, and only then, would he settle the score.

Tynan reached for the oblivion of sleep, his only hope that there would be no dreams waiting for him in the darkness.

# Chapter XVI

Since Feadain had insisted on relinquishing the largest hut to his chieftain, Tynan now had his own roof and his own pallet underneath it, across the hard-packed earth from Nara's and Tim's. But he did not sleep with his wife. Nor did he even speak to her any more than was absolutely necessary.

Nara seemed to have accepted the arrangement. Yet with every passing week, even though she took care of his and Timothy's needs without complaint, Tynan saw the light going out of her.

The cause was no mystery. None of his kinfolk, save Mary, acknowledged Nara's presence. The women, especially, took great pains to avoid her rather than risk insulting Tynan by slighting his wife. Tynan knew Nara was lonely, but he could not take her into his arms and comfort her, no matter how much he wanted to. He had to keep his distance. So he watched her sunny disposition fade, all the while doing his best to quash the sympathetic urges that tugged at his heart.

Soon. It would be over soon.

At least he had something to keep his mind off things: arming and training his men. It took every waking hour of every single day, rain or shine, but left Tynan with too little time or energy to think.

He'd assessed his men and realized that though their hunting skills were finely honed, when it came to combat, the older men were rustier than the hinges on a Roman ruin. And although the younger men were more than proficient with their longbows, loyalty and enthusiasm were the only other assets they could bring to battle.

Tynan dared not take them a single step beyond the forest until he had armed and trained them.

Aside from their bows and a few precious knives used to skin and dress the game they caught, his kinsmen had no weapons. His were the only axe, dagger, and greatsword in the camp.

So Tynan had the men collect every scrap of metal they could spare. Then he put to good use what he'd learned watching Eilean d'Ór's smith at work, supervising the smelting and then the forging of sharp tips for several pikes and dozens of arrow points. It was slow, frustrating work, for they lacked the proper tools, but by the time all the metal was used up, they had the beginnings of a respectable armory.

Once they had the metal components, Tynan and his men set about the tedious task of making bows, arrows, pikes, and staves. By the beginning of August, every man had a pike or stave, two stout longbows, and three score flighted arrows.

For protection, they were forced to rely on wood and leathern shields. But what they lacked in equipment, his men more than made up for in single-minded dedication.

Once they were armed, the training began in earnest. And train them he did. Combat training was one skill, at least, he had to thank Laird Cullum for. He'd learned the brutal art by watching the endless exercises at Eilean d'Ór. Almost every night from his twelfth year until his eighteenth, Tynan had risen while the rest of the castle slept to practice those same exercises in a forgotten cellar, using the weapons he had rescued from his father's hidden cache.

Now Tynan had briefly considered melting down his father's axe to forge it into swords, but Magnus's skill with the formidable weapon was enough to convince him otherwise. So he delegated Magnus to teach the men how to wield a battle-axe, and Feadain to train them with the dagger. The three who could lift his greatsword, Tynan himself trained.

When he wasn't doing that, he sparred with anyone who needed a partner. And the face he put on every opponent was Laird Cullum MacKay's, so every blow, every thrust only whetted his appetite for the confrontation that would never happen.

Tynan deliberately drove himself almost to exhaustion; he worked longer and harder than any of the others, thereby earning their respect and admiration. Yet with every day that passed, he worried that his chance to repay Laird Alexander for saving his life might already have slipped through his fingers.

And with every day that passed, there was always Laird Cullum to consider. For all Tynan knew, the man might have already fallen in battle.

A part of him wished Laird Cullum was dead, for that would change everything. But the larger, darker part of him still hungered for revenge.

Tynan contented himself with the knowledge that his kinsmen's training would not be in vain, no matter what might have happened beyond the forest. They'd been fugitives — outlaws — when he'd found them, but soon they would be warriors.

September was well upon them before Feadain and Magnus agreed the men were ready. Tynan did not tell Nara they were leaving until the eve of their departure.

As usual, it was almost dark before he approached their hut. But this night the closer he got, the slower his steps became.

How would she react when he told her? Tynan knew she

feared her grandfather. Now her husband was taking her to the very man her grandmother had called a monster.

Perversely, Tynan almost hoped she *would* show anger or fear when he told her . . . perhaps even lash out at him or fight back . . . anything but the wounded resignation she had worn like a cloak since they'd come to this place.

He stepped inside the hut and found supper laid out on the split-log table as usual. And as usual, beyond the fire pit, Nara lay feigning sleep on the pallet beside Timothy's.

Tynan crossed to stand above her. She was awake; he could tell by the way her body tensed at the sound of his footsteps.

He squatted low beside her. "Nara," he whispered, not wanting to complicate matters by waking Timothy. "Come sit by me while I eat. We must talk."

Graceful as a wraith, she rose and followed him to the table. How like her not to bother pretending she'd been asleep.

He motioned to the bench across the table. "Sit."

Nara's usually expressive mouth tightened, her green eyes wide with anxiety. "What is it, Tynan?" She peered at him so intently he could scarcely keep himself from looking away. "It's bad news, isn't it?" she murmured. "I can see it in your face."

After a long blink, she said, "Just tell me straight out. That's usually best in the long run, no matter how difficult it might be."

Conn's balls! The woman read his face as easily as a farmer read a summer sky. Tynan took a swig of streamwater, then picked up the joint of roast rabbit. It was still warm. She must have heard him coming, set out the food, then hastened straight to her bed.

Not that he could blame her for avoiding him. Over the

past two months he'd made it quite clear he preferred things that way.

But by everything that was real in life, how empty his arms and nights had been without her. And how grim his existence without her touch, her gentle smile, her guileless conversation.

Tynan looked across the table at his wife and felt his heart twist within him, followed rapidly by a churning in his loins. Even now, pale and worried in the firelight, she was beautiful, her shining hair almost blue-black. No matter how he'd tried to purge himself of her, he still wanted her as much as he had that first day at the waterfall.

Blast her! Why couldn't he look into those wounded, fathomless eyes without feeling guilty?

She'd asked him to be blunt, so blunt he was. "We're leaving before first light. Pack for the three of us."

She simply looked at him, her huge green eyes wide, and nodded. That was all. Tynan wanted something more from her; she always had to have the last word — gentle though it was — even these past few weeks when he'd scarcely spoken to her. But this time, she said nothing.

While he finished eating, she went woodenly about her packing. It didn't take long, since they owned little more than they'd had when they arrived, for all he was a chieftain. Then Nara lay down on her pallet and turned her back to him.

Oddly unsettled, Tynan threw the bones to the dogs outside, then settled on his own pallet and willed himself to sleep.

Nara waited until Tynan was snoring long and loud before she crept from her pallet, eased into her shoes, and wrapped herself in the warm plaid Mary had given her. Then she carefully made her way to Mary's hut. Once there, she waited outside for fully ten minutes before summoning the courage to push aside the deerskin that served as a door and whisper, "Mary? It's Nara . . ."

Inside, the hut was dark, but she heard an abbreviated snort and the rustle of fabric, then Mary came to the door, hair askew, and clutching around the shoulders of her rail a thick, woolly plaid just like the one she had given Nara. "What is it, my lady?" she whispered. "Has something come amiss with Laird Tynan?"

"Nay, nay. I . . ." Suddenly Nara's courage deserted her. But she had to know. She peered into Mary's kind face. "The men are leaving before dawn, and I with them. This might be my last chance . . ." Why was it so hard to ask? The question was simple enough.

But the answer . . . Nara shivered in the darkness when she thought of the answer.

"Your last chance, my lady?" Mary repeated, clearly confused and perhaps more than a little irritated with Nara's indirectness, "Your last chance to what?"

"To ask you for the truth," Nara managed at last. "I must know, Mary. Please tell me what happened between your people and my grandfather. All of it."

Mary glanced back toward her sleeping husband, then guided Nara out of the doorway. "Wait here," she whispered. "I'll be right out."

Several moments later, she reappeared fully dressed and led Nara to a split-log bench well away from the houses. She waited for Nara to sit, then settled beside her.

Mary drew her plaid closer against the autumn chill. "It's not a pretty story, Lady Nara. Are you certain you want to know?"

"How else can I hope to understand my husband, or the things that have happened since we came here?" Nara asked candidly.

"Aye." Mary sighed. "It must have been hard on ye, left all to yerself these many weeks."

"Everyone here but you hates me," Nara said without emotion. "Every man, woman, and child." She looked down into her lap. "They aren't evil people. I know that. So they must have good reason to feel as they do." Her gaze leveled with Mary's. "Please, Mary, tell me the truth. Hold nothing back, no matter how painful."

Mary frowned, clearly weighing Nara's request against her loyalty to her cousin and chieftain, but after a brief inner struggle, the sisterhood of women won out. She sagged. "All right, then, I'll tell ye. But not a word of this to Laird Tynan. Or to me man Feadain."

Nara crossed herself. "I vow upon my very soul, no one shall ever know you told me, not even my husband."

"Very well, then." Sparing Nara the embellishments, Mary set forth the tragic tale of Nara's parents and what their love had cost both families. When she was done, Nara sat stunned.

No wonder they hated her . . . all of them, including Tynan. His coldness made perfect sense.

As long as it had just been the two of them and Tim, he'd been able to pretend she was just Nara. But now, confronted daily by his kinsmen, he saw her for what she really was: a living reminder of Laird Cullum's barbarous treachery.

"I'm sorry, Lady Nara," Mary whispered, "but ye asked me to tell it straight, and so I have."

"Thank you, Mary." Nara managed an unconvincing smile. Her tongue felt as if it had turned to ashes, and her ears were hot from the pumping, pumping, pumping of her heart.

Dear God, she was the granddaughter of the devil himself! No matter how good she had ever been or would ever be, his blood flowed like poison through her veins.

Nara could feel her soul shriveling under the corrosive pressure of that poison. Laird Cullum had ordered her mother murdered with no more compunction than he would have ordered someone to kill a rat.

And the massacre . . . such evil, such cruelty her grandfather had wrought on Tynan's sept. His actions violated every code of honor.

No wonder the other women could not bear to look at her, much less speak to her.

Yet Mary had managed.

"Dear Mary, I am grateful to you, truly I am," she said flatly. "Not just for telling me, but for your kindness to me."

Tears of shame thickened Mary's reply. "It wasn't kindness, my lady, though God knows, it should have been. How could I hold you responsible for what happened? You were as much a victim in this as Laird Tynan."

Nara murmured the words *Seanmhair* had made her memorize: "For I the Lord thy God am a jealous God, visiting the sins of the fathers upon the children unto the third and fourth generation of them that hate me."

"Oh, child." Mary covered her mouth, stifling a soft sob.

Nara lifted her eyes skyward and stared up through the treetops into the night sky as if somehow that could stop her from dying, dying, dying inside.

Tynan had married her, knowing . . .

But why?

The question opened up inside her like a huge, hungry void, nothing but darkness at its core.

Perhaps it was better not to know. If the answer was as painful as the truth about her heritage, she could not bear it, for she loved him.

She hadn't meant to love him. But ever since that momentous afternoon on the beach, she'd been lost. So glorious it had been, so free. And that night in the monastery. And again in the crypt. Just thinking about it, she felt a powerful contraction of desire deep inside her.

But that wasn't the only reason she loved him. She respected him, too, as did his men.

All the men she had seen since meeting Tynan had only served to confirm that he was exceptional in every way. Tynan was bigger, faster, stronger, comelier, and far more clever than any of the others. And now he was a chieftain, as well he should be.

His men had chosen him because of his strength and heritage, but they followed him now because they loved him fiercely. Tynan had won that love in the two weeks since he'd been reunited with his sept.

But Nara loved him best for the part of himself he kept hidden from the others. She remembered his gentle patience with Timothy before they had reached the monastery — the way he'd laughed and roughhoused with Tim; the way he'd smiled, unguarded, when he'd thought Nara wasn't looking. How kind and patient he'd been, teaching Tim to fish and exclaiming over the small wonders of nature Tim had collected every day. That was the image of Tynan she hid in her heart, the image she held up like a shield against his coldness and rejection these past two months.

Oh, Tynan.

Her heart ached when she thought how he, more than any of his kin, had cause to hate her for the blood that tainted her very soul.

Nara rose to her feet. She took Mary's hand and kissed it, then laid it against her cheek. "Thank you, sweet Mary. I shall say good-bye now, to spare you having to look at me when we leave."

Mary enveloped Nara in an impulsive embrace, then released her. "Good-bye, Lady Nara. I shall keep you in my prayers."

"I fear this evil is long beyond praying," Nara answered. She headed back toward her lonely pallet. "May God keep you and the others safe."

With labored steps, she returned to the only home she had ever tended as a wife — a home she would leave forever in a few short hours.

Tynan rose well before dawn and wakened his men before returning home to rouse Nara and Timothy. He was on his way back to their hut when he saw their primitive oil lamp burning beyond the open doorway. Nara had already removed the deerskin that usually kept out the wind. Inside, the hut was tidy, stripped of everything portable, and Nara was sitting alongside a dozing Timothy on the bench, their meager belongings bundled neatly at her feet. Around her shoulders, she wore the length of plaid Mary Chisolm had given her when the nights had turned cold.

Mary's gift had been the only real kindness granted Nara, and that only because she was wife to their chieftain. Yet Nara now caressed the plaid as if it were the precious mantle of a queen.

When he entered, she gently shifted Tim's head aside and spoke. "All is ready. We've eaten. May I prepare some bread and cheese for you?"

"I had something with Feadain." He could see she'd been weeping, but there had been no pain or recrimination in her voice.

Tynan would have thought she'd be glad to leave behind the hostile glares and whispered asides of the women here. He inhaled a deep breath and shook his head. Even if both of them should live to be a hundred, he would never understand the woman.

But they wouldn't live that long.

"Very well," she said. "Come along, Tim." Nara hoisted him to his feet along with her. "Time to go. Tynan's taking us for another ride." She granted Tim a wistful smile. "Remember Horrible? You like Horrible. He's going to give us a nice, long ride."

"I not," Tim balked. "Huht." Planting his feet on the dirt floor, he grabbed his crotch. "Huht here to ride."

Nara colored, and Tynan almost smiled in spite of himself. He watched with barely suppressed amusement as Nara pulled on Timothy's arm in an effort to get him to surrender his grip on his privates. Until this moment, Tynan hadn't realized how much he'd missed Timothy's antics during these past weeks.

"Let go, Timothy," Nara chided, but she and Tynan both knew it was useless. On the rare occasions when Timothy took hold of his crotch, there was no getting him to let loose until he was good and ready. "Oh, for heaven's sake . . ."

"No ride," Tim grumbled sleepily. It was obvious he thought her suggestion outrageous and wanted no part of it. "It's nighttime. I tired." Crotch in hand, Tim dragged her toward the spot where his pallet had been. "C'mon, Nara. Back to bed. I tired."

Much as Tynan hated to break this up, the men were waiting. He strode over to Timothy and scooped him up as one might a small child. "Your bed is all packed up, Timothy, so you'll have to sleep on horseback. Off we go."

Nara bent to gather their things.

His arms full with Timothy, Tynan chafed inexplicably at the idea of her struggling to carry everything herself. "Leave those," he said brusquely. "One of the men will bring them."

She nodded and straightened, again without comment.

In the past two months he had told himself often enough that her efforts at conversation annoyed him, but this wounded resignation scalded his sensibilities. "Are you ill?" he demanded, knowing she wasn't.

"No. I am not ill." Nara drew the plaid over her sleek, raven hair, then walked out into the night.

Tynan stooped and angled Timothy through the doorway. But before he left, he took one last look at the structure that had been his home.

Home. How often he had dreamed of, longed for, a home of his own. And a family.

Here, he had had both, but life had proved nothing like his dreams. It took more than a roof to make a home. And more than a wife whose very existence was a reminder of the bitterness he had swallowed for twenty long, agonizing years.

Tynan turned and left their house behind with no more feeling than he'd had when he left behind those long-ago, impossible dreams.

It was a ragtag caravan of travelers that exited the forest under cover of darkness. Their departure from camp was not an easy one. Tynan knew the women were glad to be rid of Nara and Timothy, but after twenty years of hiding in the forest, the remnant of his sept had grown accustomed to living wild, free within the green confines of these woods. Political struggles and clan feuds were but distant memories — mere tales for the younger inhabitants — and he could see that the Chisolm and MacDougald women were loath to see their menfolk leave, especially to fight for Donald Balloch, a man they'd never heard of before.

But Tynan was their chieftain now. So with long faces and many silent tears, they watched their sons and husbands go. Their grief was doubtless tempered, though, by the fact that

Nara and Timothy were leaving as well.

Tynan made sure they were well away from the forest before dawn broke. He avoided the roads, lest they come upon raiders or soldiers, and kept to the rugged passages through moor and forest. With every pace, they were one step closer to the destiny Tynan had dreamed of, planned for, worked for, survived for during the past two decades. So with every pace, his blood thrummed stronger and stronger, hungry for the moment of confrontation.

Perhaps Nara was right. Scotsmen loved to fight, but Tynan would not fight without reason, and this time he had reason aplenty: In order to survive after taking his revenge, he needed all the support he could get from Laird Alexander and the Council. Fighting to free Alexander would win him that support.

Tynan's men, though, were another matter. They needed no reason beyond the dignity they would wear as warriors — bearing arms as free men instead of fugitives. The war-hunger ran deep in his men already. He could see it in the skittish anticipation on their faces, hear it in the brittle arrogance of their conversations.

Nightfall was almost upon them on the second day when Duncan Chisolm returned at a dead run from scouting the way ahead.

"Laird Tynan!"

Tynan halted and drew Horrible to a stop beside him. The other men surged forward to hear what Duncan had to say.

Gulping for air, Duncan bent over, his hands braced on his thighs, and managed, "Inverlochy Castle lies just beyond that next ridge." Long seconds passed before he had enough breath to continue. "The castle seems to be secure, but there's a huge army camped idle just beyond the walls. I saw at least six battle standards and as many fancy tents."

"Mar and Caithness," Tynan murmured to himself. "I wonder how many others have turned traitor and joined them . . ."

So he hadn't missed his chance! The battle had yet to be joined. Unless something huge and unforeseen had gone amiss, Donald Balloch would not be far away.

Tynan handed the reins to Duncan. "Well done, Duncan. Now look after Lady Nara and Timothy. Find some shelter to hide the horse and make camp." He turned to the men behind him. "Feadain and Magnus, come with me. The rest of you stand sentry around the Lady Nara. No harm must come to her, or all is lost. Do I make myself clear?"

"Aye," they said in ragged chorus. The younger men's eyes glowed with the prospect of what lay ahead, while the older men exchanged looks of grave resolution.

Tynan advanced cautiously up the next ridge, Magnus and Feadain close behind him. Near the crest, all three of them got down and crawled the last few feet for a look.

When Tynan saw the encampment beyond the stone walls of Inverlochy Castle, a tingle of dread wrapped around his innards.

Magnus nodded toward the four stout towers of the castle. "They've held out." He pointed to the center of the enemy encampment where battle standards stood staked outside the commanders' tents. "It's been a long time, but I still remember the emblems. There's the flag of Mar. There's Moray, there. And that's Seton of Gordon's standard." He squinted in the failing light. "I believe that one's Cameron. And that there is Grant. And the other . . ." He waited until a breeze straightened the banner. "Ah, that's the MacKintosh."

"Lowlanders, most of 'em," Feadain said with contempt. "But Mar . . ." He scowled. "Mar's a Highlander, as is

Moray. They ought to know better, takin' up with that Englisher James, fer all he calls himself king and wraps himself in plaid."

"There must be close to two thousand men out there," Tynan assessed.

"Aye. And we're thirteen." Feadain rolled over onto his back and gazed into the evening sky. "What now?"

"Nothing, tonight." Tynan crawled backward until he was safely out of sight, then stood. He scanned the bleak hills around them but saw no sign of another camp. Not that that meant there wasn't one. "If Donald Balloch had already been here and lost, Mar would be *in* the castle instead of camped outside it." He led the two men toward the rock outcropping that now hid Nara, Timothy, Horrible, and the others. "If Balloch had been here and won, Mar wouldn't be there at all. So it's safe to assume we haven't missed our chance to fight."

"So?" Feadain was bold to ask. "What now?

"So we find Balloch and join him."

"And if Laird Cullum is with him?" Magnus asked grimly.

"We must make certain no harm comes to him until I can stand with him before the Council." Tynan shot a baleful look at each of the older men. "Is that clear? Until I can bring him before the Council, we must all do our best to keep him safe. All of us."

Both men frowned and exchanged uneasy glances.

"I told you, there will be a reckoning," Tynan promised, "but not until after the battle. If, after all is said and done, you still wish to take your revenge, I shall not stop you."

"Fair enough," Feadain said, but his nod was less than enthusiastic.

"Aye, then," Magnus grunted reluctantly.

Tynan only hoped their agreement was binding.

The next morning, the men were still preparing to leave in search of Donald Balloch when young Alan Chisolm, Feadain's second son, leapt up from his lookout post on the ridge and headed at breakneck speed for their camp. Like his brother the day before, he arrived with scarcely enough breath to relay the news that had sent him flying. "The ground is movin'!"

"Have ye gone daft, lad?" his father was quick to ask, but Tynan wasted no time in sprinting for the ridge.

When he reached the crest, he lay down to see what Alan had tried to tell him. Sure enough, from time to time in the valley below, it looked as if man-sized patches of brush and ground were moving toward the enemy encampment.

Closer inspection revealed hundreds of men hiding behind every available means of shelter beyond the camp.

Balloch! It had to be. He was mounting a sneak attack. But unless he had held back half his troops in reserve somewhere, Balloch was outnumbered two to one.

Tynan looked to the enemy camp. A single sentry ran for the command center and disappeared inside it, but strangely, no one raised the alarm. Long minutes passed, yet no battle-cry was sounded.

Meanwhile, under cover of brush and slabs of sod, the invaders crept closer and closer.

Surely Mar hadn't been foolish enough to ignore the sentry's report! Tynan watched in amazement as the camp continued its morning routine.

That meant Balloch would have the element of surprise on his side, but Tynan didn't like the odds.

He scrambled backward and ran for camp, meeting Feadain and Magnus halfway. When he did not stop, the two men turned and trotted back alongside him.

"Balloch is launching a sneak attack," he told them, his

words punctuated by the impact of his footfalls. "He has only half as many men as Mar, but they've almost breached Mar's perimeter under cover of sod and brush. So far, no one seems to have seen them, so surprise will even the odds a bit. But every man will be needed."

Reaching camp, Tynan turned to Feadain. "Pick three men to remain behind and guard Lady Nara. The rest will follow me. We'll stay hidden until the attack begins, then reinforce Balloch's rear. But our primary objective is to find Laird Cullum and see that he comes out of this alive."

A grumble of discontent rose from the younger men, but Feadain silenced them with a glare and a shouted, "Ye! Ye! And ye!" He pointed out his son Alan, Tom MacDougald, and Braithwed MacClindon — all young, but reliable. "Stay here and keep watch over Lady Nara. The rest of ye, fetch yer weapons."

Battle-lust burned in Feadain's eyes and resonated in his commands. "It's time to kill a few traitors. But first, lads, hold." He halted them, reining in his own enthusiasm. "Remember what Laird Tynan said about Laird Cullum." Another threatening growl rose from the men. "Aye, I ken how ye feel. But remember what Laird Tynan told us. No one is to harm the knave. Leave that to our chieftain."

Tynan watched Nara stand to her feet, fear patent on her face. Then, to his surprise, she ran over and threw her arms around him. "May God keep you safe," she murmured into his chest.

Before he could stop himself, he lifted her chin with his finger and replied, "And you as well." Then he remembered himself. "Stay put, Nara. And whatever comes to pass, do not let yourself come to harm. That is an order, even if something threatens Timothy."

Her tears stopped abruptly. "But surely you don't mean

for me to allow anyone to —"

"I mean what I said," he interjected firmly. "Keep yourself safe, at any cost."

Again she met his command with a nod and wounded silence before retreating to her place alongside Timothy.

Tynan untied his axe, hefted it in his right hand, then shouted, "Magnus!" No sooner had the old man turned than Tynan let out a warning cry of "Heads up, lads," and sent the axe flying toward Magnus. The weapon's heavy, curved blade whistled ominously as it spun in a powerful arc.

Magnus caught the handle as easily as a child might catch a ball. He grinned down at the shining steel. "Ochan, but she's a beauty, my laird."

"Use her well, and she's yours." Tynan drew his sword. "Are you ready, men?"

Nine answered, "Aye," while the remaining three watched with envy.

Tynan singled out those who were to stay behind. "I know you'd rather go storming off with the rest of us, men, but yours is the harder job. No matter what happens in the battle, our future hangs on Lady Nara's safety. Guard her well, and I shall be forever in your debt."

The three of them stood just a little taller. "We'll see no harm comes to her," Alan declared.

"That's one worry, then, I won't have to carry with me." Tynan turned and led his men toward the low pass that fed into the basin at Inverlochy.

# Chapter XVII

Nara tidied up the camp and repacked their provisions three times, but nothing soothed the ragged edges from her nerves.

She could not bear to think what might be going on. The men had long since disappeared around a lesser peak, but she doubted they'd had time to reach the battle. And she heard no commotion from beyond the ridge.

If only she could go up there and steal a look at what was happening. Her guards, though, would never permit it. They stood sentry, poised and silent, around the tiny camp.

Tim plopped down beside her and leaned over, almost toppling her with his lanky frame. " 'M hungry, Nara. Eat now."

"You're always hungry," she responded without rancor. She scrounged up a stale bun, then put her arm around him and positioned him more comfortably against her.

Tim took a bite and chewed, his wayward vision circling the empty camp. "Where's Tynan?" he asked with his mouth full.

As if he suddenly sensed Nara's apprehension, his voice grew shrill. "Where's Tynan? Gone, gone?" Timothy bent forward and began to rock rhythmically. "Oh, no. Tynan's gone gone. Mooma's gone gone. Tynan and Mooma, gone gone. Just Nara now."

"Hush, Tim," Nara soothed, wishing he hadn't put Tynan in the same category as his dead mother. "Tynan will be back." He had to.

But what if he didn't come back?

Just then, she heard the sound of shouts from the ridge. So did her guards.

"Stay here!" Alan ordered before he led the others around the back of the sheltering rocks.

Nara saw Tom's head pop up above the rocks. He aimed his bow and fired.

A scream sounded, close. Then more shouts.

They were being attacked!

Another, closer cry told her one of their own men had been hit.

*Oh, please, dear Lord, don't let it be Alan.* Mary's face flashed into her mind.

More shouts, closer yet, came from the direction of the ridge. "Over there! In those rocks!" a strange voice cried.

The twang of bowstrings and whistle of arrows sounded with increasing intensity. A single arrow arced over the rocks and skittered harmlessly to the ground. Then another bounced off the rocks and fell almost at her feet.

Oddly, Timothy remained silent through it all, scarcely even quaking.

Nara reached out and grabbed the fallen arrow, holding it like a dagger. "We must be very quiet, Tim, or the bad men will find us."

His answer was strangely coherent. "No harm shall come to thee, Nara."

The words brought an inexplicable sense of peace with them. She looked back at him just in time to see a spark of intelligence before his eyes glazed over again.

All around them, it fell silent. The only sound was the whistle of the wind and the clash of a distant battle that came with it.

What had happened?

Nara huddled against the rocks for what seemed an eternity, holding Tim in her arms. When she could bear it no longer, she gave him a squeeze, then released him. "Stay here, Tim, and be very, very quiet." Watching everywhere for signs of attack, she crept out the way her guards had left.

She came upon Alan first, facedown with an arrow clear through his shoulder and another angled steeply into his thigh. She rolled him over and was hugely relieved to find he was still alive, but unconscious. Blood soaked his leg and shoulder.

Where there was life, there was hope. It wasn't easy, but she managed to drag him back to camp.

When Timothy saw her pulling Alan into the shelter of the rocks, his eyes widened briefly at the sight of so much blood, but soon wandered away. Blessedly, he kept quiet.

She dragged Alan over close to Tim. "Shhh, Tim," she cautioned. "Watch over Alan. I have to see about the others. Be very quiet, and I'll be back before you know it."

Again, she crept from behind the rocks. Not until she reached the sloping plain that led up to the ridge did she find the others. Braithwed MacClindon lay on his back, bow in hand, his sightless eyes wide and two arrows in his chest. Tom had gone down onto his side not far away.

A dozen of the enemy lay scattered and unmoving in an irregular vee, most of them near the ridge. Braithwed and Tom had slain them all, but at the cost of their own lives.

Two men young men had died to save her. Two mothers had lost their sons. Two young wives had lost their husbands. Bairns, their fathers.

They had not died for freedom or for lands or for livelihood. They had died protecting her.

Too terrible a price, for just one life saved.

Nara fought back a surge of nausea. She wanted to run,

take Tim with her and flee this madness.

But she couldn't. There was no time to waste, for she had no way of knowing when more of the enemy might top the ridge. She hastened to Tom and eased him gently onto his back.

Death had caught him by surprise. Mouth open, his face was frozen in a look of shock, and his hands still clutched the arrow that pierced his abdomen.

Nara lurched aside on all fours and lost the contents of her stomach.

They had died defending her, even though they hated her. It made no sense. Nothing made sense anymore.

*Alan,* an inner whisper chided. Quit your whining and go back to help him. Don't think. Do something!

Nara took a settling breath, then forced herself to stand. She half-ran, half-stumbled back to camp.

Tim and Alan were just as she'd left them. She surveyed Alan's wounds.

Those arrows had to come out. *Seanmhair* had told her dishonorable men often dipped their arrows in excrement, and she had no reason to think the enemy would be other than dishonorable.

Her hands shaking so hard she could barely function, she ransacked the provisions until she found some unguent and a packet of clean wool.

She tried to rip some bandages from her scapular, but the hardy fabric refused to tear until she frayed it against a sharp edge of the rock. It seemed to take hours to tear the bandages she needed, but it was probably only minutes.

Gently, she rolled Alan onto his uninjured side and ripped his shirt away from the injured shoulder to inspect the damage.

Blast! Only half of a barbed point emerged from the exit

wound in back. She'd hoped to find the entire point clear of his flesh so she could break it off, then remove the shaft, but it wasn't. That left her with only one alternative.

It took surprising force to break off the feathered end of the shaft six inches above the entry wound. She threw away the broken end, then greased the remaining shaft with unguent. Then she knelt and pulled the unconscious man into a sitting position against her own shoulder.

Nara crossed herself. *Holy Mary, Mother of God, please intercede with the Spirit and ask that I be granted strength to do this quickly. And please, let the barb do no more harm than necessary.*

Steadying Alan with her left arm, she reached between them with her right hand and firmly grasped the broken end of the shaft. Then she braced her own shoulder against her fist and shoved as hard as she could.

For one nauseating split second, she felt the resistance of barbed metal against living muscle. Eyes clenched shut, she pushed harder, the veins in her temples throbbing with effort.

When the barb broke through, it was with such force that Nara's fist slammed against Alan's entry wound, eliciting a low groan from him.

"Oh, Alan! I'm so sorry." Hurting him further was the last thing she'd wanted to do. Her vision blurred, but she had no time for tears. Nara swiped them away. "Almost done," she said with a confidence she did not feel. "The rest will be easier."

Now that the barb was completely clear, she had little trouble extracting the bare shaft from the exit wound. This time, Alan remained unconscious, his pulse and breathing strong. He bled, of course, but not nearly as much as she had expected him to.

*Must not have struck a vein, thanks be to God.*

She salved the entry and exit wounds, stanched them with

wool, then bandaged them.

"One more, Alan," she said, praying his other wound would be less serious. "Then I'll leave you alone."

But the arrow in his thigh was no simple matter. A tentative twist and tug revealed that it was firmly lodged in the bone. She couldn't force it through.

Careful to keep his plaid modestly in place, she rolled him gently onto his back, then braced one foot on his leg and gripped the arrow with both hands. If the tip was barbed like the other, extracting it would do terrible damage, but she had no choice.

She said another silent prayer, then pulled with all her might. The arrow resisted at first, then let go so abruptly she lost her balance and ended up on her rump.

"Praise be to God!" she blurted, scrambling to her feet.

It wasn't barbed.

She had the wound salved and bandaged in no time.

What now? Tynan had told her to stay put, but that was with sentries to guard her. If she and Timothy remained where they were, they would be at the mercy of anyone who came along.

She rose. "Be still, Tim. I must see what's happening."

Again she crept from her hiding place, but this time she headed for the ridge. Long before she stepped among the fallen attackers, the stench of blood and urine and feces assaulted her, but she did not turn back. She tried not to look at the faces of the dead men she passed. Near the crest, she stooped low and risked a glance over into the valley.

To her vast relief, she found no enemy soldiers waiting to pick her off on the other side. She looked toward the castle and saw why. Balloch's forces had put the king's men to rout. With the exception of a few scattered skirmishes beyond the besieging army's perimeter, most of the fighting seemed limited to small confrontations inside the camp.

The royalists must have scattered at the first attack!

Hundreds of bodies lay among the outer tents, and the camp appeared to be in complete disarray.

Nara looked at those bodies and thought of Tynan. Her heart skipped a beat. Was he hurt? Did he live?

She closed her eyes and willed with all her might for the Sight to return and tell her, but it did not.

She had to know.

What if he was wounded? She could help him, just as she had helped Alan, perhaps even save his life.

What she couldn't do, though, was wait and hide.

She had to go down into that valley and find her husband. And she had to take Tim with her. Nara had no idea why she felt so strongly she must go, but she had never experienced such a powerful impulse before in her life. She had to act on it.

Alan would be all right. She had done all she could for him, and he was resting now.

Nara crawled backward until she was well away from the exposed ridge, then stood.

She would go down into the valley, but before she did, there was one thing she could do for Tynan's kinsmen. Grimly ignoring the nausea that threatened to overcome her with each new corpse, she systematically stripped the dead men of their weapons. By the time she dragged the armaments back to camp, she had accumulated three pikes, as many bows, six smallswords, eleven daggers, and a pulleyed crossbow.

Reserving the sharpest dagger for herself, Nara stacked the weapons beside Alan, covered him with the only blanket in the camp, then piled the rest of their provisions within easy reach of him.

"Come, Tim." She took his hand and drew him to his feet. "We must go find Tynan."

She knew seeing the dead men would probably upset him, but there was no avoiding it. The only way to the pass led right by them.

Carefully she led Tim out into the open.

Tim's reaction was not what she'd expected. As she drew him along, his gaze wandered over the fallen soldiers, and he let out a chirping laugh. "Silly mens!" he burbled. "Sleepin' on the ground, inna daytime." He laughed again. "Silly mens."

His innocence protected him from the truth, and Nara was grateful for that, but the tragic irony of Tim's delusion shook her deeply. "That's right," she said with quavering voice. "Silly mens. Come along, now, Tim. We must hurry and find Tynan. Tynan needs us."

All the way to the pass, Tim kept lagging behind for another look at the "silly mens." She was glad when at last they put the grisly scene behind them. But Tim's struggling gait made progress agonizingly slow. By the time they reached the base of the slope she had looked down on from the ridge, almost an hour had passed, and the castle was still another thirty minutes away.

In the valley, Tynan and his men met the fleeing royalist troops head-on. His pulse pounding as much from the brisk march as from the challenge that now faced him, Tynan easily dispatched any enemies who put up a fight. The rest he and his band scornfully allowed to pass with taunts of, "Coward!"

Most of Mar's men acted more like panicked children than soldiers.

Feeling oddly detached — as if he were an observer instead of a participant — Tynan led his men toward the enemy camp. "Remember. Our primary objective is to find Laird Cullum and protect him. Whatever comes along in the meantime, we'll deal with together."

He nodded toward a fallen enemy. "Take what weapons you can from the dead," he ordered, "but keep a sharp eye out."

Tynan ducked just in time to avoid a bolt that sailed past him at formidable speed. "Crossbows! Watch for arrows!" he warned. "I'd hate to lose any of you to Balloch's archers."

Thank the gods he'd trained his men with axe, sword, and dagger, for by the time they gained the edge of Mar's camp, all nine of Tynan's men were fully armed with weapons they had liberated from fallen enemies.

Once inside the perimeter, they had cause to put those weapons to vigorous use. Suddenly they were attacked from all sides. "We're Balloch's men," Tynan cried as they entered the fray, but none of their attackers held back, so it was safe to assume they were king's men.

How in hell was he supposed to know friend from foe?

Though their armor marked the Lowlanders clear enough, there was no telling Mar's warriors from Balloch's. Tynan and his men had to settle for declaring themselves before every confrontation.

Soon all of them were moving forward, fighting hand-to-hand. His original assessment proved correct; over and over, as if by charm, his men arrived just in time to tip the balance in favor of Balloch's rear wave.

Tynan welcomed each new confrontation; he paid no heed to whether the men he helped were knights or mere foot soldiers. Instead, he imagined Laird Cullum's face on every one of the enemy and fought without fear or reservation. And all around him, his own men acquitted themselves with admirable skill and courage.

No one who came against them stood a chance.

Again and again Tynan killed, seeking catharsis with every contest, but each death-blow only left him emptier than before.

Why did he feel like a ghost warrior in a ghost war? Everything seemed unreal. Subdued. Yet the dead bodies all around him were real enough.

As soon as Tynan and his men had dispatched the latest batch of enemies, he led the way around the corner of the next tent and found himself face-to-face with a particularly large Highlander and six of his men.

"Heads up, lads," the lummox said to his men. "And what have we here?"

Tynan could hear his men positioning themselves behind him. "Long live Alexander," he declared, his pulse accelerating like a war-drum.

At last. A confrontation that brought everything into focus.

Instantly the enemies assumed fighting stances. "Leave the big one to me, boys," their leader ordered. "Ye can have the rest." As the others ran past Tynan to attack his men, the huge swordsman struck a mighty blow at him with his greatsword, but Tynan blocked him cleanly, the impact sending shock waves clear to this spine.

From the corner of his eye, he saw a beleaguered swordsman with a silvered shield being forced back by a lone attacker. Though fighting for his life, the man called out, "Balloch's men are badged with heather."

Hearing the revelation, Tynan's opponent made a brief, but fatal, error. The man glanced to the source of the shout, and in that instant, Tynan dispatched him with a lethal arc of his greatsword, releasing a tide of blood that soaked his own face and clothing. Tynan wiped the blood from his eyes and turned to see his ally take a thrust to his shoulder. But before the man's attacker could deliver the death-blow, Tynan whipped out his dagger and hurled it into the enemy's exposed chest. The hapless fellow looked at Tynan in shock, then fell across his intended victim.

Tynan retrieved his dagger, then turned back to his men and was glad to see that they had made short work of the other six Highlanders. "Did you hear that, lads?" he called to them. "Balloch's men are badged with heather."

A labored chorus of ayes came back to him.

"Then find you a sprig of heather and fight on."

The fallen ally shoved the dead enemy off him with his good arm and sat up. Using his gold-hilted sword, he forced himself to his feet. "Here." He pulled the sprig of heather from the scarf tied to his arm, tore it in two, and extended half to Tynan. "Take this. You earned it, killin' the bastard who laid me low."

"I'm obliged." Tynan thrust the sprig securely into the small braid hanging from his temple.

"Nay. 'Tis I who am obliged to you, man." The wounded warrior extended his bloodied hand with a wince.

Tynan took it, regretting the pain the gesture caused.

The man staggered briefly when he released Tynan but managed to introduce himself. "Ranald Bane of Islay."

Tynan couldn't believe his luck. "Brother to Donald Balloch?"

"I prefer to think of Donald as brother to *me*," Bane countered, quick despite his injury. "And both of us as sons of John Mor, God rest his soul, slain by James's treason."

Here was one baron of the Council, at least, who would understand Tynan's quest for revenge. It was an odd place for introductions, but if he survived this day, he would need every ally he could get. "I'm Tynan, son of Phelan MacDougald."

Bane's eyebrows shot skyward. "The Wolf of Cothran?" He stared at Tynan. "I thought all his kin were killed along with him."

"Laird Alexander knew otherwise," Tynan clipped out, "but he kept it to himself." He glanced around and saw that the fighting had moved well beyond them.

"A bad business, that," Bane murmured. Blood soaked the plaid covering his shoulder, and he was growing paler by the minute.

"Duncan!" Tynan called.

Duncan, still flushed and panting from the kill, came forward. "Aye, my laird?"

"Help Laird Bane find his people," Tynan instructed, "and stay with him until someone tends his wounds."

"But Laird Tynan," Duncan protested, "I'll miss the last of the fightin'! Can't it wait —"

"Do as I say, or I'll run you through myself!" Tynan roared.

Chastened, Duncan bowed to his boyhood idol with a hasty, "Aye, then, Laird Tynan."

"Sorry, Bane." Tynan glared at Duncan. "My men are still green. They have a lot to learn about discipline."

" 'Tis I who ought to apologize, keepin' you and one of your men from all the fun." Bane winced when Tynan handed him over to Duncan. "I am in your debt, sir."

Tynan bowed, taking grim satisfaction from Bane's deference. For the first time in his life, a baron had treated him as a man of honor.

He'd opened his mouth to respond when he heard a shout that sliced through him like the blade of an axe.

"Help! Laird Cullum is set upon! Help!"

Tynan forgot about Bane, forgot about the fatigue that dragged his muscles, even the pain of the shallow wound in his upper arm. Everything but what he'd just heard was washed away in a surge of primal energy so powerful it fairly lifted him off his feet.

Laird Cullum could not be slain. Not yet.

Tynan turned and hurled himself toward the source of that cry.

Four tents away, a blood-spattered page saw him coming and gestured toward one of the ornate commander's tents. "In there! Hurry!"

Nara was halfway to the battleground when she saw the soldiers running toward her. Prudently, she dropped to the ground and dragged Timothy with her.

"Play dead, Timothy," she murmured urgently, "or the bad men might hurt us." Then she realized he had no idea what "dead" meant. "Lie still and be very, very quiet," she amended. "Like when you're asleep."

Timothy's roaming eyes cleared briefly. "No one will hurt us, Nara." But he did as she asked.

Nara was too frightened to take note of his stillness and clarity of speech. She waited, heart hammering in her chest, until the men had passed. Then she pulled Tim to his feet and continued toward camp.

The fleeing troops were scarcer now, and it soon became evident they were too intent on escaping to bother with a woman and her halting stork of a companion. The truth was, they didn't seem to see her and Tim at all. Still, she did her best to avoid them, dragging Timothy across the marshy ground in an erratic course.

Once they reached the bloodstained earth at the edge of the camp, Nara did her best to shield Timothy from the grisly sights all around them, but Tim seemed as fascinated as he was confused by the dead and wounded, and who could blame him?

Nara didn't understand it, either. Donald Balloch's differences with the king seemed abstract and arbitrary, hardly worth dying for.

"Don't look at them, Tim," she urged, her own soul rent by the destruction all around them. Every corpse they passed was some waiting woman's husband, some mother's child.

*Seanmhair* had been right; men did love fighting above all else, and Nara was looking at the proof.

Nara guided Timothy halfway to the center of camp before she heard the clang of sword against sword and the guttural oaths and grunts of combat all around her. But miraculously, every time they approached the sound of a nearby struggle, the action shifted away from them, almost as if she and Timothy were moving in an invisible bubble of safety.

But Nara knew better than to let down her guard. She crept cautiously forward, Timothy in tow, yet saw no sign of Tynan or his men.

By Conn's beard! How in heath and heather was she supposed to find him? In the maze of tents, wagons, and equipment, she might search all day and still miss him. Assuming she and Timothy weren't killed first.

Nara closed her eyes and said a prayer for guidance and protection, invoking Saint Jude. Then she heard a faint cry from the center of the camp.

"Help! Laird Cullum is set upon! Help!"

Her grandfather! If he was there . . .

Nara tugged Timothy in that direction. "Come, Tim. I think I know where Tynan is."

Meanwhile, Tynan raced into the tent to find Laird Cullum down on one knee, covered in blood, his sword locked with that of a richly outfitted warrior Tynan didn't recognize.

Laird Cullum snarled up at his attacker. "Kill me if you can, Caithness, but by God, I'll take you with me."

Caithness, the Earl of Mar's right-hand man! And all about him, the slain members of his retinue — servants and retainers alike. Somehow, Caithness himself had survived to get the jump on Laird Cullum.

A flicker of motion from Tynan's left drew his attention to a bleeding guard who struggled to his feet and staggered, sword lifted to strike, straight for Laird Cullum's back. Tynan's dagger sent the craven attacker to the Yonder World before he hit the ground, toppling into Laird Cullum's field of vision.

Without looking back, Laird Cullum managed through teeth gritted in effort, "Whoever's responsible for that, I thank you."

He glared up at Caithness. "Is this how you defeat your opponents, sir? By having one of your men creep up to do them dirt from behind?"

"Considering *your* methods, MacKay, I suppose I should take that as a compliment," Caithness ground out. The two men were evenly matched, and he seemed unable to press his advantage.

While the struggling men exchanged insults, Tynan retrieved his dagger, checked to make sure there were no more of Caithness's men lurking about, then circled the impasse at the center of the tent.

When Cullum saw who had come to his rescue, his face went livid. "So it's you." Already contorted by effort, his expression was further misshapen by contempt. "This is no business for a stableboy! Get out! Leave this to me!"

Laird Cullum's insult sent a tide of rage through Tynan,

tempting him beyond all reason to lop the man's head off on the spot. Furious, he raised his sword to do just that.

But a cold, inner voice pulled him back from the brink of murder: No! That would be too easy, too honorable a death. And you need him alive.

It took every ounce of his self-control to rein in the shuddering, all-consuming urge to kill, but somehow he managed.

Panting from the effort, he executed a shallow bow to Caithness. "Allow me to introduce myself. I am Tynan, son of Phelan MacDougald, the Wolf of Cothran. And much as it pains me to do so, I'm afraid I'll have to ask you not to harm Laird Cullum, there."

"I don't give a rat's ass *who* you are," Caithness ground out through gritted teeth. "Get out! Didn't you hear the man? This is a fair fight between peers and none of your concern."

"Fair?" Tynan chuckled dryly. "It's only fair because I made it so." Sword down, he leaned close to Caithness. "But fair or foul, I must tell you that any fight with Laird Cullum is very much my concern."

A spark of admiration brightened Caithness's face, but he kept his eyes locked on his opponent. "Doubtless you want to kill him yourself. Well, get in line. I was here first."

"Go to hell," Laird Cullum spat out, "both of you!"

"All in good time," Tynan said smoothly. "All in good time." He had to get Caithness away from Laird Cullum. Then he remembered Feadain's story of how Cullum's son had goaded Laird Morgan into striking.

Tynan drew his dagger and circled Caithness. "Fight me instead."

Neither man was willing to break the straining, unrelenting deadlock, but Caithness responded, "Would you strike me from behind, like a craven coward?"

"Nay," Tynan said quietly, thrusting his face close to

Caithness's. "I do not subscribe to *your* methods, Caithness. But I have no intention of leaving." In one swift move, he kicked Laird Cullum free of the deadlock and carved an insulting slash up Caithness's cheek. Then, in another blindingly smooth parry, Tynan sheathed his dagger and brought both hands to his greatsword just in time to cut off Caithness's answering blow.

Cullum let out a squeal of indignation, but Tynan was too fast for either man. He dispatched Caithness, slid his bloodied sword into place along his back, then turned and bowed to the man he hated more than anyone in the world. "That makes twice I have saved your life this day, Laird Cullum."

"Who asked you to? I had no need of saving, especially by the likes of you!" Furious at the insult to his dignity, MacKay shot to his feet and raised his sword to strike, but a simple sentence from Tynan stopped him cold.

"I've found her." Tynan said calmly, unflinching before his attacker. "Kill me, and you'll never see —"

Nara's cry of alarm cut him off. "Hold!" She stood just outside the tent's opening, bathed in sunlight.

Tynan scowled. What in blazes was she doing *here?*

Laird Cullum spun around and looked at her as if he were seeing a ghost. He didn't even seem to notice Timothy. "Eideann!" His sword fell to the ground with a dull clunk.

For the only time since Tynan had known him, Cullum MacKay wore the look of a man who still possessed a soul. "Thanks be to God!" Drinking in the sight of her, Laird Cullum dropped to his knees. "My love, more beautiful than the day you left me. But how . . . ?"

Nara did not respond. She had eyes for Tynan alone. "Tynan! He was going to kill you!" She pulled Tim inside the tent. "Sit, Tim, and stay there." Then she rushed past her grandfather and clung to Tynan. "Dear God! So much blood. Are you hurt?"

Tynan merely shook his head. It was all falling into place, just as he had dreamed. He should be happy, but instead, anguish rose up inside him.

Laird Cullum struggled to his feet and turned, visibly shaken by what he was seeing. "Eideann? Don't you know me?"

"She's not Lady Cullum," Tynan announced with grim satisfaction. For two long years — two hungry, homeless, searching years — he had waited for this moment, and now it was really happening.

He grasped Nara's arm and roughly turned her so her grandfather could have a good look. "Allow me to present my wife, the Lady Nara. She is your granddaughter and sole surviving heir."

"My granddaughter?"

Tynan took even more satisfaction from seeing the hope drain out of Laird Cullum's face.

Suddenly MacKay looked like an old man. "My granddaughter," he murmured, understanding.

"As agreed." Tynan urged Nara closer. "I am returning her to you, herewith. Safe and sound. Now it's up to you to keep your end of the bargain."

Nara looked up at him in confusion. Then what he'd said sank in. "Ah, the bargain." She gripped Tynan's upper arms and peered into his face. "Tynan, why are you handing me over to my grandfather? I'm your wife. My place is with you." A thin thread of hysteria edged her voice. "Would you really abandon me to the very man who once threatened to kill me?"

"I have long since repented of that impetuous notion, child." Laird Cullum closed his eyes and passed a weary hand over his face. "That rash threat cost me the only woman I have ever loved. I've suffered for my mistake with twenty long, lonely, wondering years."

"*You* suffered for it?" Tynan growled. "I won't even mention what you did to me. But what about her? Your own granddaughter has spent the past twenty years literally living underground in fear, and you claim you have suffered —"

"Aye, I've suffered. And done my best to put things right." Laird Cullum's interruption was defensive. He turned to Nara. "I offered any boon within my power to grant," he explained, "to the man who could return you or your grandmother to me."

Nara stiffened, her breathing rapid. "Oh, I know all about your offer."

She looked to Tynan, and her eyes told him she was beginning to piece together the truth — the dark, dreadful truth that he had used her all along.

"Is that all I've meant to you, Tynan," she whispered, "even after what has passed between us? Am I just the means to getting your land back, nothing more? Do the vows you took before God signify nothing?"

A deadly spark animated Laird Cullum's features. "True, I did agree to restore your lands and grant you the right to lead your own sept. But I never said anything about marrying my granddaughter. I'll have it annulled." He glared at Tynan in contempt. "She couldn't possibly have consented to the union. Why, you're not fit to lick the soles of a MacKay's boot!"

Tynan didn't rise to the bait. Instead, he said casually, "An unforeseen complication." He arched an eyebrow. "It was Lady Cullum's idea, actually. She refused to let me take Nara, otherwise."

"Eideann?" Laird Cullum's eyes narrowed, the hope returning. "She's alive? But where? Why didn't she come with you?"

"Because she hates you," Tynan said coldly. Every revelation was like a sword-thrust straight to Laird Cullum's heart, wounding but not lethal, and Tynan meant to make the most of what he knew. "It seems your lady wife, sir, fears you almost as much as she hates you." He smiled, watching that sink in. "And she has taught her granddaughter to fear you, as well she should."

Nara felt physically ill, watching the poisonous exchange between her husband and her grandfather. "Tynan, don't," she pleaded, even though she knew that nothing she said would make a difference. How could it, after what her grandfather had done? "I know what he's done to you, and to your people," she blurted out, "but all that is over now. You've won."

For the first time since she had entered the tent, Tynan really seemed to hear her. His grip tightened like a vise on her upper arm. "How do you know?" he demanded. "Who told you?"

"It doesn't matter how I found out." She'd broken her sacred vow to Mary and would likely burn in hell for it, but Nara couldn't think about that now. "All that matters is I know the truth, all of it. I do not blame you for hating him." Her head dropped. "Or for hating me." She sought Tynan's eyes. "But it's over, Tynan. You have your land back. You are chieftain to your people. Let it be enough."

The dark purpose in his gaze told her it would not be enough, and for the first time since she had gotten to know him, Nara truly believed he could harm her.

Pulling at the fingers that dug into her arm, she took a step backward. "What do you mean to do, Tynan?"

"The Sight didn't tell you?" He did not let go.

Dear heaven, she could almost see the darkness welling up within him, obliterating everything that was good and sane. "You know I haven't had the Sight since we consummated our marriage."

"Consummated your marriage?" Laird Cullum spat out. "I shall not hear this! My granddaughter, and this . . . this . . ."

"This *chieftain*," Nara retorted, pivoting on him. "And rightly so, by your own vow. Accept it, Grandfather. He was born to be your equal, but you took that away from him, made him a slave." She confronted Laird Cullum without fear, her green eyes blazing. "By law, he is now your equal again, a baron well and true, for he kept his side of your cursed bargain."

Nara felt Tynan's grip ease and snatched her arm free of him. She stomped across the tent and pulled Timothy to his feet with surprising strength. "As for me . . ." She glared from her husband to her grandfather and back again. "I think Tynan is twice the man you will ever be, but the devil can have you both."

"And just where do you think you're going, little girl?" her grandfather shouted. "In the middle of a battle!"

Already three strides beyond the open tent flaps, Nara halted and glared back at them over her shoulder. "In case you two haven't noticed, the battle is over. Listen."

Silence, all around them.

She patted Tim's hand. "Tim and I are going to seek the hospitality of the castle. After that, who knows?"

She scowled, her lovely face as hard as stone. "Alan Chisolm lies wounded at the campsite on the other side of the ridge, Tynan. Braithwed and Tom died defending me. I suggest you send litters for them all. Have Alan brought to me in the castle. I'll see he's taken care of." She pivoted and

290

dragged a grinning Timothy toward the liberated castle.

"The headstrong chit!" Laird Cullum exclaimed. "Why, she's as bad as Eideann."

Much as he hated to admit it, Tynan was proud of the way she'd stood up to the both of them. He turned to Laird Cullum. "Mind your tongue, sir. Your granddaughter is now my wife; do not forget it."

He started out of the tent, then paused. "When and where does the Council of Lords meet next?"

Laird Cullum seemed surprised by the question. "On the morrow, if there's no counterattack," he answered, clearly begrudging the change of status that obliged him to do so. "Why?"

"Lady Nara is yours only until then. Bring her with you when the assembly convenes. I mean to claim her there, as is my right, with the Council as witness."

"We shall see." Laird Cullum strode past him, leaving Tynan alone with his plans. And his regrets.

# Chapter XVIII

That evening, the muddied waters that lapped near the base of Inverlochy Castle ran red as Tynan and his men, along with the rest of their victorious allies, washed the blood of battle from their naked bodies and their clothes.

They had spent the afternoon alongside Balloch's men — MacLeods of Coll, MacDuffies of Colonsay, MacQuarries of Ulva, and MacKays of Rhinn — finding their wounded, tallying their losses, and stripping almost a thousand of the king's men of their wealth and weapons.

Now prisoners and the lowest echelons were collecting slain enemies and tossing them into a mass grave.

Balloch's own high-ranking dead were being prepared for a final journey home. The remainder would be laid to rest in hallowed ground with proper ceremony on the morrow.

At Tynan's request, the bodies of Braithwed MacClindon and Tom MacDougald were to be bathed and wrapped for transport back to their hard-won freeholds, there to lie beside their ancestors.

Tynan couldn't help contrasting this afternoon's postvictory activities with those of four years ago. In that campaign, his size had earned him the right to fight for Laird Alexander, but no sooner had the battle been won than he was handed a shovel and sent to bury the enemy.

But this day was different. This day, he and his men had been treated as honored allies, as warriors should be.

Rinsed clean of his enemies' blood, Tynan gave his clothes a final swish, then rose from the cold water to the lively splashing of his own men's high-spirited horseplay.

They thought they had earned their freedom this day, and he would let them go on thinking that. But it was Nara who secured both their freedom and their lands, and Tynan couldn't forget it.

Troubled by that irony, he watched the rough play of men who had stared death in the face over and over again and emerged victorious.

Let them have their fun. They had earned it. As for Tynan . . .

He tried not to think about what he must do on the morrow.

Fate had granted all he had planned for, down to the smallest detail. Now it was up to him to finish things.

Suddenly the water was no longer refreshing; it felt icy cold, sending a deep chill through him. Tynan waded ashore to the relative warmth of a sunny breeze. He had just finished wringing out his clothes and putting them on when a page approached at a trot along the shoreline calling, "Laird Tynan MacDougald! I have a message for Laird Tynan MacDougald."

By Odin, but it sounded good to hear himself summoned by his name, his whole name, instead of, "Boy!"

Tynan raised his hand. "Here!"

The messenger stopped at a respectful distance and bowed. "Laird Tynan MacDougald?"

"Aye." By then his men were crowding around Tynan, dripping and curious.

"Laird Donald Balloch bade me invite Laird Tynan MacDougald and his men to celebrate today's victory at a banquet in the Great Hall of the castle this night."

A tight buzz of excitement passed through his men, but Tynan had reservations. He would not be laughed at. "Tell Laird Donald that I humbly thank him for his invitation, but none of us has the proper clothes for such an exalted occasion."

Amid a chorus of disappointed muttering from Tynan's men, the page bowed and sprinted for the castle.

Only Feadain was bold enough to speak out. "Unless these past twenty years have changed things more than I think they have, there will be meat on the table tonight in the Great Hall," he reminded Tynan, "and ale aplenty. Our lads lost two of their best this day and more than earned a good meal. Might I ask ye to reconsider?"

"Would you have them mocked, then, Feadain, for their rough clothes and lack of manners?" Tynan asked with all sincerity. "Nay. Better to go hungry and maintain their dignity."

Feadain shrugged. "Just think about it. That's all I ask."

Tynan was doing his best to ignore the glum faces of his men when the page returned a half-hour later. "Laird Tynan," the boy gasped out.

Tynan stilled, suddenly wondering if his refusal might have been misconstrued as an insult. "What is it?"

Though they tried to pretend they weren't listening, Tynan's men fell silent all around him.

"My master, Laird Donald Balloch, bade me answer Laird Tynan thus." The lad paused, his lips moving without sound as he rehearsed the message so as to get it right. Then he nodded and rattled off, "Laird Tynan and his men have clothed themselves this day in the blood of our enemies. There is no finer raiment. Laird Donald Balloch will expect Laird Tynan and all his men in the Great Hall by sunset. None present shall be served until all are in attendance."

Clever of Balloch. No man in his right mind would risk alienating a hall full of hungry warriors by not appearing.

Ignoring Feadain's grin, Tynan bowed to the inevitable. "Convey my grateful acceptance to your master. We'll be there." He scanned the hungry smiles of his men. "All of us."

The men let out a cheer. Overcome by anticipation, they descended on Duncan Chisolm, picked him up, and hurled him, laughing, back into the river.

Tynan almost smiled with them. It was the best day he'd had in twenty years.

If only he could stop the sun from rising on the morrow. But he couldn't, so he settled for savoring the pleasures of this one shining day, fleeting though those pleasures might be.

Inside Inverlochy Castle, Nara sat in awe on a featherbed. The chamber she'd been given was warmed by thick, colorful rugs and hung with brilliant tapestries. Never, in all her life, had she seen such splendor.

Seven maids ran back and forth from the corner to the door, relaying buckets of hot water for the massive copper tub her hostess had sent for Nara's use.

A bath, with hot water. The extravagance of it was almost more than Nara could fathom.

And the clothes! She wiped her grimy hand as clean as she could on her torn apron before caressing the lovely dress laid out for her. When asked if she preferred a certain color, she had thought of her mother and told them her favorite color was deep pink.

Lo and behold, her hostess had provided a gown in just that shade, its rich damask color shot with gold and bordered in white fur. The pale pink silken undergown was sheer as gauze, with deep sleeves that floated like butterflies' wings whenever they moved. Below the lacing on the front of the undergown was a sumptuous panel of gold brocade, designed to show just above the soft leather shoes she'd been given. Even the rail laid out on the coverlet had pink flowers embroidered around the neck and hem.

Who would have imagined?

And to think she had worried they might not receive her when she'd taken Tim through the open gates to the castle. She had been more than anxious when she'd told one of the soldiers inside that she was Lady Nara, wife of Laird Tynan MacDougald and granddaughter of Laird Cullum MacKay.

Despite her tattered appearance, the guards had taken her at her word. Their captain had bowed, ordered three of his cohorts to escort her to their mistress, then run ahead to announce her presence. By the time Nara had reached the front door, the mistress's lady-in-waiting was there to meet her, so solicitous of Nara's "ordeal" that it was all Nara could do to keep from telling the woman she was not some fragile flower that wilted at the first sign of trouble.

The only thing that had kept her from doing so was the deference the woman granted Timothy. Why, she'd treated him as if he were just like anyone else, dispatching the master's own manservant to see to Timothy's bath. The lady-in-waiting had even assured Nara that Tim would be given new clothes after his bath and returned to her.

At first Tim had been reluctant to go with the stranger, but after a little coaxing from Nara, he'd allowed the manservant to lead him away. Nara had watched carefully as he left and was pleased to see that the servant was quite gentle and deferential to Tim.

And now here she sat, surrounded by luxury.

A serving girl entered bearing food and drink. "My mistress bids the lady eat," she said shyly, her eyes lowered.

"There's mead, meat pies, and dumplings." She set the tray on the table beside the bed, still not looking directly at Nara. "Does my lady require anything else?"

"Nay." Nara's belly let out a horrendous growl which she hoped vainly the girl hadn't heard. She hadn't realized how hungry she was until she saw the food.

Ravenous, she was reaching for a pie when one of the bath attendants brought over a shallow copper bowl half-filled with warm water and a dainty towel. Eyes downcast, the bath attendant asked, "May I wash the lady's hands?"

Nara did her best to rise to the formality of this exalted household. "By all means." She extended her hands, wondering if her grandfather's house was this opulent or this formal.

The warm water felt like heaven, sending pleasant chills up Nara's arms. Once her hands were clean, though, she saw how grimy this day's ordeal had left the rest of her, but she was too hungry to bathe before eating.

Thirsty, too. She sniffed the mead, judged it sweet, and took a healthy swig. It was the most wonderful substance she'd ever put in her mouth. The golden liquid tasted the way laughter felt, and it warmed her almost as much as one of *Seanmhair*'s hugs. The meat pies and dumplings were delicious, too. In almost no time, her trencher and cup were empty and her stomach pleasantly full.

By then, all but two of the maids had left the room, closing the door behind them. As soon as Nara had finished eating, the remaining two maids approached the bed, one of them holding a thick sheet of cotton damask. They stopped a respectful distance away and waited, eyes downcast.

Waited for what? Suddenly Nara was all too conscious of her ignorance. "Yes?" she asked.

"Whenever milady is ready," the maid responded.

Her answer left Nara as much in the dark as ever. Though

she had no wish to expose her ignorance, Nara had neither the disposition nor the talent for deception, so she decided to be honest. "Waiting for what?"

The maids fidgeted but remained silent, eyes downcast.

"For heaven's sake," Nara said, "why won't anyone in this house look me in the eye?"

"It's not permitted," the elder of the two volunteered primly. "Not proper."

"I see." Nara didn't like that one bit. "Well, it makes me nervous. So I'm asking you both to look at me."

The younger did as she asked immediately, clearly fascinated, but the elder managed only an alarmed glance before dropping her gaze back to the floor.

"Please," Nara coaxed her. "You can do it. I promise not to tell anyone."

After considerable inner struggle, the woman looked at Nara, but her expression betrayed her fear that someone might come in and see her flaunting the rules.

Nara hopped off the bed, crossed to the door, and closed the bolt. "There. Now no one can interrupt us."

The two maids exchanged troubled glances.

"Oh, dear." Had she displayed bad manners by locking the door? "Is that against the rules, too?"

Both maids shrugged. Nara might as well have been a talking pig, for the looks on their faces.

"Where were we?" she murmured, trying to quash the awkwardness she felt. "Oh, yes." She approached the two women. "You were waiting, and I asked for what."

"To help milady undress and bathe," the younger said.

Nara's eyebrows shot up. Tynan was the only person in the whole world besides *Seanmhair* who had ever seen her naked. She wasn't at all sure she could strip in front of two total strangers. But then again, she'd already given the servants cause enough for gossip. Swallowing her embarrassment, she lifted her arms to each side. "Very well. Undress me."

It wasn't as bad as she'd feared. First the younger woman untied Nara's belt, then asked her to sit. She sat, and each maid took a foot and removed the shoe and stocking. They then asked Nara to stand, and when she did, the older woman averted her eyes and held up the sheet of damask to shield Nara from both of them while the younger girl deftly pulled first Nara's scapular, then her gown and rail over her head. With expert swiftness, the two maids wrapped her in the damask without exposing her nakedness.

Relieved, Nara clutched the covering around her and crossed to the tub.

Exotic oils and bath salts clouded the water, and rose petals floated on the surface. Before she could ask what came next, the two maids stationed themselves on either side of her, their backs to her and the tub, then pulled the damask free to serve as a screen while she stepped into the tub.

Once safely up to her chin in the cloudy water, Nara let out a satisfied sigh. "Heavenly."

The maids set about bathing her arms, legs, face, and hair with sponges. It felt divine. Nara reveled in every warm, perfumed minute of her bath. But when the younger of the two maids reached toward her submerged torso, Nara stayed her arm and took the sponge. Coloring, she murmured, "I prefer to do that myself."

An hour later, her hair had been combed almost dry and fashioned into a sleek figure eight on the back of her head. After that, six maids helped her dress, catching in the elegant gown's fullness just below her breasts with a golden sash secured in the center by a brooch of rose quartz set in gold.

Nara felt like a queen as she sat in a backless chair while a proficient young woman offered an elaborate, heart-shaped headdress of deep rose-colored velvet and satin for her approval.

"Goodness," she blurted out, "that looks heavy."

"Only a trifle, milady." The hatkeeper sniffed. "But well worth the inconvenience. It's the latest fashion in all the courts of Europe. Her ladyship will be wearing one much like it to the banquet." She added haughtily, "Of another color, of course."

"Her ladyship?" Nara still had no idea who her hostess was.

The maid became even haughtier. "Why, Lady Alasdair, of course."

Whoever *that* was. "Of course." At least Nara now had a name for her hostess.

She eyed the dense roll of fabric that formed the headpiece's thick, heart-shaped circlet. Golden cords spiraled around the roll, binding it to the velvet skullcap. "May I hold it?"

"As you wish, my lady," the maid said with barely disguised disdain.

Sure enough, the thing was as cumbersome as it looked. And stiff. Those velvet panels on the sides would cover her ears completely. They'd be hot and interfere with her hearing.

Nara looked into the box of hats the lady's maid had brought with her. "What about that one?" She pointed out a simple openwork caplet of golden filigree. "And that veil, there." She indicated a length of sheerest pink silk. "That should look lovely with my gown."

Clearly disapproving, the maid extracted the items she had chosen. "Madame has not worn those for years, my lady. But if milady insists . . ."

"Milady insists," Nara retorted, feeling every bit as regal as she looked.

No sooner was her hat in place than a knock sounded at the door. The maid hastened to answer it.

"It's John, the laird's manservant," she announced, "and Master Timothy."

Nara was on her feet before the words were out of her mouth. "Have them come in."

Timothy — spanking clean and dressed in clothes that were finely made, but far too short and far too wide for him — dragged a smiling John into the room. "This's John, Nara," Tim chirped. "He's nice. A lotsa food, an' good. An' I had a bath."

Obviously, John had treated Tim kindly. Nara granted the manservant a heartfelt, "Thank you so much, John. I can see to him now."

John shot her a subtle flash of masculine approval before dropping his gaze and bowing. "It was my pleasure to attend Master Timothy, my lady. He is a most exceptional gentleman."

*Master Timothy.* That was rich. Nara grinned outright, but managed to recover her dignity. "He is special, indeed, and dearly loved, so it pleases me to see him treated well."

"I am at Master Timothy's service." John started to leave, then paused. "Will Laird Timothy be joining milady in the Great Hall for supper?"

Nara looked for and found the subtle signs of fatigue in Tim's face. "I don't know. He seems tired." She tried to meet Tim's eyes. "Are you tired, sweeting? Would you like to stay up with Nara or go to bed?"

Tim's response was to lope across the room, crawl up onto Nara's bed, and close his eyes. "G'night, Nara. I tired."

Nara chuckled.

"We have prepared an adjoining chamber for Laird Timothy, my lady. Shall I take him there?" John said, clearly worried that Tim had just appropriated the bed intended for her.

"No." Nara crossed to the bed, drew Tim's frail legs aside, pulled the covers from underneath, then tenderly tucked him in. She kissed his cheek. How comforting it was to see him warm, well fed, and happy. No matter what else came of this day, she could give thanks for that much, at least. And for Tynan's safety.

Nara turned back to John. "Let him stay where he is. I shall take the adjoining chamber."

"Ah . . ." John coughed, suddenly awkward. "But the bed in the adjoining chamber is rather narrow." His cheeks flushed with embarrassment. "Fine enough for one, my lady, but certainly not large enough for Laird Tynan, as well. That is . . ."

Tynan. Nara hadn't even considered that her hosts would logically put them in the same room.

"Humbly begging milady's pardon," John said, "but with all of Laird Donald's men in the castle, not to mention Laird Alasdair and the others, we're a bit short on accommodations."

"How thoughtless of me. I should have realized." Nara regretted embarrassing John, especially in light of his kindness to Timothy. She turned and took Tim's hand. "Come, sweeting. John has prepared a very nice bed next door, just for Tim."

Tim frowned and rolled back onto his side. "I wanna sleep with Nara."

Now it was Nara's turn to color. "Not tonight." She grasped Tim's shoulder and resolutely drew him into a sitting position. "But I will sit with you until you fall asleep. Come along, Toady-boy."

Begrudgingly, Tim obeyed.

He was sound asleep within five minutes. Nara left him under John's watchful eye. She had made her way halfway down to the Great Hall when she remembered that she and Tynan had been assigned only one bed.

The prospect of sharing that bed with him in the luxurious privacy of their chamber brought a fresh surge of color to her cheeks. She was still blushing when she entered the festive gathering in the vaulted hall.

The noise level was daunting, as was the rough brand of banter these warriors were engaged in. There must have been more than two hundred of them crammed into the spaces between the long tables.

Nara halted, more than a little overwhelmed. With the exception of the serving women who were putting the finishing touches on the tables, she couldn't see a single woman present from where she stood.

"Ah, and there she is!"

A man she assumed to be her host rushed forward, trailed at a more dignified pace by a stately woman in blue. Her hostess? Nara decided she must be, for the woman was wearing a dark blue headpiece quite similar to the one Nara had refused.

"Lady Tynan, I presume," her host said.

Nara forgot her manners entirely. "Aye."

Her host paid no attention to her blunt response. "Allow me to introduce myself. I am Alasdair Carrach, Laird of Lochaber east of Lochy, and as such, host of this joyous occasion." His smile broadened to a leer. "What a lovely young bride you are."

His eyes still on her, he called toward a group of men at his left. "Cullum, you knave, you should have told me your granddaughter was so beautiful!"

Laird Alasdair turned to the woman on his right. "My dear, allow me to present the Lady Tynan. Lady Tynan, this is my wife, the Lady Alasdair."

"I am so pleased to see you refreshed and well," the older woman said with sincerity.

Nara liked her immediately. "Thanks to my lady's generous hospitality," she responded, "I am most refreshed." Remembering her manners, she dropped into a deep curtsy, but before she sank as low as she intended, her hostess caught Nara's elbow and urged her back aright.

"I am not a queen, dear child," Lady Alasdair offered, clearly embarrassed by Nara's excessive deference, "merely your hostess, and right honored to be so."

Another gaffe. Nara resigned herself to making many more before the evening was over. But all she could do was her best.

Her grandfather emerged from the group her host had called to. He approached Nara head-on, bowing slightly when he reached her. She could have sworn she saw agony on his face when he looked at her.

Was it her hat that so discomfited him? For a fleeting moment, she regretted turning down the stylish headpiece. Then she realized he was looking at her face, not her hat.

Such longing, such sadness were reflected in his eyes. As the true reason dawned on her, Nara felt herself softening toward him. He looked at her and saw *Seanmhair*.

Did he love *Seanmhair* that much? she wondered.

Then she remembered why *Seanmhair* had fled her husband, and the softness she felt quickly solidified into distrust.

Laird Alasdair put his arm around Laird Cullum's shoulders and nodded toward Nara in approval. "Lovely as a queen. Had I known about this one, Cullum, I'd have insisted you save her for one of my sons."

Nara didn't like being talked about as if she weren't there. "Too late," she countered archly, not caring that she hadn't been addressed. "As you know, my laird, I have a husband already." She leveled a challenging gaze at her grandfather. "I am married to Tynan MacDougald, chieftain of his sept and, as of this very day, freeholder of his father's lands."

Laird Cullum glared back at her, the tension between them thicker than the smoke that rose from the torches that lit the hall.

Mouth pursed, the master of Inverlochy Castle looked skyward, but it fell to Lady Alasdair to extract Nara from the deadly silence. "Come, my dear. I know everyone is anxious to meet you." She tucked Nara's hand into her elbow and guided her through the laughing, jostling victors.

Once they were safely beyond Laird Cullum's hearing, she said to Nara, "Your husband's valor this day has earned you both a place at the head table. I'll show you to your seat."

As they worked their way in that direction, Nara's hostess selectively nodded and spoke to her guests, introducing Nara only to the higher-ranking barons and earls.

It was all very confusing. Too much noise, too many strange men, too many faces. By the time they reached her place near the end of the head table, Nara felt as if her skull would burst with the jumble of names, titles, and holdings of the men she'd met.

It didn't help matters, either, that she was one of only a few women present.

And so far, she'd seen no sign of Tynan.

One by one, the chairs around her began to fill, but the seat beside her remained empty. She made every effort to appear casual and relaxed, but inside, Nara was miserable.

Then she looked to the open doors at the back of the hall and saw him, towering above his men.

Nara's throat tightened with pride. Despite his humble clothing, Tynan looked like a golden warrior-god.

Then she remembered this afternoon's coldness, and her heart contracted. How would he react to her here, in front of all these people? She sat very straight, trying to brace herself for the worst.

Nara watched as his men were led to seats at the lower tables, while Tynan was escorted toward the head table. As he made his way through the remaining crowd, a tight murmur of excitement followed in his wake. He reached the center of the head table and bowed to their host and the guest of honor, who received him warmly.

At Tynan's approach, the man just beyond Donald Balloch rose to his feet. He wore a sling on his right arm but used his left to strike a good-natured clout on Tynan's shoulder. The wounded knight's hearty welcome told Nara he was glad to see Tynan. She strained to hear the introductions, but they were lost in the rising tide of conversation all around her.

One thing was clear, though. These powerful leaders were doing their best to make Tynan feel welcome in their midst.

Nara looked for her grandfather and saw that he had been seated at one of the lesser tables. Conscious of the slight, she nevertheless had no wish to rub his nose in it, so she looked away before he made eye contact.

Tynan was growing increasingly uncomfortable as man after man he had helped this afternoon praised his prowess. Still, he was grateful to whatever dark deity had brought about such opportunities. He and his men must have come to the rescue of half the Council, it seemed. But Tynan knew better than to count too heavily on the flattery now showered upon him, for many of the same men who now praised him had once looked straight through him back at Eilean d'Ór when Tynan had helped them onto their horses.

He had just accepted Donald Balloch's thanks when Ranald Bane rose beside his brother. Bane gave Tynan's shoulder a congratulatory whack with his good fist. Then, despite his injuries, Bane leaned across the head table and grasped Tynan's forearm. "And there he is, the man of the hour." Grinning, he released Tynan's arm and subsided into his chair.

"Look you, Donald," he said to his brother. "He's as big as I told you, aye? You should see him wield a greatsword," he added with affection. "Ochan, but it's a thing to behold. Stirs my blood just thinkin' about it."

"What blood you have left, little brother," Balloch said with a smile. He studied Tynan closely. " 'Tis more than my brother's life I have to thank you for, MacDougald. You came to the aid of some of my most valued allies this day. I am beholden to you."

"Given the chance, any man here would have done the same," Tynan responded truthfully.

"Ah, but any man here did not. There were only you and your men, and that by Divine Providence. None here shall soon forget it."

Balloch leaned forward so as not to be overheard. Eyes narrowed, his voice dropped. "Before he surrendered himself to King James, Laird Alexander vouchsafed certain documents — and certain secrets — of the Council to me, as senior member at liberty of the Donalds. I know of your vow."

Tynan tensed. "And . . ."

"And . . . allow me to assure you, Laird Tynan, that in my cousin's absence, his promise as head of the Council will be honored. The matter has already been discussed." His voice went lower still. "Laird Cullum has his allies on the Council, but they are few, and even those cannot deny the justification for what you've sworn."

Straightening, Balloch sighed, weary under the burden of leadership. "So, unless some unforeseen calamity occurs, most of the Council will stand behind you. As they would have in any event. It's only just."

He looked past Tynan to Laird Cullum with both contempt and regret, then turned to stare at Nara, his expression hardening. "Pity. A sad business and a waste." Balloch's piercing gaze focused back on Tynan. "But, for all our faults, we are, after all, men of honor, not beasts. Soon or late, honor must be served."

So. Honor would be served.

Tynan took no satisfaction from hearing that all would be as he had planned. He felt, instead, as if he'd just received his own death warrant instead of Nara's.

Nara watched with pride as baron after baron rose to offer Tynan thanks. He had almost reached her when she met his eyes and smiled, in spite of herself. His reaction was not what she'd expected.

Tynan took one look at her and stopped cold. A dozen emotions seemed to struggle just below the surface, but there was no reading his expression. Only one word could accurately describe the way he finally ended up looking at her: haunted.

That look went through her like a cold wind, but she managed to maintain her polite smile.

Before Tynan could take another step, a woman dressed in scarlet approached him from behind. Her face seemed naggingly familiar.

"Tynan," the woman oozed. "Our hero. I was hoping you'd come." Taking Tynan's arm, she granted Nara a condescending glance. "Ah, niece. How very quaint you look this evening, all dressed in pink just like your dear, departed mother."

Lady Margaret! And she had her claws on Tynan as if she owned him.

Nara's chest tingled with a surge of territorial jealousy so strong it left her queasy. She leveled her gaze with her great-aunt's and, to her own horror, heard herself respond, "How bright you look in scarlet, Aunt Margaret. I must say, it becomes you far better than the color you were wearing the last time we met. It was so late, the hue wasn't easy to tell. Brown, wasn't it? A rather monastic shade."

Conn's balls! Where had *that* come from?

Amazed, Tynan stifled his surprised chuckle and ended up making a sound halfway between a sneeze and a muffled belch.

Lady Margaret was anything but intimidated. On the contrary, her feral smile spread to a genuine grin of approval. "Well done, child. Blood will tell."

Dear heaven, Nara thought, she's right. The poison had come to the fore, and all it had taken to overcome her better instincts was a little jealousy.

Lady Margaret turned her attention back to Tynan. "Much as I would like to talk over old times, I'm afraid I must sit beside my brother to sup." Her cold eyes glistened. "How it must gall him to see you up here, while we've been relegated to the company of lesser lights."

She started away, then turned back to him. "Come see me after dinner." She shot Nara a wry glance. "Alone." Lady Margaret chuckled. "We have much to talk about, Tynan." She pressed her scarf over her heart and drew close again, so that only Nara and Tynan heard what came next. "I'm sure you remember, Tynan, how very unpleasant I can make things for those who refuse my invitations." Then she laughed like a young girl and left them without a backward look.

Nara's outrage sent her heart pumping even faster. So this was her birthright — evil, pure and simple. Unable to look away, she watched her great-aunt sit beside Laird Cullum and whisper into his ear. He shoved his sister roughly away with absolute disgust on is face.

What had she told him? Nara hesitated to imagine.

Tynan provided a welcome distraction by sitting down next to Nara. She'd been so caught up with her great-aunt, she hadn't even seen him round the table to join her. As he settled into the backless chair beside her, she could feel his presence drawing at her.

Surely he had to be aware of the charged forces that seemed to throb between them. Yet he did not even speak to her.

Stung by his rejection, Nara introduced herself to the stranger on her right, but he responded only with monosyllables, obviously resenting anything that took him away from the business of eating and drinking. So she eventually gave up trying to engage him in conversation.

Tynan, on the other hand, made no effort to speak to the man to his left. He simply sat and watched the celebration all around him as if he were merely an observer instead of a guest. As course after course was served, he said little and ate even less. Amid all the talking, jesting, laughing, and drinking, he kept himself an island of isolation.

What was going through his mind?

A casual observer might interpret his silence for modesty, even shyness, but Nara knew better. Underneath his grave demeanor, Tynan was grieving.

When she had finished eating, she turned to him and ventured, "I'm so sorry about Braithwed and Tom. They were good men."

"What?" Tynan frowned just as she used to whenever

310

*Seanmhair* had caught her daydreaming.

"Braithwed and Tom," she repeated, sorry now she'd brought it up.

"Oh, aye," he said absently. "A grievous loss."

But not the one that's grieving you, she realized.

Nara decided to try the direct approach. "You're quite a hero, Tynan. Everyone here has sung your praises to the heavens. Yet you seem troubled, distant." She tried to see past the grim mask he was wearing, to no avail. "Please tell me what's bothering you. I'm your wife; any burden that affects you is also mine to bear."

Tynan's vacant gaze cleared; he peered at her with searing intensity. "Trust me, Nara, you do not want to know."

"But I do," she said with conviction, "no matter what it is. Please, Tynan. I would gladly share any burden, no matter how heavy."

Again, that haunted look claimed his features, deepening the lines beside his mouth. "I told you. You do not want to know."

Everyone else in the crowded, boisterous hall seemed to melt away. Nara was conscious only of Tynan and the secret burden that he bore.

"Oh, Tynan. Don't you see?" She had to touch him. She laid her hand on his muscular, sun-browned forearm. Taking courage from the solid warmth of his flesh, she said what she had known for months. "I love you. I don't know how it happened or even why, but I've loved you since . . ." Unable to bear the emptiness in his great, golden brown eyes, she turned her gaze to her lap. "The truth is, I can't remember not loving you. It's as if you were there all along, hidden away in some secret part of me, and I was waiting, waiting, waiting, and then . . . everything fell into place, just as it was supposed to."

She glanced up, only to see that he had closed his own eyes in agony.

"Tynan, what *is* it?" Fear began gnaw at the edges of her hope.

He opened his eyes and regarded her with longing, but his words brought neither solace nor enlightenment. "God knows, there's precious little love in this world, Nara. Do not waste yours on me, for you will hate me soon enough." She could see him dying inside. "And do not ask me for the truth; it will only destroy you."

"Nothing you say or do can ever make me stop loving you, Tynan." She had that much to hold on to.

"I would give my soul to believe that, Nara, but destiny has already decreed otherwise." Almost reluctantly, he withdrew his arm from her touch. "This much of the truth, I have given you: You shall hate me, soon and till your dying breath. That is truth enough."

As if he could no longer bear being so close to her, Tynan rose, drawing the attention of those at the head table. He bowed to Alasdair Carrach. "Laird Alasdair. Laird Donald. Pray excuse me. This has been a most enjoyable celebration, but I fear my duties require that I take my leave at once."

"Must you rush off, man?" Laird Alasdair asked, his speech slightly slurred from drink. "Why, I haven't had a chance to toast your prowess."

"All in a day's work, my laird." Tynan offered his host a cold smile. "Your safety and that of our allies is acknowledgment enough, sir. Now I must beg your leave."

Laird Alasdair's disappointment was obvious, but Laird Donald seemed to understand. He shot Nara a penetrating glance, then nodded his permission for Tynan to leave.

Outranked, Laird Alasdair could only comply. "You shall be missed. But come and see me tomorrow. I wish to express my gratitude in more concrete terms."

Tynan bowed. "I am at your service." And then he was gone.

Feeling as if the whole world had just become a desert, Nara stayed until her eyes grew heavy. She must have dozed off, because the next voice she heard was Donald Balloch's. "Lady Tynan? I fear the entertainment is about to become unsuitable for a gentle lady such as you. Might I beg the honor of escorting you to your chamber?"

She looked up and saw infinite compassion in his face. "Thank you, my laird. The honor would be mine."

They said little until he reached her door and opened it for her. Then, an odd look on his face, he stepped back into the hallway and asked, "Are you a woman of faith, Lady Tynan?"

What a strange question. Nara was so taken aback, she didn't even have the wherewithal to challenge his reason for asking such a thing. Instead, she answered honestly, "Oh, aye. Prayer has been my greatest comfort in this life."

"Then I suggest you pray for a miracle," he said. He bowed, turned, and strode away so briskly she could only stare after him, wondering what in the world he was talking about.

Confused and exhausted, Nara entered her room and carefully closed the door behind her. She crossed to the connecting door and peeked in on Timothy. He was snoring soundly, his mouth wide open. Nara closed the door with a smile.

So tired she could scarcely keep her eyes open, Nara removed her veil, hat, and gowns, then carefully laid each item across the large trunk at the foot of the bed. After a long-overdue appointment with the chamber pot, she unbound her hair, shook it free, and crawled into the big, inviting bed. Though she knew it would take hours to get the tangles from her hair the next day, she hadn't the strength to plait it.

She had almost drifted to sleep, her mind struggling sluggishly to sort out the mysteries of this evening, when she remembered she hadn't said her nightly prayers. With Tynan gone, she had the luxury of saying them aloud.

Nara crawled out of the bed and knelt on the thick rug beside it, head bowed and hands folded. "Heavenly Father, almighty and everlasting God, I give Thee thanks," she whispered, "for the blessings of this day. I give Thee praise for answering my prayer about Alan." If only she had prayed for Braithwed and Tom, as well. "And I beg your forgiveness for only asking You to protect Alan. I should have prayed for the others. All I can do now is beseech You to take them to heaven." Sleepily, she directed her rambling prayer back to her blessings. "And thank You for keeping Tynan and Timothy safe; and me; and for the victory you granted; and for the hospitality of this wonderful place — how kindly they treated Timothy — and Laird and Lady Alasdair's generosity in providing this room and the bath and the lovely clothes and the food. And the *mead*." She was rambling again.

The image of Tynan's face took shape behind her closed lids, and her heart twisted. "But most of all, dear Lord, I thank You for the gift of love and the courage to tell Tynan how I feel, even though he cannot return that love. I will not ask You to let him love me. I ask only that he might love You, because only Your love can bring light to end the darkness that consumes him." That would be miracle enough. "Use me as You will to bring that about," she prayed fervently. "I hold nothing back, not even my life."

As always when she prayed sincerely, she felt the peace of communion flowing through her, soothing, quieting the questions and restoring the joy that had nothing to do with circumstance and everything to do with God's grace.

Then she remembered Laird Donald's admonition. "And Father, I humbly ask You to grant us a miracle." Nara had no idea *what* miracle, but she was confident that God, who knew all, would. Crossing herself, she concluded with, "I offer this prayer in the name of the Father, the Son, and the Holy Ghost. Amen."

She climbed into bed and murmured one last supplication before she slept. "And if it's all the same to You, dear Lord, please protect Tynan from Lady Margaret and bring him safely back to his own bed, where he belongs."

Confessing her jealousy would have to wait until she could honestly renounce it. Nara closed her eyes, her last waking thought the hope that she would dream of Tynan . . . and of love.

And dream of love she did.

She had no idea how long she'd been asleep when the dream became so real that she opened her eyes and found herself cradled in Tynan's arms. His breath was hot against her hair and smelled of whiskey, just as it had in her dream. Nara's femininity flexed involuntarily at the scent.

She let him go on thinking she was asleep until he shifted to pull away. Then she twined her fingers into the soft hair at the nape of his neck, refusing to let him go. "I was dreaming of this," she said huskily.

Without the candle, he was a dark silhouette beside her. The rest of the castle had grown quiet.

"Go back to sleep," he whispered brusquely.

"No," she murmured. Driven now by desire and an inexplicable sense of urgency, Nara kissed him with all the hunger that welled inside her. Her breasts hard against his chest, she felt his rapid heartbeat grow even more rapid, his skin hot through the thin fabric of her rail.

When he tried again to pull away, Nara shamelessly slid her hand up his inner thigh until she found the pulsing resistance of his erection. "Take me, Tynan. Let us have that much, at least."

He held back, still battling his inner demons.

Nara closed her fingers around his erection and slid them rapidly up and down again. His gasp of pleasure told her this one prayer, at least, had been granted.

# Chapter XIX

"What about Tim?" Tynan protested, but he did not take his hands from her ribs. "We might wake him . . ."

Nara was burning, burning. "Lightning could strike this very room without waking Tim, and you know it." She kissed Tynan again, and her kiss succeeded in igniting the flame of his own need.

But there was something different about the way he responded. Before, Tynan's kisses had always been forceful, hungry, and demanding, yet this night his lips were tender and lingering.

He grasped her hands and stretched her arms full-out on the pillows above her head, his teeth finding her nipples through the sheer fabric of her rail and teasing them aright. Shifting his weight to one knee alongside her, he slowly ran his palms up the sides of her legs, pushing the rail ahead of them. When he freed the dark vee between her legs, he bent and kissed her there, sending a tremor of pure ecstasy through her.

Impatient to remove anything that came between them, Nara finished stripping away the rail herself, then she unbuckled his belt and fumbled with the lacings of his shirt. Tynan did not bother with the lacings. He reared up and snatched off his plaid, then shucked out of his shirt.

Nara could see only his silhouette in the darkness, but as always, the wild, male scent of him drove her almost to distraction. Gripping his hips, she curled forward and boldly kissed his erection.

So hot. So smooth.

Tynan groaned and threaded his fingers into her hair, drawing her lips closer. Then he eased her back down and continued exploring her body with his hands, his lips, his fingers, kissing, parting, stroking with uncharacteristic deliberation. It was as if he were memorizing the taste and feel of every square inch of her.

Gone was the fierce urgency he had shown her before. In its place, he savored her with the lingering sweetness of a last farewell. Once, twice, he took her to a shuddering release, but withheld his own. Each time, he renewed his deliberate assault on her senses.

When she could endure it no more, Nara threaded her hand between their bodies and grasped his erection. "Come inside me," she whispered raggedly. "I cannot bear this emptiness one second longer."

Slowly, Tynan entered, filling her by degrees until the seat of her desire made contact with the crisp curls of his loins. But he did not thrust. Again he took her hands and extended them above her, kissing her forehead, her ears, her eyes, her neck.

Exquisite torture, it was. Nara arched against him. Then she curled to his chest and nibbled at the tight buds of his nipples. Tynan gasped with pleasure, and inside her, his member leapt.

She pulled her hands free of his and gripped his buttocks, her short nails digging into the hard, muscular flesh. Almost instinctively, her legs wrapped around him, and she flexed to draw him in even farther.

At last he lost control. Tynan took hold of her waist and held her close against him as he reared back onto his knees, thrusting into her again and again, faster and faster until a guttural exhalation told her he had spent himself inside her.

Drenched and panting, he collapsed atop her.

Lost in her own afterglow, Nara let her hands roam up and down his back. By Glory, but he felt good.

Tynan made to lift himself off her, but she wrapped her arms around him and would not let him. "Stay, just a little longer."

She felt him tense.

"Tynan, I know something is wrong. Again I ask you, please tell me what it is, so I might help you."

Silence. Tynan lifted his face to peer at her in the darkness.

Unsettled, Nara let go of his back to stroke his cheek. The moment she touched his face, he jerked away from her, but not before his tears had wet her fingertips.

Not tears of joy. The realization set loose a cold, numbing tide of fear inside her.

He rolled free of her and sat on the side of the bed, his back to her as he gazed into the darkness. Then he collected his clothes and put them on with expert quickness.

Nara tried to make her voice light. "For once we have a real bed, and you choose not to sleep in it."

He paused, but said nothing.

She hated herself for having to ask, but she asked it anyway. "Will you go back to Lady Margaret, then? Is that why you are leaving me?"

"Nay." His voice was harsh. "You know better than that. She has nothing to do with it."

"Then she did not try to seduce you into her bed?"

"She tried to seduce me, all right," he said bitterly, "but not into her bed."

"No?" Nara said skeptically. She drew the coverlet over

her nakedness. "If not into her bed, then into what?"

"Murder," Tynan clipped out. "She invited me to kill your grandfather."

Nara could scarcely believe what she was hearing. "But he's her *brother*. What kind of woman —"

Tynan cut her off with, "I told you what kind of woman she is: She's a MacKay, and the same venom flows through her veins that flows through your grandfather's." He stood. "They're very much alike, she and Laird Cullum." Tynan hurled the words at her like weapons, as if he were suddenly determined to put as many obstacles as possible between them. "Lady Margaret has two grown sons and wants to see one or both of them in control of Laird Cullum's holdings."

"Does she think you a fool?" Nara whispered, dazed by her aunt's reckless, evil proposition. "They'd hang you for killing my grandfather."

"She's counting on that, just as she's counting on my hatred. But I will not kill him, and I told her so. That would be too easy."

"Too easy?" Nara went still. "What *do* you mean to do, then, Tynan?" When he did not reply, she asked, "Did she say anything about me?"

"No," he said, "but don't fool yourself. You know too much. Lady Margaret would not hesitate to get rid of you." Tynan bent closer in the darkness. "Doubtless she thinks of you as an inconvenience, and a temporary one at that."

The hostility in his voice caused Nara's heart to shrink. "Why are you telling me this, Tynan? What's happened?"

"Nothing . . . yet." He picked up his sword.

Something indefinable made her wonder if she would ever see him again. "Where are you going?"

"To be with my men. After what I said to Lady Margaret, I do not think she will dare to do anything to Laird Cullum this night. But just in case she does, I shall need witnesses, lots of them, to swear to my presence elsewhere."

"When will I see you again?"

Tynan stood looking at her in the darkness for some time. When he answered, it was not in anger, but softly, with regret. "Tomorrow, at the Council of Lairds." Then the hardness returned. "Laird Cullum will take you there. Be ready when he calls for you."

Then he turned and left her to lie awake and wonder what would happen when he came for her. One thing was certain: Tynan had something planned — something he would not tell.

Early the next morning, Nara was given breakfast in bed while John discreetly took Timothy away to see to his needs. No sooner had she finished eating and relieving herself than four of Lady Alasdair's own attendants arrived bearing an even more splendid outfit than the pink one.

This regal ensemble had a sheer ivory-colored underdress with a front panel of deep purple brocade, its long sleeves decorated with sheer petals of silk that trailed to the floor like exotic feathers. The overgown was fashioned of emerald-green wool so soft it reminded Nara of a kitten's tummy. An intricate pattern had been embroidered in gold thread on the outside in a leafy design that echoed the shape of the underdress's sleeve hangings. And there was rich, ebony mink on the outer garment's deep neckline, fitted elbow-length sleeves, and hem. Purple flowers with dark green leaves graced the neck and hem of the freshly pressed rail.

Clothes fit for a queen.

The outfit was completed by green leather slippers and a deep purple girdle heavily tooled in gold.

"Laird Tynan will be honored today by the Council," the

321

attendant in charge explained. She made no effort to conceal her excitement. "In observance of such a special occasion, my mistress wished to provide these garments as a token of her esteem."

Still out of sorts from Tynan's abandonment, Nara wondered crossly if everyone knew everyone else's business in this place. True to form, Tynan had neglected to mention that he was to be honored, leaving Nara to find out from complete strangers. It rankled. She consoled herself with the possibility that that was the secret he'd been hiding, even though — deep down — she knew it wasn't.

"Please convey my thanks to Lady Alasdair," Nara said. "I shall make every effort to see that the garments are returned in good condition."

"Returned?" All four attendants pivoted in undisguised amazement.

The one who had spoken first looked askance at the others, then said smoothly, "Forgive me, my lady, for not making it clear. The clothes are a gift, for milady to keep, of course."

"To keep?" Nara inspected the sumptuous offering in grateful disbelief. The very idea that someone could part with such exquisite raiments . . .

"If milady will stand," the sympathetic attendant requested, "we will help her dress. I fear we are rather pressed for time. There is still Lady Margaret to assist."

"Of course." Nara hastened to her feet. "Forgive me. The magnitude of Lady Alasdair's generosity touched me so, I quite forgot my manners."

Nara turned her back and changed into the fresh rail, then allowed the maids to lace her into the underdress. Next they carefully lowered the outer gown over her head, feeding the underdress's elaborate sleeves through the arm holes in advance of her hands. In no time, the front of that was laced, as well. It fit as if it had been made for her. Then they assisted her in donning her stockings and the supple slippers.

"Goodness." Nara hiked up her skirts for a look at her shoes. "What are these slippers made of? They're so comfortable. And so warm."

"Kid leather, lined with shearling," the attendant answered. "Now, if milady will stand . . ." She held out the girdle. When Nara obliged, she placed the girdle just below Nara's breasts and fastened the golden buckle made in the image of a dragon's head. Once that was done, all four of the women set about arranging the folds that fell from the high waistline.

It occurred to Nara that she would get little done taking this long to dress every day, but she kept her thoughts to herself.

The four attendants stood back and surveyed the results of their efforts.

"Magnificent," was their consensus.

"Green is definitely milady's color," the attendant in charge declared, to the murmured agreement of the others. "It brings out the lovely emerald color of milady's eyes."

"Aye," said the second. "And the underdress makes milady's skin look as smooth and white as cream."

Nara shifted uncomfortably in the face of such flattery.

"Now, as to milady's hair and hat —" the first began.

"Please. I prefer not to wear a hat, thank you," Nara interrupted, remembering the heavy headdresses her hostess and Lady Margaret had worn.

Self-conscious, she finger-combed the tangled hair drawn over her shoulder. "Just help me find a becoming style to get my hair off my neck. That will be sufficient."

"As milady wishes."

By the time her grandfather was announced, her hair had been drawn up into a coil of braids on her crown, and she had been sitting, ready and anxious, for almost an hour.

"Please show him in."

What would she say to him? And he to her?

Laird Cullum sighed deeply when he saw her. "Ochan, lass, but you are beautiful. Every bit as beautiful as your dear grandmother, the day we wed."

"I am complimented, sir."

Was this how it was to be, then? Stiff and stilted?

He crossed to sit in the high-backed chair facing her. At length, it was he who broke the awkward silence. "Today's congregation of lairds is a solemn occasion. You must not speak unless you are questioned directly." He did not say it as if he were scolding her, but Nara bristled at his subtle reference to last night's outburst.

He seemed to sense her defensiveness. "These are treacherous times. In the Council," he explained, "even a single idle word can start a war. Best to stay silent, child."

"I am not a child, Grandfather," she said quietly. "I am a woman full-grown. A married woman."

He looked at her so intently she could almost see the questions he wanted to ask, but for some reason could not. Instead, he rose and walked to the high, narrow window. His back to her, he finally managed one question, at least. "What, then, are your feelings for the MacDougald?"

From small talk to this.

Nara answered him honestly. "I love him, Grandfather." She saw his shoulders sag. "But more than that, I respect him," she added. "In spite of everything he's been through, he's a good man at heart. A woman could not ask for more in a husband."

Laird Cullum turned on her, anger patent on his face. "A

good man?" He gripped the hilt of his jeweled dagger. "Have you known so many men, then, that you can judge? I think not." He paced closer. "Why, you're scarcely more than a child. You cannot know —"

"*Seanmhair* had been married to you for seven years and mother to your son for five years when she was my age!" Nara interrupted, scalded by his condescending manner. "And it is you who know nothing, sir, of my life."

She rose, her cheeks burning. "In the past three months, Tynan has saved my life a dozen times, and I his. We've survived the worst circumstances imaginable. And we did it together. For all the darkness you planted in his heart, he has been a good husband to me, and kind in ways you could never understand. I will not have you speak ill of him."

Laird Cullum's brows lowered along with his voice. "I'll have it annulled."

"No, you won't." Nara met her grandfather's glowering mien with one of her own. "*Seanmhair* granted my marriage to Tynan. It was properly performed, witnessed, and recorded. Nothing you say can change that. And no matter how many bishops you might have in your pocket, I shall not consent to an annulment." Her hand went to her belly. "I am with child, Grandfather."

Laird Cullum's breathing became even more rapid. He grabbed her arm, his grip far from gentle. "Is this true?"

Nara straightened to her full height. "I never lie." She glared down at the fingers that gripped her so roughly. "Unhand me this instant, or I shall scream for help."

"Fah!" Laird Cullum snatched his hand away.

Nara forced down the anger that had risen within her. Anger accomplished nothing.

"The child I carry is your great-grandchild," she offered in a more conciliatory tone. "Yesterday you told me your rash oath cost you the one woman you have ever loved. Were you telling the truth when you said you'd long repented of that oath?"

Laird Cullum did not answer. Instead, he sank into the chair and lowered his head into his hands.

"Grandfather, this is your chance to make things right. Let go of the past. Allow Tynan and me to go our own way. God willing, there will be more children to come. Only you can assure that there will be peace between us."

"They killed my son." The words sounded as if they'd been torn from him. "My only son." He glared up at her, the hatred in his eyes so strong Nara knew it was useless to reason with him. "No man can forget that."

"And *you* killed a hundred of theirs! Was that not revenge enough, even for you?" Frustrated beyond measure, she gripped her upper arms and cried, "Dear God, when will it end? Would you destroy us all?" Desperate, she knelt before her grandfather. "Grandfather, please, I beg you; let it be enough." Hard as she tried, she could not stop the tears that overflowed. "On my knees, I ask it: For the love you bear my grandmother, for all my children yet unborn, forgive! Let us go in peace."

"Never." Laird Cullum would not be moved. She'd succeeded only in adding contempt to the hatred in his eyes.

Nara wiped the tears from her cheeks and rose. Cold, so cold she felt inside, and weary as an old woman. "Very well, then." She could not, *would* not let his hatred contaminate her. "Then you are none of mine, sir. I renounce you and the bloodline that spawned you. From this day forward, you have no authority over me. I swear it before God."

"Swear what you will," he snarled, "the law is on my side."

John chose just that moment to knock. Nara hastened to the door to find him waiting in the hall with Timothy.

No sooner had he seen her than Timothy engulfed her in an awkward bear hug. "Mornin', Nara. I missed you."

She hugged Tim back fiercely, drawing strength from his innocent embrace. "Good morning to you, sweeting."

John bowed. "Laird Alasdair bade me inform Laird Cullum that the Council is assembling." Noting Nara's reddened eyes, he asked, "Would it suit milady for me to care for Master Timothy until such time as milady is free?"

"God bless you, John," she responded, extracting herself from Tim's arms. "I would like that very much."

The Council. She had to get a grip on herself.

Nara shot an anxious glance back to her grandfather, who was pacing by the window. "But, pray, keep Timothy close to the Great Hall," she murmured. "Laird Tynan and I might be leaving in a hurry."

John lowered his voice and sidestepped so Laird Cullum couldn't see his face. "Shall I have Laird Tynan's horse made ready, then? And packed with provisions and milady's belongings?"

"Dear John, you're an angel." She hesitated, then whispered, "The utmost discretion is required." She shot an anxious glance toward her grandfather.

John understood. "Then I shall be most discreet."

Nara gave the manservant an impulsive peck on the cheek. It flustered him completely but broke the tension she had felt. "Pray, wait until Laird Cullum and I have gone downstairs. I do not wish anyone to know we're leaving. Not yet."

"As my lady wishes." John bowed, then led Timothy away.

Nara announced to her grandfather, "Our presence is required by the Council, sir." Without looking back, she made for the Great Hall, where Tynan — and her destiny — were waiting.

# Chapter XX

Nara paused at the closed doors of the Great Hall. All around her in the vestibule waited petitioners and lesser nobles whose overlords were absent.

She was the only woman present. No sign of Lady Alasdair or Lady Margaret.

Her grandfather caught up with her, taking her elbow from behind.

"I will not have you shame me in front of the Council," he said tightly.

"Then do nothing to provoke me, sir, and I shall have no cause," she answered evenly.

The heavy doors were opened.

Nara took a deep breath and entered.

Gone were the festive decorations of last night's banquet. The tables had been taken away and the floors had been scrubbed clean, scattered with fresh rushes. But the gathering was no less impressive. All around the perimeter of the room, the Lairds of the Isles sat in ornate armchairs, their vassals and freeholders in attendance.

Only two chairs were empty: one centered at the far end of the room and higher than the rest vacant, no doubt, in recognition of Laird Alexander's absence — and a second chair near the rear doors.

Nara noted that Donald Balloch sat next to Laird Alexander's seat. He was deeply involved in earnest conversation with a bishop and several men she could only assume were the Council's advisers.

Many of the earls assembled wore the golden circlets of kings. And all were armed as if for battle.

The same men who had cavorted, laughed, and drunk most of the night away now sat deadly serious, the tension so strong Nara could almost taste it.

The signs had been subtle, but that tension had grown even stronger when she and Laird Cullum entered.

Nara searched the hall for Tynan but did not see him.

She did, though, notice that everywhere she looked, eyes averted.

Why would no one meet her gaze? Tynan was about to be honored, yet she couldn't help feeling as if something terrible was about to happen. Keeping her head high, she did her best to ignore the tightening in her stomach.

Laird Cullum led her to the vassals gathered behind Angus Dubh, leader of the MacKays. When she realized what her presence there implied, she considered moving away but had no idea where she should go. She decided to remain where she was only until she found Tynan. Then she would go to him.

Donald Balloch brought the Council to order. He stood. "My lairds!" All conversation ceased. "His Grace, our eminent bishop." He bowed to the cleric. "Distinguished nobles and honored guests."

He turned to Nara, his expression oblique, and bowed. "My Lady Tynan."

Then Balloch addressed the assembly. "We thank our host, Laird Alasdair, and his lady wife, not only for their generous hospitality, but for their courage and patience in remaining loyal under siege."

The thud of fists on wood and sword-hilts on shields thundered through the hall, pounding out the warriors' approval in savage rhythm.

"We give thanks to God for this victory . . ." More pounding, louder than before. Balloch waited until it subsided to continue. "And we honor now those who gave their lives in loyalty to our cause." Balloch paused, head bowed, as did the others.

After the tumultuous responses that had preceded it, this silence spoke far more eloquently than words.

Nara tried not to dwell on the stark images of death that came with thinking of Braithwed MacClindon and Tom MacDougald; instead she bowed her head and offered up a silent prayer for their souls.

She was still praying when Balloch resumed. "As our first order of business, we would like to recognize one whose valor and prowess in battle, along with that of his men, have earned our heartiest gratitude." He paused dramatically, then announced, "I present to the Council Laird Tynan MacDougald and his warriors."

As the doors swung open, a single thud of approval was joined by another, and then another, until the thundering cadence resounded from the vaulted stones above. With every shuddering throb, Nara's heart beat prouder.

All eyes watched a grim-faced Tynan march in at the head of his men. Nara was especially pleased to see Alan Chisolm present, even though he could scarcely limp along on his crutch. The rest of the men were anything but grim. Pride was written on their faces, and Nara rejoiced to see them standing tall and proud before this illustrious company.

But Tynan did not look at her. Not once.

"Laird Tynan. Honored warriors," Balloch intoned when they were assembled before him. "The leaders of the Council have met in chambers concerning your timely assistance in yesterday's conflict. As head of the Council in my cousin's absence, I have been delegated to invite you to sit as one of us." Balloch motioned to the empty chair at the back of the room.

Nara gazed at her husband. At last he was vindicated. Surely this great honor would go a long way toward reconciling her grandfather to her marriage. But when she looked to Laird Cullum's face, she saw only jealousy.

That was the last straw. Before her grandfather could stop her, she stepped forward, dropped a deep curtsy to Donald Balloch, then marched behind Tynan and his men to take her place beside his waiting chair.

The action set loose a ripple of subdued comments around the room, but blessedly, Balloch said nothing. He merely waited for Tynan's response.

"My lairds. Your Grace. Distinguished nobles. Honored guests." Tynan's voice carried strong and clear across the assembly. "My men and I have done nothing but what every other warrior in this company would have done under similar circumstances."

Murmured disagreement rose from the assembly.

"But . . . I am deeply honored by your offer. On behalf of my sept, I gratefully accept this seat among you and pledge my life, my sword, my lands, and my assets to the service of our cause."

Cheers erupted along with the thunder.

Tynan pivoted smartly and took his place on the Council, his grinning men behind him. Yet still he did not meet Nara's gaze.

"Our next order of business," Balloch announced when the tumult had subsided, "is of a sensitive nature, so I must request that all nonvoting members of the Council, save Lady Tynan and Laird Cullum, leave the hall." He looked to the

331

disgruntled allies he'd just displaced. "You will be readmitted as soon as this matter is concluded."

Now the speculation rose in earnest. Two-thirds of those present filed out, including Tynan's men. Then the doors were not only closed, but barred.

Watching the lairds slide the heavy timbers into place, Nara felt a tingle of foreboding. She laid a hand on Tynan's shoulder and felt him flinch from her touch.

This was not good. Not good.

*Dear Father,* she prayed earnestly, *whatever lies ahead, please, I beg of You, help me to acquit myself as You would have me. My life is in Your hands, Dear Lord. No matter what happens, I trust Your love. Send me Your Spirit, that I might have courage to do Your will and do it gladly. This I ask in the name of the Father, Son, and Holy Ghost.*

She opened her eyes just as Balloch motioned her and Tynan forward. "Laird and Lady Tynan."

He nodded to a glowering Laird Cullum. "Laird Cullum."

As Laird Cullum stepped from behind his overlaird's chair, Angus Dubh shot him a look that said clearly he was on his own.

Donald Balloch waited until the three of them stood before him, Nara in the middle, to produce a timeworn parchment. "My lairds," he read aloud, "the following charges have been brought against Laird Cullum of the MacKays: First, that Laird Cullum did in the year of Our Lord 1411 maliciously, in violation of every known law and code of honor, order the murder of his daughter-in-law, the Lady Grainne, born to the MacDougalds."

An agitated hiss of shock passed through the assembly.

"This charge is substantiated by the written confirmation" — he brought forth another yellowed missive — "of none other than Laird Cullum's own wife, written, dated, and properly witnessed on the very day the murder took place, but delivered to me only recently."

The hiss rose to a murmur.

Balloch referred back to the charges. "Second, that Laird Cullum did on a subsequent date three months hence maliciously, in violation of every law and code of honor, attack and massacre more than one hundred of the MacDougald men, women, and children, with no one spared, including Laird Morgan of the MacDougald, a loyal baron of the realm and member of this Council in good standing. These charges were made, inscribed, properly witnessed, and sworn in the presence of Laird Alexander on August seventh, the year of our Lord 1429, by one Tynan MacDougald."

Nara looked to Tynan, but he remained rigid, eyes forward.

Balloch leveled a steely glare at Laird Cullum. "What answer do you make to these charges, then, sir?"

"As for the charges attributed to my wife, they are clearly forgeries, concocted by my enemies. All here know that my wife disappeared twenty years ago. As for the first charge itself," Laird Cullum railed, "I remind this Council that the domestic affairs of any household, freehold or noble, are beyond the jurisdiction of their authority."

"You consider the murder of your daughter-in-law — sole heir to a noble and respected family — to be merely a *domestic matter?*" The question came from Angus Dubh himself. "Conn's balls, man! Can you not even give a reason for what you did?"

"She was a MacDougald!" Laird Cullum roared. "An enemy, at my very hearth." He pointed to the gathered nobles. "Admit it! Any one of you would have done the same!"

When he met only stony silence, he spat out, "What a pack

333

of hypocrites! Well, I will not grovel nor make excuses. I did what had to be done." His eyes narrowed. "You've used me well enough for that, over the years."

He pointed out one laird. "You, Cameron! Remember that lout who deviled your village so, how you said you wished he'd simply disappear? You questioned nothing when I asked the man out huntin' and he didn't come back. You used me well enough then."

Cullum pivoted to another. "And you, Lofton! It didn't seem to bother you when I took care of that wench who threatened to go to the cardinal about your bishop's bastard."

Sagging, Nara covered her ears. What she was hearing made her physically ill. Was there no depth to her grandfather's depravity? Or to his arrogance?

"Keep your comments to the matter at hand!" Balloch demanded. "Have you no defense?"

"I need make none!" Laird Cullum responded.

"Very well." Balloch turned to Angus Dubh. "Laird Angus, your vassal has made no defense to these charges, and so stands hereby summarily convicted. Do you agree?"

Angus Dubh nodded reluctantly. "So I must, for he made no defense."

"Very well." Balloch drew out yet another document. "Before we act further on this matter, I offer on behalf of Laird Alexander the following oath for the consideration of this body: I, Tynan MacDougald, make this declaration as son of Phelan MacDougald, who lived and died as a loyal vassal and baron of this land, grievously and cravenly murdered along with all save me of his kith and kin. As sole surviving heir to my bloodline, I do hereby claim by blood oath my right to avenge the aforementioned crimes. I alone shall be sole executioner, and no crime shall be laid to my charge on that account. This blood oath I invoke in accordance with

Holy Writ and the law of this land, life for life. Hereby recorded and sworn by Tynan MacDougald and witnessed and *affirmed*" — the emphasis was lost to no one — "by the hand of Laird Alexander himself. Dated likewise to the charges and signed in blood by the mark of Tynan MacDougald."

An ominous silence filled the hall.

Every man there understood, and probably supported, Tynan's right to take vengeance. Laird Alexander's affirmation simply sealed the matter.

Laird Cullum looked to Angus Dubh for support, but the overlaird frowned at him and shook his head. More defiant than ever, Nara's grandfather stepped past her and spat in Tynan's face. "Kill me if you can, you sorry excuse for a —"

"As I told you yesterday, MacKay," Tynan said with deadly calm, "I have no intention of killing *you*."

He'd uttered it so softly, Nara wasn't sure anyone but she and her grandfather heard, yet his words robbed her of her very breath.

Oh, please, dear God, it couldn't be true! Nara turned glazed eyes to the man she loved. How could he do this?

And then she knew. He'd planned this all along.

All along . . . all along

*You shall hate me, soon and forever.* The words came back to haunt her.

Yet she didn't hate him. She loved him, so his calculated betrayal came as a mortal blow.

He'd made love to her, knowing what lay ahead.

Nara blinked back tears of disbelief. This was the source of darkness she had sensed, the terrible secret he could not share. Everything made perfect, hideous sense. The "riddle" had played out.

*She* was the damask rose's thorn, hiding away beneath the earth, buried for all those years. And Aunt Keriam,

*Seanmhair*'s twin, was the "dark reflection." Her aunt had glimpsed Tynan's blood oath and tried to break it by forcing him to marry Nara, but it hadn't worked. And now her husband would kill her, as coldheartedly as Laird Cullum had killed all those women, children, and babies twenty years ago.

A cruel revenge, but just, for Laird Cullum would have to live on alone, the way he'd forced Tynan to live on — alone, but for the ghosts of the past and his regrets.

She stared at Tynan's classic profile. Even now, the sight of him tugged at her shattered heart. Such a heavy burden he had borne these past months.

It took several moments for the truth to dawn on Laird Cullum, but when it did, his eyes widened in horror.

He stepped between Nara and her husband. "Did you hear what he just said?" he called to the lairds. "I'm the one he wants, yet he plans to slay my granddaughter! Surely you do not mean to let him. Only a coward would kill a woman thus."

Laird Cullum slapped Tynan across the face. "Your quarrel is with me. Settle it like a man!"

Tynan stood as still as stone.

Desperation crept into Laird Cullum's voice for the first time. "I am one of you! You cannot let him do this!"

Balloch's gaze polled the Council, prompting nods from first one laird, then another. In the end, it was unanimous.

"The Council supports Laird Tynan's right to take vengeance for the crimes against his family."

Ranald Bane leaned over and whispered something into his brother's ear. Balloch nodded, then said to the assembly, "In light of the unusual nature of the sentence, though — and the esteem my brother and I bear Laird Tynan and his lady — we feel this matter is not suitable for our eyes."

He stood and turned his back. Beside him, Ranald Bane shot Tynan a look of compassion, then rose and turned his back as well.

Angus Dubh started to turn next, but Laird Cullum's cry stopped him, if only briefly.

"Angus," Laird Cullum pleaded. "You were godfather to my son! Don't let them do this. I'll take whatever punishment you wish to lay on me, but do not let him snuff out my seed forever, before my own eyes."

Nara recoiled. He hadn't asked them not to kill *her*, he'd asked them not to let "his seed" be wiped out! She meant nothing to her grandfather but an extension of his line.

"The punishment is fair, Cullum," Angus Dubh replied. "You brought it down upon your own head twenty years ago. We looked the other way then about the massacre only because we thought you'd killed anyone who could prove you were responsible. It's only fitting that we look the other way now, so that justice may be served." With that, he turned his back.

One by one, the others stood and turned until the three of them were alone in the circle of death.

Laird Cullum thrust Nara aside and drew his sword on Tynan. "I'll not let you kill her." He crouched, his sword circling, circling, anxious for the confrontation. "You'll have to come through me. And if you kill me, the blood oath is satisfied, so you *cannot* then kill her and live."

Tynan moved so quickly, Nara could scarcely follow the motion of his sword. The next thing she knew, her grandfather was gripping his bleeding hand and his sword had clattered to the stone floor. Tynan kicked it far out of reach.

Laird Cullum drew his dagger. "I could have killed you a thousand times," he taunted Tynan. "I should have, but it was far more amusing to watch you suffer."

Seeing the two men go at each other was more than Nara could bear. "Stop! Stop it, this instant!"

If this was the world she was destined to live in, she no longer wanted it. Nara stepped between her husband and her grandfather. She gazed into the torment in Tynan's eyes. Her heart had taken blow after blow and kept on beating, but now, seeing the agony that welled within him, she felt her very soul shatter into a thousand pieces.

He had been wounded so cruelly, suffered so long. If her death would put an end to that suffering, then so be it. In that decision, she found at last the peace she'd been looking for.

Detached now, she looked at Tynan and recited, "Death from life and life from death is born." She grasped the tip of his sword and placed it just above her girdle at the base of her breastbone. It was almost a relief, thinking that she would soon be with her mother. "If my death will bring you peace, Tynan, then I give my life gladly."

He stared at her, dumbstruck.

"No!" Laird Cullum started forward, but Nara turned her head and cried, "Hold, or I'll drive the blade home myself and add my soul to the guilt you bear!"

The threat was enough to stop him.

She took one last, lingering look at the man she loved, the man who had broken her heart. "Do it, my love," she implored. "But strike swift and sure. I do not wish to linger here."

"Nara." Tynan condensed the pain of a thousand hells into that one word. She saw it now, in his face. "Dear God," he groaned out. "For twenty years, my brain has echoed cries for vengeance from my people, yet now, when I look into your eyes . . ." His head dropped forward. "Why can't I do this?"

Nara actually felt pity for him. "You would gladly die for your honor, Tynan. Can I do any less?" She smiled at him.

"End it, and be done. Honor must be served."

Tynan's eyes glazed with tears, but still he did not strike.

Nara felt her courage begin to falter. She pulled the blade tighter against her. "Do it, Tynan. If not for honor, then to end the torment of this betrayal. I cannot bear to live another day knowing you would use me thus."

Before Tynan could respond, a dull thumping battered the barred doors.

"Let me in!" came a muffled cry from beyond. "I must see Nara and Laird Cullum!"

Clearly relieved, Balloch turned and ordered, "See who it is."

Four of the lairds closest to the door removed the bar, then pulled the heavy portal open only wide enough to see what all the ruckus was about.

Nara's gasp was echoed by Laird Cullum's when a resolute nun pushed past them and strode into the hall.

*Seanmhair* or Aunt Keriam?

Nara couldn't tell from this distance, and apparently neither could anyone else.

The nun took one look at Tynan's sword to Nara's breast and screamed, "Hold! Do not harm her!"

Her cry prompted the rest of the Council lairds to turn and see who had dared interrupt these solemn proceedings. Intent on this development, neither Nara nor any of the others took note when another woman discreetly slipped in before the lairds closed and barred the doors. Instead, everyone was watching the first intruder. The air fairly crackled with suspense until she reached the front of the hall.

Nara knew it was Aunt Keriam long before then, but as she drew near, Laird Cullum focused on her face and breathed, "Eideann. It is you at last."

When he started toward her, she held up a staying hand. It

was heavily bandaged. "Nay," she said, not without compassion. "Not Eideann. I am Keriam, her sister." Her eyes sought Nara's. "Eideann is dead."

"No!" Nara let loose of Tynan's sword and crumpled to the ground. "No, no, no." She hadn't thought there was enough left of her to feel such pain, but this final loss was too much, too much. Weeping uncontrollably, she rocked back and forth, her arms wrapped tightly around her.

She was only vaguely aware of Aunt Keriam's comforting embrace. "There, there, my darling. Aunt Keriam is here. The worst is over now. Everything will be all right. You'll see."

Abruptly Nara inhaled a spasmodic breath. An eerie calm came over her. "No," she said. "It's not over. Not yet, not ever, until I am with *Seanmhair*."

"Precious," Aunt Keriam hastened, "you don't know what you're saying. Let me take you from this place." She drew Nara to her feet.

Nara looked into Aunt Keriam's eyes. Not *Seanmhair*'s; those eyes would never be *Seanmhair*'s. She stroked the cheek of that beloved face. Not *Seanmhair*'s face . . .

"Dead?" Laird Cullum repeated numbly. "How?"

Aunt Keriam sighed, her arms still around Nara. "When I told her what had happened — about Tynan's finding us and taking Nara back to her grandfather — it was more than she could bear. She'd feared just that for so long . . ." Keriam looked at Tynan in reproach.

"She had a stroke. It didn't kill her outright." She closed her eyes. "We nursed her for more than a month, hoping she would come around, but the soul was gone out of her. She died at peace a month ago."

Laird Cullum brought his fists to his own eyes.

"I came looking for Nara as soon as I could." Keriam faced Tynan. "But no one would tell me where you'd taken her. I was about to give up when I met the strangest man . . ."

She leaned her head against Nara's. "He seemed to come from out of nowhere. He was halt and palsied, thin as bone, but he spoke well enough, though I never could manage to meet his eyes. Said his name was Timothy."

Nara and Tynan looked to each other in shock.

"When was that?" Tynan asked.

"Three weeks ago, in Wester Ross."

"But Timothy was with us then, in the forest," Tynan argued.

Keriam shrugged. "There are hundreds of Timothys in the world —"

"Not like this one," Tynan insisted. Something was happening inside him; Nara could sense it, but she felt too numb to wonder what.

Aunt Keriam's coming had changed nothing. Nara pushed away from her, breaking the last tie with the living. "Leave us, Aunt Keriam. I do not wish you to witness what must happen."

"Why was your sword to her breast?" Keriam demanded of Tynan. Her eyes narrowed. "Do not lie to me. Remember, I have the Sight, Tynan."

At that, many of the Lairds made the sign against the Evil Eye and murmured incantations to block her power, but Tynan said nothing.

Nara neither knew nor cared what he was thinking. She only longed to cross over to the Yonder World, even more so now that *Seanmhair* was waiting for her there.

"The Sight showed me of your terrible oath, Tynan, but it also showed me something more." She looked to Laird Cullum. "It all lies in your hands. Everything. Think what my sister would want, Laird Cullum. Pray, and it shall be opened unto you."

"I am damned already," Laird Cullum spoke like a broken man, at last. "God does not hear the prayers of the damned."

"Nay, sir. If that were so," Keriam said gently, "all of us would be destined to hell, for all have sinned and fallen short of the glory of God."

Laird Cullum bowed his head, and everyone in the hall waited in tense silence.

When he raised it up again, it was with a look of resignation. "My lairds!" he called. "Witness this now." He unsheathed the jeweled dagger that was the emblem of authority among his people and held it up by the blade like a cross. "I do hereby freely and without coercion name Tynan MacDougald as my successor. All my holdings and all my authority I grant to him now, before this Council. Nothing that happens subsequent to this shall be charged against him —"

"Noooo! You can't! I won't let you!" Like a Fury, Lady Margaret hurled herself from her hiding place behind one of the chairs, her own dagger raised to strike at Tynan. "Cullum, you lying bastard!" she screeched. "You promised my boys would succeed you!"

Before Tynan had even unsheathed his own dagger, Laird Cullum's blade found its mark deep in her stomach.

"Dear God!" Aunt Keriam averted her eyes, making the sign of the cross, but Nara watched as if she were a fetch already, unaffected by the torments of the living.

Lady Margaret, her weapon still raised, looked down in surprise at the hilt sticking out of her stomach, then back to her brother. "My boys!" she gasped with her dying breath. "You promised. I slept with you, and you promised!" Then she toppled to her side, eyes glazed.

Laird Cullum strode over to her and withdrew his dagger. "This changes nothing."

He approached Tynan and stood before him. As custom

342

demanded, he turned the dagger's hilt toward his successor, laying the bloodied blade toward himself. "Take it."

For the first time, Nara saw a spark of hope in Tynan's eyes. She watched him reach out and grasp the jeweled hilt.

Laird Cullum placed his hand over Tynan's, officially granting his blessing. "Let all here bear witness. Nothing that now happens shall be accounted to Laird Tynan's charge. His is innocent, absolved completely, for I have grievously harmed both him and his people, for which I do now confess and repent before God and these witnesses. What I do, I do of my own free will."

Nara thought he was referring to naming Tynan as his successor until she saw her grandfather smile at Tynan, grasp his successor's elbows, and impale himself on the jeweled dagger Tynan was holding.

Caught completely off guard, Tynan retreated immediately, but not before the deed was done. With every beat of Laird Cullum's heart, blood spurted from the wound.

"The oath has been satisfied," Laird Cullum gasped out. "Let this be an end to it." His eyes turned past Nara to Aunt Keriam. He reached a bloodied hand toward her. "Hold me, my love, this one last time."

Aunt Keriam did not correct him. Instead, she knelt beside him and gathered him close, just as her sister would have. "May God have mercy on your soul," she murmured, bathing his face with her tears. "You've done well, Cullum. Take that with you. In the end, you've done well."

He looked to Nara and whispered, "I have forgiven MacDougald. Pray, forgive me if you can." Then he died in Keriam's arms.

Nara stood transfixed. She could not think, could not feel. Dared not hope.

Then Tynan's arms were around her, holding her so

tightly she could scarcely breathe. "It's over, Nara, and we're alive." His huge, warm hands framed her head and tipped her face back to his fevered gaze. "Don't you see? We're alive, and free."

Oblivious to everyone but her, he kissed her with all the pent-up longing of the past three months. Then he cradled her head against his chest. "It's a miracle, my love. A miracle." His own soul awakening to the wonder of it, he said as much to himself as to her, "We can live out our lives together. We can have children. Nara, it's over, at last."

A miracle. The word was like a beacon, piercing the fog that clouded Nara's mind. She'd prayed for one and God had granted it — a miracle as just and terrible and merciful as the very nature of God Himself.

With shaking hands, Nara circled Tynan's waist and held on.

The child! How could she have forgotten? With all that had happened before the Council, she'd never once considered the child within her.

Nara smiled. She would tell Tynan, but not now, not here. This was a place of death.

*Death from life and life from death is born.*

The riddle had played out, after all.

Donald Balloch broke the silence. "My lairds, we must be careful how we interpret what has just happened here." He scanned the somber, nodding faces that ringed the room. "It is my opinion that Laird Tynan would make a far more suitable chieftain than either of Lady Margaret's sons. What say you?"

Agreement was unanimous.

"So," Balloch concluded, "from the looks of this, I think it would be reasonable to say that Lady Margaret fell by her brother's own hand even as she slew him. What say you?"

344

"Aye," came the heartfelt response.

Balloch's solution was an elegant one. If the truth got out, Lady Margaret's sons might well challenge Tynan's right as chieftain, and the last thing the Council needed was another feud within their number.

This way, Nara's grandfather could be given a proper burial with all honors and laid to rest in hallowed ground. Since in the end only God could judge the state of Laird Cullum's soul, Nara felt nothing but relief at Balloch's suggestion.

"We shall hold a memorial service this afternoon with all present," Balloch informed Tynan. "Laird Tynan shall stand at my right hand. That should ensure an orderly transfer of power."

He looked to Angus Dubh. "Angus, please see that Lady Margaret's sons are in attendance. Make sure they understand the tragic calamity that claimed their mother's and their uncle's lives."

"Aye," Angus Dubh agreed. "And I'll be certain they know Laird Tynan has my full support." He shot Tynan an apologetic grimace. " 'Tis the least I can do, considering."

Tynan bowed without letting go of Nara. "We are most grateful, my laird."

Balloch nodded to Tynan. "I shall look for you in the chapel this afternoon, Laird Tynan. The ladies, of course, will be excused allowing to their grief."

His face weary, he dismissed them at last. "Remember well what has been said within this chamber, but take it to your graves unspoken. The truth has been decided. After the memorial service, you are free to return to Eilean d'Ór. I shall summon you only if we are unable to defeat Moray within the month."

"Donald," Angus Dubh inserted, "I think I shall have

need of Laird Cullum's nephews in that campaign." The request guaranteed Tynan at least a month to take over his new holdings without opposition.

"A most politic suggestion," Balloch agreed.

Nara marveled afresh. As always when God had a hand in things, an insurmountable crisis had been perfectly resolved — worked out down to the smallest detail.

"You are dismissed."

*Thoom!* The impact of sword on shield echoed through the hall.

*Thoom!* Another joined it, and another.

*Thoom, thoom, thoom!* The pounding rhythm swelled and grew until every laird present was pounding out his tribute.

They kept on pounding, even as the doors were unsealed.

And then the sound was the beating of her heart, miraculously made whole again.

Tynan turned to leave, supporting her in his arms even then. Aunt Keriam took her place alongside them. The three of them gave the bodies of Laird Cullum and Lady Margaret wide berth as the doors swung open.

They had almost reached the outer hall when Nara remembered something Aunt Keriam had said. "Aunt Keriam, there's something I want to know about that palsied man who told you where to find us. You must meet Timothy and tell me if he looks anything like that man." There had to be a logical explanation.

A roar of speculation rose all around them as the waiting crowd poured into the hall and saw the grim tableau inside, but Nara was too anxious looking for Tim to pay any attention. She caught a glimpse of John on the other side of the throng. "John!" she called, then turned to Tynan. "He has Timothy. Do you see them?"

346

"I see John over there," Tynan answered. "But no Timo-thy."

They were halfway across the outer hall before the crowd thinned enough for John to reach them. "Laird and Lady Tynan." Visibly distressed, he bowed before them. "I don't know how it happened. One moment, he was right beside me. The next thing I knew, he was gone." He snapped his fingers. "Just like that. I've had the whole household looking for him ever since, but he must have gotten outside somehow. He's nowhere to be found indoors." John wrung his hands. "I swear, my laird, I hardly took my eyes off him for a second —"

"Calm down, John. You have no cause to reproach your-self." Tynan spoke with the quiet assurance Nara had always wished for him. "This isn't the first time Timothy's es-caped."

"Aye," Nara added. "He got away from me once, the same as he did with you." She did not mention the dire conse-quences of that escape.

"Don't worry, Nara," Tynan assured her. "We'll find him."

They spent the better part of the day searching, along with those few members of the household who could be spared, but no one found a trace of him. Tynan interrupted his search only long enough to go to the memorial, then he resumed looking. The sun was low on the horizon before John and Tynan returned, empty-handed, to the bedchamber where Nara and Aunt Keriam were waiting.

"We've covered every square foot of this place," Tynan said, "but no luck."

Just then a page came running down the hallway. "Laird Tynan! Message for Laird Tynan!"

"Here!"

Nara and Keriam leapt to their feet.

"Master Timothy," the page panted out. "He's been seen."

"Where?"

"On a hillside just south of the castle. One of the sentries saw him. Shall they send men to fetch him?"

"Nay." Tynan took Nara's hand. "That might frighten him off. We'll go."

Nara smiled, glad that he knew she would want to be there. "Come, Aunt Keriam. You and John may be needed."

The page went to the window and pointed down. "There's a back exit that lets out just at the base of the wall. I'll show Yer Lairdship the way. That will put Yer Lairdship out much closer than the main gate. Just follow that glen, there, south for half a mile, and Master Timothy should be just to the west."

All four of them hastened after the page. Fifteen minutes later, Inverlochy Castle lay behind them as they scanned the rolling hills between them and the setting sun.

Aunt Keriam pointed to a halting silhouette on the hilltop ahead. "There! Is that not he?"

To Nara's vast relief, it was.

"Tim!" She raced toward him, the others close behind. But Tim only turned and grinned. She was still more than fifty yards away when she saw what looked like a huge brown dog loping up to Tim.

"Tynan!" Nara cried, panic speeding her pace. "It's the wolf!"

Miraculously, the wolf did not attack. Instead, it reared up on its hindquarters and placed its paws on Tim's chest.

Nara's paces slowed erratically until she was standing in amazement, watching the wolf lick Timothy's face.

She'd have sworn such a huge animal would have easily knocked Tim flat on his back, but he stood steady as a rock, laughing.

Tynan came up behind Nara. "Do you see what I see?"

Nara nodded. "Dare we approach them?"

"Nay," Tynan advised. "It might set the wolf off."

John and Aunt Keriam arrived behind them.

John's eyes widened. "Would you look at that."

But Aunt Keriam scarcely seemed to notice the wolf. "Why, that's him," she said. "The one who told me where to find you."

"It can't be. Timothy was fifty miles from there, in the woods with us," Tynan argued, transfixed by the unlikely sight before him.

"I may be old, young man, but I still have my mind." Aunt Keriam waggled her finger toward Tim. "A fellow like that isn't easy to forget. It's him, all right."

Then, in the blink of an eye, Tim and the wolf were on the crest of the next ridge.

All four of them looked at each other in disbelief.

Tynan's eyes widened. "Did you just see what I saw?"

Nara nodded, as did the others. They turned as one.

The sun was halfway down, a huge orange semicircle behind the clear silhouettes of Timothy and the wolf. One moment, they were there, cavorting on the hilltop. The next moment, there was a blinding flash of light.

Nara watched in amazement as Timothy straightened within that flash, no longer frail and palsied, but sound and strong, his clothing transformed into robes of incandescent white. And then he was gone, the wolf with him.

"Did you see that?" Nara tugged at Tynan's arm. They had just witnessed another miracle. "Tynan, tell me you saw what I saw."

He nodded, incredulous. "Aye, I saw it."

"And I," John chimed in.

Aunt Keriam merely smiled, her face as smug as a cat's

with a mouthful of cream. When all three of them looked to her, she shrugged. "Deny your hospitality to no one, for thus have some entertained angels unawares."

She took John's arm and started back down the hill. "Come, John. Let's leave these young people to themselves. They've had precious little privacy this afternoon, and no doubt have much to discuss."

Nara was still smiling when the two of them disappeared down the far side of the hill.

At last they were alone, with all the glory of nature spread before them. Nara stretched out her arms in the evening wind and slowly turned. Then she paused, arms outstretched, the afterglow of twilight golden on her eyelids and the cool, cleansing wind whipping at her hair and clothes. "Oh, Tynan," she murmured, "I'm as light as a feather. No. As light as a bird soaring high above the world."

Tynan came up behind her and took her outstretched hands in his. "Teach me how to fly, Nara." The wind in their faces, he stared past her to the golden horizon. "I've been earthbound so long."

Nara turned in his arms and kissed him, a tender kiss that said they had all the time in the world. "You only have to believe, my love."

She saw peace in his eyes when he looked at her, and wonder. "I believe in you," he said.

"Don't settle for that, Tynan. There's so much more." She nuzzled her forehead against his chest. "You saw what happened to Tim. Do you not believe in that?"

"Aye, I must confess, I do." Tynan chuckled, the sound warm and full. When he spoke now, he sounded . . . young. New. "For so many years, I believed in nothing. And now, suddenly, everything seems possible." He sighed. "Truly, I want to see life as you do, but I'll need your help, my love."

"My help has always been yours and always shall."

"Somehow I knew that all along, even when I couldn't admit it to myself." Tynan held her close, the words he'd wanted to say for so long pouring out at last. "I love you, Nara, and never want to lose you. I want to stay with you forever and take my last breath in your arms. I want to plant my seed inside you and watch our children grow up to have children of their own, then sit by the fire when we are old and tell our grandchildren about the miracles of this day."

"We shall do all those things, Tynan. Of that I am certain," she said seriously.

Tynan took her face tenderly into his hands and gazed into her eyes. "How can you be so sure? Did the Sight tell you?"

"Nay, my love." *This* was the joy at the end of darkness! "But I have seen it in my dreams."

"Then I believe."

# *Author's Note*

I have long been fascinated with the ancient Greek myth of Hades and Persephone, but since I find some of the elements of that story objectionable, I've always wanted to write my own version. *Damask Rose* is my interpretation of that age-old account of the struggle between light and darkness.

*Damask Rose* is also a parable of faith that shows the transforming power of sacrificial love. I hope you've enjoyed reading it as much as I enjoyed writing it.